About the Author

Don Townshend was born in Hackney, East London but has lived in Essex for over forty years. He retired from a senior post in local government and now shares a hobby, of collecting vintage children's books, with his wife Barbara. He has always liked writing and storytelling. Don is also passionate about conservation of the natural world.

A Kind of Retribution

Don Townshend

A Kind of Retribution

Olympia Publishers
London

www.olympiapublishers.com
OLYMPIA PAPERBACK EDITION

A CIP catalogue record for this title is
available from the British Library.

ISBN: 978-1-78830-938-7

This is a work of fiction.
Names, characters, places and incidents originate from the writer's imagination.
Any resemblance to actual persons, living or dead, is purely coincidental.

First Published in 2021

Olympia Publishers
Tallis House
2 Tallis Street
London
EC4Y 0AB

Printed in Great Britain

Dedication

For my wife, Barbara, the love of my life.

He woke up with a start. Where was he? The last thing he remembered was having a drink at Terry's house. He must have passed out. But this certainly wasn't Terry's place. It was pitch black and cold. He had a horror of the dark and panicking, he stood up. He put his hands out in front of him and felt a wall.

As his eyes adjusted to the dark, he could just make out walls all around him. He appeared to be inside a very small room. He cried out in anguish until his voice became croaky. He slumped to the ground. He just couldn't understand what was happening to him and suddenly he was overwhelmed with another fear. Surely, if someone had placed him in this hell, they would at least have to bring him food and water.

What he didn't yet know, was, that he would never leave this room alive! He was a prisoner and it was a death sentence!

Chapter One

Four weeks later, Detective Inspector James Halstead was sitting in his office in Lewes, in East Sussex. Halstead, just turned thirty, was handsome in a rugged sort of way. He had neatly trimmed, black hair and was athletic in build, having played football and cricket for police teams. His only sport now was golf and he didn't play often enough to get his handicap down to single figures. He was well regarded by his bosses, because he had a good record of solving cases. James Halstead was slightly old fashioned but he was also tenacious and surprisingly tough, when the need arose. Detective Sergeant Jill Trent knocked on his open door and walked in without pausing to be invited.

James Halstead looked up.

"You're in a hurry this morning Jill. Where's the fire?"

"No fire; a dead body!"

"Where?"

"At the old co-op building. You know, the one they're demolishing to make way for new shops."

"Let's go and have a look. We can take your car," said James, as he jumped up.

Jill Trent was a real go-getter. She was tall and very attractive, with shoulder length, brown hair and at twenty-seven, her ambition was to make Inspector before she reached thirty. She kept fit by going to the gym. As they drove to the demolition site, Jill reflected that she always seemed to do the driving in her pale blue Fiat 500. James Halsted, at six feet two, was a little cramped in the passenger seat and Jill always smiled to herself when she saw him trying to get comfortable.

"I wish you would get a bigger car, Jill."

"We could always take yours," said Jill, in a matter of fact voice.

James Halstead didn't answer but smiled to himself.

He had the greatest respect for Jill and admired her abilities as a Detective. She sometimes threw herself into situations, rather than consider the dangers first but he wasn't immune from this himself. Jill was fiercely loyal to James Halstead. She liked him both as her boss and as a person. Outside of work they regarded themselves as friends and this enabled them to trust each other completely, when working on cases.

When they arrived at the demolition site, there was a police car and a forensic investigations van. Police tape was all around the site entrance and a uniformed police officer was on guard. Halstead greeted him.

"Morning Tom. Where's the body?"

"There's a basement area, with a small room. The body is inside. Doctor Grant is down there, with the forensic team."

Doctor Grant was an experienced pathologist. She was a middle-aged woman with a strong sense of humour. Halstead and Trent donned protective suits, handed to them by one of the forensics team. James Halstead spoke to Doctor Grant.

"Hello Doc, what have we got?"

"Don't call me Doc, he was one of the seven dwarves!"

"Sorry, Doctor Grant." He smiled.

They always had some banter, even when meeting under grim circumstances.

Doctor Claire Grant turned to James.

"Dead male, probably forties. Been dead for about a month at a guess, but I'll know more after the autopsy."

"Thanks Doctor. Now all we have to do is find out who he was, and cause of death."

"Well, I can help you with your first question. He was Arron Kelp. I found this wallet. It was inside his trouser pocket."

James hadn't actually entered the small room and stretched out a gloved hand to grasp the wallet. It contained cash and a battered credit card as well as a driving licence. James flicked through the cash.

"Not a robbery then?"

"No, but that's your job James; wallet was sticking out of his pocket. Couldn't really have been missed," said Claire Grant

"By the looks of this door, he must have got locked in. We need to speak to the workman who opened the door," said James, studying the now, broken lock.

Later that afternoon, Charlie Denis, the workman who found the body, was sipping coffee in an interview room, sitting opposite Jill Trent. He was quite relaxed but kept eying the coffee.

"Not very nice, this coffee. Do you lot have to drink this horrible stuff every day?"

Jill Trent pulled a face.

"You get used to it after a while. Now, if you've finished complaining I want to know how you found the body. The door to the room was damaged and I'm assuming that was down to you?"

"Yes, it was. The governor asked me to have a look around in the basement before we started the demolition. I saw the door and tried to open it. The lock was a bit rusty. There was a key in the lock but it wouldn't turn. I tried plyers but the key didn't budge so I got a sledgehammer and a few clouts against the lock, did the trick."

"So, the key was on the outside?"

"Yes, it was. The door had definitely been locked from the outside."

"Then what did you do?"

"I saw a pile of rags and then realised there was a body. I got out of there as fast as I could and ran to tell my governor. He called you lot."

"Did you touch the body?"

"You're bloody joking! No, I couldn't get out fast enough. Not much more I can tell you."

"Did you touch anything inside the room?"

"Touch anything? You must be joking."

"Were you wearing gloves?"

"Yes of course. Oh, I know what you mean. Fingerprints."

"We have to ask in case there are any unidentified prints at the scene."

"Yeah, I've seen it on TV cop shows."

"OK, we've got your details Mr Denis. We'll be in touch. Enjoy the rest of your coffee."

"I'll give it a miss thanks."

When Jill Trent got to James Halstead's office, he was staring at his computer screen. Without looking up, he said,

"Arron Kelp. Unusual name, isn't it? Seemed familiar and I've just found out why."

"Known to the police, was he?"

"Yes. Do you remember the court case a while ago, when some bastard was convicted of cruelty to his dog? Well, it was Arron Kelp!"

"Now you mention it, I do. Can't remember what he got for it," said Jill.

"He got five weeks in prison, suspended, and a fine of £350, plus £440 court costs. He locked the dog in a cellar under his house, without food and water. It was found dead by RSPCA officers, while they were investigating a complaint that the dog had been barking on and off for days."

"And Kelp is then found dead in a cellar!"

"Yes, I know exactly what you're thinking Jill."

"Probably the same as you."

Chapter Two

Simon Wells was sitting in the dining room at The Grand Hotel, Eastbourne, in East Sussex. This was The Garden Restaurant and it was quite busy for a Thursday evening. Wells was a wealthy man, and drove a Bentley Continental convertible, just to let everyone know how wealthy he was. He was mid-forties but overweight in his well-cut, expensive, blue, chalk stripe suit and loud tie. Sitting at the table with him was Ludo Chambers. Ludo was a nickname, but he had used it since childhood and most people didn't know his real name. He was slimmer, than Wells and wore his hair quite long. This made him look quite roguish. Like Wells, he was wealthy but a few years younger. The two men had known each other for twenty odd years and had made their money in the antiques trade and in 'import and export'; a description that was both ambiguous and possibly secretive. Neither man had ever run foul of the law, but those who associated with them knew they had probably sailed close to the wind, over the years.

A third man was seated at the table and he knew all about sailing. Ryan Ledbetter owned a large cabin cruiser, which he kept moored at Eastbourne's Sovereign Harbour. Ledbetter was very different to his two companions. His weather-beaten face spoke of time spent at sea. He also owned a night club in Brighton. Ledbetter was well-built and looked as if he could handle himself.

Simon Wells raised his glass of wine.

"Well gentlemen, I think we should toast the success of our latest venture together."

The others raised their glasses. Ledbetter grimaced as he joined in the toast.

"It doesn't get any easier but we owe ourselves this toast. I think we did very well," said a cheery Ludo Chambers.

Ledbetter gave an ironic smile.

"Yes Ludo. Nothing's impossible if you don't have to do it yourself. Rough seas and rough weather mean nothing to you!"

Simon Wells chided him.

"Keep your voice down, Ryan. I don't think they quite heard you at the other tables."

Chambers responded before Ledbetter could take offence.

"Let's just enjoy our meal. We can talk in my suite later. Let's order more wine."

Later that evening after coffee in the lounge, the three men were relaxing in Chambers' suite. Ledbetter was standing by a window which looked out over the sea. It was pitch black, punctuated by spots of light from vessels, miles offshore. There was also the regular flashing light from the Royal Sovereign light tower, located a way offshore. This light gave Ledbetter some comfort because he had often used it as a reference point when approaching Sovereign Harbour during his nocturnal boat trips.

"Do you want a nightcap, Ryan?" asked Chambers.

"Yes, a brandy would go down well."

Simon Wells looked at his two companions.

"To business gentlemen. We made forty grand from our latest venture and there's more where that came from. Can you arrange for another pickup in a fortnight's time?"

Ledbetter stared at him

"Look Simon. Things are getting a bit bloody tight. I can't keep making the odd trip at night without raising suspicions. The 'Cormorant' security system is really efficient. If it wasn't for my inside information, it would be impossible to do anything. It's time to give it a rest. You'll just have to concentrate on your legitimate antiques business for a while. You're both good at that, so you keep telling me."

As usual Ludo Chambers, exuding charm, tried to calm Ledbetter down. "Now, now, Ryan, we know you take most of the risks but…"

"Most of the risks? I'd say I take all of the risks. I'm out there, dodging security, while you sit on your backside sipping wine."

"That's a bit harsh," chided Chambers. "Simon and I put a lot of money into this venture."

Ledbetter scoffed.

"I put money in too and I've supplied the means to move the merchandise."

Simon Wells put both hands up.

"Enough, please. It's pointless arguing because it isn't getting us anywhere. We all take risks and OK, Ryan, I'll admit that you bear a very big risk moving things in and out by boat. Don't forget the risks I've taken recently. The antiques are red hot! The French dealers all know my name."

"Mine too," exclaimed Chambers. "Let's just talk about this without getting into criticising each other. OK, Ryan, Ludo?" said an exasperated Wells.

Chambers and Ledbetter agreed to let it go and concentrate on the next steps. It was true that their luck had held for a while now, but it couldn't last indefinitely, if they got too greedy. There was another reason for their success and it wasn't down to luck. It was inside information, which was supplied by a silent partner.

Ledbetter downed a whiskey.

"Just get real for a minute." He raised his hand. "Hear me out. Moving the antiques is tricky, but they're all small items, so I can hide them fairly easily. The difficult cargo is the cannabis."

"You've never told us how you get it ashore, Ryan," said Chambers, sipping his drink and looking directly at Ledbetter.

"No, and I'm not fucking well going to. The fewer people who know, the lower the risk."

Chambers looked hurt.

"It's OK for you to keep secrets but don't forget that Simon and I provide the working capital."

Ledbetter stood up.

"So you keep reminding me! I think we should let it drop, before I lose my temper and spoil the evening. One thing's for sure. We have to take a break on the antiques for a while. There's a full-blown police investigation going on and I'm not going to take unnecessary risks. Let's just cool it all down for a while."

Wells and Chambers nodded their agreement.

The men had a few more drinks and then Ledbetter and Wells, made their drunken way to their separate rooms. They all lived in East Sussex and the stay at the Grand Hotel was one of several venues they used, for a get together every five weeks or so. Simon Wells had an antiques showroom in Lewes and Ludo Chambers had a similar sized showroom in Eastbourne. Ryan Ledbetter had a flat at Sovereign Harbour, where his boat was berthed. He also had a flat above his club in Brighton. Although they argued and bickered with each other, they were tied together by business. It was a lucrative arrangement and none of the men wanted to pass up the opportunity to make money.

Wells and Chambers were involved in all sorts of shady dealings. Ledbetter was on a different level. He had lots of business interests. The cannabis smuggling was just part of his illegal activities. The south coast was an area of beauty and a traditional holiday destination. Ledbetter, operated in an altogether, darker world.

Chapter Three

It had been two days since the body of Arron Kelp had been discovered. DI James Halstead had instigated a forensic search of Kelp's house. Jill Trent thought that Kelp's conviction for starving his dog to death and then being discovered in similar circumstances himself, was too much of a coincidence. James Halstead had reminded her, that Kelp's cause of death had not yet been established. Despite this, they wanted to get some idea about when the man was last seen alive.

James and Jill were discussing possible lines of inquiry, when Doctor Grant walked in, carrying three take away cups of coffee from the local coffee shop. James looked at the cups.

"Good morning Claire. You are very welcome if the coffees are for us."

"Well I know that the coffee from your machine tastes like dishwater, so I come bearing gifts." Jill Trent took her coffee and produced some chocolate biscuits.

"This is all quite civilised, James," said Claire Grant.

"Well, I do like to look after my favourite pathologist."

"No need for soft soaping. I know what you really want is the PM results on the late Mr Kelp."

"Well, now you mention it Doc, err sorry, Claire; it has been a couple of days."

"Yes, I know. We're very busy at the moment, but I've got the report here."

James opened the file and read it briefly.

"So, Kelp died of dehydration?"

Claire Grant looked over the top of her glasses.

"Well yes, he did but he also starved. A body can go without food for longer than going without water. Dehydration is the final cause of death. There was no indication of injury on the body, except for his fingers. I would surmise that he was trying to get the door open and made his fingers bloody. Eventually, he probably became too weak to do anything and drifted into a coma, before dying. I would put his age at around late forties. It's all in my report. Not sure how much help that will be though."

"We'll be able to get his actual age, linked to his driving licence. The part with his date of birth is badly rubbed and illegible. The next line remains the same. We're running checks now," said James, savouring his coffee.

Jill Trent looked at her boss.

"So, he was locked in the room from the outside, which means it was a deliberate act. Whoever locked the door would surely have known that there was no food or water in the room."

Halstead finished his coffee.

"Well, in the unlikely event that someone just turned the key in the lock without knowing Kelp was there, I think we should consider it a murder investigation; until we find out what happened."

"Good luck with that, James. My part looks the easy bit. Thanks for the biscuits Jill, I must be on my way."

After Claire Grant had gone, Jill Trent looked pensive.

"Claire's right to wish us luck. Proving intent to commit murder isn't going to be easy."

"Not easy, but certainly not impossible," mused James.

Jill wasn't so sure. She wondered if even James' hero, the fictional Sherlock Holmes, would have been able to crack this case.

James Halstead had got in touch with the police officer who had been involved with the cruelty case against Kelp. It was Police Sergeant Rosemary Mires. She wore her blond hair in a bob cut and was in her late twenties. She was seated in James Halstead's office and Jill handed her a coffee from the machine. Rosemary Mires looked at the coffee and gingerly sipped from the plastic cup.

James kicked off the questioning.

"I've looked at Kelp's conviction online and read the case notes. His house is in Eastport Lane and his dead dog was found in the cellar."

"Yes sir. The RSPCA were involved and the case was prosecuted about a month after their investigation."

"Is there any indication that Kelp had friends in the area?"

"No sir. I think he was a bit of a loner. I spoke to his immediate neighbours and they said they had never seen anyone visiting him. He apparently kept himself to himself. The poor dog was his only companion. They had heard it barking, but not loudly. I put that down to the fact that it's barking was muffled by being in the basement."

"And the dog was definitely starved and deprived of water?"

"Yes sir. The RSPCA vet did a post-mortem. The poor dog died of dehydration."

James and Jill looked at each other.

"Have I said something wrong?" asked a concerned Sergeant, Rosemary Mires.

Jill Trent reassured her.

"No Rosemary, nothing wrong at all. It's just that Kelp had the same cause of death."

"So, are you thinking that someone did the same to him in revenge for what he did to his dog, sir?"

"Thinking it, yes Rosemary, but proving it might be more difficult. There's a pub near Eastport Lane, I can't remember the name of it."

Answering together both Jill and Rosemary said, "The Grange."

James smiled.

"Thank you both. I think that's it for now Rosemary. If you think of anything, however small, please let me know. We need all the help we can get with this."

"Yes sir."

Rosemary Mires left the room, still clutching her half full cup of coffee, no doubt intending to pour it down the toilet!

"What's our next move?" asked Jill.

"Let's take a stroll to The Grange pub, via, Chez Kelp, shall we?" said James. They arrived at Kelp's house. One of James Halstead's officers had been there with a forensic team but had found nothing of significance. They had gained entry with a locksmith and fitted a new lock. James had one of the keys in his pocket in an envelope. James and Jill entered the property and were aware of a sour smell.

"Get a window open, Jill. This place stinks."

Jill opened a window and James found an air freshener in the kitchen. He sprayed it liberally, but the heavily scented vanilla mingled with the sour smell; hardly making it more palatable.

"Well, the forensic team didn't find anything," said James.

"What exactly are we looking for?" asked Jill, pulling a face as the sickly smell assailed her senses.

"I don't really know, Jill. I just wanted to have a nose around. Nose being the right word. The vanilla is making me a bit queasy."

"Me too," said Jill, as she held a tissue over her nose.

They walked around the house and discovered the source of the bad smell. There was a festering, half-used, four-pint milk container in the fridge, which apparently wasn't plugged in. Covering his nose with his hand, James poured the offending milk down the sink and flushed it with cold water. The smell subsided, but not by much.

They walked around the property and, on a shelf, in the corner of the living room, were a couple of highly coloured glass vases. Next to them were some old metal cars.

"Dinky Toys," said James, picking a car up and looking at the base plate.

"Did you have any when you were a boy?" asked Jill.

"Not like these. They must be very old. Look at the shapes of the cars. Vintage models, I would guess."

There were also some old music boxes and some quill pens, in a large ornate inkwell.

They carried on looking, hoping to find some paperwork but were disappointed. They really wanted to find something that would show family or next of kin.

"The forensics' team didn't take anything away, I assume," said Jill.

"No, they didn't find anything of any use to us. The fingerprints mostly belonged to Kelp, with a few unidentified ones."

"Do you know, James? It's almost as if all the paperwork, like bills and bank statements have been taken."

"Yes, I was thinking the same. But why?"

Still with his hand over his nose, James said,

"Let's get out of here and go for some lunch at The Grange, shall we?"

"That's the best idea you've had today, James."

They walked into the bar at The Grange. They both went to the toilets to wash their hands because they felt dirty after the tour around Kelp's place.

"What will it be, Jill?"

"Just a coke please."

"Two cokes please." "Want a sandwich?"

"Yes please. Despite that awful smell of sour milk, I'm hungry. Cheese and tomato, if they've got any."

"Two cheese and tomato sandwiches with the cokes, please."

They found a table near the back of the bar. Jill munched her sandwich. "How's things going with Sandra?"

She was referring to Halstead' ex-wife.

"Oh, she's being a bit of a pain about the divorce settlement. I suppose on the plus side, her family have got shedloads of money and Sandra's not short of a bob herself. She's already got a flat, which her parents gave her."

"Well, what's the problem James?"

"It's not really a problem but there's a dispute about which items in our former matrimonial home belong to who. In her mind, lots of it is hers."

"Are we talking music collections?"

"No, we're not talking music collections. Believe it or not she has been harassing me over the cat."

"The cat?"

"Yes, the bloody cat has gone missing and Sandra actually accused me of giving it away."

"Did you?"

"No, of course I didn't. Tell the truth, it was quite old and had started weeing indoors, so I wouldn't have objected to her taking it with her."

"So, what else does Sandra want?"

"Oh, silly things really. She wants some of the china, a duvet and an old table that we got in a Brighton flea market, years ago. With all her money, I can't see why she would want bits and pieces. Anyway, at least she doesn't want me to sell the flat. She says I can keep it and she doesn't want half the equity."

"Well that's a result, at least you won't be homeless."

"Yes, you're right. I don't have a big mortgage and I'm quite comfortable there."

They finished their lunch and turned to the business in hand. The team that checked Kelp's house didn't find any photographs of him. In fact, there were no photographs of anyone. They were able to access Kelp's photo from his driving licence but from the first time Halstead had seen it, he thought it wouldn't be much help. The face staring out from the driving licence was certainly not a man in his forties. It was a much younger Arron Kelp.

Halstead approached the man behind the bar, who had served them and flashed his ID.

"Wonder if you could help? Do you know a man named Arron Kelp?"

"I know him. He's the piece of garbage who starved his dog to death. It was all over the papers. What's he done now?"

"Just an inquiry. He didn't live far from your pub. Did he drink in here?"

"Yes, he did. I banned him after he killed his dog. A lot of my regulars said he should have been strung up for what he did."

"Do you know the names of anyone expressing those views?"

"Now wait a minute, nobody was serious about stringing him up, and it was just a heat of the moment thing when they read it in the papers."

"I'm sure it was just a figure of speech, but we are interested to speak to anyone who spoke against him."

"Look, I've said too much already. It was just general banter. I can't remember who said what. Just casual comments, that's all." "That's not very helpful."

"Sorry but I've said all I can say."

"We might need to talk to you again. Here's my card. Give me a buzz if your memory comes back," said a disappointed James.

The man looked thoughtful for a moment.

"There is one thing I can tell you. There's a guy called Oz. He was one of my regulars until I banned him for being drunk and obnoxious."

"Does Oz have a surname?"

"Probably, but I don't know it. Everyone just calls him Oz. I don't like the guy, never did and I was pleased to find a reason to ban him."

"And you are telling me this because?"

"Well, when people were slagging off this Kelp bloke, Oz started defending him and said he knew the guy and he hadn't meant for the dog to die. Just punishing it for barking."

"Any idea where I can find this Oz?"

"Yes, he drinks in The Swan, in Mountfield Road. I'm friends with the landlord there. He knows I banned Oz from here and keeps an eye on him. Apparently, he's in The Swan most Friday nights. Plays dominos, I'm told."

"Thanks for that."

"Don't thank me too much. Oz is a bastard when he's tanked up with booze and he's a big bloke."

"Don't worry, my Sergeant is quite tough herself!"

Jill gave James a glance and shook her head.

The two Detectives made their way back to the police station and James asked Jill if she would accompany him to The Swan on Friday night.

Neither liked the sound of this Oz and they planned to arrive in the early evening, hopefully before Oz got tanked up. Today was Wednesday and there weren't any other leads to follow until they spoke to the man.

That evening Jill Trent was sitting alone in her flat in Station Road. She didn't have a current boyfriend, having broken up with the last one several months ago. Jill was an attractive woman and had plenty of 'offers' to go out on dates. The big turn off for most of these suitors was her job. For some reason, whenever she told them she was a Detective Sergeant they just lost interest. One man had been very interested to know if Jill had a police uniform. She had no illusions, why he had asked!

Her flat was comfortable and she had got used to the sound of trains, pulling in and out of Lewes railway station. In fact, she was almost unaware of the noise after two years. Jill poured a glass of merlot and sat watching the local news on TV. It was the usual mix of bad news, led by council funding cuts. There was an interview with a couple of men who were complaining that fishing had been banned from the end of Eastbourne Pier, by the new owner; health and safety etc. Then an item caught her eye. There were reports that cats had been going missing in Lewes. An angry man was staring into the camera and blaming 'foreigners!'

Chapter Four

It was Thursday morning. Three men and two women were strolling along Grand Parade, on the Eastbourne seafront. One of the men was really tall and well built. He was in his late twenties and wore jeans and a t-shirt, with short sleeves rolled up over his muscular arms. His hair was cut in the style of an American Marine, with shaven sides. He was good looking in a sort of brutish way.

The other two men were shorter and considerably less well-muscled than their companion. They were mid-twenties. Both wore shorts with long t-shirts and sported crewcuts. The two women both had long, blond hair and wore vests and shorts which did little to hide their figures. They could easily have been athletes. Both wore make up and were attractive. They were late teens, early twenties.

One of the women grabbed hold of the big man and said, in a little girl voice,

"Can I have an ice-cream?"

He gave her a disdainful look.

"I'm not in the mood."

"Go on Terry, buy Angie an ice-cream," said Tracie, the other woman.

The two younger men said nothing. It didn't do to upset Terry and it was best to keep quiet when the women were teasing the big man.

Terry was known for his violent nature, but the woman knew he wouldn't lift a finger against them. Indeed, that's why they teased him. Poking the tiger with a stick and all that!

Truth be told Terry liked this horseplay with the women and quite fancied Angie. She kept pestering Terry until he finally gave in. Handing her a twenty-pound note, Terry said,

"Get yourself a bloody ice-cream. Get one for everyone. I don't want one."

The two other men, Sean and George, looked at each other. Terry never seemed to be short of cash.

The group were approaching Eastbourne Pier, when Angie said,

"Hang on Terry, look at those three lads on the beach."

The three lads were throwing stones at a group of gulls and laughing loudly, as the birds jumped out of the way.

Angie said, "Come on Tracie."

The two women walked over to where the three lads were throwing stones. Angie was annoyed.

"Stop throwing stones. If you hit a gull, you could kill or badly injure it."

One of the lads turned to face Angie and Tracie.

"What the fuck has it got to do with you? Piss off before we throw stones at you." Angie moved forward and hit the lad hard in the face.

Before he could recover from the shock of being hit by a woman, Tracie kicked him on a knee and he went down holding his leg and swearing. The other two lads were motionless and stared down in disbelief, at their injured friend. The downed lad got to his feet and grabbed Angie by the vest. Before he could do anything, Terry was next to Angie. He hit the lad full in the face. The lad went down with blood spraying from a broken nose. He was laying on the beach unable to get up and writhing in agony. The other two lads ran off.

A group of people were having refreshments at one of the beach deck cafés. One man came over to attend to the injured lad. He was a big, middle-aged man and shouted at Terry.

"I saw that, you bastard. He's just a lad. You shouldn't have punched him like that. Pick on someone your own size."

Without replying, Terry hit the man in the stomach and then caught him with a hard punch to the side of the head. Despite his size, the man went down, clutching his stomach. A couple more men came over and were about to get involved, when Angie got hold of Terry's arm and led him away. Tracie put her arm through Terry's other arm and they walked back up the beach. The two newcomers helped the fallen lad and the injured man. Terry and his companions left the beach area and made their way along Terminus Road, just off the seafront and into the town centre. They ended up in a coffee shop.

Meanwhile, somebody at the seafront had called the police and ambulance services. Two police officers and two medics attended the injured. The lad was in a bad way with a broken nose and suspected concussion. The middle-aged man was still rubbing his stomach and the side of his face was swollen and discoloured.

Several witnesses gave their names and addresses to the police and brief statements were taken. The injured were taken away to hospital for precautionary checks and the beach returned to normal. About two dozen gulls were casting watchful eyes, for anyone foolish enough to leave their food unattended for a split second.

Chapter Five

Wednesday afternoon found James Halsted sitting at his computer. He was about to get a coffee from the station machine, when Jill Trent walked in with two coffees and two doughnuts.

"Jill, you must be a mind reader. I was about to get a coffee. Doughnuts too!"

"Thought you might like real coffee and a sugar rush," said Jill. "I've been talking to Rosemary Mires about the Kelp case. I told her about this Oz character and she told me to take care."

"I've been thinking about Oz, myself. It might be an idea to have a couple of uniforms nearby in case this bloke kicks off."

"You told the barman at The Grange that I could handle him," smiled Jill.

"Yes. I'm sure you would have a go, but I prefer my team to be in one piece."

"All joking aside, I agree with you that back up would be wise," said Jill.

"But who knows? This Oz might be a pussycat," smiled James.

"Talking of pussycats, did you catch the local TV news last night?"

"No, why, anything interesting?" asked James, as he munched on his doughnut.

"Well, it might be interesting to you. Apparently, lots of cats have gone missing in the Lewes area."

"And you think my cat is one of them?" asked James, raising an eyebrow, Roger Moore style.

"I didn't say that, but it's a bit of a coincidence don't you think?"

Before they could explore the great cat mystery any further, Halstead's telephone buzzed. "Yes OK, what time? Ten minutes. Fine, thanks." He hung up.

"Problem?"

"Don't know. Super wants to see me. Her secretary never gives much away. A chat apparently. Just enough time to eat my doughnut."

Detective Chief Superintendent Lorraine Marsh was a career police officer. She was a university graduate and had risen through the ranks at breakneck speed. She had plenty of experience at the sharp end of policing but the further up the ranks she travelled, the more 'political' she had become. She admired James Halstead because she appreciated his skills as a Detective and his clear up rates. She knew about his marital problems and was impressed by his professionalism. Of course, James Halstead would never have suspected that Marsh liked him, because she was very professional herself and always business-like in her dealings with him. At thirty-eight, she was relatively young and was looking for the next step up.

James walked into the Super's office. A few moments before, he had been grateful to Jill Trent for pointing out that he had sugar from his doughnut stuck to his chin.

"Hello James, come and sit down." Marsh gestured towards a comfortable settee and armchairs, which surrounded a modern coffee table.

"Coffee?"

She had her own filter coffee machine, which was a big step up from the less than satisfactory, station machine.

"Yes, please Ma'am."

Marsh asked her secretary for two coffees.

"I just wanted to discuss a couple of matters with you James. Are you making any progress with the body in the basement?"

Just as James was about to reply, Marsh's secretary placed a tray on the coffee table and left.

"Not much more than my original briefing note, I'm afraid. But I am following up a lead on Friday. I'm hoping to speak to a person who may be able to provide a link to the dead man."

"You're working on the premise that it's murder?"

"Yes, we think Arron Kelp was locked in the basement and left to die."

"Because of what he did to his dog?" asked Marsh.

"Yes, it does kind of link together. He killed his dog and then died himself in almost identical circumstances."

"You think his death was a kind of retribution?"

"It's possible, but proving it and finding a perpetrator, isn't going to be easy."

"OK James, please keep me posted on the case."

James sipped his coffee and savoured the taste.

"Better than the station machine coffee, isn't it? Privileges of rank James," said DCS Marsh, smiling.

"Is there anything else, Ma'am?"

"Well, as a matter of fact, there is. What do you know about the epidemic of missing cats?"

"Err, well, I think it was reported on the local TV news the other night."

"James, I know that you probably think it has nothing to do with us, but I have been coming under a bit of pressure from local councillors and our MP. They want to know what we are doing about it."

James Halstead looked a bit pained.

"I can see that you are not exactly enthusiastic about this, but I would like you to at least make some enquiries, so I can tell the councillors and MP that we are investigating. Perhaps you could ask Sergeant Trent to set something in motion."

"I'm sure she will relish the opportunity, Ma'am."

Marsh smiled. "I'm sure she will. And James, I am serious about this. We need to keep everyone on side. The bigger picture and all that."

"The bigger picture, yes Ma'am."

James returned to his office and smiled at Jill Trent.

"You look happy, James."

"Yes, and now I'm going to make you happy."

"How so?"

"The super wants you to investigate the case of the missing moggies."

"Seriously?"

"Yes, seriously. It's all about the bigger picture, apparently. She specifically asked that you investigate it."

"James, you know that the rest of the station will refer to me as 'Cat Woman' don't you?"

"Jill, I told the Super that you would relish the opportunity to take the case."

"Thanks James. I'm so glad the Super has confidence in me."

Chapter Six

Friday night, and the meeting with Oz loomed. James and Jill had arrived at The Swan early and were sitting outside, enjoying the summer evening. They had checked inside the pub. There was one man, sitting at a table with dominos in front of him. He was around sixty and obviously not Oz. They assumed that if Oz was playing tonight, he would turn up sooner or later. If not, it was a nice evening to just sit outside for a while. Jill Trent was wearing a skirt but having had time to think about it, she wished she had worn trousers. Halstead was wearing a sports jacket (police casual) and chinos. His open-neck shirt gave him a vaguely informal look.

They were both drinking coke to keep clear heads and importantly, if there should be any confrontation with Oz, it would have been unwise to have alcohol on their breath. A police car with two uniformed officers was parked just around the corner from The Swan. Jill had her radio in her bag, so everything was nicely set up. What could possibly go wrong?

As they had no idea what Oz looked like, the plan was to go into the bar a little later and see if there was a game of dominos, then just ask if Oz was there, pull him aside for a quiet word and then go home. Simple! Of course, the potential for problems with the plan was well understood by both of them but it was important to make progress with the case and Oz seemed like a potential lead. They sat sipping their cokes for half an hour as the pub began to fill up. There were young men and women, obviously out to get blotto and some older men who were just out for a social drink. And hopefully, perhaps, some domino players.

Eventually, James and Jill sauntered inside the bar and their vacated garden table was immediately grabbed by a group of young men and women.

In the corner of the bar, sat several men playing dominos. There were four in total and one was a rough-looking man with ferocious stubble and a pint of Guinness in front of him. He appeared to be downing a short and burped loudly, which raised a cheer from his fellow players. The older man, who had been waiting earlier, was a member of the dominos group.

The Detectives edged over to the domino players and the big man, suddenly aware of their presence, looked up.

"You're crowding us."

Not a good start thought Jill. James stepped forward.

"Sorry, we didn't mean to crowd you, but we are looking for Oz."

"Who wants to know?"

As discreetly as he could, James leaned towards the big man.

"Detective Inspector James Halstead. If you are Oz, we would really appreciate a few minutes of your time."

"You would, would you? Well, I don't want to talk in here, it's too crowded."

Halstead was a little apprehensive but remained calm, at least on the outside. He did get a few jitters but pressed on.

"Tell you what, let's go out to the garden and we can have a quiet chat. Nothing to be worried about, I can assure you."

The big man rose from the table and downed his pint of Guinness in almost one gulp. He burped, again, getting another cheer from his companions and wiped his mouth on his sleeve.

"Can't leave that behind, cos these bastards will drink it."

James and Jill half smiled, as all three made their way outside. The man obviously drank very quickly. Perhaps they should have gone back inside the pub earlier, before he got tanked up. There were no vacant tables. James had really wanted to have this chat sitting down to make it appear informal and non-threatening. They found a quiet corner of the pub garden away from the tables full of people. Everyone was having a good time and took no notice of the trio as they stood together,

35

apparently, in casual discussion.

James spoke. "Can you confirm you are Oz?"

"What a stupid question, of course I am. I thought you already knew who I was."

Jill Trent responded in her most calm and unthreatening voice.

"Sorry, but we have to make sure we're speaking to the right person."

"What the fuck do you want?"

Ignoring the swearing, James responded.

"We believe you know Arron Kelp."

"Are you bastards still harassing him over that dog business? He went to court over that and still you can't leave him alone."

"No, we're not still after him. We just wanted to know if you are a friend or acquaintance."

Oz was looking very red. More accurately, his face was an angry hue of reds and blues. He was about to kick off and the two Detectives were ideal targets for his anger. Jill Trent stepped back as Oz came at them like an enraged bull. He aimed a massive roundhouse punch at James Halstead, which, had it connected, would have put him down and out. Fortunately, James was fit and quicker on his feet than the clumsy Oz. The roundhouse punch had been thrown with such force, that after missing Halstead's head, the momentum had caused Oz to stagger and fall, face down on the grass, like something out of a comedy. He went down so hard that the combination of booze and the face first landing had winded him. He had both arms stretched out in front of him. They had clearly not softened his abrupt landing.

Without hesitation, Jill Trent sat down heavily on the prone figure of Oz. Ignoring the fact that skirts are really unsuitable for ground wrestling, she pinned the struggling Oz, as she spoke into her radio and called in the cavalry. Halstead in the meantime had handcuffed this lumbering giant. The people at the tables all gave a drunken cheer as Jill Trent tried to stay seated on the struggling Oz's back.

Fortunately, the two uniforms arrived within minutes and the still dazed Oz was formally arrested. Still handcuffed, he was bundled into the back of the squad car. As the car drove Oz to the police station for a night in the cells, on a charge of attempted assault, James and Jill looked at each other.

"Are you all right Jill? That was very brave of you to jump on him like that,"

said James, smiling.

"I'm glad you aren't hurt. If that punch had connected with either of us, we would be in hospital, or worse now."

"Why are you smiling James?"

"Relief I guess and just a thought. I don't want to be called sexist, but skirts are not really suitable for wrestling with violent men!"

"Funny you should say that; I had a similar thought myself. Should have gone for trousers."

"Well, I think we should give Oz time to sober up and get a good night's sleep in custody. Are you up for interviewing him on Saturday morning?"

"Yes, on one condition."

"What's that?"

"I'm starving. Let's find a restaurant and eat."

Chapter Seven

Saturday morning came around very quickly. James Halstead and Jill Trent had eaten in a restaurant in Lewes town centre the previous evening. Then they had gone their separate ways. They had reflected on how lucky they were, that Oz had not inflicted any damage on either of them. Now they had to interview him. Not a very appealing prospect!

They had commandeered interview room one, which was the largest of three rooms. James felt that they needed a bit of space in case Oz kicked off again. They were both seated on the same side of the securely bolted down table. The Duty Sergeant entered the room with a dishevelled Oz and got him to sit in a chair opposite.

"Do you want me to stay, sir?" asked the burly sergeant.

"No, that's fine."

The Sergeant gave a quizzical look, before exiting.

James studied a folder, which was on the table in front of him.

"Can I start off by establishing your real name? Apparently, you told the custody officer that you are John Wayne. When the officer looked at your personal effects, there was a driving licence in the name of Osbert Francis. The photo on the licence was definitely you."

Oz gave a pained look.

"I didn't ask to be given the bloody name. I've had to put up with taunting when I was at school and as soon as I left, I told everyone to call me Oz."

"Well, Oz, we don't mind going along with you, because we aren't formally charging you. At least not at this point."

"Look, I'm really sorry about what happened at the pub. I'd had a few drinks and you were annoying me."

"Well, because your attempted punch missed us both, we're just going to ignore it. Your night in the cells, was just to sober you up."

The violent Oz had now been replaced with a contrite Oz. He looked at Jill Trent.

"You really jarred my back when you jumped on me."

"Sorry Oz, I just wanted to hold you down," said a half smiling Jill.

There was a knock on the door and a police officer bought in a tray with tea and biscuits. Oz grabbed a biscuit and sipped his tea.

James looked into the big man's eyes.

"Look Oz, I don't want you to kick off again but there's a good reason why we were asking about Arron Kelp. We're not after him. I'm afraid he's dead!"

"Dead?"

"Yes, we haven't released any information yet. There will be a news release this afternoon. I'm only telling you now because I want your help."

"Help, for what?"

"We suspect that he may have been murdered and we need to speak with anyone who knew him. Your name came up and that's why we wanted a discreet chat, not a fight."

"OK, but I didn't really know Arron that well. We used to meet sometimes and have a few beers in The Grange. Then he got a big fine and suspended prison sentence and the bloody landlord barred him."

"We heard that you were defending him in an argument with regulars."

"Too right. He wasn't a bad bloke. Don't think he meant to kill his dog, but he still got a hefty fine and the threat of prison."

Jill Trent finished her tea, despite the fact that it was as ghastly as the station coffee.

"Do you know if he had any other friends or drinking mates?"

"Well, there was a bloke; he seemed to know Arron. He was very keen to hear all about the court case and was asking him all sorts of questions. Think his name's Terry."

Jill looked at her boss and continued.

"When was this?"

"Just after Arron was fined. About five or six weeks ago now."

"Did they meet up very often?"

"About three or four times and the big guy was always buying the drinks. Arron was never a big boozer, but he used to get really tanked up when he was with his friend."

"Did you drink with them?"

"At first, but the bloke collared me in the toilet and told me to fuck off."

"And what did you do?"

"I left the pub."

"Without a fight?"

"Yeah. Look, I know I'm a big bloke and can handle myself, but this guy was an even bigger bastard. Different class! He looked like he could really cause some damage. Could've even have been a boxer. Not an ounce of fat on him. I'm not stupid enough to take on someone like that."

"So, was that the last time you saw them both together?"

"Not the last time, no. I didn't drink with them after my warning, but they were in the bar a few more times. I stayed well away. The last time I saw Arron was when he staggered out of the bar and the big bloke, Terry, was almost having to hold him up."

"Do you know where this Terry lives?" asked Halstead.

"Not a clue, sorry. I didn't want to get involved with him. He was Arron's new best buddy."

"Can you describe him? Other that the fact he was a big bastard!"

"Yeah, he was about thirtyish, built like he went to the gym a lot. Massive muscles. Short hair, shaved at the sides. Not the sort of bloke you'd want to get in a fight with."

"Oz, have you any idea what Arron Kelp did for a living?" asked James.

"No. As far as I know he didn't work. He was never short of a bob or two. Think he did a bit of buying and selling."

"Like what?"

"Oh, old stuff. Load of junk, as far as I could see. He had a van. Did a lot of car boots."

"One of his neighbours said Mr Kelp had a van. Any idea where it is?"

"Nah, not seen it around recently. Think he must have got rid of it. Perhaps someone nicked it."

"Apart from this Terry, did Arron have any other friends or associates?"

"Not really. He was a bit of a loner. After the court case, nobody wanted to know him."

"Do you know if anybody threatened him?"

"Yeah, the whole pub did a bit of name calling. Then Arron got barred and the place settled down after that."

"And you defended him."

"I just argued back and it fizzled out. Nobody wanted to take me on."

"Is there anything else you can tell us, Oz?"

"No, sorry. I'd like to find out who killed Arron, but I've told you everything I know."

Halstead stood up and offered Oz his hand. Oz shook it and said,

"No hard feelings, mate."

"None at all."

Oz offered his hand to Jill Trent, who took it and gave a brief shake. He almost smiled, but not quite.

"If you want to have a return match, you know where I drink."

"Thanks, I'll bear it in mind," said Jill.

Oz collected his personal belongings from the custody officer and left.

James closed the folder and Jill, who had been making notes, turned to her boss.

"Well that was interesting but where do we go next? A big bastard, named Terry, about thirty, and who you wouldn't want to pick a fight with."

"Yes, it's not much to go on but we know more now than we did yesterday. There's not much more we can do today. Let's call time and start again on Monday morning. You need to give a bit of thought to your great missing cat case."

"Yes, I have been thinking of nothing else."

Chapter Eight

Charles Massey was the Master of the Uckfield Hunt. He had recently appeared on local television following an incident with hunt saboteurs. His wife, Isobel, had been filmed whipping a masked man, who was trying to unseat her during a drag hunt. She had been charged with assault, but the case had been thrown out of court on a technicality. There had been some ugly scenes involving protesters outside the court and Isobel Massey and her husband had to be smuggled out, via a back door.

The television interview had shown Charles Massey to be an arrogant man who blamed class envy and hatred of anyone deemed posh, for the anti-hunt mob's dislike of him and his friends. In truth the hunt had broken the terms of the Hunting Act 2004 several times, but it was difficult for the anti-hunt brigade to get enough evidence for a prosecution.

Saturday evening found Charles and Isobel Massey dining at the Magpie Inn, which was just outside the East Sussex village of Cross in Hand. They were a party of four couples and the booze was flowing as Charles Massey shouted, "Ladies and Gentleman, a toast to the legal system and one in the eye for the garbage protesters!"

The group laughed loudly and a braying man shouted his support for the toast.

Seated at the bar were three men and a young, blond woman. They were the same people who had been involved in the assault on Eastbourne seafront a few days ago. The young woman was Angie and she was getting very agitated, watching the noisy group. Terry was angry to witness the laughing and shouting coming from the table in the dining room, because it was clearly upsetting Angie.

"I've had enough," said Terry.

"Don't Terry," said George, grabbing his arm. Terry shrugged him off, but Sean stepped in front of him.

"Don't kick off in front of all these witnesses. Just wait."

Terry was about to push Sean away but thought better of it. George spoke into his ear, in a whisper.

"We don't need the attention. We all agreed to keep a low profile. You'll blow it for all of us. Just calm down, for fuck sake!"

After another round of drinks, the three men and the woman left the pub and Terry looked daggers at the table of braying hunters, as Angie whispered in his ear.

When they got outside, Terry shouted at his companions.

"I want to smash the bastards. Did you hear what they were saying? These people think they're the ruling class. They don't care what people think of them."

George put his hands, on Terry's shoulders. He knew he was risking a punch in the mouth, but he persisted.

"Look, Terry, you can't just beat people up in public places. What you did on the beach was risky. Suppose the police had been nearby. You could've got arrested and who knows where that would have led?"

Terry removed George's hands from his shoulders and patted his cheek, Godfather style.

"You're right. Let's go and get some fish and chips, then all back to my flat. We can pick Tracie up on the way."

"Yeah, great," said his two companions.

"I'm coming as well," said Angie, grabbing Terry's arm. Terry smiled to himself. He wasn't a really a hunt protester at all. He just fancied Angie and hung out with her and her friends, to get close to her. But he would've enjoyed smashing the posh bastards!

That night, Jill Trent had also had a fish and chips takeaway and was sitting on her settee with a big glass of her favourite merlot wine. After she had left the police station following the interview with Oz, she had started to plan her investigation into the disappearing cats. There was no way on earth that she really wanted to get involved but as the request for her to investigate came from on-high, she had little choice. Jill planned to open a few lines of enquiry and when, as she fully expected, it went nowhere, she could point to lack of evidence.

Despite her lack of enthusiasm, she had actually contacted the local television station that ran the 'cat' story, to get the name and address of the angry cat owner featured in the piece. Fortunately for her, one of her ex boyfriends, worked for the television station and with a vague promise of a drink, she was able to obtain the information. The angry cat man was Cyril Blake who lived in Sun Street, not far from Lewes town centre. She had nothing planned for Sunday morning and had decided to pay Cyril a visit. Technically, she should not make visits without advising her boss where she was going. Although it seemed unlikely that Cyril, who looked like a senior citizen in his TV interview, was actually a serial killer, she knew she should really have followed protocol.

It was about ten o' clock. Not too late to ring James Trent. She rang his mobile and he answered almost immediately.

"Hello, Jill, what's the matter, can't you sleep?"

"Hi James, sorry to disturb you."

"No problem. I've just had a takeaway and I'm on my third Peroni. What can I do for you?"

Jill had explained her plan to visit Cyril Blake and James had given her the go-ahead. She had reflected that she and her boss had both been sitting at home with takeaways and booze, on a Saturday night. Two lonely people? No, of course not. They were both alone, but surely not lonely. A second large glass of merlot had ensured that her thoughts about lonely lifestyles had subsided into sleep, as soon as she got into bed.

Early the next morning, Jill's eyes opened and her headache was telling her that she was dehydrated after the wine. Dehydration, she reflected, was exactly the cause of Arron Kelps demise. Not a very pleasant thought! She drank several cups of coffee and had some buttered toast. Then after a shower, she felt human again. Her headache had gone and she squeezed into a pair of complaining jeans and a crisp, white t-shirt.

She arrived at Sun Street at mid-morning. She found the house and rang the doorbell, which played a tune. Because it was a very long tune, Cyril Blake had opened the door when it was only halfway through. Jill introduced herself and showed her ID. Cyril Blake was pleased to see her.

"It's about time the police took an interest in what's been going on. We pay our council tax and get nothing!"

"Well, I'm here now, Mr Blake and I want you to tell me all about the missing cats."

Blake led Jill into a well-furnished living room. She was taken aback at how modern everything was. It was almost like a room in a film. There were some small antique vases, but they didn't seem out of place in the modern setting.

"Please sit down, Inspector."

"Sergeant actually," said Jill, as she sat on an uncomfortable, modern armchair.

"Oh there, I've just promoted you. Coffee, tea?"

"Coffee would be nice."

While Blake was making the coffee, Jill looked around the room. There were several paintings on the walls. Jill didn't know much about art, but the pictures were garishly coloured and made no sense. They must be modernist, she thought. Blake entered the room with a tray of coffee and some after eight mints.

"I see you are admiring my paintings. I'm an artist and these represent my best work. I've got some being exhibited at the Towner Centre, in Eastbourne. Mints OK? Help yourself to sugar and milk."

Jill helped herself to a mint and felt obliged to lie about the paintings. She had thought that if these are the best, what must the others be like?

"Very nice, very colourful."

"Yes, I love colour. My late partner, Henry, was very partial to colour. In fact, the red one was his favourite."

Jill drank her coffee and was on her second or third mint. She had her notebook in her lap.

"Now, Mr Blake."

"Oh, please. Call me Cyril."

"Cyril, can you tell me about your missing cat."

"Well I'd had Sebastian for six years, then one night he didn't come in when I called him."

"Was that unusual?"

"Well, yes. I always used to let him out last thing at night to do his business and that last time, he didn't come back. I put a few notices on trees, with Sebastian's photo and offered a reward of fifty quid for a safe return."

"I assume nobody came forward."

"Absolutely right. Then I found out that cats had gone missing from all around the area. I'm sure it's got something to do with foreigners!"

"Have you any particular person in mind?"

"No, but it's the sort of thing they do, isn't it?"

"Cyril, you can't just generalise. You shouldn't make such accusations without any evidence."

"Well, who else would kidnap cats?"

"We don't know that cats have been kidnapped. That's why I'm making enquires."

Cyril Blake looked downcast.

"If Henry had still been here, he would have been so upset. He did so love Sebastian! Anyway, the RSPCA told me that they were concerned that there could be a gang, stealing cats for their fur and shipping it abroad. So many have gone missing, you know. It's just so sad!"

"OK, Cyril. I'll talk with the local RSPCA office and see what they can tell me."

"Thanks for the coffee and biscuits. Here's my card. Just give me a buzz if you think of anything else."

"Thanks, I really appreciate you coming out on a Sunday. I expect you would rather be with your boyfriend at weekends."

Chapter Nine

Monday morning found Jill Trent sitting at her desk outside James Halstead's office. James Halstead arrived about ten minutes later, with a newspaper under his arm.

"They've got the Arron Kelp case on the front page."

He put the paper on Jill's desk and she looked at the headline story.

Death of local man

The body of Arron Kelp, 46, was discovered last week, in the basement of the disused former co-op building, which was being demolished. A workman made this grisly discovery when he broke into a locked room. According to a police statement, the body had been there for about a month. A post-mortem examination found that Kelp had died from starvation and lack of water. It is believed that he had been locked in the room and the police are treating the death as murder. The police spokesperson declined to comment on the theory that Kelp's death was a retribution, for the killing his dog.

Arron Kelp had been given a suspended prison sentence and had been fined for starving his dog to death. The police are pursuing several lines of enquiry and are asking for anyone with information to contact Lewes police.

Jill Trent looked up.

"We only have one line of enquiry and that's going nowhere at the moment."

"Our only lead is this big guy, Terry and without some more information, we will need to get really lucky, to identify him."

"By the way, you made the inside page!" smiled James.

Jill opened the newspaper, and on page five was a photo of her, sitting on the fallen Oz. Someone in the pub garden must have taken the photo. It showed James Halstead in partial shadow. The heading under the photo read:

Punch up at The Swan Pub.

Two men and a woman were involved in a fight in the garden of The Swan pub. The woman had clearly won the first round with a pin. The police arrived soon after and took one man off in handcuffs. The other man left with the woman.

"What an embarrassing picture. I'm glad they didn't get a full-face shot. There's no mention that we were police."

"Don't worry Jill. I'll speak up for you if you are on a police brutality charge!"

"Thank you for your support, sir."

"How did you get on with your missing cats' investigation on Sunday?"

"I met a nice old guy named Cyril Blake. He told me all about his missing cat, Sebastian."

"Sebastian?"

"Yes, imagine calling him in at night."

"Did you get anything useful?"

"Only that Cyril Blake blames 'foreigners'."

"Not a very PC thing to say."

"I don't think he even considered that to be honest."

"What next?"

"I'm going to talk to the local RSPCA, to see if they have any ideas."

"The Super is expecting a breakthrough, Jill."

"Yes, I'm sure she is."

Jill had typed up the Oz interview notes and had put them in the very thin, Arron Kelp file. This case really was going nowhere fast. James Halstead had to go to a meeting later that morning. It was a regular 'partners' meeting where Social Services, Probation, Education and

Local Council got together with the police. Halstead's boss had nominated him to represent the police. As far as he was concerned, it was an opportunity for everyone around the table, to blame the police for everything.

This gave Jill Trent the opportunity to contact the local RSPCA office in pursuit of what she privately called, 'Operation Moggy'. She had arranged to meet an Inspector named Roy, at a local coffee shop. Jill arrived at the coffee shop and was approached by a short, stocky, black man, in uniform, with a prominent 'Roy' name badge. They ordered coffee and croissants and after a short debate about who was going to pay, Jill handed over a ten-pound note and got very little change back.

Roy stirred his large cappuccino and took a sip, leaving a moustache of chocolate and milk on his top lip. Jill gestured towards Roy's mouth and he laughed.

"My wife normally keeps an eye on me when I have cappuccino. Thanks Sergeant, not a good start is it?"

"Please, call me Jill. As I told you on the phone, I'm looking into the missing cats."

"Oh, I bet you drew the short straw. I can't see the police taking it that seriously."

"I was asked by our Superintendent to investigate and I thought you could give me some background. I've interviewed Mr Cyril Blake, the chap who was on TV and he told me that the RSPCA were involved."

"Mr Cyril Blake was bending my ear for ages on the phone. He was on about foreigners kidnapping his cat. When I called at his home, he gave me a funny look. My grandparents were originally from Uganda and when he clapped eyes on me, he must have been a little embarrassed."

Jill smiled. "So, he told you all about Sebastian?"

"Yes, including his nightly toilet habits."

"So, what can you tell me Roy?"

"The reason I wanted to meet face to face is to hand over a copy of our investigations. I suppose 'investigations' is a bit grand really. It's more a series of notes showing names and addresses of people who have had cats go missing. Even got some photos of their beloved animals. Everyone seems to take mobile phone shots of their pets, these days."

Roy handed a file over to Jill. It contained nearly two dozen or so sheets of foolscap paper. Jill reflected that it was considerably thicker than the Arron Kelp file, back at the office.

"How many missing cats are there?"

Roy grimaced.

"There are twenty-three cats, reported missing and that's beyond coincidence. In a typical month, we normally have about four maybe five cases and generally, the cats have been handed in to us and are returned to their owners."

"So, twenty-three missing cats is an unusual occurrence?" "I'd say so. Especially as only three cats have been handed in to us for the last six weeks!"

"So, what do you think is happening?"

"Illegal fur trade!"

"Really? I didn't realise there was such a thing."

"Well, in truth, there's quite a market across the channel. It's all undercover but the fur is being sold as faux fur. You know, around hoods on coats and cuffs and the like. Apparently, some of it is finding its way back to the UK."

"Well now you mention it, I did see a report that Trading Standards have been investigating market stalls in some parts of the country."

Jill suddenly had a picture in her mind of the unfortunate Sebastian, decorating a hooded jacket.

They finished their coffee and croissants and Jill left with the file. She reflected that the police didn't really have the resources, nor the inclination, to interview twenty-odd cat owners and was grateful to Roy for supplying the information. She could add her Cyril Blake, interview to the file. But 'Where to go next?' was the question.

Chapter Ten

That evening, Charles Massey and his wife Isobel were driving towards the gates of their estate near the East Sussex village of Willingdon. It was still light and a very pleasant evening. They had the hood of the Bentley Continental down. Charles Massey had downed a couple of beers, but felt he was still under the drink drive limit. Anyway, there weren't often police around in this rural setting. As they were slowing down to trigger the automatic gates, Isobel pointed to the side of the road.

"Stop Charles! Look, there's someone on the side of the road."

"What the hell!"

He stopped violently and he and his wife got out. It was a woman. What on earth was she doing here?

As they approached the prone figure of a woman, she suddenly sat up. She wore a scarf over her face. In his usual arrogant way Charles Massey, barked,

"What the bloody hell are you playing at? I could have run you over and killed you."

A voice from behind them said,

"Yeah, you're used to killing things, aren't you?"

The Masseys both turned to see a big man, with a scarf over most of his face. They could see his eyes, which seemed to match the anger in his voice.

Charles Massey was not a man to be intimidated.

"You're one of those hunt saboteurs. You bastard! Fuck off before I give you a good hiding!"

The big man stepped forward and hit Charles Massey hard in the stomach, which made him double-up. He was then smashed violently, in the face by the attacker's knee and went down hard. Isobel Massey rushed towards her fallen husband and glared at the masked man.

"You cowardly bastard. If I had my whip, I'd…"

Her words were cut short by a blow to the back of her head. The previously prone woman had hit her with a stick and blood was already running down Isobel Massey's neck. She fell face down next to her husband. Charles Massey was barely conscious but managed to speak.

"You bastard," he screamed.

The woman with the scarf, spoke in a calm voice now.

"I saw you and your posh friends braying and laughing in The Magpie. You thought it was great that your bitch of a wife had got away with whipping a protester. You and your kind are the real vermin. Not foxes. Well, you won't be killing foxes for a while." With that, she kicked Charles Massey violently on an ankle and then on a knee. The woman did the same to Isobel Massey, who screamed in agony.

As they were leaving, the violent couple kicked the side of the Bentley. They strolled off up the lane and then cut across fields and were soon gone, leaving the bloodied Masseys laying in the road.

Chapter Eleven

The following morning DI Halstead and DS Trent, were outside the Massey's house in Willingdon. The Masseys had been discovered in the road next to their Bentley, by a dog walking couple. Both had been carted off to Eastbourne Hospital. Both had knee and ankle injuries which needed surgery. Charles Massey had a badly bruised face and swollen nose. Isobel Massey had a deep gash in the back of her head, but a scan had shown no permanent damage. Their condition was described as comfortable, but they were both in some pain and required pain killers. They were, in reality, far from comfortable.

The police Duty Officer had initiated a forensic search but the area around the attack had been well trampled. DI James Halstead was advised that there really was nothing useful in what was, a contaminated crime scene. James and Jill had wanted to interview the injured couple as soon as possible, but their doctor had advised that they needed a period of rest. The interview would have to wait. They had been told by the Duty Officer, that the Masseys had a daughter, Sarah, living at home and they had asked to speak with her. Which was why they were now outside the front gate. James spoke into an electronic box, announcing their presence. The gate slowly opened and Jill drove her Fiat 500 through the gates and up a long drive. After what seemed like ages, a large house came into view, as they rounded a bend. There were mature trees, a substantial lake, with a rowing boat on the shore and a tennis court.

James shook his head.

"How the rich live."

"Jealousy is a terrible trait!" smiled Jill.

She parked between a Bentley and a red MX5 sports car. As they approached the rather grand-looking front door, a man opened it.

"DI Halstead and DS Trent, to see Sarah Massey."

The rather haughty man, a butler, guessed James, responded without emotion.

"Yes, Miss Massey is expecting you. She's by the pool."

They followed at a sedate pace, as the immaculately dressed man led them to the pool. There was a young woman lounging on a padded wooden recliner. She was wearing a bikini and sipping a Martini.

James was a little embarrassed by this young woman's attire, or lack of, which left little to the imagination.

"Miss Sarah Massey?"

"Yes. Come and sit down. Martini?"

"Err, thank you, no."

"Oh, sorry, it's that old TV police thing where you say, 'not while you are on duty!"

"Something like that." "What about tea or coffee?"

"A coffee would be nice."

"Yes please," added Jill.

Sarah Massey nodded, almost imperceptibly, to the man. He was obviously well trained because he disappeared without speaking a word.

James sat down, as did Jill. She took out her notebook and placed it discreetly on her lap. She then spoke to the young woman.

"Miss Massey, we are so sorry to learn about your parents. We've been told by Eastbourne hospital, that they're are both comfortable."

"Yes, that's what they said to me. I saw them late last night and they looked far from comfortable. The attackers damaged their knees and ankles and my mother is lucky not to have a fractured skull!"

Jill Trent responded.

"Yes, from what we've been told it could have been far worse."

Just then the man appeared with a large silver tray with an impressive silver coffee pot and expensive-looking, antique-looking china.

"Please help yourself to coffee," said Sarah Massey, smiling at James, who poured while Jill Trent continued the questioning.

"We know that your parents were found, laying in the road just outside your gates, by a couple of dog walkers."

"Yes, that's right. They were both pretty bloodied and couldn't move. We know the dog walkers because they used to take our old dog out on occasions."

"What happened when they raised the alarm?"

"They spoke to William, our butler, on the gate intercom and he alerted the police and ambulance. I went out with William, to comfort my mother and father. Two police officers took a few details and when the ambulance got here it took my parents off with sirens and lights, blaring down the lane." "Yes, the police officers recorded the incident. Have you any idea who would attack your parents, Miss Massey?" asked James, trying, without success to look her in the eye.

Before she answered, she pulled a large towel over her bikini top, much to the relief of James, who was finding her semi nakedness both embarrassing and distracting.

"Well it could be those hunt saboteurs. My mother had a run in with some of them a while back. She was taken to court for whipping one of them. Fortunately, the case was thrown out. We were celebrating in the Magpie at Cross in Hand last Saturday evening. There were eight of us. My parents, me and my boyfriend and two other couples. I must admit that we got a bit raucous, but it was a good evening."

"Did you recognise any hunt saboteurs in the Magpie that night?"

"No, of course not. They always wear masks, when they harass us."

Jill took over.

"Miss Massey, would it be possible to let me have the names and addresses of the two couples and your boyfriend? I assume he doesn't live here."

"No, he lives at East Dean. I'll have to look the two couples up on my father's computer address book. They're his friends."

Jill handed her a business card.

"My email address is on the card. Just email the information in the next day or so. Oh, including your boyfriend's address and contact details please."

James looked thoughtful.

"Miss Massey, I noticed a CCTV camera in the trees near your front gates. I don't suppose you have any footage from last night."

Sarah Massey looked surprised.

"Now I know why you're a Detective. The camera is camouflaged and not many people spot it."

"Why not make it obvious to deter intruders?"

"My father has got no end of cameras around the outside of the house and gardens, which are clearly in open view. I've no idea why he hid the one near the gate."

With that, she rang a small, silver bell and as if by magic, William appeared.

"William, can you get a copy of the footage from the CCTV gate camera, from last night?"

The inscrutable William nodded.

"Certainly Miss Sarah. Will a flash drive copy, be acceptable?"

James nodded and William glided back into the house.

"So, your mother and father are both active with the hunt?" asked Jill Trent.

"You know full well that hunting foxes has been illegal since that ghastly Blair got it banned," said a suddenly animated Sarah.

"Of course, I should have said drag hunting."

"Exactly, they just follow a scent trail, but the bloody working-class activists and townies just can't leave us alone, the bastards!"

Just as the temperature was rising, William came out and handed over a flash drive.

"All the footage from last evening is on there, Miss Sarah."

She passed the flash drive to James.

"Thank you. If we need to see any earlier footage, I assume you keep it."

"Yes, most certainly sir. We back it up regularly and keep it for about two months."

"Is the camera monitored from a computer screen?"

"Yes and no," said Sarah Massey.

"It's monitored some of the time by our security guy, but he's also the gardener and he cleans the cars. I guess to call him security is a bit of a stretch."

"And last night?" asked Jill.

"I'm afraid not. Our guy, Stewart, was away in Brighton, visiting his mother."

"So, nobody thought to look at the footage?"

"No, we were too concerned for my parents to think straight. If you hadn't mentioned the security camera, it wouldn't have registered. I guess I wasn't thinking straight."

James said, in his most soothing voice,

"Don't beat yourself up, Miss Massey. I'm sure you would have thought about the camera at some stage."

James Halstead and Jill Trent said their farewells and got into Jill's Fiat. As they drove out along the drive, Jill taunted her boss.

"That bikini was very small. I thought she was going to fall out of it at one stage."

"I hadn't really noticed."

"Really?"

"Well yes, it was a bit revealing. I was glad when she covered up."

"Yes, I bet you were."

"Changing the subject, the camera footage might be a bit of help. Let's get back and play it."

Jill smiled to herself. She knew James would have been embarrassed by Sarah Massey's tiny bikini because he was very proper; probably the last of the gentlemen. She had detected some reddening of his neck, when he first saw the young woman.

Chapter Twelve

Both Detectives were keen to review the security camera footage. Jill Trent inserted the flash drive into her laptop and they spent the next hour watching the country lane, with very little happening. Several dog walkers came and went and a couple of cars zoomed past. Then, just as they were getting a bit bored, two figures appeared right on the periphery of the screen. One was big and the other was small, probably a man and a woman. Jill pointed at the screen.

"Hard to tell at this range but the smaller figure is slimmer than the big one." James nodded and said,

"Look, the smaller one seems to be laying down at the side of the road. Damn! Why can't they be in the centre of the frame?"

"Looks like the old carjacking ruse. Body in the road, car stops and an accomplice jumps the driver."

"Yes look, the bigger figure is hiding in the bushes over the road. Come on matey, turn and look at the camera! Great! He's got a scarf round his face."

A few minutes of footage later, a Bentley makes a fast stop. Enter Charles and Isobel Massey. The big figure comes out of the bushes and assaults Charles Massey. The other figure, also masked with a scarf, hits Isobel Massey on the back of the head and knocks her to the ground. There seems to be some dialogue, which is inaudible. The big figure gestures to the fallen Masseys. Then the smaller of the two figures, delivers sickening kicks to the prone bodies and the two assailants casually stroll off down the lane. The smaller figure is holding what appears to be a stick or broken branch of some sort. The rest of the footage shows two people with a dog, attending to the Masseys. A concerned looking William appears. Sarah Massey comes into view and is comforting her parents until a police patrol car and an ambulance appear on the scene.

The rest of the footage shows a police forensic team, examining the area and then driving off in their van.

Jill Trent sat back in her chair and stretched.

"Well, now we know how the attack happened, but we don't know why."

"Unless of course, Sarah Massey is right and it's the anti-fox hunting lot," added James.

Jill was looking reflective.

"The big figure was definitely a man and the way he hit Mr Massey, suggests he is used to violence."

"Well yes. But there must be lots of men who fit that description."

"But at least we have the video footage. Jill, get our tech team to run it and get some screen captures of both figures. It's a long shot with the covered faces but someone might recognise them if we circulate some photos."

The following morning, James and Jill were at Eastbourne Hospital. They had been advised that the Masseys could be interviewed. They met a nurse in reception, who took them to a private room. She cautioned them not to overtax the injured couple. Jill Trent expressed surprise that both Mr and Mrs Massey were sharing a room. The nurse explained that they had insisted on being together and as they were paying for private treatment, they expected to call the tune.

The Detectives entered a smart looking room. There was a big television on the wall and a settee with a table in front of it. Mr and Mrs Massey had comfortable looking single beds, side by side. Both patients had tubes going into their arms. Understandably, both looked grim. James observed that Isobel Massey looked like an older version of her daughter, Sarah. Mercifully, she was wearing pyjamas, so wasn't exhibiting acres of flesh like her daughter.

"Good morning, I'm DI Halstead and this is DS Trent."

Charles Massey glared at them.

"About bloody time you lot came to see us. I pay a lot of council tax and expect the police to act a bit faster."

"Mr Massey, we wanted to see you and Mrs Massey yesterday, but the doctor told us to give you more time to rest."

"Another bloody excuse!" shouted Charles Massey.

Jill said in her calm voice, that she always used in these situations,

"Mr Massey, we really did want to see you both sooner, but we have to follow medical advice. Now if you don't mind, we would very much like to ask you some questions."

Massey calmed down.

"Look, I didn't mean to have a go at you, but we are both in a lot of pain. These drips are liquid painkillers. Without it we would be in agony! Ask your questions."

James drew breath.

"Well, before we ask you questions, we would like to share the fact that your daughter, Sarah, gave us a copy of CCTV footage from your hidden security camera." Massey looked concerned; Isobel's eyes flashed.

"What right have you to get a copy of private security footage?"

James was taken aback.

"It's a very important part of our investigation. If you want to complain about it, you are welcome to write to our senior Officer."

"Oh, do stop Isobel. If it helps to get the bastards who attacked us, all well and good," chided Charles Massey. Isobel said nothing.

James continued.

"As I was saying Mr Massey, when we reviewed the footage, we saw exactly what happened. One person was laying at the side of the road, getting you to stop your car. Then another person comes out of the bushes and hits you." Isobel became animated.

"Yes, and the little bitch jumped up and hit me on the back of the head with something. I'm lucky not to have serious brain damage or worse!"

Jill spoke in her calm voice again.

"Yes, it was fortunate that you were not more badly hurt. We got the impression from the video footage that your attackers were speaking to you, although, there was no sound."

"Bloody right they did." said Massey. "I called the big one 'a bastard' and then he hit me."

"What did they say?" asked Jill, still trying to be calm and soothing.

"The woman said she saw us with friends at the Magpie Pub in Cross in Hand. Said we were braying and celebrating."

"And were you? I mean celebrating."

"Too right we were. Isobel had been taken to court for thrashing a hunt saboteur, with a whip. The bastard had tried to unseat her from her horse; bloody dangerous thing to do. Anything could have happened. Anyway, the case was thrown out and we had dinner at the Magpie with my daughter and her boyfriend and two other couples. Yes, we were making a noise but, the pub made a lot of money out of us. Cost me a fortune!"

"So, your attackers were possibly in the pub? Did you see anyone looking at you? Perhaps a big man?"

"No, I didn't. We were out for a celebration and didn't take any notice of anyone else," said a disgruntled Massey.

James looked thoughtful.

"Has anyone threatened you recently or acted suspiciously?"

"Apart from the anti-hunting bastards, no. But I know the attack was linked to fox hunting."

"In what way?"

"If the camera picked it up, you probably saw on the video footage that our attackers kicked us both in the ankles and knees. Well they said, "You won't be doing any fox-hunting for a while"."

Isobel Massey was tearful now. "My knee is damaged and my ankle ligaments are torn, so no, I won't be riding anytime soon."

"Same goes for me, except that my ankle is broken and my knee was dislocated. She knew what she was doing, so our days with the hunt are over, at least in the medium term."

Halstead nodded.

"Your daughter tells me that your hunt does drag hunting, which is not the same as fox hunting."

"Well the townie, metropolitan bastards in Parliament think the law will stop us but…"

"Mr Massey, I understand your anger, but this is not really the occasion to discuss the merits of the law."

"Oh yes, don't want to get arrested," he said with a sly smile, followed by a painful grimace.

James looked at his watch.

"I think we've taken enough of your time. Thank you both, you've been very helpful. I'll leave my contact details on your bedside cabinet."

"I hope you catch the bastards."

"Goodbye., I hope you recover soon," said James.

When they were well clear of the hospital, James Halstead turned to Jill. "What did you make of them?"

"Arrogant and feeling very sorry for themselves."

"I know what you mean but we, of course, are impartial. A spot of lunch would be nice. Let's drive over to Sovereign Harbour and get something, we deserve a lunchbreak."

Chapter Thirteen

Later that evening, large crowds were making their way to the famous Devonshire Theatre in Eastbourne. Some of them were in good spirits after having an early evening meal at a local Italian restaurant. Several of the restaurants in the area catered for theatre goers, by serving food in plenty of time before the curtain went up at the Devonshire. Tonight was special, because tonight and the following night, top of the bill was Fancy Carter, who revelled in the title of The King of Comedy.

Fancy Carter was in fact Norman Carter. He was the kind of old-fashioned showman that used to grace light entertainment shows on television and was, at one time, very big indeed. He had made a considerable fortune from his television days and had invested his money in all sorts of lucrative ventures. He didn't really need to perform any more but it was in his blood and he was fond of saying, "It's not the money. I just want to give something back to the people."

A more cynical interpretation would be that he was getting reasonably well-paid performing in theatres and he had an ex-wife to pay for. So, why not?

He was in his mid-fifties and getting a bit heavy because he lived well. Or more accurately, he ate and drank well. Too well! He had to let some of his show costumes out a little; especially his trouser waists, but what the hell? His hair was also getting a bit thin on top but he was just about hanging on to it. Of course, the hair dye didn't help and certainly for a man in his fifties, jet black hair made his face look white. In his act he often used a line attributed to the late President of the USA, the ex-film actor, Ronald Regan. A woman had allegedly shouted to President Regan, "Hey Ronnie, you look younger now than when you were in the movies. Have you dyed your hair?" To which Regan had replied. "No, I had my face lightened!"

Fancy Carter stole the lines and told audiences the story but adapted it and inserted himself into the exchange. As it was obvious Carter dyed his hair, he thought by making himself the butt of the story, it would prove he had no vanity. Of course, in reality he was one of the vainest men in show business. A title that was surely, well contested.

Finally, it was time to go on stage. Although he was still top of the bill, he often had to share shows with acts that he thought were beneath him. Naturally he never said anything to his fellow acts, but in private he thought many of them were not in his league. On tonight's exciting bill was a female singer from a TV talent show, who had come an unimpressive fifth. A performing dog, with a glamourous lady trainer. They had actually won their particular TV talent contest but were probably on the way down. There were traditional 'hoofers'. Dancing girls in the old days but now celebrating under the title of just 'dancers'. There was a bit of juggling and a ventriloquist whose mouth obviously moved; almost more than the dummy in fact.

At last the magnificent Fancy Carter was in the spotlight. He did some jokes that inexplicably got roars of laughter. Probably down to the half time alcohol, served in the bar. He did a bit of hoofing himself and several songs, ending with a dramatically overacted version of Sinatra's 'My Way'. He did a carefully rehearsed, impromptu curtain call and left the stage to a rousing ovation. After the final curtain call with his fellow performers, Fancy Carter made his way to his dressing room. Although not in any way as palatial as dressing rooms from his heyday, it was the largest one in the theatre.

As Fancy Carter was changing into his street clothes, he was making a call on his mobile.
    "Hello my sweet, I've just come off stage. Did you have a nice meal? Ah good, see you in your room. Won't be long. Bye my love"
    Fancy Carter had met a young woman while he was in the bar of his

seafront hotel, the previous evening. Although he was only starring for two nights at the theatre, he had arrived two days ago and was booked at the hotel for the whole week. Carter's main residence was a nice flat in Brighton. He did lots of shows around south coast towns and always booked into hotels rather than drive back to his Brighton home. The young woman had told him she was a big fan. As unbelievable as this might seem, his vanity had got the better of him. She had a room at the same hotel and had made it obvious that she wanted to become close to him. Tonight, was the night! The thought of making love to a young woman excited him. He didn't for one minute, think that this might be some sort of set up. After all he was, in his mind, still attractive to women and he had lots of money to splash on willing bed partners.

Soon, Carter found himself standing outside the young woman's room. He gulped down a blue, oval-shaped pill, which would hopefully prevent any embarrassment 'downstairs'. He rapped on the door, which was opened by a woman with blond, shoulder length hair. She was wearing pyjama shorts and a pyjama top.

"Hello Christine," said an almost slathering Carter. Christine was tall and although she was not exactly slim, she was very athletically built.

Carter shook off his jacket and sat on the large double bed.

"Drink darling?" purred Christine.

"Err, yes please my lovely."

She poured him a large gin and tonic and he gulped it down.

"Steady on Fancy, you'll make yourself ill, drinking that fast."

"Yes, my love, you are quite right. Don't want to see it again!" Christine smiled.

"Before playtime, I wonder if you could do me a big favour."

"Anything you desire," said a slightly impatient Carter.

"Well, it's just that I left my mobile in my car. I need to send a text to confirm an appointment for tomorrow. I know it's a pain in the backside, but I must send it."

Reaching into his discarded jacket, Carter took out his mobile and handed it to her.

She looked at the screen.

"It's got the security lock on. What's the four numbers?"

"Oh sorry, can't be too careful. It's 4678," said an increasingly impatient Carter.

"Thanks, won't be a second." Christine sat on an armchair and crossed her legs. The shorts showed them off a treat and Carter felt the first stirrings of his blue pill. She sent a text, deleted it afterwards and handed the mobile back to him. He was now getting a bit hot under the collar and was expecting a great night with this good looking, young woman. He thought, if only my third-rate fellow performers could see me now. Then he thought, perhaps not! Carter hurriedly took his trousers off and threw them over a chair. Next came the socks and he almost fell, while trying to stand on one leg. Then, his shirt was almost ripped off and the Marks and Spencer vest was discarded. He kept his boxer shorts on, because he didn't want to fully expose himself to this attractive woman. Well, not quite yet anyway.

Christine eased herself on to him and sat astride his fat stomach. Carter grunted as she let her weight go but still enjoyed the experience. She then began to slowly unbutton her pyjama top. Carter was now beside himself with excitement and things were happening downstairs. Come on, he thought to himself, get that bloody top off. He looked up at this athletic woman and was about to make his next move, when he suddenly felt sleepy. Surely the tablet would see him through. He couldn't fall asleep now, could he?

The answer to his question was, yes, he could, and he drifted into a deep sleep. Christine gently slapped his face a couple of times. The great showman was soon snoring like a pig. Christine got off him and covered him up with the duvet. She then took his gin and tonic glass and washed it under the bathroom tap. Unfortunately for Carter, the crushed sleeping tablets had worked faster than the blue pill. Had he not been so keen to make love, he might not have swilled the gin and tonic in one go. He might even have noticed the slightly different taste. He was out for the night now. Christine then got dressed and felt inside Carter's jacket pockets. She hooked out the entry card to his room.

Christine looked along the corridor and it was empty. Carter's room was just two doors along and glancing around again she let herself into the room. She opened the wardrobe door and stared at the room safe, with its digital lock. She had taken a gamble on what the combination might be. She was a student of human nature. People have to remember so many security codes for all manner of things. They sometimes double up for ease of remembering numbers. Would her gamble pay off? Or would she have to endure another bedtime adventure with the hideous Fancy fucking Carter! The swearword that came to mind, instantly made her shudder. Suppose he hadn't fallen asleep! Too horrible to imagine! Her contingency plan was to say she felt ill. Not completely convincing, she thought.

Her finger was poised next to the number pad. Slowly she pressed the sequence: 4678. There was a barely audible click and the door of the safe opened. Inside was a small laptop. Christine removed it and sat on the bed. Now for the next big challenge. She opened the lid and to her absolute joy, her luck had held. The screen opened up and there before her, was everything she was hoping for. Carter was no computer geek! She entered the word 'fancy' and lo and behold, she was in. She inserted a flash drive and within twenty minutes, had downloaded everything she wanted.

Christine closed the laptop and placed it back in the safe, punched in the same code and it locked. She made her way back to her room and to her great relief, Carter was still doing his farmyard impressions as he lay open mouthed on his back. She quietly packed her holdall. She only had toiletries, pyjamas and some underwear and then after replacing Carter's room card in his jacket, she blew an ironic kiss towards the noisy figure and went to the hotel reception. She asked for her bill and explained that she had to leave unexpectedly due to a family crisis. She insisted on paying for this evening as well, handed her room card to a sympathetic receptionist and was gone.

Chapter Fourteen

For Christine, whose real name was Jackie Read, the night was far from over. She drove to Brighton and was soon ringing the entry bell to some modern flats.

"Yes," came an answer on the intercom.

"It's me."

The door opened and the now, Jackie Read made her way to a top floor flat. Greeting her was a man in his late thirties. He was a tad under six feet tall, with greying brown hair, worn in a crewcut and piercing blue eyes. He was DI Bob North from the Brighton Police station. Jackie Read was in fact a Detective Sergeant at the same office. They kissed and North said,

"I couldn't believe it when you rang me. You got the lot. Brilliant." Read gave him a strained look.

"What I did was break the law! I don't know why I agreed to do it. He lives in Brighton. Suppose he recognises me?"

"Don't be daft, what's he going to say? 'Hey, you're the tart that ran out on me, just as I was going to give you one'?"

"Don't even joke about it."

"You wouldn't have gone through with it, would you?"

"No, I bloody wouldn't but it was a close thing. I was sitting astride his horrible, fat belly, really taking my time unbuttoning my pyjama top. I was worried that your so called 'special sleeping tablets' weren't going to work!"

"Oh, so you gave him a treat then?"

Read scowled. "You bastard!"

"Is that any way for a DS to talk to her DI?" chided North.

"Anyway, do you want to see what's on the flash drive?"

"Nah, it can wait 'til morning. I've got a better idea. Why don't you get topless for me? I don't want sleeping pills though."

"North, you really are a bastard."

With that they headed for the bedroom.

The next morning Jackie Read woke up to the smell of coffee and bacon. Bob North was in the kitchen, hovering over a cooker. He greeted his DS. "That was really great last night!"

"Yeah, wasn't bad."

"Wasn't bad? Do you want bacon and scrambled egg?"

"Yes. But I must have a coffee, my mouth feels like a hamster cage."

After breakfast and lots of coffee, they both showered and dressed. Read inserted the flash drive into North's laptop. She clicked on the icon and there was a list of files. Some were just scripts containing jokes. Another had forthcoming dates and venues for shows.

North was impatient.

"Come on Jack, find his bank details."

Jackie gave him a withering look.

"If you think you can do better, why don't you take over?"

"OK. Keep your hair on, it's just that I need the information."

"He doesn't file things under proper headings. It's a real mess."

She clicked more headings and then scrolled down the file list.

"Bingo! Here we go. This icon is his bank statements."

North leaned forward and Read increased the type size.

"Would you look at all that money going in and out? There's lots, of activity. This must be a business account."

Read looked more closely.

"Could be. Looks like you were right, it all looks a bit dodgy, although there could be a reasonable explanation, except we can't exactly ask him. Nothing we have here is admissible evidence."

"Yeah, having sex with him to get hold of his laptop, doesn't help."

"I didn't have sex with him!"

"No, but the boss wouldn't approve of your methods."

"My methods?"

North dropped the discussion. Although he and Read were intimate, he was ruthless enough to ignore what could have happened with Fancy Carter. They searched through the rest of the stolen files and then got into the emails. There were several from theatres and a couple from Carter's agent. One of these explained that he couldn't get higher fees for bookings. Apparently, Fancy Carter was not as marketable as he thought and the agent suggested that it could have been a lot worse.

Jackie Read moved some deleted emails from 'trash' and reinstated them. North grabbed Jackie's shoulders.

"Well, would you look at that? An email from an anonymous sender which says, 'Same place, usual time tonight.' That was four weeks ago."

"So how does that help?"

"I don't know. Look Jack, you have to trust me on this. I'm looking for an angle. I know Carter is involved with some people. I can't tell you any more at this stage, but your undercover stuff has shown large sums of money going in and out of Carter's bank account."

"Yes, but I can't see anything illegal. He's apparently a wealthy man and he has money going in and out. What does that prove? I don't understand what you're after."

"You don't need to darling, just trust me"

North looked at his watch.

"Whoa! I'm running late! I've got to see the boss at 10.30. See you at the office. Close the door behind you."

After North left, Jackie Read sat at the breakfast table and rubbed her face. Things were getting a bit heavy! What was the real reason North wanted Carter's files? It didn't make much sense and she had the feeling she was being played.

Chapter Fifteen

James Halstead and Jill Trent were sitting at a table in one of the interview rooms at Lewes police headquarters. James had wanted some peace and quiet, to go over the Arron Kelp file with Jill. Although his own office was just up the corridor, it was in the corner of the CID room and this morning it was busy, with general hub bub coming from four of his Detective Constables. Two men and two women were munching on bacon sandwiches and planning interview visits for the day ahead.

"Now, let's go over what we've got on Kelp," said James.

Jill spread out the sparse papers from the file.

"Well, so far we've got the notes from the interview with Oz, that describe a big guy, thought be named Terry, who threatened him and told him to stay away from him and Kelp. The PM on Kelp states cause of death is dehydration, from lack of food and water. Kelp was done for cruelty, locking up his dog with no food or water. The dog died from dehydration."

Halstead scratched his jaw.

"Not much to show, is there? We keep going over this and it's a big fat zero."

"That's all we've got," said Jill. "My missing cat file is much thicker!"

"OK speculation," said James, leaning back in his chair.

Jill paused and then said,

"Well, the obvious point is the very similar deaths of Kelp and his dog. Someone wanted Kelp to die like the dog did. We know beyond doubt that the body was Kelp, from his driving licence."

"How did Kelp end up in the basement of a semi derelict building? If this mystery man, the big guy, took Kelp to the basement, he had to get him into the building and then into the room. Lock him in and walk back out into the road." James was on a roll now.

Jill nodded.

"It could certainly have happened like that. If it was premeditated murder, but perhaps whoever locked the door thought Kelp would be discovered and released. Perhaps he only just wanted to frighten Kelp by giving him a taste of his own medicine."

James agreed.

"Yes, it's a possibility that it happened in the way you describe, but it's also just possible that the person who locked the door was prevented from retuning. An accident perhaps. Something unexpected."

Jill gathered up the papers. Just as she was putting them in the file, Detective Chief Superintendent Lorraine Marsh appeared in the doorway.

"Hello James. Your team told me you were hiding here." Halstead and Trent stood up.

"Not hiding Ma'am. Just trying to get some quiet time, to review the Arron Kelp case."

"Any progress?"

"Not really Ma'am. We're just exploring some possibilities. A witness told us that Kelp had been seen drinking in the company of a big guy, named Terry, but that's all we have."

"You need to find, the big guy, then?"

"Yes, Ma'am but apart from his size and name, there's no other description."

"Just keep the investigation ticking over. In the meantime, I have another case for you. Both of you in fact," she said, turning to Jill. Come to my office at 3 p.m. today and I'll brief you. Oh, and Jill, I hope you have made a start on the missing cats."

"Yes Ma'am, ongoing investigations. I've met with the local RSPCA inspector and I've interviewed the man who was on the local TV news the other day," said a less than enthusiastic Jill.

"Look, I know it's not exactly top priority but as I told DI Halstead, there are local councillors and our MP, asking questions. Let me see your case file and I can show them we are looking into it."

"Yes Ma'am, I'll bring it with me this afternoon, if that's OK?"

"Yes, that's fine. See you both later."

As DCS Marsh was leaving, she turned and looked at Jill.

"I saw a photo in the local paper. There was a woman who looked a bit like you pinning a man down. Apparently, it was a fight in the gardens of a pub." Without giving Jill a chance to respond, she was gone.

James smiled. Jill, whose face had gone just a little pink, said nothing. Then quickly changing the subject,

"Wonder what this other case is?"

"Probably more disappearing moggies, DS Trent," grinned James.

She gave a sour look and went back to her desk.

Dead on 3 p.m., Halstead and Trent were sitting on the comfortable settee, drinking the good quality coffee. DCS Marsh was sitting opposite.

"Right, I expect you're wondering what this meeting is about."

"Yes ma'am," said Halstead, sipping his coffee and wondering if he dares risk dunking a bourbon biscuit.

"There has been a spate of robberies in Brighton and the surrounding area. Not opportunist stuff. More speciality based. All the stolen items have been antiques."

"Are we talking furniture Ma'am?" asked Jill Trent.

"There have been some items of furniture, but nothing larger than small antique cabinets and a couple of bible boxes."

Jill didn't like to ask what a bible box looked like, but James Halstead jumped in.

"Some of the really old bible boxes are worth a lot of money."

DCS Marsh shot him a look over the top of her glasses but didn't comment on this seemingly clued-up remark from her DI.

"The vast majority of stolen items are small antiques, like silver boxes, Japanese ivory carvings, Chinese vases and the like. There has been lots of antique jewellery taken, much of it valuable, because of the gold and gems content. Do you have much knowledge in this field James?"

"Err, a little Ma'am."

"Good, then you will feel at home on this case."

Jill gave James a quick glance. Her boss obviously had hidden depths.

"Anyway, the point is, that several of the people, who have been robbed are quite wealthy members of society. Some live, in expensive properties and despite having alarm systems, the thieves have been able to somehow get around the security and make off with the valuables."

James was about to speak when the DCS continued.

"It has been decided that additional resources are needed to help with the investigation. They are a bit stretched in Brighton, due to several high-profile investigations, including an ongoing case at a former children's home."

"Is there a time frame Ma'am?" asked Jill Trent.

"Initially a week and then a progress review. By the way, I know Lewes is not that far from Brighton; I would like you both to stay in the area. No hotel I'm afraid. You will be staying at a currently disused police safe house. It's got four bedrooms and plenty of mod cons. Look, I know it must seem a bit odd asking you to stay in Brighton, but I have my reasons. I can't tell you much more, except to ask you to keep your eyes and ears open. See if everything adds up. Or if it doesn't. If you discover anything, I want you to report to me personally. Tell nobody else."

James and Jill looked at each other.

"Not a problem is it?" asked the DCS, looking over the top of her glasses again.

James looked puzzled.

"I can only speak for myself but isn't it a bit irregular? As you say, we both live just up the road from Brighton. I really don't understand why we would have to stay overnight for a week."

"James, you are right of course. It's extremely irregular and I can't actually order you to do it."

"I'm sorry but the orders are vague. Can you be more specific? Keeping our eyes and ears open for what, exactly?"

"I can only tell you that something is going on in Brighton.

Something which could embarrass the force and create negative publicity."

"Surely there would be an internal investigation if that was the case."

"Look, as I have said, I can't order you to stay at the safe house, but I am requesting that you do. You won't be restricted to staying put in the evenings when you are off duty. You would be free to do as you please in your free time. I just want you to live there for a week. It's a delicate situation and I am just asking you to take what I say at face value. It's very important that you are known to be staying in Brighton, by Officers in the local force."

James and Jill were silent. Then James spoke.

"If it's that important, I will agree to stay at the safe house, but I would respectfully request that you record my concerns about the irregularity of the request."

Jill jumped in as soon as James had finished.

"I have the same reservations as DI Halstead, but I am willing to comply with your request Ma'am."

Lorraine Marsh looked relieved.

"I would like to thank you both for your cooperation. Your reservations will be duly noted on file," said Marsh, looking from one to the other.

"Right, I want you to report to DCI Sandy Charteris first thing Monday morning. He'll brief you and introduce you to the rest of the team."

"How many of us will there be on the team?" asked James.

"Four altogether. Now if there are no other questions," said the DCS, obviously meaning, there will not be any other questions!

James and Jill got up to leave and Jill handed her missing moggy file to the DCS.

"Oh, thanks for this Jill. I hope this will demonstrate that we've been investigating the case."

Jill nodded, but didn't speak.

"And good luck in Brighton next week," said a relieved Lorraine Marsh.

When they got back to James' office, Jill looked at her boss.

"I wasn't aware you knew about antiques."

James smiled.

"Truth is, I saw a bible box on The Antiques Roadshow and it was worth a fortune. I bet the owner was straight down the local auction rooms after the show."

"So that's the extent of your knowledge then?"

"DCS Marsh was impressed, wasn't she?"

"Yes, I could see the surprise on her face. Anyway, looks like we're stuck together at a police safe house next week."

"You don't mind, do you Jill?"

"Depends if I can hear you snoring in the next room!"

"My ex never mentioned snoring in the divorce papers, so I think you'll be OK."

They both laughed.

Jill looked serious.

"Do you know this DCI Charteris?"

"Yes, I bumped into him a couple of times on cases. He seems a reasonable bloke for a DCI. Can get a bit stroppy though. Not a man to upset."

"James, what do you suppose the DCS meant by seeing if everything adds up?"

"I don't really know what to make of it. Makes me wonder about the reason she prefers us to stay in Brighton, when it's not exactly the other side of the world from Lewes. It seems a bit odd, doesn't it?"

"I smell trouble," said Jill

"Look, we are both Detectives. I'm sure we can sniff out anything that doesn't look right. Our problem will be who to trust!"

"I've never been asked to do anything like this before. It goes against procedure, doesn't it?"

"Just a bit!"

James went back to his office and handed over the Arron Kelp file and the Charles and Isobel Massey investigation, to his team. They already had more than enough cases but could keep things ticking over. James told them to ring him on his mobile if the Masseys kicked off, hoping that they wouldn't.

He didn't really like to leave cases in the middle of an investigation. He particularly asked to be kept updated on Kelp, especially if the mysterious big guy could be located.

Chapter Sixteen

Early on Monday morning, James and Jill were at the Brighton Police station. DCI Sandy Charteris was indeed, a nice bloke. He was a burly Scot and resembled the man in a vest on the porridge oats box; although he was older and more careworn. He greeted them both and took them to the canteen for refreshments.

"How long is it since we last met, James?"

"Probably about two years ago on the East Dean burglaries, sir."

"Yes, I remember now. Cut the sir, while we're in the canteen, James; we're a bit more informal in here. I know your DCS likes the formalities but she's a career officer and will probably end up as Chief Constable."

"Yes, I think she will sir, err Sandy."

"And what about you Jill? How do you like working with James?"

"Oh, I have to put up with a lot but we get on OK," she said, smiling.

After the relaxed canteen meeting, they went to a large room, laid out with a large round table and chairs. On the wall was a map of East and West Sussex, with red pins which marked out lots of individual locations. There were folders on the table with lists of the stolen antiques. Each list had photos of the actual items. There were estimated values next to each photo. These were cross referenced with statements from the owners of the stolen property. DCI Sandy Charteris was going over the details with them when two people came into the room. One was a tough looking man and the other was an attractive woman, with blond hair.

DCI Charteris immediately introduced them all.

"DI James Halstead and DS Jill Trent, this is DI Bob North and DS Jackie Read."

Handshakes were exchanged and everyone took a seat. DI North was a hard-looking man with greying, brown hair and a crewcut which made him look severe. He had stubble, which was close to becoming a beard. He was probably late thirties, early forties, thought James. His crumpled, navy, linen suit, had obviously seen better days. He was probably just under six feet tall, and his thickset build suggested that he was not a man to cross.

Jackie Read was a tall, athletic woman. She had blond, shoulder length hair, tied in a ponytail and her minimal make up made her look attractive. She wore a short light blue dress, with a light blue linen jacket. She was probably a tad taller than Jill and looked as if she worked out or played some sport. Jackie Read stole a look at Jill Trent but looked away when Jill looked up. This was to be a brief planning meeting before the detailed case work started.

DCI Charteris nodded towards the lists.

"We're splitting the interview lists in two. Each folder has the most up to date information. Each team will have a folder for each burglary and the addresses of near neighbours. You will also have a master list showing every property that was robbed. So, each team will know what the other team is investigating. All the interviews with the actual burglary victims have been completed. As you will see, there has been no fingerprint evidence at any of the crime scenes. The person or persons responsible are obviously clued up on forensic evidence. In a lot of cases, the burgled houses are detached properties. Some of their immediate neighbours have been interviewed but there are lots of gaps where people have either not been seen or we need to do follow ups. As you know people sometimes remember little bits of detail that prove important. The plan is that you do the visits in pairs. There are a few names and addresses of ex-cons who are known to be alarm experts. A couple of these ex-con bastards are a bit tasty, but they might think twice about kicking off with two police officers."

Jackie Read looked at Jill.

"If any of these bastards kicks off, you can jump on them!"

Jill looked surprised and was about to speak, when Bob North butted in.

"We heard about the arrest you made in that pub garden."

Jill gave North a hard look.

"I didn't realise I was so famous," she said, without smiling.

James Halstead said,

"The guy we arrested was drunk and throwing punches. He learnt not to mess with Jill."

There was a brief silence and straight away, Jill thought she wasn't going to get on with Jackie Read.

Bob North seemed to like conflict and said,

"Don't worry darling, if you fancy a rough and tumble, I'm your man."

DCI Charteris interrupted this conversation and abruptly closed down the issue.

"Bob, show a bit of respect. We don't speak to each other like that."

James Halstead was annoyed that this oaf had taunted Jill like this but didn't say anything.

Charteris continued.

"On the wall behind us is an up to date information timeline, plus any ongoing queries. I want it kept up to date with the results of your witness interviews. That way you will all have a visual record of the overall investigation. Is that clear?"

Everyone nodded.

The rest of the meeting continued in a slightly frosty atmosphere and when it was over, both teams picked up their files and stood up. DCI Charteris said,

"OK, you work in pairs and check back here at four p.m. each day, to compare notes and discuss any issues that come up. I want all your interviews typed up and logged on the main file before you break for the night. By the way James and Jill will be staying in Brighton at a safe house."

North looked puzzled.

"Staying in Brighton., but why? They only live up the road in

Lewes," he said, looking at Charteris.

"The decision comes from above," said Charteris, as if to close down the conversation. "Right you two, I'll take you to your accommodation now so you can dump your bags. You'll have to follow me in your car because I've got a meeting in an hour."

"See you both later," said North, without much enthusiasm; as Jackie read looked Jill up and down.

James and Jill got into Halstead's car. It was a black BMW three-series and was two years old — a nice comfortable car and plenty of leg room. James had thought of asking Jill to bring her Fiat 500, but didn't want to spend a week crammed into the passenger seat. They followed DCI Charteris. He drove a new Jaguar XJ. After a short journey, they arrived at the police safe house. DCI Charteris handed the door keys to James.

"Here you are James. There's food in the freezer but you'll need to get some shopping for day to day stuff. Just get receipts and I'll reimburse you. Any wine or beer, you pay for yourself." He laughed. Then he was off in his Jaguar.

Jill hadn't said anything to James during the car journey. Fortunately, the house had off road parking to accommodate several vehicles. In Brighton, this was a bonus. James parked up and they removed their bags from the boot. James unlocked the door and they entered. Neither was expecting very much in terms of this ordinary looking house. They were very surprised when they saw a modern, well-fitted kitchen with an electric range cooker, large fridge freezer and expensive, black quartz worktops. The living room was furnished with a comfortable looking settee and some armchairs. Upstairs, all four bedrooms were a decent size with fitted bedroom furniture. Two had en suite bathrooms. These were the rooms each chose.

James looked at Jill and said,

"You didn't like North and Read, did you?"

"No, I didn't! You know I don't mind a bit of banter, but I draw the line at sexual innuendo and being called darling by a senior officer."

"You especially don't like Read, do you?"

"No, I don't. I like to think I'm professional and she just got under my skin. I didn't know our fight with Oz was that widely known."

"Look Jill, don't beat yourself up about it. If you hadn't jumped in when you did, we could both have been hurt before the uniforms arrived. I, for one, am very grateful to you. And besides we're a team and we take care of each other."

"Wow James, that was quite a speech. Seriously, it's nice to hear what you really think. Anyway, I've got a feeling that we're going to have to watch each other's backs with our two fellow team members."

"Did you notice that DI North knew we lived in Lewes?"

"Yes, I did. Not much is secret in the force, but I wonder why he had to mention it."

"No idea. Bit of machismo, probably."

They unpacked and then sat down in the kitchen to look at the case files.

"The first potential witness is Mrs Sandra Temple living in Brighton, at Stanford Avenue, near Preston Park. It's next door to the house that was burgled," said Jill.

They studied the details of the burglary from the victim's statement and decided to contact Sandra Temple. Apparently, she hadn't been available to be interviewed previously.

Jill took out her mobile and rang the number in the file. They were in luck. Sandra Temple was at home and available to see them that morning. James put the address in his sat-nav and they were soon on their way. He knew that driving in Brighton was akin to driving in London. The parking in this bustling, seaside metropolis was difficult. Everywhere was controlled by paid parking and James doubted that his 'Police' sign, would be respected by traffic wardens. He was always reluctant to put the notice in his windscreen. Might as well put up a sign saying 'Police, feel free to vandalise!'

They arrived at Stanford Avenue, which even with a sat-nav was a torturous journey. They were relieved to see that the property had off road parking and James carefully manoeuvred his BMW next to a brand new, mint coloured Fiat 500.

"Somebody has taste," observed Jill.

James just smiled.

They rang the doorbell, which gave a harsh ring. A dog barked, then squealed with excitement and they heard a woman saying,

"Don't worry Alfie, it's only the bell."

The door was opened by a slim, attractive woman in her mid-fifties. She was holding the collar of an extremely excited, gold spaniel, which obviously wanted to jump on these two visitors and probably slobber all over them.

"Mrs Sandra Temple? I'm Detective Inspector Halstead and this is Detective Sergeant Trent." They both flashed their ID cards.

"Oh hello. I'm glad I was at home when you rang earlier. I've been away in Scotland, so haven't been able to speak to the police. It's about the burglary next door, isn't it?"

James gave a pleasant smile.

"Yes, it is, Mrs Temple."

"Won't you please come in? Don't worry about Alfie, he just wants to greet you. He always goes a bit mad when the bell rings. I tell him every time to calm down but he never does, until he sees who it is."

Mrs Temple led them to a comfortably furnished sitting room. There were two expensive looking settees and a large screen television on the wall, above the fireplace. She let go of the struggling Alfie and he excitedly made a beeline for Jill, who had just sat down. He put his front paws on her lap and tried to kiss her. Jill rubbed his ears and he calmed down.

"Sorry about that; he loves people."

"Don't worry, I love dogs. I grew up with a springer spaniel," said Jill, still rubbing Alfie's long, dangling ears. He's a working cocker, isn't he?'

Mrs Temple nodded and smiled at Jill.

Alfie soon quietened down after his boisterous greeting. He went over to his dog basket in the corner and flopped down. He kept watching the two visitors.

"Would you like tea or coffee?" asked Sandra Temple.

"No thanks," said both Detectives.

"OK. Now what is it you would like to know?"

James took the lead.

"As you obviously know, your neighbour was robbed several weeks ago."

"Yes, poor John and Marion, they were so upset."

"Do you remember anything or see or hear anything on the 12th May?"

"I heard a car outside just after midnight. It woke Alfie up and he started barking. I looked out of my bedroom window and saw a couple of rear car lights in the distance. I'm afraid it's probably not much help."

"And you don't know what make of car it was?"

"No, it was too dark and I'm not very good at recognising makes of cars. I couldn't even make out a colour."

Jill looked around the room.

"You seem to have some nice antiques. Have you ever seen anyone hanging around outside?"

"No, can't say I have."

"Have you got an alarm system?"

"Not a conventional one, but Alfie is the next best thing. He makes such a noise if he hears the slightest sound, so I suppose that would deter most intruders."

"Your neighbours told our original investigating officer, that you have each other's spare door keys. Is that right?"

"I hope you're not suggesting…"

"I'm not suggesting anything, Mrs Temple. I was going to ask if you still have their spare key. It hasn't been lost or anything."

"No look, this is their front door key, on my keyring," she said, pointing to a key.

"If they go away for any amount of time, I go in to water their houseplants. I suppose I'm incriminating myself, but they have given me the house alarm code, so I can turn it off and on."

"Don't worry, Mrs Temple. According to the interview notes, they already mentioned this when they were questioned. They said you were a brilliant neighbour," said Jill, in her most reassuring tone.

"They are lovely folks and I feel so sorry for them. It must be terrible to have your house invaded by criminals. I only wish I could be more helpful."

James stood up.

"Don't worry Mrs Temple, you can only tell us what you saw. DS Trent has taken some notes. At this stage we aren't taking official statements, just notes but if we need one in future, we'll call on you again."

Sandra Temple stood up as well.

"There is one thing I remember."

Jill looked up. "About the night of the robbery?"

"Well, err, no. I've just had a thought. You asked me about alarms earlier. It's just that about two months ago a man called at my door and said he was in the area fitting burglar alarms and wondered if I wanted a quote. I told him I didn't."

"Did he have a van or a car?"

"Not that I saw. I'm so sorry, you must think I'm a bit scatty, not mentioning it before."

James smiled.

"Not at all, Mrs Temple. We all have things that slip our memory, from time to time. What did this chap look like?"

"He was quite short and a bit furtive."

"Was he young, old?"

"Oh, I'm not very good at ages. I'd say forties, perhaps. Could be older."

"What about his face and hair, what colour was his hair?"

"His hair was brownish with grey streaks and he had it in a ponytail. It was probably down to his shoulders. His face was pale and he had one of those long moustaches, like they wore in the 1970s. Oh, and he had an old leather, pilot's jacket. You know. A sheepskin jacket with a big collar. It was very dirty. Brown or black, I think."

"Anything else about him?"

"Yes, his teeth were bad. That's about it, really."

"I'd like to send someone to see you to get a photo fit of your caller. Are you OK with that?"

"Well yes, I suppose so. If you think it would help."

James reassured the woman.

"You've been a great help already, Mrs Temple. We've got your contact number; I'll arrange for someone to get in touch with you."

They started walking towards the door and Alfie didn't seem to feel it necessary to say goodbye. He just opened one eye, peered over the top of his basket and closed it again.

They walked up the road and noticed that the house on the other side of the burgled property was empty and had a 'Sold Subject to Contract' board in the front garden. As they got in the car, Jill said,

"A house-burglar, alarm fitter?"

"Yes. Either we've just had a bit of luck or it's just a coincidence," said James.

Chapter Seventeen

Meanwhile, Bob North and Jackie Read were sitting in a very posh front room at a house in Seaford. Just over the road, was a large town house which was on the list of burgled properties. Opposite them sat Jonathon Greelish. He was smartly dressed in expensive-looking clothes. Greelish was in his late forties and had an obvious comb-over hairstyle. He hadn't offered the Detectives a drink and was nervously rubbing the side of his large nose. Jackie Read was the first to speak.

"Mr Greelish, I would like you to think about what you said to Detective Constable Westmore, when he visited you three weeks ago."

"Haven't you got it written down?"

"Yes, but I would like you to just go over what you said please."

"What, about hearing a car?"

"Yes. Perhaps it would help if I told you what you said. You were awakened by a car turning around in the road outside your house. You got out of bed and looked out of the window and saw a car driving away. Have you anything to add to that, now that you have had time to think about it?"

"Err, perhaps it was a van."

"What makes you say that? You said it was a car," said North, in a brusque manner.

"Well, it could have been a van."

"Or it could have been a car," said North, with barely disguised impatience.

"Yes, I suppose so."

"Relax Mr Greelish. The whole reason for this follow-up is to just go over your original interview," said Jackie Read, shooting a look at North.

"Mr Greelish," said Bob North, fixing him with a stare.

"You say you were in bed and the noise of a car, apparently turning outside, woke you up."

"Yes, that's what happened."

"You must have jumped out of bed very quickly, to see a car or van disappearing."

"Well I wasn't asleep. I was sitting up in bed."

"That's not what you said in your original interview," said North

"Look, I'm sorry but I got a bit confused. I suffer from insomnia and had taken a sleeping tablet that didn't work. I got a bit confused when I spoke to your colleague Mr err…"

"Westmore. Detective Constable Westmore," said an increasingly tetchy North.

Jackie Read stepped in.

"Mr Greelish, don't worry about it. We only wanted to see if anything else had occurred to you since your interview. Anything else at all? No matter how small."

"No, I'm really sorry. I don't know the people who were robbed. They don't really speak to me and there aren't any other near neighbours. Sorry."

"No need to apologise, Mr Greelish. I think we're finished here now," said Jackie Read, attempting to reassure Greelish, who looked worried.

The two Detectives got up to leave and Jackie Read gave Greelish her business card. When they got back to the car, North was annoyed.

"Fucking waste of time that was!"

"Did you have to make it so obvious that you were pissed off with him?"

"Oh, was it that obvious?"

"Yes, it was and it was uncalled for. It was just a follow up. He could only tell us what he saw."

"Yeah, first he was asleep, then he was awake and the car might have been a fucking van. Or was it a car?"

"Bob, what's wrong with you?"

"Nothing's wrong, I just think we're wasting our time interviewing prats like him."

"It's part of our job. There's been little progress on the burglaries and that's the reason for the follow ups. Someone might remember seeing something. You know how it works."

"Yeah, I know how it works. I need a drink."

They parked up in a lay-by, munching take-away burgers and drinking coffee. North said, between mouthfuls,

"Come on. You've hardly said a word since your lecture about interviewing. What's up?"

"Nothing's up."

"What do you mean, nothing? You've had a face like a slapped arse, all morning."

"You're a bastard."

"So you told me last night, but it didn't stop us having 'How's your father', did it?"

"Shut up! If you must know, I didn't like the way you were leering at DS Trent. I bet you weren't joking when you said you'd love to wrestle with her!"

"Oh, is that it? Jealousy isn't a good look."

"It's not jealousy, it's just that you made yourself look a prat. It's the first time we've met them both and you have to open your big mouth."

"Don't forget my rank, darling."

"Try to act like an Inspector then. James Halstead gave you such a look when you mentioned wrestling with Jill Trent."

"I bet he's slipping her a length."

"You're so crude. We've got another visit to do in South Heighten."

"Another waste of time. I've looked at the file. A Mrs Littlejohn. The note says she's in, afternoons. She didn't see anything on the night of the burglary. Why are we bothering with this crap?"

"Because she's on our list to follow up."

"It's going to be the same old story. Nothing to add."

"Let's just drive over to see her. It's only up the road from here."

As it happened, Bob North was right about Mrs Littlejohn. She had nothing of any use to add to her previous interview. This time he had behaved himself and was quite charming. This was mainly because Mrs Littlejohn was an attractive woman, in her thirties. Jackie was going to comment on Bob North's demeanour when they got back to the car after the interview. In the end, she didn't want another argument. It wasn't easy working with him at the best of times but recently, it had become much worse. More aggressive and techy.

At 4 p.m. both teams were back at the police building typing up their notes from the day's interviews. Both teams had seen potential witnesses but the only item of any real interest, was Sandra Temple's story about the burglar alarm specialist who had called on her. Halstead could not help noticing that North was very interested to learn about this. He asked to read the notes, which Jill had just printed from her computer.

James asked North.

"Does that description ring any bells with you?"

North feigned disinterest and handed the sheet back to Jill.

"Nah, not really. I just don't think it's much of a lead. Could be a genuine caller."

"Or it could be a burglar alarm specialist who disables systems before burglaries," said James. "Anyway, I'm getting a photo fit made up, so we can circulate it."

North was about to snap back to disparage the notion but suddenly thought better of it. Instead he said,

"Look, you two. I think we got off on the wrong foot this morning. I didn't mean any offence. I can be a bit of a prat, sometimes."

"Sometimes," mumbled Jackie Read.

North gave her one of his looks but before he could respond, James said, "Yes, we are supposed to be a team and I think I speak for Jill as well when I say, let's make a fresh start." Jill slipped him a quick glance but nodded her agreement.

North looked pleased with the response.

"Tell you what. Why don't we all go out for some nosebag tonight? I know a good restaurant and I can probably get us a nice table. It's never that busy on a Monday night. What do you say?"

Jill looked at James and they both agreed to go for a meal. It was arranged for 8 p.m.

"Great," said North, warming to this thaw in the relationship.

"Here's a business card for the Apple Tree restaurant. The parking is hell, so let's meet there just before eight. Get a taxi. All the cabbies will know it. It's not far from the Brighton Pavilion."

Jill had noticed that Jackie hadn't said much while the arrangements were being made.

The two teams split up and as James and Jill were driving back to their temporary home, James said,

"You don't mind going out with them, do you?" "No, I don't mind. You know James, we are almost behaving like a couple, rather than DI and Sergeant."

"Sorry, I didn't mean to…"

"Don't be sorry, James, I was just winding you up."

When they got back to the house, they both had showers and got ready for the evening. James was sitting in the lounge, wearing a light blue jacket with cream trousers and a dark blue t-shirt. He was running through his text messages and emails when Jill came into the room. She was wearing a short, light green dress with a light green jacket. James could not resist looking at her as she sat down opposite him on the settee. As she crossed her legs, his eyes were drawn to her knees. Seeing him, looking, Jill asked, "It's not too short is it?"

"Err what?"

"My dress, it's not too short?"

"No, no, it's great. I mean it looks nice."

"James, we're off duty you know. You are allowed to pay me compliments."

"Jill, you look stunning."

"Thank you very much. You don't look too bad yourself. I've never seen you in that outfit before."

"Well, we've not lived together before. Err, what I meant is…"

"I know what you meant," laughed Jill.

"While you've been getting ready, I found a local cab company. The cab is booked for twenty to eight. Apparently, the restaurant isn't that far from here."

"You are a resourceful man, James."

"Yes, I know. Did you notice how interested Bob North was in Sandra Temple's comments about the alarm systems guy?"

"Yes, I did. He seemed very interested, but then seemed a bit put out at the suggestion of a photo fit."

"It might be because he's been working on the case, before we came along. Perhaps he thought it was a first lead to us." "Yes, but then he seemed to go cool on the idea."

"Could be nothing. We mustn't start seeing things that aren't there. But all the same, it was a reaction."

Just then there was a hoot from outside. The taxi had arrived, dead on time. They made their way outside and confirmed their destination. The driver was Italian and gave them a running commentary on Brighton.

Chapter Eighteen

Bob North and Jackie Read were waiting outside the restaurant, when James and Jill got out of their taxi. North was wearing a dark suit with a white, open-necked shirt. Read had obviously made a big effort to outdo Jill. She had a very short skirt, with a revealing blouse that left little to the imagination. She greeted James with a peck on the cheek. North did the same with Jill. To a casual observer, they appeared to be old friends. That of course, was far from the truth. Jill thought that Jackie had dressed to make a statement. A statement which said, 'look at me'. That was Jill's initial thought anyway.

North had got them a table in the front window of the restaurant. He seemed on good terms with the manager, named Carlos, who was everyone's idea of an Italian caricature. In reality he was of Spanish origin, but he played an Italian to perfection. He was a portly figure, slightly balding, with grand hand gestures. He had kissed Jackie's hand and then did the same to Jill. He shook hands vigorously with James and Bob.

They ordered merlot and Sancerre wine for the table and all four had gin and tonic to start. Jackie's thoughts went back to the Eastbourne hotel room, when the gin and tonics arrived. She thought about Carter, swilling his drink down. Despite the undertones of unease on James' and Jill's part, the meal was going well. As Bob drank more wine he blurted,

"Hey, I've just twigged." Pointing to the two women he said in a loud voice, "You two are Jack and Jill. Ha, ha."

He barely noticed that neither woman, nor James found it amusing, but nothing was said.

Apart from that one moment of embarrassment, nothing else happened until they were eating pudding. Outside the window, stood a rotund man with obviously dyed black hair. He was wearing a tight-fitting, blue suit which would have benefited from being let out a little. He was with another man who, wore round 'John Lennon' glasses, which magnified his eyes and gave him the appearance of a worried owl. The man in the tight-fitting suit, stared through the window at the four Detectives.

Jackie Read looked as if she had seen a ghost. It was the very thing she had warned North about. It was shear bad luck, bad timing, call it what you like; but it was happening. The others hadn't noticed her worried reaction because they were looking at the man who was looking at them. Then, North suddenly realised who the man was.

The great Fancy Carter entered the restaurant, with his owlish companion who was quite short. He was shielded from view by the much larger figure of Carter. He stared at the four in the window table, as he was led to a table at the far side of the room. Jackie was feeling a little sick. She stood to go to the toilet, just as Carlos was all over Carter.

"Ah, Senior Carter, what a pleasure to have the famous star in my humble restaurant!"

While this hero worship and buttering up was going on, Jackie slipped discreetly past the noisy scene, into the ladies' toilet. She resolved to brass it out because other than hiding in the toilet for the rest of the evening, she had no choice.

Jackie freshened up her makeup, took some deep breaths and casually walked past the table, where Fancy Carter was swilling a large gin and tonic. She was almost past when Carter stood up.

"Christine, where the bloody hell did you get to? They said you'd checked out. The chamber maid found me asleep on your bed. What's going on?"

Jackie was mortified but she didn't let it show.

"Sorry, I think you've made a mistake. My name isn't Christine. Are you drunk or something?"

Carter looked flummoxed, then staring at her said,

"Come on love, I'd remember those lovely legs anywhere."

She just walked away. She got back to her table and sat down. North looked annoyed but Jill spoke first.

"Problem?"

"No, some drunk thinks he knows me. No problem, just a clumsy attempt at a pickup," she said, a bit unconvincingly.

James looked at her and was about to say something when he felt Jill's foot touch his leg. He remained silent. Suddenly, North got up and said, "Must go to the bog."

He ambled over to the toilet. The great Fancy Carter wasn't at his table. In fact, North had seen Carter going into the toilet. As he walked in, he saw Carter standing at a urinal. North quickly noticed that both cubicles were empty, because the doors were open. Carter was about to nod a 'hello', when North pushed him hard against the urinal. Carter gasped,

"You've made me piss all over my trousers, you bastard." North, shoved Carter's head against the wall.

Carter shouted,

"Don't you know who I am?"

North put his face close to Carter's and said menacingly,

"I know fucking well who you are. You're a washed-up piece of shit, who just tried it on with my girlfriend."

"But…"

"But nothing. When you go back to your table, you will keep your fucking gob shut. If you speak to my girlfriend again, I'll make sure your face isn't fit to go back on stage for a month, even with fucking make up. Is that clear?"

"Sorry, I must have made a mistake," said a visibly shaken Carter. "I thought she was a woman I knew."

"Yeah, you made a fucking big mistake," glowered North.

Carter got some toilet tissue and tried to get the wee off his trousers. Meanwhile, North used the urinal, washed his hands and left. When he got back to the table, Jackie slipped him a look.

"Just spoken to the bloke who thought he knew you, Jack. Guess what? He's no other than Fancy Carter, you know, The King of Comedy. I told him he was mistaken. No harm done."

Jill and James looked at North. Then they glanced over to the table where Fancy Carter was sitting, rubbing his forehead and glancing down at his trousers. His owlish companion was sitting in shadow but nodding his head at something Carter was saying.

The rest of the meal was without incident and James Halstead, looked at his watch.

"We've got another day of interviews tomorrow. Shall we get the bill?"

Bob North wasn't ready to call it a night.

"Come on Jimmy boy. It's not my bedtime yet, let's go on to a club."

Jill knew that James hated being called Jimmy and Jimmy boy, was really pushing it. James was about to say something, when Jill said,

"I'm a bit tired, I think we should get the bill."

Jackie winked at her.

"Can't wait to get to bed, Jill!"

Ignoring the unsubtle innuendo, Jill just said,

"That's right, I'm exhausted."

Bob North looked from one woman to the other. He was about to make a vulgar comment about James and Jill only needing one bed but thought better of it.

"OK, boys and girls, I'll get the bill." He stood up and walked over to Carlos, who was talking to another dinner, by the till. James noticed him say something to Carlos and the man nodded in agreement. Then North turned and ambled back to the table. James had a credit card in his hand. North saw it.

"Don't worry old son, bill's settled. I'll put it on expenses, my treat."

James wasn't happy with this arrangement but decided not to dispute it.

The four said goodbyes and left the restaurant. Jill had noticed Carter having a sideways glance at them, but he quickly looked away when

North stared at him. The couples went in opposite directions after James had declined North's invitation for a shared cab ride.

"Do you mind a walk Jill, or shall I ring for a cab?"

"A walk would be nice, it's not really that far to the house. I think our exuberant cabbie took us the long way around."

"Yes, I thought the same."

"What did you make of that business with Carter?"

"Well he seemed pretty sure he'd met Jackie before," said Jill.

"I'd say he was very sure, even though he called her Christine."

"Perhaps our Jackie has been moonlighting."

James looked thoughtful.

"Did you see Carter rubbing his head after he came out of the toilet?"

"Yes, and it was right after North had put him straight."

"Yes, something is going on, but what?"

There was a few moments of silence and Jill put her arm through James' arm as they walked. He didn't say anything; it seemed a natural thing to do. Just an ordinary couple out for a walk; would hardly be swinging their arms, military fashion. Just natural to be arm in arm. Good colleagues, off duty.

"Something worrying you, James? Apart from me holding your arm."

He laughed at her last remark.

"No, I like it. I am worried about the bill for our meal. I don't think North paid anything at all. We both know he can't claim it on expenses. He didn't have cash or a credit card in his hand. He just said something to Carlos and walked back to the table."

"It looked like an arrangement on the face of it, but North may have a charge account there."

"You don't really believe that any more than I do Jill."

"No, I don't."

They finally arrived at their accommodation after only briefly getting lost once. They both went to their rooms. Jill called out,

"Do you fancy some hot chocolate as a nightcap, James?"

"Have we got any? I didn't see any in the cupboard."

Jill emerged from her room, carrying two sachets of Cadbury's instant chocolate drink.

"I bought these with me, but I'm happy to share with you."

James smiled. Jill was wearing pyjamas and looked very fetching.

He was wearing jogging bottoms and a t-shirt. Jill made two hot chocolates and sat down next to James on the settee.

James felt relaxed and was reflecting that it was a long time since he had been in the company of a woman in a domestic setting. Jill looked at James. She also felt very relaxed.

"James, are you happy being divorced?"

"Once custody of the bloody cat gets sorted."

"Seriously James?"

"Suppose I am really. Yes, I definitely am. Sandra is very difficult to live with. I think it's because she was spoilt as a child and her parents gave her a lot of money. She always rubbed it in about having more than me. Terrible cliché, but we drifted apart. Sandra didn't like it when I was on a late duty. Wanted me to get a nine to five job."

"It's not easy for anyone married to a copper, James. You always see that on TV police shows. The phone rings while they are out for a meal, or the police officer misses an important family event."

"I know and some of it rings true, doesn't it? What about you, got anyone in your life at the moment?"

"No, I'm just not interested really. Funny how you get used to your own company. Nice glass of wine, takeaway and a TV show, that doesn't get too complicated and I'm happy."

"Are you really happy, Jill?"

"I can honestly say 'yes'."

"And here we are, you in your pyjamas and me in my jogging gear, just sitting, talking and speaking for myself, quite relaxed."

"Me too, James."

Both were really enjoying the informality of being together. They had worked as a team for a while and could never have imagined that they would be with each other in a domestic setting, outside of work. They had been out for the odd meal together, but it had never been what could be described as a date; more of quick bite after work. James reflected that it would be so easy, natural even, to jump into bed together. He considered Jill to be a good Detective and someone he could totally rely on. He also considered her to be an attractive woman. Jill harboured similar thoughts about James. She too, could imagine the two of them enjoying an intimate relationship. They had both been lost in companionable thought, when James broke the silence.

"Jill, I think we need to watch ourselves with the dynamic duo."

"You stole my thoughts. Do you think they are part of the reason we were asked to stay in Brighton?"

"To be honest Jill, I just don't know what to think. It's very odd. I've never heard of any situation where police officers are asked to stay overnight in a house when they live so close, without a clear explanation. It breaks so many police protocols."

"Let's hope we don't live to regret agreeing to do it, James."

"Well my reservations are apparently being noted. Or so the boss said."

They each went to their separate bedrooms, bidding each other goodnight. Both were a little confused about their feelings, but maybe it was something for another time. At the moment, they had a job to do.

Chapter Nineteen

That same evening Bob North and Jackie Read were sitting in the kitchen of North's flat. They had taken a cab and Bob North had been silent for most of the short journey. The driver had tried to make conversation but North had just responded with monosyllabic replies. Jackie Read had at least tried to be pleasant and replied when the driver had asked if they had a nice meal. She was feeling a bit apprehensive because of the incident with Fancy Carter but tried to put it out of her mind.

Bob North poured himself a brandy, but Jackie preferred a coffee. She looked at him as she sipped her drink.

"I told you that fat bastard Carter might recognise me. What are the chances of meeting him a restaurant?"

"Fucking good chance, it seems!"

"And it would have to happen in front of Halstead and Trent."

"Yeah, just bad luck."

"What did you say to him in the toilet?"

"Told him he'd made a mistake."

"And?"

"And what?"

"What did Carter say?"

"Nothing much, he was too busy wiping piss off his trousers. And before you say anything, I just roughed him up a little to get his attention."

"Oh Bob, why do you always have to take things too far?"

"Look, he got the message. He won't bother you again. I'm more worried about our new partners."

"Worried, what about?"

"I don't trust them. When Sandy Charteris told us we were getting help, he said it was down to lack of resources. The children's home investigation and a couple of other high-profile cases and all that crap!"

"What are you getting at?" asked Jackie, draining her coffee cup.

"How normal is it for two Detectives who live and work in Lewes, to be asked to stay in Brighton for at least a week? They could easily commute, and still work on the case. It's only about burglaries. Think about it. Why do we need help?"

"Well, before I was drafted in it was only you and DC Westmore. You must admit that there's still a lot of interviews and case note updates outstanding. You only did preliminary interviews and a couple of follow ups."

"Yes, but you replaced Westmore and then our bosses drafted two outsiders in. What does that smell of?"

"It smells of additional resources."

"Jack, you are so fucking naive sometimes!"

"What do you mean by that?"

"So, you don't think they have been sent to have a look at what we've been doing?"

"Why would you think that? Bob, are you involved in something you're not telling me about? Is it to do with Carter's laptop? What have you got me into?"

"Grow up Jack. All I've done, well to be more accurate, all you've done, is to get information without going through channels."

"All I've done? You really are a bastard!"

"Coming to bed?"

"No, I'm not. I'm not staying tonight!"

"Suit yourself. Bet you wouldn't say that if James Halstead was asking."

"Oh, grow up."

"I saw the way you looked at him. Jill's quite a stunner. Perhaps we could do a swap."

Jackie didn't reply. She was ringing for a cab, which was promised within ten minutes. She left without saying anything else. Not even a 'goodnight' or 'see you in the morning'.

When she got to her own flat, she got ready for bed and sat there for a while. She was thinking about what North had said about the case. She was also worried about Carter. Suppose he didn't take notice of the warning? And what was North into? She had only been working on the burglary case for a short time. Everything looked normal and according to the case notes, procedures had been followed by North and DC Westmore. But at the back of her mind, something was nagging her.

Perhaps she was worrying about nothing. She finally laid down in bed. She thought about James Halstead. Yes, he was a good-looking guy. She wondered how close he and Jill were. And what of Jill? She seemed like a nice person. She wished she hadn't taken the micky about her jumping on that bloke. All joking aside she could have been badly hurt. Jackie drifted into a fitful sleep.

Chapter Twenty

The next morning, James and Jill were up early. When Jill came into the kitchen, James was trying to prise slices of a cut loaf apart.

"Problem James?"

"I forgot to get this bread out of the freezer last night."

"Stick it in the microwave on the defrost setting."

"Why didn't I think of that?"

"Is there any coffee?"

"Only instant."

"While you're making toast, I'll check what provisions we need and make a shopping list. Should have done it yesterday."

"This is like being married," said James, instantly regretting his remark.

"What I mean is…"

"I know what you mean, James." Jill smiled.

James returned her smile and defrosted the loaf in the microwave.

They had toast and because there was no milk, black coffee at the breakfast bar. It was a comfortable atmosphere and they decided what shopping was needed for the week. When they had finished, James got the case files and spread them over the worktop.

"What's the plan for today?"

"There are another ten witness interviews to do as well as an alarm expert, called Jason Mitford. Apparently, he's been going straight since he got out of prison four months ago."

"When do you want to see him?"

"Well, he lives at Alfriston and so does one of the witnesses. I thought we could ring the witness, a Major Peter Carmichael and see if he's available today. If not, we can switch to a Frank Crawshaw, who lives in Brighton at Hartington Road."

James rang Major Carmichael and he was happy to see them any time after 11 a.m. They drove out to the lovely village of Alfriston, which was nestled in a valley in the South Downs. They drove along the scenic route on the A259 as far as Seaford, and then onto a B road which gave way to a steep descent into Alfriston. Jill thought how lovely this place was. She had been here before with a former boyfriend. There were tearooms and a lovely old church, as well as some shops. There was also an antiquarian book shop.

They found the Major's house, which was located next to a green opposite the church. James found a parking space and they knocked on the door of what could only be described as a picturesque cottage. A ruddy-faced man opened the door and fixed them with a suspicious stare.

"Good morning, Major Peter Carmichael?"

"Yes."

"I'm DI James Halstead and this is DS Jill Trent."

Both held out their warrant cards and the Major gave them a detailed inspection.

"We spoke on the telephone earlier this morning."

"Ah yes, come in."

The Major led them through to a cosy sitting room. The walls were adorned with military scenes from historic battles. One depicted the charge of the Scot's Greys at Waterloo. There was a two- seater settee and two armchairs. On a large table, were two opposing armies of model soldiers.

"Do sit down."

James and Jill sat on the settee and the Major sat in an armchair opposite.

"Now, you said on the phone, it's about the burglary, next door."

"Yes, I know you have already been seen by the police," said James, looking at his file.

"We wanted to follow up on it, in case you have remembered anything else."

"Anything else?"

"We often find that people remember some little detail or something they had forgotten," said Jill, who as usual, had her notebook on her lap.

"All I remember, is seeing some headlights outside. I was in bed and the headlights went out. I assumed that it was a neighbour and went back to sleep."

"Your next-door neighbours have a burglar alarm, according to our information. Did you hear anything at all?"

"I already told the other officers that I didn't hear anything. Not surprising, considering the bastards disabled it, is it?"

Jill looked up from her notes. "How do you know that?"

"Frank and Amanda are good friends. They told me. Nothing wrong with that, is there?"

"Of course not. I just wondered, that's all."

"Look, I really can't tell you anything I've not said before. Sorry, but that's it."

"By the way Major, out of interest, what regiment are you with?"

"I'm retired but I'm afraid I can't tell you. Hush hush. National security and all that," he said, tapping the side of his nose.

James and Jill looked suitably impressed. They left a contact card with the Major and said their goodbyes as they walked out to the car. James was looking at the files.

"I wonder why the address on the other side of the burgled house has a file but is crossed out on the interview list?"

"Don't know. It might have been missed when the interview sheets were printed. Must be crossed out for a reason," said Jill, looking at the paperwork.

"While we're here, we might just as well check it out."

They walked up the short path to the house. Jill rang the bell and they heard a feint ring. A shadow appeared behind the door, which was opened by an elegantly dressed woman in her thirties. James held up his warrant card.

"Sorry to disturb you. I'm Detective Inspector James Halstead and this is Detective Sergeant Jill Trent. Can I ask your name?"

"Susan Bolton. Err Miss Bolton. Would you like to come in?"

"We're making enquiries about a burglary next door."

"Oh yes, poor Frank and Amanda. But I was wondering why you are asking me again. I told the other Detective everything I know. Was my information of any use to you?"

Jill spoke.

"I'm sorry, Miss Bolton, but we haven't got the interview notes with us."

"Oh really! Talk about a waste of our council tax!"

Ignoring the remark, Jill pressed on.

"We had to come to Alfriston anyway and now we're here, I wonder if you could add anything to what you originally said."

They walked into a nice country style kitchen. The smell of coffee seemed to be luring them in. They were glad that Miss Bolton seemed to have forgiven them for daring to waste her council tax. They gratefully accepted her offer of coffee.

They were seated on kitchen stools. Sipping his coffee, James asked,

"Can you just recap for me, anything you saw on the night of the burglary?"

"Yes, I can. Wait a minute, I've still got a note of the registration number of the van."

She went to a pile of papers and found what she was looking for.

"Here it is. It was a dark coloured van, registration AE61 BUS. As I told your colleague Mr, err, hang on he gave me his card. Here it is, Westmore, it woke me up. I heard a vehicle arrive but it went quiet. I tried to get back to sleep but I couldn't. I was just getting a glass of water when I heard an engine start up. I looked out of the window and saw the van just driving away. I noticed the registration number and remembered it because of the word BUS. I thought it was odd for someone to be out at that time of night."

"And you told all this to Mr Westmore?"

"Yes, he was nice and friendly, wrote it all down. I haven't got anything to add to what I told him."

"I'm sure your interview notes are back at the police station. Thanks again for your information," said James, handing Miss Bolton his business card.

"Is there a problem Inspector?"

"Nothing to worry about. Thanks again for your time."

After finishing coffee and thanking Miss Bolton, they decided to walk into the centre of the village for lunch and a comfort break. Over more coffee and toasted teacakes, they briefly discussed, in low voices, what had just happened. Their case notes clearly had Miss Bolton's address crossed out. It was strange that there were absolutely no notes, about a van or any interview details with Miss Bolton. Their brief had only been to interview specific people. All the burglary victims had given official statements with accompanying inventories of their stolen antiques. There was no instruction to interview any of the victims, just specific neighbours, as indicated on the master list.

When they had finished lunch, they visited the antiquarian bookshop. They browsed for about twenty minutes and James had considered buying an old book about the South Downs. Considered it, that is, until he saw the price inside the front page.

Afterwards, when they were sitting in the car and could now speak freely without being overheard, James Halstead said,

"This is a bit odd. Perhaps someone has misplaced the original interview."

"Well, we need to have a word with Westmore. If he's based at Brighton, he shouldn't be that hard to find. Let's find out when we get back," said Jill, shuffling her paperwork.

"We need to think about our approach, Jill. I agree that we need to see Westmore, but I want to take it softly. We know the burglary enquiries were under-resourced and it's possible that corners have been cut. We don't want to come across as criticising the accuracy of the investigation, without good cause."

"I'm not looking forward to our next interview. His offending record doesn't paint a very nice picture," said Jill, as she leafed through the file.

James punched Jason Mitford's address into his sat-nav. Mitford was, by all accounts, a professional burglar who was known to be a dab hand at disabling alarm systems. According to the file, he was going straight after serving two years for burglary. There was no phone number for Mitford and so far, he had not been interviewed. There was no evidence that Mitford had been involved in the antiques burglaries. Some of them had taken place while he was a guest of Her Majesty. A couple had been committed after his release. The interview was to be informal at this stage; merely an initial contact to see what he had to say. If it was deemed necessary to take it further, a formal interview under caution was an option. The first stage was actually making contact with the so far, elusive, Jason Mitford.

As it turned out, Mitford lived just on the edge of Alfriston. James and Jill pulled up outside an old cottage. The front garden, like the cottage itself, had seen better days. They knocked on the dilapidated front door. There was no answer. After about five minutes, they were just about to write a note to push through the letterbox, when they heard a voice from behind a gate, at the side of the cottage.

"Who's that?"
    "Police," said James.
    "Piss off."
    "Just want a word, can you come to the front, please?"
    James looked at Jill
    "Take care, OK?"
    Jill nodded.
    Then a scruffy-looking man walked through the side gate. He could have been any age between forty and sixty. He had a grey beard, which stuck out at angles. A large, reddish nose protruded from the hair which seemed to have overrun his cheeks. The hair above his mouth was stained with nicotine. Certainly not the sort of man anyone would want to meet in an alley, or anywhere else for that matter!

"Mr Mitford?" said James, holding out his warrant card.

The beard parted to expose a slash of a mouth with brown and yellowish teeth.

"I told you to piss off!"

Jill stepped forward, ignoring the body odour that seemed to fill the air, as he stood in front of her.

"Mr Mitford, we wondered if you could just spare us a few minutes and answer some questions."

"I've got nothing to say to coppers!"

"We haven't asked you anything yet, Mr Mitford. We can always do this back at the police station in Brighton."

Jill shuddered at the thought of having to put up with the body odour all the way to Brighton. Mercifully, Mitford seemed to have second thoughts.

"What do you want to know? You can't use anything I say, without my solicitor present."

Jill moved straight into her well- rehearsed, calming mode.

"Mr Mitford, this is just an informal chat. No need for a solicitor. We just want to know if you remember what you were doing on these dates." She showed him two dates and times, which she had written in her notebook.

"I know bloody well why you're asking. It's those bloody burglaries, isn't it? Well, I've got news for you."

Mitford pointed to one of the dates.

"I was in hospital in Eastbourne on that date. Overnight stay. Check it if you want." Pointing to the other date, he said,

"I was night fishing off the beach at Seaford."

"Can you prove that, Mr Mitford?" asked James Halstead.

"Can you prove I wasn't?"

"Anyone with you?"

"Yes, Charlie and Trev."

"Their surnames and addresses?"

"No idea, only know their first names. They live in Seaford but I don't know where. We meet up on the beach."

"How do you get there?" asked Jill.

"In my old van, over there," said Mitford, pointing to an almost antique Austin van, with old black and white number plates. Nothing like the number they had been given by Miss Bolton. Much too old.

Satisfied that there was not much more they could do at this stage, they turned to leave. James handed Mitford his contact details. He had handwritten the Brighton phone number next to his printed Lewes number.

"Thanks for your cooperation Mr Mitford. If you do find out the surnames and addresses of your mates, I would appreciate a call. Use the Brighton number."

They drove back to Brighton, for the 4 p.m. session.

"James, what are we going to do about the missing interview notes?"

"Nothing yet, Jill. I want to find out about this Westmore chap and check out the car registration. As I said, we need to tread softly. Let's just keep it to ourselves at this stage. Just type up the Bolton interview but we won't put it on file yet. Just save it for the time being."

"Do you think something's going on, James?"

"Don't know but we'll need a bit more information before we say anything to anyone. Could just be a cock up."

"Wonder if this is what the Super meant about keeping our eyes and ears open?"

"Perhaps. Let's go and see our new colleagues and see what they've got."

Chapter Twenty-One

James and Jill walked into the police station meeting room. It was just after 4 p.m. and they were surprised to see it empty. Jill opened her computer and started typing up the interviews from her notes. She read the notes from the discussion with Susan Bolton but for now, nothing would be put on the main file. James leaned over and copied down the vehicle registration number from Jill's notebook.

"AE61 BUS. Won't be a minute, I'll get them to run the number for us."

He left the room. Jill carried on working and it was now twenty to five.

She was wondering what had happened to her colleagues, when Jackie rushed in.

"What a bloody day, I've had. Two dead end interviews and one no reply, despite making an appointment. Where's James?"

"Oh, little boys' room. Where's Bob?"

"Don't speak to me about Bob. He phoned me this morning and said he needed to stay close to his toilet! Some bug, he thinks. I reckon it's more to do with booze."

"Why, does he like a drink?"

"No more than the rest of us, but he reckons he has a couple of glasses of Glenfiddich before turning in. Claims it helps him sleep."

"So, have you been out on your own?"

"No, I got DC Westmore to come out with me. He's a good lad and he used to be on the burglary enquiries, 'til Sandy Charteris took him off and I took over."

James came into the room with two coffees. "Oh. Hello Jackie, where's Bob?"

"Staying close to the toilet today."

"Oh dear!" said James, trying to keep a smile from his face. "Would you like a coffee?"

"No thanks, I need to go and check with DC Westmore. He's typing up today's notes." With that, she left.

"DC Westmore, now there's a coincidence," said a surprised James.

"Apparently Westmore worked on the burglary investigations before Jackie. He was working with Bob North and Jackie replaced him."

James stroked his chin.

"Very Sherlock Holmes, James."

"What?"

"Stroking your chin. I thought you were about to solve the mystery of the missing interview."

James laughed.

"If only! The number plate is phoney. Big surprise. How many burglars go out in their own vehicle, when they do a break-in? Not many, unless they're stupid."

"I agree; another big, fat dead end. By the way, I'm going to the gym before we eat tonight. Do you fancy coming along?"

"Err, no thanks. I can drop you off though. Where's your gym stuff?"

"Back at our house. Sounds really weird, our house!"

James nodded his agreement, just as Jackie came back.

"What are you two up to tonight? Out on the town?"

"No, Jill's hitting the gym and I'm cooking a meal later."

"Sounds very domesticated. Tell you what Jill, do you mind if I come to the gym with you?"

"No, not at all," said a slightly quizzical Jill.

It turned out that Jackie Read belonged to the same gym chain as Jill. Members could use any club locations, even though Jill's membership was based in Lewes. Arrangements were made and Jackie said she would pick Jill up from the house, to save James taking her. Jill had wondered if she had misjudged Jackie, but James had told her to be on her guard.

The absence of Bob North looked a little odd, but who knows? He might really be sticking close to the toilet, thought James.

Jackie arrived at the safe house as arranged and both women went to the fitness club. They had a good workout followed by a sauna. Jill suggested a quick drink in the bar, but Jackie suggested that they go back to her flat, which was quite close by. Jill had agreed because she was curious to see where Jackie called home.

As they parked up, Jill's mobile rang.

"Yes, Yes, OK. I'm just outside Jackie's flat, we're having a quick drink and Jackie's running me home. OK, fine. Yes. Any preference? Right, I'll choose then. Bye."

"What was that all about?" asked a slightly curious Jackie.

"Oh, it's James, he wants me to get a bottle of wine and some cornflakes."

Laughing, Jackie said,

"Hmm, sounds like a great meal."

They both laughed.

"Tell you what, the mini market is just over the road," said Jackie, pointing to a small row of local shops.

"You go and get your shopping and I'll go on ahead. I'm flat four on the first landing. I'll leave the door ajar. The main door entry code is 2001. You can't forget that, can you?"

"No," said Jill, thinking that James would love the 'Space Odyssey' reference.

Jackie entered her flat and as she was wedging her front door open, she sensed that something wasn't right. Then she thought she was being silly and walked through to her lounge. She was just rearranging the scatter cushions on her large comfortable looking settee, when a voice made her jump.

"Hello, Bitch!"

She turned around to see a man staring at her. She was trained to observe and, in that instant, she was weighing up possible actions. The man was in his forties, about five feet eight and wearing faded blue jeans, with a white t-shirt. He was wearing round, John Lennon glasses. In the short time it took for her to take all this in, she focused on the knife he had in his right hand. He was wearing black, leather gloves.

"I've seen you. It was in a restaurant the other night. You were with Fancy Carter."

"How observant of you Christine, or should I say, DS Jackie Read?"

"What do you want?"

"I want to know why you got friendly with Mr Carter and why you accessed his computer, while he was knocked out."

"Knocked out."

"Don't give me that surprised shit."

"He knows someone copied some of his files and he wants to know why. He couldn't understand why a woman looking like you would make a play for him, but he didn't want to turn you down. Thinks you're a good-looking woman. Pity to spoil your looks!"

Jackie kept her eyes riveted on the knife. She didn't know if it was just a threat or if he intended to stab her. The man moved towards her, making side to side movements with the knife. This was deadly serious. Jackie was trained in self-defence and had faced knives as part of the training. Except that the knives had been soft rubber and couldn't hurt anyone if a mistake was made. Disarming a man with a real knife was not easy. Downright dangerous in fact! She knew she had to watch the knife and await a chance. Maybe just one chance and if she misjudged her move, it would in all probability be fatal.

"I'm not going to kill you bitch, but I am going to cut you. Call it a warning." His eyes were wild and the John Lennon glasses, made them look even bigger through the round lenses.

Just then, Jill entered the room. The man's attention was momentarily diverted towards her. Jackie took her chance and grabbed his arm. She managed to get a lock on it, but he still held onto the knife. Jill rushed forward, grabbed his arm and put pressure on his wrist, while desperately trying to avoid the deadly blade. The man was very strong, despite his diminutive size. Both women were a couple of inches taller than him and had more leverage, but still they couldn't dislodge the knife. The man suddenly shouted in pain as the pressure by both women loosened his grip. The knife finally flew out of his gloved hand and across the room.

Having disarmed him, the women were now trying to force him down. Jackie still had a firm grip on his arm. Jill was pulling the struggling man towards the settee, which was right next to them. Although the man was strong, he was getting exhausted. The women almost had him on the settee now. Jackie forced him, face down on his front and stepped over his trapped arm. She was now able to use her thigh as a bar to bend his arm in a direction it wasn't intended to go.

Jill meantime had lifted his legs onto the settee and then knelt on the small of his back. The man's strength had almost deserted him, as he felt the pain of Jill's knees pressing into his back. He then made a desperate effort to get up. Wrenching the trapped arm almost vertical, Jackie sat down heavily on his upper back, at the same time, crossing her legs over his trapped arm. He screamed in pain but was unable to move under their combined weight. The dangerous knife man had no more strength. He was pinned down and in pain. Jill changed her position from kneeling to just sitting on his back. Both women were gasping for breath. Jackie still held the arm lock and now her legs were firmly crossed, trapping the man's arm and neck with her thighs.

Jill gasped. "What the hell is all this about."

"He threatened me with the knife. I thought I'd had it. Thanks for your help. I really mean it. I couldn't have held him if you hadn't joined in."

Jill got up briefly to retrieve her mobile, which was on the floor. She sat straight back down on the man just in case he managed to struggle free. She called for assistance and was promised it would be under twenty minutes. She then rang James and told him what had happened. He asked for the address and said he was on his way. Jackie, somewhat hesitantly, gave Jill her postcode.

Jackie said,

"I really didn't want to call for help. We've taught this little creep a lesson. We could just have got off him and let him leave."

Jill looked surprised.

"Jackie, he had a knife; he could have killed you!"

In the meantime, the man was starting to moan.

"You've broken my fucking ribs and my wrist. Get off me you fucking bitches!"

The women just ignored him and waited for the cavalry to get there.

The police backup arrived and two uniformed officers arrested the bruised and battered man. He again complained that his ribs were broken and so was his wrist. The officers bagged the knife for evidence and the man had to be helped up after being virtually squashed. He looked in a bad way.

"Better take him straight to Brighton Hospital," said Jackie. "Get him looked over and then take him to the Custody Sergeant at the nick. We'll be there later to press formal charges."

As he was being led out of the flat by the two uniforms, James came bursting in.

"Jill. Are you OK? You're not hurt, are you?"

"No, I'm fine," said Jill.

"I'm not hurt either, thank you James," Jackie said, with a slightly annoyed expression.

"Sorry. I'm glad neither of you are hurt. How did he get into your flat? Was the front door forced?"

Jackie was rubbing her arms. "No, he must have unlocked the door somehow. If I'd seen any signs of a break in, I wouldn't have entered. He was a strong little bugger. Took two of us to overpower him. We had to use Jill's favourite technique, to subdue him."

Jill gave a little smile, but she did think they had been lucky. If he had been younger and stronger, things could easily have ended differently.

James quietly asked Jackie,

"Did you know your attacker?"

"No, he just broke in. Burglary gone wrong probably. Look, I'm going to have a soak in the bath. Why don't we all meet up at the station later?"

James nodded.

"OK, we'll go home and have a bite to eat. Give me a ring later and we can hopefully sort all this and find out what's it's about."

As they were leaving, James noticed a pair of John Lennon glasses on the floor, near the settee. He bent down to pick them up, disguising this action by picking a cushion up.

Jackie ran her fingers through her hair and was wearing a worried frown.

Jill took her arm.

"Are you sure you're all right, Jackie?"

"Yeah, I'm fine, really."

James had his mobile in his hand.

"Better get forensics here to examine the room."

"No James. You two go home. I'll phone it in. Can't see them finding much. Not with all of us milling around."

"OK, Jackie. See you later."

Chapter Twenty-Two

As soon as they left, Jackie was on the phone to North. She told him what had happened and he said he would sort it. Things were getting out of hand. The lid had to be kept on. There was a lot at stake!

In the car on the way home, James asked Jill,

"Are you sure you are all right. It's great that you can look after yourself, but you really could have got seriously hurt."

"James, I know you worry sometimes but you know, it's just part of the job these days."

"It's just that we're a team and I don't want you to take risks. He had a knife and it only needed one stab and that could have been that!"

Jill privately thought it was really sweet of James to be so concerned. She knew it was professional concern, but she also thought it was a little bit more than that. They had worked closely for a while now, but in the last couple of weeks she had been involved in two fights; both potentially dangerous. She genuinely liked James and staying at the house was a little strange professionally, but also very nice.

They ate the meal that James finally prepared. It was a very quick pasta bake, followed by some fresh fruit. They had decided not to open the wine, because they were going to the police station later, to see if they could get to the bottom of the attack on Jackie.

Jill hadn't mentioned the glasses, while they were in the car or while they were eating their meal. Then Jill said, "James, why did you pick those glasses up?"

"Was the attacker wearing them?"

"Well yes, at least I think so. They probably flew off at some stage during the struggle."

James got them out of his pocket and put them on the table.

"Do you recognise them Jill?"

"Well, only that they're like the ones that John Lennon used to wear."

"Right, but do you remember seeing anyone wearing a pair recently?"

Jill looked thoughtful and then suddenly realised.

"Yes, there was a man who walked into the restaurant the other night. He had a pair. He was with that awful man who accosted Jackie and kept calling her Christine. Fancy somebody or other."

"Carter', the apparently well-known entertainer!"

"That's right, Fancy Carter."

"Then if it's the same guy, I wonder why he ends up attacking Jackie Read, in her flat with a great big knife? Strange, isn't it?"

Jill was helping to clear the dishes away.

"Yes, it is. Of course, Jackie's attacker might not be the same man we saw in the restaurant. I only got a fleeting look at him when he came past. There's something else James. Our Jackie was reluctant to have the guy arrested. She even suggested letting him go!"

"Really?"

"Yes, it was me that called it in and when the uniforms arrived, she told them to take him to the hospital first, for a check-up."

"Was he that badly hurt?"

"I guess so. He was certainly moaning. Jackie must have cracked his ribs the way she held him. Normally, he would have been assessed by a doctor at the custody suite, wouldn't he?"

"Normally, yes. Still, at least we might get some answers at the nick a bit later."

Jill went to her room to change her clothes. James had just put the dishwasher on when his mobile rang.

"What! How did that happen? And there's no trace of him. What about his injuries? I see, so nothing too serious. I bet the two coppers are red-faced. Yes, so would I be. What about CCTV? Oh great! I guess it's going to be an early night after all. Thanks for letting me know. I assume you've told DS Read. OK. Bye."

Jill was standing in the kitchen, with a puzzled look, waiting for James to speak.

"You won't believe this but your burglar chum's done a bunk from hospital. Apparently, they checked him over and he's got a sprained wrist and two cracked ribs. He went to the toilet and despite his injuries, he got out through a window. One of the Constables was buying some sandwiches and the other one had a phone call. When they went in and checked the toilets, matey was long gone. Someone must have picked him up in a car, because there was no sign of him outside."

"What about CCTV at the hospital car park?" asked Jill.

"Not working. Apparently, it's being fixed. Great timing."

"Well, at least we can relax now. Anything on TV tonight?" asked Jill, picking up the remote.

James reflected that this was only their second night and already they were behaving like a couple. He did enjoy being with Jill and he hoped she felt the same. It felt a bit unreal but it was comfortable. Life would seem very empty when this case was over. Why is life so bloody complicated? he thought to himself.

Chapter Twenty-Three

While James and Jill were having breakfast the next morning, James' mobile rang. It was DCI Sandy Charteris.

He said he wanted to see them both at 9.30, before they continued with their interviews. He didn't say why. James just said they would be there.

Jill looked at James, across the breakfast bar.

"Problem, James?"

"Don't know. That was Sandy Charteris. He wants us both at his office at 9.30 this morning. Better get a move on."

When they got to Sandy Charteris' office, Bob North and Jackie Read were already there, drinking coffee. Charteris poured coffee for James and Jill and everyone sat at the meeting table.

DCI Charteris sat in silence, looking at each person in turn. The silence was deafening. Then, after what seemed like ages, Charteris looked directly at Jackie.

"OK, what the fuck is going on?"

"Going on, sir?"

"Don't give me that innocent look, Detective Sergeant. What the hell happened at your flat, yesterday evening?"

"I confronted a burglar and DS Trent came to my assistance."

"And?"

"And, we managed to overpower him and hold him down until help arrived."

"That's it?"

"Well, yes sir," said Jackie, attempting to look surprised at the questioning.

Charteris looked at Jill. All trace of informality had disappeared.

"What was your part in all this, DS Trent?"

"Just what DS Read said. We had been to the gym together. We went to her flat, but I stopped off at the local mini market. When I got to DS Read's flat, she was struggling with a burglar. He had a knife and I helped her to disarm him."

"Look, I hear that you were both brave and could have been seriously hurt or worse. But I don't understand the whole episode. What's going on?"

Jackie Read spoke.

"Look sir, we just acted as we were trained. We disarmed him and held him. That's it really."

Charteris fell silent again. After a minute or so he spoke.

"The two police Constables who came to your flat, were told by you, DS Read, to take the man directly to hospital. Why did you tell them to do that?"

"The man complained that he had sustained broken ribs and a broken wrist, during the struggle, sir."

"How did his injuries occur?"

"DS Trent and I sat on the bastard and I guess we are heavier than we thought, sir."

"Don't try to be facetious, DS Read. This is a serious matter."

"Sorry sir, but we were in real danger and did whatever we could to defend ourselves. If he got hurt, then it's his hard luck. He shouldn't have been there!"

"Point taken. Now, DI Halstead, what's your role in all this?"

"Not very much, sir. DS Trent called me and told me what happened. I drove there to see if I could assist. As I arrived, two uniforms were escorting the man to hospital. I checked that DS Trent and DS Read were OK and then took DS Trent back to our accommodation. The plan was to get the attacker to the police station, after he had been checked over at hospital. We intended to interview him that evening. That's it really."

Charteris just nodded and seemed to accept that James had a fairly minor role in the affair. Finally, he looked at DI North.

"What was your role in all this?"

"None at all, sir. I was off work with the shits."

"If that's an attempt at levity, cut it out. Is that clear?"

"Just a statement of fact, sir. I had a stomach upset and couldn't leave my flat all day. Didn't control give you my message?"

Charteris didn't respond. Then he addressed them all.

"You are aware that the burglar, attacker, however you want to describe him, later escaped from the hospital via, it seems, a toilet window."

"I've spoken with the two officers who were supposed to be watching him and frankly it was a cock up. We are expected to believe that a man with two cracked ribs and what turns out to be a sprained wrist, actually climbed out of a window."

"That's what we heard, sir," said North.

"Well," said Charteris, looking perplexed,

"I think a man with his injuries would have found it difficult to climb out of a fairly small window. One of the Constables was away getting some sandwiches. The other officer got a phone call, on his personal mobile phone. He said it was from you." He looked directly at North.

"Why did you ring him, DI North?"

James and Jill glanced at each other. Jackie Read just stared ahead.

North shrugged his shoulders.

"Just checking with him about the man's injuries and asking when he would be at the station for interview."

"PC Standish said you asked him if both he and his colleague had the prisoner in sight. He told you he was on guard on his own, outside a toilet waiting for the prisoner to come out."

"That's right."

"And you knew the Constable's private phone number?"

"Yes, sir. I've got PC Standish's private phone number in my phone directory."

"Why?"

"Geoff Standish and I go way back and I knew I could talk to him informally."

"Why informally?"

"Well sir, I'm an old- fashioned copper and I wanted first crack at the bastard. He attacked my Sergeant and I wanted a quiet word alone with him, as soon as Geoff Standish got him to the station."

"Are you telling me that you wanted to rough the offender up?"

"Well, not exactly sir. More like a man to man chat. We've all done it, sir."

"No, we have not all fucking done it DI North! It's a good thing for you personally that he got away, otherwise you could be facing charges yourself, along with PC Standish!"

"I'm sure you've never done anything like that sir, but you do understand, emotions run high when colleagues are attacked."

DCI Charteris just stared North. He didn't respond. Then he looked at Jackie Read.

"You didn't see fit to get forensics to look at your flat?"

"No sir, probably a waste of time."

With a look to the heavens, Charteris folded his arms.

Then with a resigned look, he said,

"I can see that I'm not getting anywhere with this bloody mess." He paused for dramatic effect and then said softly,

"The four of you are here to try to solve the antiques burglaries. I've read the notes of your interviews and we're not setting the world on fire, are we? Just carry on and we'll review the case at the 4 p.m. get together."

He gave them all a stare which would definitely have melted ice!

"I want you to put statements on record about the fight at DS Read's flat." Charteris made it clear that the meeting was over, by picking up his phone and gesturing for everyone to leave the room. This was one of his trademark dismissals

The four Detectives walked down the corridor. Bob North was the first to speak.

"Great, isn't it? Some maniac breaks into Jackie's flat and escapes from the hospital. And I get all the shit!"

James was first to respond.

"Look Bob. The DCI was right to ask what's going on. From his point of view there are lots of unanswered questions."

"Oh, so you're on his side now?" snarled North.

"It's not about sides, it's about understanding what happened. Like, why would a man get into Jackie's flat and then attack her with a knife?"

"Because there are some nasty pieces of shit out there who don't care who they hurt. If I ever get hold of him…" shouted a red-faced North.

He didn't finish the sentence because Jackie put her hand up.

"Just don't say it Bob. You know you don't mean it, because they would chuck you out of the force. Just let it go. Charteris is just doing his job. Let's write it up as he asked."

North was about to reply but just shrugged. Jill didn't say anything. She had exchanged glances with James when North was blowing his top but decided not to give an opinion.

The two teams gathered their files and set off on another day of interviews and probably more dead ends.

Chapter Twenty-Four

North and Read got into North's car and he drove off.

"Where are we going?" asked Jackie Read.

"For a drive. I'm pissed off with all the questions and I don't like our new team members."

"Look, I know you're pissed off, but Jill really got stuck in when that bastard attacked me."

"It's because she's a cop. Not because she likes you!"

"Why can't you ever give anyone some credit?"

"Because we've got bigger problems to sort out, that's why. When you told me that Carter's friend had been carted off to hospital, I knew it could blow everything. You could've just denied everything if he'd accused you of — offering to have sex with Carter, but some shit sticks and it might just stick to me!"

"To you? Is that all you're worried about. What about me? I was committing a crime when I copied Carter's computer files. So, the shit would stick to me, even though you were the instigator."

"Instigator? You sound like a fucking lawyer."

Jackie was annoyed and at this moment she wished she had never agreed to get involved with North's activities, whatever they were. Nothing was said for the next half hour or so. North finally pulled into a layby near the picturesque Seven Sisters cliffs. He shut off the engine and turned to Jackie. He put a hand on her knee and gradually let it travel up her thigh. Jackie grabbed his hand and removed it.

"Don't," she said, firmly.

"What do you mean, don't?"

"Just that. I don't want you to do that."

"Oh. It's like that is it?"

"Like what?"

"Don't you fancy me anymore?"

"Look, at this moment in time I'm more worried about the attack at my flat and what you've done to the guy."

"So, you don't want a little grope?"

"For fuck's sake Bob, just grow up! What's happened to the little bastard?"

"As far as you're concerned it's sorted, but if it's putting you off having a bit of how's your father later, then I'll tell you. When you rang me, I was with someone who does a bit of tidying up for me."

"Tidying up what?"

"No need for details, Jack. Just trust me. He just does some bits and pieces for me. He went to the hospital and found the two PCs. He kept an eye on them until our little knifeman had been X- rayed. He rang me to tell me that one of the cops had gone off somewhere and that PC Geoff Standish was keeping watch while matey was in the bog. As I told Charteris, I rang good old Geoff. I did ask him when he thought he would be back at the station with his prisoner."

"And how comes your friend knew which copper was Standish?"

"He described him to me. Can't mistake his bushy moustache. Standish is an old mucker of mine. We've done a few bits of business together, outside of work. I just asked what was happening with his prisoner."

"What, just so you could beat the bastard up in an interview room?"

"Made a good story, concern for my sergeant and all that. But it was just a cover. Meanwhile, my man went into the bog and lifted matey out of the window. Strong as a fucking horse. You and the lovely Jill wouldn't have stood a chance if it was him coming after you!"

"Yeah, yeah, but what happened after that?"

"My guy just walked outside and got matey into his car and drove off. The CCTV outside wasn't working. Pure luck. The CCTV inside would just show a guy with a hoody going in and out of the bog. Pretty clever and it's saved you from any embarrassing questions, if the bastard had been interviewed."

"Where is he now? Matey, as you call him."

"End of information, darling. Best you don't know."

"Best I don't, but it won't stop me worrying. And, you know what I think? The business with Carter's computer is just crap. You've got me into something that I don't understand!"

Bob just gave her one of his, 'what me?' looks.

"Now, where were we? Ah yes, I was moving up your thigh!"

"Just stop it Bob. It's called sexual harassment!"

"What! After what we've done together? You must be fucking joking."

"I'm just not in the mood and certainly not in a public layby. Now let's get on with our interviews. We're supposed to be working."

Jackie turned in her seat and looked into Bob North's eyes.

"And I don't believe for one minute, you were ill yesterday. You were up to something!"

North just started the engine and drove off without another word.

Chapter Twenty-Five

Meanwhile, James and Jill had carried out two interviews with witnesses. That was a misnomer because neither had witnessed anything in addition to their original interviews. No mysterious vehicles in the early hours or suspicious men with droopy moustaches. Both witnesses were located in Eastbourne, so Halstead and Trent decided to have lunch there. It was a nice sunny day, so they decided to get fish and chips at Eastbourne Pier. They had settled down at one of the picnic tables on the decking of the pier. They sat talking and eating with a wary eye on some large herring gulls, which were casting beady eyes on their lunch. It only needed a second's distraction, or a meal left unguarded and it would have been all over. These bandits would swoop in, grab anything they could and fly off. Jill had witnessed this on a couple of occasions and was eating her fish and chips with deliberate caution.

"Not a very good morning so far," said James.

"No. These burglars seem to be very organised. I was really hoping the registration plate might have helped. We still don't know why DC Westmore didn't record the interview and registration."

"I've been thinking about that a lot and I've decided to confront him."

"Confront him?" asked Jill.

"Well, have a quiet word with him. It could be a simple mistake, but we need to find out one way or the other."

"Problem is, he was working with Bob North and I just get the impression that something isn't quite right where DI North is concerned. His temper goes from nought to one hundred in seconds."

They carried on eating lunch and afterwards they took a stroll around the pier. There were lots of happy people having picnics at the various tables.

At the end of the pier, there were people knocking back beer and large glasses of wine. The two Detectives looked just a little out of place, because James was wearing a lightweight, dark blue suit and a white open-neck shirt. Jill wore a cream, knee length skirt with a dark jacket over a navy t-shirt. Everyone else seemed to be in shorts. A couple of women were sitting with large glasses of wine, wearing low cut vest tops which barely hid their breasts. James just looked straight ahead as they passed the women. Jill couldn't resist a little smile, as she saw James pretend not to see the acres of flesh on display.

They had one more call to make in the village of Willingdon and then, depending on the length of the interview, it would be time to get back for the usual 4 p.m. get together.

Chapter Twenty-Six

Later that day, all four Detectives arrived back at the police station. As usual, Jill typed up her interview notes. Jackie Read got four cups of coffee and there was a distinctly uncomfortable silence in the room. James broke the silence.

"Any idea where I can get hold of DC Westmore?" he asked nobody in particular.

"Now, why would you want him?" asked a surly Bob North. "Oh, just wanted to compare some notes. He interviewed one of the people we saw and there are a couple of points that need clarification."

James was trying to make it all sound casual but Bob North had for some reason, adopted a defensive attitude.

"It's only something we need to speak with him about. Sure, it can be sorted out, if he's around," said Jill, trying hard to placate the surly North. Jackie thought that North was still a bit prickly about what had happened in the car earlier and felt the need to counter her partner's bad manners.

"DC Westmore should be in the main office upstairs. If you take a stroll up there now you should catch him."

"Thanks, Jackie," said James, trying hard to sound grateful and ignore North's grim face.

"I'll go and see if I can catch him."

James finished his coffee and left the room, after exchanging an almost imperceptible glance with Jill.

James walked into the main office and there were three men and two women sitting at desks, working at computer screens. They all looked at James.

"I'm DI James Halstead from Lewes. I'm looking for DC Westmore. A slim, black man stood up and offered his hand. As they shook hands, he said with a worried look,

"I'm Peter Westmore, what can I do for you, sir?"

"I want to have a quick word with you about the antiques burglaries. I understand that you have worked on the case."

Peter Westmore looked relieved.

"Oh, yes. I was on the case for a few weeks but was moved onto another job. I was with DS Read just for the day this week, because her DI wasn't available."

"Is there an interview room we can use?" asked James.

The others in the office all looked up at the two men and then went back to their work.

"Err, yes, I think so. Interview room two is probably empty. We can go and have a look."

The two men made their way to the room and found it empty. There was a sour, body odour smell and DC Westmore reached into a cupboard just outside the door. He grabbed a fresh air spray and the room now smelt of violets, with undertones of body odour.

"Sorry about that. Some of the clients don't spend money on deodorants."

"Tell me about it," said James, with a smile.

"What did you want to speak to me about, sir?"

"No need for formality. I just wanted to ask you a couple of questions."

"Do you recall interviewing a Susan Bolton, who lives next to one of the robbery victims in Alfriston?"

"Yes, I do. Lovely location, opposite the old church."

"That's right. Do you recall her giving you a vehicle registration number?"

"Yes, I do. I remember it because it ended in the word BUS. It's all in my report."

"Well, that's what I wanted to ask you about. Did you type up your report for the case file?"

"Yes, I did. I'm a real stickler for procedure and always log reports."

"Well, unfortunately I can't find your report. It's not on file. Any idea why not?"

"No idea at all. I can show you the report on my computer, if you like. It's definitely logged on the main case files."

"Perhaps the hard copy got mislaid. Do you remember putting it in the case files?" asked James.

"Hum. I didn't actually put it in the case file. I handed it to DI North."

"Did you do a check of the vehicle registration?"

"No, DI North told me he would do it."

"And you didn't do any follow up?"

"Well, no. I was replaced on the investigation by DS Read. Don't know if she did anything about it. You say it isn't on the file?"

"Well, I can't find it," said James.

"If you come back to the main office, I can run you off a copy."

"That would be just great, Peter."

James Halstead collected a printed copy of the interview with Susan Bolton. He had a good feeling about DC Peter Westmore. He seemed efficient and was obviously surprised that a hard copy of his interview report hadn't been put in the case files. When he got back to the meeting room, Jill was printing off file copies of their latest interviews. There was no sign of North and Read. He looked at Jill with a quizzical eye.

"Where have our two colleagues gone?"

"Both gone home. They finished writing up their interviews and called it a day."

"Why don't we do the same?"

Chapter Twenty-Seven

James and Jill arrived back at their house. They flopped down on the settee and James stretched his arms. Jill sat back and rested her head on the back of the settee. James had told Jill about the missing report in the car, and the fact that North had apparently not filed the hard copy in the case notes file.

James laid back on the settee.

"Something isn't right, Jill. What possible reason would North have to not file the report?"

"Good question. It could be that he didn't want anyone checking the vehicle registration."

"Except that it's a phony. It doesn't implicate anyone."

"No, but it might just be that it bought a bit of time for the driver to take the vehicle off the road," said Jill, brushing something off her skirt.

"You know Jill, I think DI North is more than just a nasty bastard. I think he's bent!"

"Well if he is, then it's not really up to us to investigate. We could just pass it on to the Super, and she could put some wheels in motion. Look, this is our third day here and we may have uncovered something or nothing. We don't have a definitive brief. Just a vague instruction to see if there is anything going on. That's the reason we are staying in Brighton, instead of going home every night isn't it?"

James stretched his back.

"I think we need to get a better idea about what's going on. Frankly, I think we need to unwind. Rather than cook tonight, why don't we go out for a meal."

"What, in Brighton?" asked Jill.

"No, let's go out of town. It's a nice evening. Fancy a drive over the

South Downs to Eastbourne?"

"Yes, sounds like a lovely idea but aren't we supposed to stay put in Brighton?"

"We were asked to stay over at the safe house, but nobody said we couldn't go out of town in our own time."

"Got a restaurant in mind?"

"As a matter of fact, I have. Smart casual; it's an upmarket place. No flip flops and shorts."

Jill laughed. They both showered and were soon driving over the South Downs. They drove along the Eastbourne seafront and turned off into town at the statue, of the seagull-dropping-stained head, of the Duke of Devonshire. There was plenty of parking and they got a space at the far end of the road. It was only a two-minute walk from the restaurant. James pointed to their destination. It was an Italian Restaurant called Giuseppe's.

They walked through the door and to Jill's surprise a woman came out from behind the reception counter and kissing James on each cheek, she said, "James, it's so nice to see you again. It must be a couple of months."

She looked at Jill.

"Is this your partner?"

Hiding his slight embarrassment well, James replied,

"Err no, this is Jill, my work colleague."

The woman greeted Jill with two kisses.

"Table for two?"

She indicated a table in the window. It was in the middle of two tables set out for four people.

"That's lovely," said James, waiting for Jill to sit down. The woman handed them both a menu and told them she would give them time to decide.

"What shall we have to drink?"

"I normally have the house white. Is that OK, or do you want something else?"

"House white is fine."

"A bottle of the usual then, please."

The woman smiled at the couple and left them. Jill looked puzzled.

"You seem very well known here James."

"Yes, I used to come here quite a lot in the old days."

"With Sandra?"

"Yes, but those days are long gone. Now I'm with a work colleague," he said, laughing.

"Why don't I think that lady believed you?" Jill smiled.

"DS Trent, it happens to be true," said James, still laughing.

Their wine arrived and after they had ordered their food, the starters arrived. They both went for the deep-fried king prawns and James cautioned Jill to watch out for the juices. They ate happily and to the other diners, they could easily have been a married couple or perhaps, boyfriend and girlfriend. They laughed and talked as if they knew each other intimately. Before the main course arrived, the owner of the restaurant who was greeting everyone, came to their table. He shook James' hand vigorously.

"James, it is so nice to see you. And who is this?" he asked, looking at Jill.

"This is Jill. She's a work colleague."

"Ah, a colleague," he said gently, taking Jill's hand.

The word colleague was greatly emphasised, suggesting that it was a title of convenience, rather than a fact. Jill's slight blushing didn't go unnoticed by James. He thought it was nice, because it was something, he himself, wasn't exactly immune to.

They were both extremely full after the main course and couldn't face a sweet. They ordered two expresso coffees and then called for the bill. When the waitress arrived, James asked if she would cork the wine bottle so they could take it with them. Jill smiled at this. She knew it was because he was driving and he had limited himself to just one glass.

James paid the bill and after lengthy goodbyes and a promise to return to the restaurant soon, they strolled back to the car. It was about 10 o' clock and James suggested that they put the wine in the boot and stroll to the seafront. It was a balmy night and as they came out at the top of the road, next to the seagull-spattered, Duke of Devonshire, they could smell the sea. Jill had almost without realising, linked arms with James. The promenade lights gave the seafront an almost magical look. They headed towards the pier. There were groups of young people, students probably, sitting on the beach. They could see the tiny pinpricks of light from cigarettes and brighter lights from mobile phones. There was laughter and some general horseplay, but it all seemed good humoured.

They were just walking past the famous Eastbourne carpet gardens when James suddenly stopped. Jill gave him a worried look.

"What's wrong, James?"

"I've just had a sudden thought."

"What?"

"Well, remember when North was telling Charteris about making a phone call to PC Standish at the hospital?"

"Yes, he said he knew Standish and had his personal phone number."

"And he gave an explanation as to why he rang him. He said it was to have a word with the offender, man to man, because he had attacked his DS."

"Yes, that's what he said," mused Jill, looking puzzled.

"And PC Standish happened to be on his own, standing outside a toilet waiting for the attacker to come out."

"That's what North said," nodded Jill.

"And remember that the other copper was away getting some sandwiches at the time."

"Yes James. Is this another of your Sherlock Holmes moments?"

"Well yes! It could be. I'm wondering if the whole story is just a smokescreen for something else."

"Like what?"

"Just suppose that North was at the hospital and saw that PC Standish was on his own. He then rings his mobile from somewhere just out of sight. PC Standish engages in conversation and North asks him when the prisoner will be at the police station. All above board. Wants to see the bastard who attacked his DS. Standish is distracted by the call and meanwhile, someone goes into the toilets and helps the prisoner to escape."

Jill looked thoughtful. She was silent for a while and James waited for her to mull over his theory. They sat down on one of the benches in front of the carpet gardens. Jill turned towards James.

"You want me to play Doctor Watson? OK. I can see that your theory might work. But even if it's actually, what happened," Jill paused.

"Yes?"

"The big questions are: one — how did North know about the attacker being taken to hospital? We both know the answer to that one, is Jackie, two — how did he organise it? and three — Why would he want the guy to escape?"

James thought for a minute.

"Jackie knew that the guy had been taken to hospital because she told the uniforms to get him checked out before taking him to the station. So yes, the answer to question one, is obvious.

Question two — I don't know how he organised it, but I assume that they did x-rays and it wouldn't have been a quick in and out. Not with the waiting times and even accompanied by coppers, it must have taken time to process matey.

Question three — I've got no answer at all. All I do know, is that DI North is involved in something. Is there a connection between him and the attacker? And if so, what could it be? Plus, the missing report on the vehicle registration could well be down to him."

"James, we need to find out the 'whys'. We can't really say anything to DCS Marsh, without any real proof."

"Yes, I know, but we both keep coming back to our suspicion, that something's going on!"

They got up and walked to the pier. They crossed the road and looked into the lounges of the big seafront hotels. There were people nursing drinks and, in some hotels, the sounds of entertainers could be heard. 'I

Did It My Way' seemed to be popular. It was about 11 o' clock when they got back to the car. They decided not to drive back to Brighton, over the South Downs, in the dark. Instead, they went through Eastbourne town centre via the ring road and then out to the bypass, to Brighton. They got back to their house just before midnight.

As they pulled onto the drive, they were surprised to see a white mini, tucked away at the side of the house. They got out of their car and looked around. No sign of anyone lurking in the shadows.

"I don't like the look of this, James," said a concerned Jill.

"Just stay behind me as we go."

"But James…"

"Don't argue, just stay behind me!"

They opened the front door and cautiously entered the hallway. They had left a small lamp on in the living room when they had gone out earlier. They stepped inside and a figure was sitting in one of the armchairs.

"You keep late hours," said DCS Lorraine Marsh.

"Yes Ma'am," said a surprised James.

"Sorry to startle you both, but I didn't want to see you in a formal meeting at the office. I didn't expect you to be out 'til midnight."

"We went out to a restaurant, Ma'am," said Jill.

DCS Marsh didn't comment. She looked at them and for some reason, they both felt a little guilty. Marsh seemed to pick up on this.

"No problem. I don't blame you for taking some leisure time. After all, I hear that you've been involved in another rough and tumble Jill. I take it there are no incriminating photos doing the rounds this time."

Her smile made Jill relax.

"Bit of a fight Ma'am, but luckily I was on the winning team."

Seeing the Super's smile made James relax.

"Would you like a drink, Ma'am? Tea, coffee, something stronger"

"A strong, black coffee would be nice. I need something to keep me alert for the drive back."

James poured the coffee and the three of them sat down. James and Jill sat on the settee. Without thinking Jill had removed her shoes and James had taken his jacket off. Lorraine Marsh privately reflected, momentarily, that they looked very much at home.

Dismissing this thought she said,

"I suppose I should have telephoned you but it was really a spur of the moment thing. I was speaking to DCI Charteris earlier and he told me about the attack on DS Read. Jill, he told me the two of you disarmed the attacker and held him until help came. I was disturbed to learn that the man later escaped from hospital, while being guarded by two PCs. I also understand that the attacker was not known to DS Read and she thought it was just a random burglary, which ended in a confrontation with a knife."

"That's exactly right, Ma'am," said Jill.

"What was your role in all this, James?"

"Not very much. DS Trent rang me from DS Read's flat, where they were holding the attacker. When I got there, the man was just being taken away by the two PCs."

"Why was he being taken to the hospital in the first place? If he had been taken to the police station, he could have been medically assessed by a police doctor and then taken to hospital if it was felt necessary."

"Well," said Jill, hesitantly, "DS Read ordered the PCs to take him straight to hospital. As it turned out, the man had two broken ribs and a sprained wrist."

"And did you agree with her order?"

"I didn't really say anything," said Jill. "I didn't feel it was appropriate to argue about it in front of the two PCs."

"Don't worry Jill, I'm not trying to catch you out. I was just double checking what actually happened."

"Ma'am, if you don't mind me asking. What's this all about?" asked James.

"What, you mean my interest in the so-called burglary?"

"Why do you say, so called?"

"Sorry, James, it must all seem very confusing to you both."

"Put it like this. You ask us to help with the antique robberies case. You ask us to stay in Brighton when we only live a few miles away in

Lewes. Then, you tell us to keep our eyes and ears open, but we don't know what we are looking for. I'm sorry to put it so bluntly but, yes, it's very confusing."

Jill was looking from one to the other. She was hoping that James hadn't gone too far, but she felt she should say something.

"James, err, DI Halstead speaks for both of us, Ma'am."

Lorraine Marsh put her empty cup down and fixed them both with a stare, that suggested they had gone too far. She then surprised them.

"Look, I'm as pissed off as you. Let's drop the Ma'ams and rank and just talk openly. I haven't told you any more because I don't know any more. The Assistant Chief Constable ordered me to send two of my best and most trusted officers to Brighton, to work on the antiques robberies. He particularly wanted you to work with Bob North and Jackie Read. He has apparently heard some whispers that something isn't right. He doesn't want a full-scale investigation through official channels at this time. He thinks that something serious is going on and he doesn't yet know the extent of it."

James and Jill were speechless and just looked, first at each other, then at their boss. Taking up her invitation to ignore the protocols of rank, James replied.

"Thanks for being so open about it Lorraine, but is there nothing else you can tell us? Something to point us in the right direction?"

"What do you think about Bob North? Be frank and don't beat around the bush!"

James exchanged glances with Jill again.

"We both think he's up to something, but we have no idea what it is."

They told Lorraine Marsh about the missing interview sheet, the apparent dismissal of a possible lead identifying a man who cold called a house next door to a burglary victim, and their suspicions about North's possible involvement in the hospital escape. They also told Marsh that they had decided not to raise these suspicions with her up 'til now, because there was no actual proof that North had acted improperly.

Lorraine Marsh didn't interrupt during James Halstead's summing up. When he'd finished, she asked

"And what about Jackie Read? Do you think she's implicated in any activities connected to North?"

Jill answered.

"Jackie Read works hand in glove with North. He's her DI and they seem quite close."

"Closer than you and James?"

Jill felt her face reddening but tried to remain composed.

"James and I have worked closely for a long time. We're a team and we watch each other's backs. So yes, we are close."

Lorraine Marsh put her hand up as James was about to add something.

"Thank you both. I just wanted to know what you think. This is only your third day in Brighton, well fourth day, Thursday now," she said, looking at her watch. "Look, I know I'm asking a lot, but you may need to spend next week here as well. Is it going to be a problem?"

James and Jill both slowly shook their heads.

"No, if it's that important to you and the ACC, I think I can speak for both of us and say, we will stay," said James.

Lorraine Marsh stifled a yawn. "By the way, I'm sorry to just let myself in, but I did check that you weren't here. For your peace of mind, all the spare keys are in the station safe. DCI Charteris just loaned me one. Perhaps you would return it for me." She then said her goodbyes and left. They watched her drive off and closed the front door.

Jill yawned. "I must get some sleep. It's been a long day. Thanks for a lovely evening."

"Glad you enjoyed it. Let's call it a night. We can run through what Lorraine told us in the morning."

They both went to their rooms.

Chapter Twenty-Eight

It was very late; well after 1 a.m. Fancy Carter had fallen asleep on his settee after drinking a few gin and tonics. He had suddenly awoken from a disturbed drunken slumber, sweating like a horse. His Brighton flat was very plush and the walls were adorned with theatre bills, featuring the self-proclaimed King of Comedy. He lay there reflecting on what had happened. The recent Eastbourne booking had gone well, despite the supporting acts being third rate, in his opinion. His private life hadn't gone quite as well. The young woman who had promised a good time, had not delivered. In fact, she had deceived him and it turned out that she was a police officer.

His associate, Steve Daynes, had found out all about her. He had also checked Fancy's laptop and had discovered that someone had copied files. He wished he had not confronted the woman in the restaurant the other night. In hindsight, he should have kept a low profile. Her boyfriend had roughed him up a bit in the gent's toilet at the restaurant. In fact, it had been most unpleasant because he had been shoved against the urinal in full flow, soiling his expensive trousers. Very unpleasant! The man had also banged his head on the wall and Carter still had a slight discoloration above his eye.

Carter had thought long and hard about the woman's offer of sex in the hotel room and had concluded that it couldn't have been an official operation. Women police officers would surely not have got semi-undressed and then drugged him, to steal files from his laptop. Besides, there wasn't anything incriminating as far as he knew. His bank records were in order. No sign of any of his other business activities were on the computer.

The reason Carter had woken up with a start, was because Steve Daynes had told him that the woman needed teaching a lesson. He had dreamt that Daynes had killed her. She was probably looking for information for some blackmail scam. A police officer, freelancing in her own time. Yes, that was it. Well, Jackie was going to find out the hard way, that nobody gets one over on Fancy Carter. Not even a cop. If her hard man boyfriend was to get involved again there were people who could deal with him. Steve had said he was going to cut her, to teach her a lesson. The worry was that Steve hadn't been in touch, since going to see the woman. This was what was troubling him. Normally, a few gin and tonics would send him to the land of dreams for hours. It was the not knowing that was disturbing him.

Carter suddenly jumped. There was a knock on his door. Someone had bypassed the external security door and was now outside his flat. He composed himself and walked down the hall. There was a shadow, just beyond the opaque glass of the front door. He immediately thought it was Steve Daynes. He was about to open the door when he suddenly became cautious. He shouted from behind the door.

"Who is it?"
  "Police, can you open up?"
  "What do you want?"
  "Open up, sir."
  "I need to see some ID," said a still sweating Carter.
  A wallet, with a warrant card, was shoved through the letterbox. He looked at it and the name on it was DI North.
  "OK, wait a minute." Carter unbolted the door and foolishly, as it would turn out, took the security chain off.
  Suddenly, Carter was face to face with the man who had roughed him up in the toilets. The recognition was instant and he desperately tried to push the door shut. DI North shoved the door open wider and stormed into the hall. He pushed Carter so hard, that he lost his footing and went over onto his back.

"You and I need to have a word, you fat bastard!"

"What do you want? Do you know what time it is?" asked Carter, trying a bit of bravado.

"You sent a piece of garbage to rough up one of my officers. Get up!"

North grabbed Carter by his dressing gown and hauled him to his feet. He then dragged him into the living room and shoved him hard, onto the settee. Carter was very frightened but managed to speak.

"You're a police officer, you can't treat me like this. I'll report you to the Chief Constable. We're members of the same lodge!"

"Ha ha, don't give me that Freemason's crap. Just shut your fat mouth and listen to me."

"But you can't…"

Carter didn't get the chance to finish the sentence, because North slapped him hard around the side of his head. He reeled back into the settee and rubbed his head, both in pain and in shock. North made himself comfortable in an armchair opposite the now, extremely distressed Carter.

"Just listen to me, you fat bastard. Your friend, the one you were with the other night at the restaurant, threatened my DS with a knife. Well, he came unstuck and got hurt. I know you sent him because he mentioned the hotel room. Bet you were really disappointed when you missed out on a shag!"

"What's happened to him? Is he in custody?" asked a worried Carter.

"As it happens, he had to go to hospital because my DS broke his ribs. He escaped from the hospital and hasn't been seen since."

"You won't find him here."

"I know. It's you I came looking for."

"What do you want?" asked Carter, still rubbing his face.

"I want a bit of your business."

"What, show business?"

North stood up and slapped Carter's face, catching his nose and causing blood to trickle from one of his nostrils.

"Don't make fucking jokes, you aren't that funny!"

Carter could feel the blood running down his lips and chin. All his bravado had gone. He was a frightened man.

"What business?" he asked, meekly.

"Your little side business. You know, the drugs. And if you deny it, I'll really hit you hard."

Carter was open-mouthed and was about to say something but thought better of it.

North put his face close to Carter's.

"I know you're into drugs. I want the name of your main supplier."

Carter looked frightened and garbled.

"Look, I'm shit scared of you but the people I associate with are far worse. I can't mention any names, they'll kill me!"

"And you think I won't?"

"You're a police officer. I don't think you'd kill me. Whatever you do to me, I won't and I can't tell you."

North stood up.

"OK, you fat bastard. I'm going to give you a deadline. One week from today. Next Thursday, I want the name of your supplier."

"I can't do it, Mr North, I just can't. I just told you, they'd kill me!"

"One week, Carter. The alternative is allegations of underage sex. A couple of young ladies I know would be willing to swear in court, that you assaulted them and forced them to have sex with you. Understand?"

Carter was still sweating like a horse. Blood had stained his dressing gown and his face was wringing wet. He looked nothing like the bouncing entertainer displayed on the theatre posters around his room. He looked diminished. He sat with pleading eyes but said nothing else.

North looked down on the pitiable wreck that was Carter.

"I didn't think for one minute that you would have anything on your laptop about your business venture. It was just a fishing exercise to let you know that I can get really close to you, if I want to. Have another drink. I'll be in touch."

North turned away and strolled down the hall and out of the front door. The deflated Carter just sat there. Tears were now mingled with the trickle of blood from his nose. He needed a double gin and tonic.

Chapter Twenty-Nine

James and Jill had showered and dressed and were now enjoying scrambled eggs on toast. James was a dab hand at cooking, but Jill had been ready first and had made breakfast. They were sitting at the breakfast bar and both were thinking about last night's surprise visit by DCS Lorraine Marsh.

Jill was just eating her last piece of toast.

"What do you think last night's nocturnal visit was really about?"

"I think Lorraine Marsh is genuine enough, but I smell some politics here. The big question is why aren't our Professional Standards people running with this? If North is bent, why don't they just investigate him? One way or another, it would be sorted."

"Honest answer Jill, I think we are either being set up or we're going to end up right in the middle of something. Either way, it could be us that will take any flack."

"So, what do we do?"

"We just carry on working on the antiques robberies and see what comes up. We've got to mention the missing Susan Bolton interview notes to Bob North at some stage."

"He's so prickly most of the time. I think he will take it as criticism if we mention it to him, head on. James, perhaps I should casually mention it to him, rather than you tell him. He's not quite so bad with me. I think he sees you as a rival and has to act the tough DI."

"I can see your logic Jill. I don't like passing the buck to you but it makes sense. After all, there may be an innocent explanation," said James, getting up to put the breakfast plates in the dishwasher.

"Incidentally," said James, "do you think Jackie Read is involved in something dodgy with North? Apart from a personal relationship."

"I really don't know. They were pretty close in the restaurant on

Monday night but who knows? Maybe they are sleeping together," replied Jill.

"Well if they are, it's their business. Won't be the first time, people working closely together have fallen into bed."

Ignoring a slight feeling of butterflies in her tummy at James' piece of wisdom, she looked at her trousers.

"These are my last clean pair of trousers. I need to get some more clothes if we're staying another week."

"Me too. We'll have to sort out some clean clothes at the weekend."

They opened the case files and James pointed at yet another address that had been crossed through.

"Some Detective I am. I've looked through these interviews and lists lots of times and I hadn't noticed that this address in Addison Road had been crossed through. It's next door to a burglary victim."

Jill, who was just slipping some shoes on looked puzzled.

"What do you mean, James?"

"Well, remember the other property next to the burgled house? The one DC Westmore interviewed but the hard copy wasn't on file. Well, I wonder if this is the same."

"Could just be a coincidence. Our brief is to interview neighbours who haven't been contacted or follow up some to see if they remember anything new. This one might have been dealt with and just crossed off," said Jill, putting her jacket on.

"I know we mustn't get paranoid but why don't we just drop in and do a follow up?"

Jill smiled. "You, paranoid James?"

They drove to the crossed-out address in Addison Road, which was to the west of Brighton town centre. The name of the owner was Alan Braithwaite. To their surprise and relief, there was a parking space near the address. Although the sat-nav was a little vague on the final destination, this was clearly the place. The house they were looking at was a large Victorian town house, next door to an even grander house, which their notes indicated had been robbed of silver boxes and Victorian jewellery.

They rang the bell of the Braithwaite property. A young woman dressed in what looked to James, like a boiler suit covered in paint, opened the door. James showed her his ID and introduced himself and Jill.

The woman smiled at them.

"I thought you lot had given me up. Come in. Sorry about my appearance, I'm painting. I'm Tricia Brathwaite. My father's in London, I'm afraid."

James and Jill were shown into a large, bay-fronted room. There were paintings all around the room. Some showed wild eyed figures almost jumping out of the canvass. Others were more traditional landscapes, in idyllic settings. The two Detectives took in the whole room.

James felt obliged to comment.

"You've got some nice paintings here."

Tricia Braithwaite laughed.

"Please don't feel obliged to comment on my work. Some people think the wild, modernist stuff is a load of crap! Most prefer my landscapes, but they don't sell as well as the crap!" She laughed even more. "Ironic, isn't it?"

The two Detectives smiled. Jill privately thought that the modernist stuff was ghastly. Just like the paintings that Sebastian the cat's owner had on his walls.

James got down to business.

"Miss Braithwaite, you said you thought we had given you up. What do you mean?"

"Oh, it was just that the police interviewed me and Dad a couple of weeks ago and said they would send someone round to make up a photo fit of the guy my dad and I saw, on the night of the burglary."

"Do you know the name of the police officer?"

"Yes, wait a minute." Tricia Braithwaite looked on top of a paint covered sideboard.

"Here it is. DC Peter Westmore from Brighton police station. He was such a nice guy. Loved my modernist paintings."

"And you've not heard from anyone since?" asked Jill, with her notebook in her hand.

"Not a sausage. Thought you weren't interested, or you'd caught the bugger."

"What did this guy look like, Miss Braithwaite?" asked James

"I can do better than describe him. After your colleague left, I did a little paint sketch, just in case I forgot any detail."

She rummaged through a pile of canvases and finally came upon her picture.

The little canvass showed a man with long hair and a drooping moustache. His face was in shade and not full on, but it bore an uncanny likeness to the man an earlier witness, Sandra Temple, had described.

"He looked a bit like that bloke in the old TV series, err Department, something or other."

"Department S," said James, ignoring a sideways look from Jill, who thought it was typical of James that he would know something like that.

"Jason King," he added.

"That's right," said Tricia Braithwaite, obviously impressed. "Yes, Jason King. The series has been running on a Freeview TV channel."

Ignoring the fact that James had made a great impression on this arty woman, Jill asked,

"Can I take a photo of your drawing, please?"

Tricia Brathwaite was enthusiastic in her response.

"Yes, of course. Take the canvas with you if it's of use to you," she said, looking straight at James and ignoring the fact that it had been Jill's request.

"Is there anything else you want to know?" enquired a now buoyant Tricia Braithwaite.

Jill broke the spell of the woman's gaze at James.

"Yes, how did you and your father come to notice this man?"

"Oh, my dad had taken me out for a meal with my mum. They're divorced, but still get on well. I think they might get back together, sometime soon. Hope so anyway."

"And what about seeing the man?" prompted Jill, trying to get Tricia Braithwaite back on track

"Oh, we had got our taxi to drop Mum off at her place and then me and Dad, got home about midnight. Dad decided to have a nightcap. We put some smooth jazz on and lit a candle. The lights were out and Dad was talking about Mum and asking me if I remembered some of my childhood adventures, with my brother."

"Go on," said Jill, who was getting a bit impatient at all the meanderings.

"Well, we must have been talking for over an hour. Dad had just poured another drink when we heard a car outside. Thought nothing of it at first but it obviously wouldn't start. We glanced out of the window and saw the man in my picture. He had the bonnet up and suddenly the car started."

"So, he wasn't the driver?"

"No, someone else was driving. Didn't see his face. Mr Moustache shut the bonnet and glanced up at next door's window. He obviously didn't see us because we only had a candle on and the curtains were pulled."

James, who had been taking some notes while Jill had been talking, looked up pen in hand.

"What happened next?"

"Oh, they just drove off. Funny thing though. They had forgotten to put their lights on."

"What sort of car was it?"

"Oh, I'm not much good at cars. It looked like a black van. Might have been any dark colour but it looked black, especially with none of its lights on."

"OK, don't worry. I think that's it for now, unless you can think of anything else," smiled James.

"No, nothing else comes to mind. Just the man with the moustache and the dark van. I'm sorry I can't be of more help."

James held out his hand which was eagerly shaken by Tricia Braithwaite, even though her hand had dried paint all over it. Jill also shook hands, but Tricia Braithwaite was not as enthusiastic as she was with James.

As they left the property, Jill said,

"Thanks again for the portrait. If we need to ask you to do a photo fit as well, we'll definitely get in touch."

They got back to James' BMW, which as luck would have it had not fallen victim to the enthusiastic parking wardens.

They sat in the car and Jill was looking at James with a big smile on her face.

"What are you smiling at?"

"You. That arty girl was all over you. She was hanging on your every word."

"Really? I didn't notice."

"She was obviously impressed by your knowledge of old TV shows. You need to watch yourself James!" said Jill, as an even bigger smile lit up her face.

"I think we should grab a coffee and a sandwich," he said, changing the subject.

"Good idea James, it's your shout today," said a still smiling Jill.

Chapter Thirty

Further along the South Coast, the day at Eastbourne had started a bit cloudy. But as often happened, the sheer height of the South Downs had broken up the cloud and it was turning into a bright, sunny day. Eastbourne was soon basking in the sun and a gentle breeze was playing with the flags that fluttered on the seafront. People were strolling along the promenade and the Dotto road train was making its leisurely way along the seafront; the driver ringing the bell, in case anyone needed reminding to keep out of the way.

The gulls were keeping a beady eye on anyone eating an ice cream, ready to swoop down and grab it, if there was a moment's carelessness by an unsuspecting victim. All the seats along the front of the famous carpet gardens were taken by people in their senior years. There were some floppy hats on display, to keep the sun off.

There were shirtless, young men in baseball caps and young women in skimpy shorts and vest tops. All seemingly oblivious of the dangers of sunburn and were most likely destined to have an uncomfortable night, with bright red skin. There were large groups of boys and girls. Many were foreign students, which must have made some older people wonder if they actually spent time studying.

People were sitting at picnic tables on the refurbished pier. Others were just strolling along the pier and making a circuit. Several had stopped off for a beer or wine at the pub at the end. Everyone was just enjoying the weather. Although the golden age of the seaside town seemed long gone, days like this hinted at a revival of fortunes.

Suddenly some people at the very end of the pier were looking anxiously over the railings, into the sea. The tide was coming in and something was in the water, being gently washed towards the shore. A woman screamed when she and her companions realised, to their horror, that the something was a body. Several people were quickly using their mobile phones. The woman's scream had attracted lots of people to gawp over the side of the pier as the body made its way slowly towards the beach, on the gently rolling waves.

On the beach next to the pier there was sudden activity. The sea was too shallow for a boat to reach the body. In any case, it would soon make its way to the shoreline. There were police officers on the beach now, moving people onto the promenade and asking them to stand back. Their patrol car must have been close by, to have arrived on the scene so quickly. Children were being taken away by their parents. Some people were attempting to take photos and videos of the body. The police were trying to stop them. Others were shouting their disgust at the amateur photographers. It seemed that nothing was out of bounds with camera phones, these days!

Gradually, the body washed up onto the beach and the police immediately tried to pull it further up. They couldn't set up a police cordon, because the tide would come in a lot further and the body would be moved with it.

The body itself was that of a man. Mercifully, fully clothed.

The idyllic seaside scene with people enjoying themselves, had been transformed by the horror of the body, intruding upon their enjoyment.

Eventually, when the police and various emergency services had got the body onto the beach, people were trying to see what was happening. One of Doctor Claire Grant's team had eventually arrived and took charge of the body after a preliminary examination. The police had erected some screening around the scene and had moved the public away.

Later in the day, the body would be examined by Doctor Claire Grant. She had been contacted and would soon be making her first assessment.

The police would want to determine the cause of death. Sometimes an apparent drowning is far from that.

Chapter Thirty-One

James Halstead and Jill Trent had finished their lunch and were sitting in James' car, ready to make another visit. James had decided to ring DC Peter Westmore to ask him about the Braithwaites. James put the call on speaker, so Jill could hear.

"Hello, can you put me through to DC Peter Westmore please?"

"I'll check to see if he's available."

"DC Westmore, who am I speaking with?"

"Oh, hello Peter, it's James Halstead."

"What can I do for you? Not another missing file, I hope?"

"Well, funny you should say that Peter. We've been talking with Tricia Braithwaite."

"I remember her, she's an artist. Great paintings, modern stuff!"

"Yes, perhaps not to everyone's taste. She said you interviewed her father about the burglary next door."

"Yes, hold on a second. Here it is. I've just got the interview sheet on my laptop. Alan Braithwaite, Addison Road. He and his daughter saw a man trying to get a van started, on the night of the burglary."

"That's right. Miss Braithwaite said you were going to send someone round to put a photo fit together."

"That's right."

"Well, she hasn't heard back from us."

"That's strange, have you got a copy of my interview notes with you?"

"Well no. All I have is the name and address on my list, but it's crossed through."

"Crossed through? Those files are a bit of a mess. We did so many interviews and victim statements. Seems the admin's not up to much. If you're in the office later, I can run off a hard copy and leave it on your table."

"That's fine, Peter. Just one more question."

"Yes?"

"Why didn't we send someone to do the photo fit?"

"I'm not sure. I gave DI North a copy of my interview and as far as I remember, he said he'd organise a photo fit. Shall I remind him or are you sorting it?"

"No, don't worry, Peter. Miss Braithwaite has given me a portrait painting of the man she saw and it's quite lifelike. Not at all modernist! We can probably do a photo fit directly from it."

"Is that all you need from me, sir?"

"Yes, and thanks Peter. Bye."

"Bye sir."

Jill looked at James. "All paths lead to DI North!"

"Why on earth would he say that he would organise the photo fit? DI's wouldn't normally do that."

"No, they would delegate," said Jill.

"This is the second time DI North has, at best, apparently delayed the investigation or at worst, obstructed it."

"But why? Every interview is on computer files," said an exasperated Jill.

"Yes, but it would buy a bit of time if the report wasn't printed off. Anyone using the interview folders wouldn't be aware what was missing."

"James, I know our bosses think something is going on and DI North may be implicated. Suppose it's just slapdash admin or forgetfulness. We've got no actual evidence of obstruction."

Letting that thought hang in the air, they drove off to their next interview. This turned out to be routine. No revelations and no missing reports. It was just a follow up and nothing new was added. The couple involved were due off on holiday in two days' time and were more interested in preparing for it, than the burglary at their neighbour's home. Their third and fourth interviews were really a waste of time. James and Jill had hoped to make better progress, but no new information had been forthcoming.

James and Jill walked into the meeting room at the police station, just after a quarter past four. There was no sign of DI North or DS Read. Jill got on with putting the interview notes on her laptop and James was reading the interview report DC Westmore had left on the table. It had a post it note saying, 'Sorry', attached to it.

They had finished their admin and were sitting drinking vending machine coffee. It was better than their Lewes police station fare, but still not exactly tasty. It was just after 5 o'clock, when DS Jackie Read strolled in. She didn't look too happy but nodded a 'hello'. She had a takeaway coffee and a doughnut.

"Late lunch," she said, holding up the doughnut.

"Hi Jackie," said Jill. "Where's your boss?"

"I'm here. Why the interest?" said a glowering DI North.

"Just making conversation," said Jill, thinking that this didn't seem like a good time to ask North about missing files, or for that matter, anything else.

North looked like thunder.

"I don't know why the fucking hell you're so concerned about my whereabouts!" he said, stepping towards Jill, who stood her ground.

Seeing that Jill didn't appear to be intimidated, North glared at her.

"I know you probably think you're a tough bitch but believe me, I'm tougher."

James immediately stepped in front of Jill and stood very close to North.

"Just back off. Don't talk to my DS like that. You're out of order."

"So, you're sticking up for your bit of stuff. Bet you love being alone in that house, so you can slip her a length!"

With that, North swung a punch at James but it didn't connect. James blocked it with his arm and shoved North, who stumbled backwards. He didn't make an attempt to come back at James. He just walked out.

158

Jackie Read looked at both her colleagues.

"I don't know what to say. He's been like this all day. I'm really sorry."

James spoke calmly.

"I appreciate that Jackie. I'm sorry I reacted like that, but I don't like his mouth and I don't like his aggression."

Jackie shook her head. She put a hand on Jill's shoulder.

"Just ignore him Jill. He's a bit of an arse at times."

Jill nodded.

"So, it seems. Forget it Jackie!"

With that, Jackie collected her bag and laptop and walked out of the room.

"Are you OK, Jill?" asked a concerned James.

"Yes, I'm fine James. I thought all that macho abuse against women in the force ended some time ago. I was wrong. And James thanks for what you did. I could have hit him, but I didn't fancy striking a senior officer."

They both smiled, gathered up their files and belongings and headed out of the door. They hadn't noticed the figure of DCI Sandy Charteris emerging from the next room. He looked thoughtful, then made his way to his office.

Chapter Thirty-Two

After the altercation with James Halstead, Bob North was sitting in his car in the police station carpark. Jackie Read approached and North glowered through an open window.

"You are a complete arse; do you know that?"

"Just fuck off, Jack, I'm not in the mood."

"What's got into you?"

"Nothing you need to know. I'm going home and I don't want you around!"

"OK by me," shrugged Jackie, as she walked away towards her car.

North got a pay as you go mobile phone out of his glovebox. He pressed some buttons and waited.

"My flat, in an hour," he rasped.

Then hung up and drove off, throwing a shower of gravel in his wake.

James was driving at a more sedate pace as he and Jill made their way back to their house. Neither cared to admit it but they were both a little shaken by the incident with North. Jill knew that the normally thoughtful, placid James must have really been annoyed, to shove North. But it was self-defence and he was standing up for her.

When they arrived home, they both flopped on the settee in the living room. James was looking at Jill.

"What is it, James?"

"It's what North said about us. Do you think other people think the same?"

"What, that you're slipping me a length?"

James laughed. "Very ladylike, Jill. Yes, that's exactly what I meant."

"Does it matter what people think? We are work colleagues and we've been placed into a social situation. Let them think what they like."

There was a shared silence which was broken by James.

"I don't fancy cooking tonight, do you?"

"It's your turn James, so you get to decide what we do about food."

"Let's find a restaurant here in Brighton and have a few drinks. After our tussle with North, I need to unwind. What do you say?"

"Yes, let's stroll into town and get a cab back. It looks a lovely evening," said Jill, kicking her shoes off.

Half an hour later, they had both showered and James was sitting reading a magazine, when Jill walked in. She was wearing a short, but fairly modest dress with a cardigan. James had a lightweight, cream, linen suit, with a navy shirt. Jill thought he looked very good. Jill sat down and put her shoes on. James thought his DS looked very attractive indeed. Jill had a trim figure and at five feet nine, she was an elegant woman. She was wearing sensible shoes with a small heel. Even so, she wouldn't match his height. As she sat there, James couldn't help but look at Jill's long legs. He glanced away when he saw her smile at him. He thought what the loutish North had said. Yes, he thought, under different circumstances, he would like to make love to this lovely woman. Not very politically correct but he couldn't help his feelings. What was happening to him? This was so unprofessional.

His thoughts were broken when Jill said,

"Come on, I'm getting hungry. Now you've refused to cook tonight, we'd better find a restaurant."

They both smiled as they got up and James checked that he had the door key. It was a wonderful, balmy evening as they strolled along the road to the town centre. As was becoming her habit when they were off duty, Jill hooked her arm around his. Anyone observing them would conclude that they were a couple. This was certainly not the way colleagues would normally behave. It was as if they had both ignored the discipline of the police service and rules. They talked about everything except work. Neither wanted thoughts of North to intrude into this lovely evening. They found a little Italian restaurant and were soon drinking

Jill's favourite merlot. Although work was definitely off the agenda, they talked about Tricia Braithwaite's paintings.

"So, Peter Westmore liked Miss Braithwaite's modernist paintings? I've never understood why people can be in raptures over something that looks like a small child has painted it."

James nodded his agreement.

"Did you know about the chimpanzee that painted?"

"Is this the start of a joke, James?" asked Jill, laughing.

"No, it's a true story. Apparently, a chimp did a painting and it was put on show with other modern art paintings. Turns out, the public couldn't tell which one the chimp had painted!"

They both laughed and Jill raised her glass.

"A toast. To modern art."

"Modern art," they both said, as they clinked glasses.

At the end of the evening, they decided that it was too early to get a taxi home. They strolled along, talking and laughing and enjoying each other's company. When they got home, Jill changed into her pyjamas and James put his jogging suit on. They sat contentedly watching the local news. There was the usual assortment of stories. The local bus company was changing some of the bus routes; much to people's anger. Seagulls had made a bombing raid over a car park in Brighton and irate car owners were saying something had to be done. An expert pointed out that the gulls were protected by law and had to poo somewhere.

Then, a serious bit of news. A body had been found in the sea, near Eastbourne pier. Police were unable to identify the body, which was a man, possibly in his late forties, early fifties. Death by drowning was suspected but a preliminary post-mortem had been inconclusive. The police were going to circulate a photo of the victim, in the hope of getting an identification. As the weather forecast came on, Jill said,

"I wonder if anyone will come forward?"

James nodded, "Yes, I wonder."

Changing the subject, he said, "It's Friday tomorrow. The week's gone quickly. We'll have to check with DCI Charteris about weekend duty. Hopefully we'll get a chance to change our wardrobe."

When they got back to the house, they had both gone to their rooms, thinking what a nice time they'd had and how it would be so different, going back to their own flats when this case was concluded.

Chapter Thirty-Three

DI Bob North had not had such a pleasant evening. The person he had telephoned from the office carpark had been delayed. In fact, it was nearly midnight when the visitor arrived at North's flat. The big man sat in an armchair drinking a glass of North's malt whiskey. The mood in the room was grim.

North's earlier bad mood had not subsided, as he poured himself another whiskey.

"All I asked you to do was look after him and keep him on ice for a while. And what do you do? You fucking kill him!"

The big man, Terry Dalton, just stared at North, sipped his whiskey and putting his glass on the table, he spoke quietly,

"First off, I didn't kill him. It was an accident."

"Accident! He's still dead whether it was an accident or not."

"Just hear me out. I had him locked up in a boat shed. I gave him food and drink and all he did was fucking moan. He told me he had connections. People who would sort me out but if I let him walk, he'd just forget it."

"So you killed him?"

"How many fucking times do I have to tell you? I didn't kill him. Forget you're a cop for just a minute and listen," said a clearly irritated Terry.

North took a few deep breaths and calmed down a bit. He spoke slowly.

"So, what happened to him, before he was washed up on a beach at Eastbourne?"

"A mate of mine has a little fishing boat. We went out the other night and took your friend with us."

"Why the hell did you do that?"

"Because I wanted to keep an eye on him; didn't want to leave him in the shed. My mate doesn't ask questions. I just said I was keeping the bloke on ice for a few days."

"So, the three of you went out on a cosy little night fishing trip?

Do you know how ridiculous you sound? A night fishing trip with a prisoner in tow. What a fucking brilliant idea!"

"Well it's all right for you. 'Just keep him on ice,' you said. You don't fucking care how I do it, just as long as you're not inconvenienced. While I'm keeping an eye on the bastard in a boat shed, you and the lovely Jackie are tucked up in bed!"

"Terry, I make sure you get a fucking good cut from the business; more than a lot of people would get. So don't start bad mouthing me, just because you've fucked up! I'm still waiting to hear what happened to the guy you didn't murder. So, you were all out for a bit of night fishing. What happened? Did he decide to go for a midnight swim to Eastbourne?"

"Well in a way, yes. All the time I was with him he was moaning about losing his glasses. Said he couldn't see more than an arm's length, in front of him. Should have heard him bleating about it when I lifted him up to that toilet window at the hospital. Said he was virtually blind and his ribs were killing him. Couldn't find his glasses. When I got around to the other side of the window, he was just standing there. When I shoved him in the car, he didn't know where he was. Couldn't even see my face, he said."

"All very interesting but what's all that got to do with what happened to him?"

"That's just the point. He was virtually blind without his glasses. While we were fishing, the stupid sod fell over the side of the boat!"

"Fell over the side? You mean you didn't tie him up?"

"No need; he wasn't going anywhere while we were at sea."

"Only over the fucking side!" growled North.

"Look, I'd put an old life jacket on him. Problem was that it wasn't up to much. I thought at least it would stop him drowning. I was wrong! We looked for him all around the boat and then just gave up and left."

"Leaving his body to wash up at Eastbourne?"

"Yeah, but nobody will know who he is. He didn't have any ID on him. I checked his clothes. He must have emptied his pockets when he went around to attack your girlfriend. He wasn't very good, if he couldn't overpower a woman!"

"Jackie wasn't alone, she had a DS named Jill Trent with her. They both jumped on him and broke his ribs."

"Some hard man he was then."

"He wasn't a hard man, he's just a mate of Fancy fucking Carter. Don't know why he thought he could take on Jackie. Anyway, never mind all the crap. Did you do anything to him before he went for a midnight swim?"

"Nothing at all. Unless he got hit by a boat or something, while he was in the water, he won't have a mark on him. He probably just drowned because of the cold and the distance from the shore. Probably couldn't even see the shore."

"Yeah, apart from the broken ribs and damaged wrist, nobody will know him, will they? Now what about that bastard Ratty?"

"I told him to lay low, like you said." "Right, keep an eye on him. He was seen during at least one burglary. I've tried to delay any circulation of his photo fit but if it gets circulated, he's no use to us. He'd blab his fucking mouth off if he was ever picked up."

"I've told him to keep his face covered on jobs."

"It's worse than that. The stupid sod did a house call to see if the owner wanted an alarm system."

"Shit."

"Yeah, shit's the word. He's made a lot of money deactivating house alarms and the stupid bastard has to do some freelancing! What a fucking mess. One dead body and one idiot!"

The two men had another whiskey and North was a little more relaxed, now that he knew Fancy Carter's little friend had conveniently drowned, rather than being murdered. He had thought all along that it was unlikely that the guy would have implicated Jackie, because of what he was into himself. But people sometimes do unpredictable things under police questioning. There was a lot of money at stake. It was a complication North could do without. Now it was hopefully solved, at least as far as the prat opening his mouth about Jackie.

Terry was looking at his watch.

"Need to get going. When are we going to do some more antique collecting?"

"We're giving it a break for now. Things are getting complicated. Besides, we're a man down and it could soon be two."

"And do we get a new van?"

"I'll leave that to you Terry, but we may be out of the antique business. Might have to just concentrate on our main money-maker."

Both men exchanged a knowing glance as Terry left.

Chapter Thirty-Four

Jill Trent was on breakfast duty that Friday morning. James was a bit bleary eyed after last night's wine drinking. He had showered and shaved and felt better now than he had earlier. Jill didn't look like she had been drinking at all. She was fresh eyed and dressed in a smart trouser suit. She had an apron, displaying a rude joke on the front. James had given it a double-take and laughed.

"Found it at the back of the kitchen cupboard," smiled Jill. "Bit rude, isn't it?"

"Glad it's your turn to make breakfast," said James, looking at the apron.

While they were eating scrambled egg on toast, James was wondering about the body washed up on the beach.

"Do you suppose Doc Grant will be involved with that drowning case?"

"Could well be."

Just as they were pouring coffee, there was a ring at the front door. James went to answer it and came face to face with DCI Sandy Charteris.

"Morning James, hope I'm not disturbing you."

"No sir, you're not. We're just having breakfast, come through.'

Jill almost stood up when Charteris walked into the kitchen but resisted doing so. "Morning sir; coffee?"

"Morning Jill. Yes please, black no sugar. Interesting apron."

There was an uncomfortable silence as Jill handed Charteris his coffee. He sat at the breakfast bar and looked around.

"Not a bad place this. Good job it was empty; nobody needing to stay safe. Are you both OK, staying here?"

"Yes, we've settled in sir," said James, wondering what the purpose of this early morning visit could be.

Charteris drank some coffee and glanced at the two Detectives.

"Look, I'm not one for beating around the bush," he said, after beating around the bush since he'd arrived.

"I'm going to tell you something you already know. You're here for another week. DCS Marsh contacted me and said you'd agreed to stay in Brighton. I know you wonder what the hell is going on, but you will have to trust your senior officers on this one."

James and Jill were expecting Charteris, to continue, but he didn't elaborate any further. Finishing his coffee, the DCI said in an almost hushed voice,

"I heard what happened in the operations room yesterday evening."

Before either Detective could respond, he said,

"I know that DI North is a rough character. He sometimes sails close to the wind and always seems to be one step away from a disciplinary hearing. He gets lots of convictions but his methods are questionable. So far, nothing has stuck to him but it's probably only a matter of time, before he goes too far. I assume that neither of you are reporting him for what happened yesterday?"

James shook his head.

"No sir," said Jill.

The DCI looked relieved.

"You have every right to complain about the incident but if you are not minded to do so, then I'll ignore it. Fortunately for me, I didn't actually see anything, so I'm not minded to act either." Another silence. Then DCI Charteris looked deadly serious. He steepled his fingers and seemed to be considering his words carefully, before speaking.

"One of the big strengths of modern policing is the transparency of everything that we do. We have to ensure that we are squeaky clean, when investigating crime. We also have to ensure that people we interview on suspicion of crimes have access to proper legal representation. We do not make our own judgements on guilt or innocence. But we gather the facts and present the case for legal appraisal."

James and Jill just looked at the DCI and made no comment. Hands still steepled, he continued.

"I know you are both looking at me and thinking we know all this. Why is he telling us? Well, I'm telling you because the Assistant Chief Constable, DCS Lorraine Marsh and I, as well for that matter, are going out on a limb. We're asking you to carry out an investigation into the antiques burglaries as part of a team, knowing full well that at least one member of the team could be bent and another could be straying into dangerous territory. I'll say it out loud. It's possible, probable even, that DI North is involved in something that will ultimately bring the Sussex Police into disrepute or worse."

James had to speak.

"I'm going to be blunt sir, because I have to. Both I and DS Trent are honest officers. We don't break the rules. We investigate according to laid down procedures. We are now in a position where we're investigating the burglaries, but in reality, seem to be keeping eyes and ears on DI North and DS Read. We have found some inconsistencies in some of the case notes and suspect that an attempt has been made to delay certain actions that might help towards solving the case. We have agreed to stay in this house, rather than commute the short distance between Brighton and Lewes; which is not really normal procedure, but we can live with it if so ordered. There also seems to be no intervention by our Professional Standards people. So sir, we are out on a limb as well, don't you think? Sorry if I've overstepped the mark, but it had to be said."

Jill added,

"For the record sir, I support everything DI Halstead has said."

Charteris folded his arms and smiled.

"That little speech is exactly the reason you two were chosen. DCS Marsh said you were both top officers and can be trusted to act in an appropriate way. I want you to carry on, with the understanding that you have the full support and confidence of the ACC."

"If DI North is going to slip up, I want you right there if it happens. When you come to the office this afternoon, I will announce that you are both staying on the team for another week. Just watch yourselves and come to me if you have a problem you can't resolve."

"Yes sir," said both Detectives.

DCI Charteris got up to leave.

"By the way, I know you are normally rostered to work some weekends but take this coming weekend off; go home recharge your batteries and all that. See you both later."

After Charteris had left, James and Jill cleared away the breakfast dishes and didn't say very much. Then James smiled at Jill.

"Guess it's a weekend of washing and ironing for me."

"Me too," laughed Jill.

They were suddenly both serious.

"What have we got ourselves into, James?"

"I really don't know. What I do know, is that I'm enjoying our time together socially."

"So am I James. It's so difficult to separate work from our off-duty time. I know exactly what you mean because I'm feeling it too. I know I've said it already, but when this case finishes, we'll have to see how we feel. I think we both know already but we really need our wits about us and…"

"Jill, no need to say it. We both know what's happening. Let's just keep it professional. Hard as that is, for me."

"And me James!"

They got their files together and set out on another day of interviews. Their previously unspoken feelings were now out in the open. They were both single and perhaps their close proximity in the house and spending off duty time together had inevitably exposed hidden feelings. They had been close work colleagues for a while now. They had shared some off-duty meals but only as DI and DS; nothing personal at all. Lots of their work colleagues met up for social activities. A night at a bowling alley or darts in pubs. No big deal. With James and Jill, it was different altogether.

Chapter Thirty-Five

Friday morning had been the usual meeting between Doctor Claire Grant, the police pathologist and her team. They had been discussing several ongoing post-mortems but the latest case of the drowned man found on Eastbourne beach had been at the top of the agenda.

Both the preliminary investigation and subsequent follow up had pointed to drowning as the cause of death. The man had not been in the sea for very long and had not been nibbled by sea creatures. He had not been hit by boats or propellers. The condition of the body was just as would be expected for someone who had drowned recently. The body was fully clothed, except for two missing shoes. Normally a body in the water would sink and later, due to gases, bob to the surface. The man had been wearing a long, waterproof coat which had allowed air pockets to form and provided some buoyancy. He also had a partially-deflated life jacket, which had perhaps helped to keep him afloat; not enough to prevent drowning. It was thought that the man hadn't been in the water for more than five or six hours. It was likely that he had fallen from a boat and the tidal currents had propelled him to the shore before he had sunk to the depths. There were some injuries: two recently broken ribs and a minor wrist sprain, which was initially picked up from some discolouration.

There was no wallet or driving licence. No papers, receipts or anything that would help to identify the victim. The police had been keen to establish cause of death in case it was a murder investigation. As far as Doctor Grant was concerned, this was just a tragic drowning. There would have to be an investigation to try to find the identity of the man. The police photographer had taken some close-up head and face shots. Because the body had only been in the relatively cold water for only an apparently short time, the facial features had not deteriorated sufficiently to render identification impossible. There was also the possibility that dental records could determine who the victim was. The fingers would still, in all probability, yield up prints. In fact, as a matter of routine, all the standard identification methods would be fully deployed.

The initial efforts would involve circulating the photo of the face, both around the various police stations and offices and the local press. There was also the question of how the man came to be in the sea. The fall from a boat theory seemed the most plausible answer. An accident while night fishing perhaps. It was not thought that he had jumped off the nearby cliffs, because the body was undamaged. The life jacket would certainly have been incongruous.

Nothing was ever dismissed though, until it could be categorically ruled out.

Chapter Thirty-Six

DI North and DS Read had met up in the car park at Brighton police station. North was in a slightly better mood today, but not by much. Jackie Read had parked up and walked over to North, who had just lit a cigarette. As he puffed smoke out of his car window, Jackie Read said,

"Time you gave that up, Bob."

North just scoffed and blew out more smoke.

"I hope you're in a bit better mood today. We don't need another bust up with our partners."

"Fuck our partners! I don't know why we can't just carry on with this case the way we were."

"What you and DC Westmore, you mean?"

"Yeah, it was going along OK. We don't need help."

"So, you didn't want me on it either?"

"Not really. I was supposed to get another DS and DC, until they got dragged off onto that children's home case."

"Yes, along with half a dozen others Bob."

"Anyway, it is what it is. I didn't get much choice."

"And now you're stuck with me and our two colleagues from Lewes!"

"Yep. That's it then. Let's get going. My car?"

"If you can keep your hands to yourself!" said Jackie, giving North a serious look.

"Just get in the fucking car, Jack. Don't piss me off. I know where I stand now."

James and Jill were on their way to East Dean, which was inside The South Downs National Park. They had telephoned a Mr Reginald Prentis, who lived quite near to a property that had been burgled. The drive from Brighton was pleasant and they enjoyed the scenery. It was the upside of policing in Sussex, but the distances and in some cases the remoteness of villages, made it difficult to keep an eye on these locations.

James had put the address in his sat-nav and eventually they were at the home of Reginald Prentis. He had another of those doorbells that seemed to go on forever, when Jill pressed it. They heard the sound of loud barking and howling and a voice saying, "Calm down." There were some scrabbling noises behind the door. A small, rotund man in his fifties opened the door and was desperately trying to control two boisterous Springer Spaniels, without much success.

James held out his warrant card.

"DI Halstead and this is DS Trent. Mr Prentis?"

"Yes," said the still struggling Prentis.

"Sorry about this but they always go mad when the bell rings. Please come in. They won't bite you or anything."

"Don't worry about it, Mr Prentis," said Jill, apprehensive none the less, about her smart trouser suit.

Despite the attention of the two dogs, they were shown into a comfortable living room. A woman came out of the kitchen and offered them tea or coffee. They opted for coffee and sat on a large, comfortable settee. The two dogs sat at their feet and were anxious for attention. James and Jill rubbed the dogs' ears and then things settled down. Both dogs sprawled on the carpet in front of the settee. Reginald Prentis sat in an armchair. Coffee arrived and the woman introduced herself as Barbara Prentis. She was probably in her fifties but could certainly be described as a handsome woman. She was dressed in tight fitting jeans, with a t-shirt bearing the legend, 'Barbados' on the front. This was in stark contrast to her conservatively dressed husband who wore baggy, green trousers with an old, off white, polo shirt that was past its best. Barbara Prentis left the room.

James eyed the chocolate biscuits that had accompanied the coffee.

"Do help yourselves to biscuits, but watch out for the dogs, they are little sods when food is around."

As if the dogs had understood these words, they both sat up and eyed the plate of biscuits. When James and Jill helped themselves to a biscuit each, two pairs of eyes followed their every movement and both dogs licked their chops.

Jill had her notebook out as James led the interview.

"Mr Prentis, I see from the file that you have been interviewed by Detective Inspector North about the burglary of the property near you. As I explained on the phone, we are reviewing the case files and just want to go over some details with you. Now, on the night of the burglary I understand that you heard a car in the road at 2 a.m., on Wednesday the 10th of January."

"Yes, I not only heard it, I got out of bed and saw a van moving off."

"You saw it?"

"Yes, that's what I told that other Inspector."

"The notes say you heard it."

"Well yes, but I did see a van. I guess I wasn't too explicit when I spoke to the other Detective. I think I said that I saw a van but couldn't be sure if it was just passing by. I didn't actually see it driving away from next door. I assume your colleague decided that it wasn't explicit enough to note down."

"Yes Mr Prentis, I'm sure that must be the reason. Is there anything you want to add to your original interview?"

"Not really."

"What about the days leading up to Wednesday the 10th of January, Mr Prentis. Did you see anyone hanging around or sitting in a vehicle?"

"No, unless you count a couple of blokes walking on the downs."

"Were they in the vicinity of your property?"

"Oh, no. I was out with Fred and Buster."

He saw the bemused faces of the two Detectives.

"Ha, sorry, Fred and Buster are these two scallywags," he said, pointing towards the two dogs, who had clearly given up on snaffling a biscuit.

"We were way over to the south of here. I take them for a couple of miles a day. Springer's need a lot of exercise. Anyway, I saw two men. One was big and one was small. Proper 'Little and Large', they were."

"Can you describe their faces?"

"No, not really, they were quite a way from where I was. The big one had sort of combat gear on. The little guy had an old flying type jacket. You know, the ones that wartime fighter pilots used to wear."

"And you had no idea what they looked like."

"No, as I said, they were too far away. In any case they both had woolly hats with scarves wrapped around their faces. It was bloody cold in the wind. I had my hat with ear flaps as well as a scarf."

Jill had jotted this down and asked,

"Was that the only time you saw the two men?"

"Yes. Come to think of it, apart from the almost comical disparity in size, I did wonder what they were doing so far from the road, but on the other hand we get lots of walkers on the downs. I can't really help you, I'm afraid."

Sensing that they wouldn't get much more from Reginald Prentis, they stood up. Both dogs had gone from lazy to fully alert in the time it took for James and Jill to get to their feet.

"Now, come on boys, don't start all that again," said Prentis, addressing the dogs as if they understood his every word.

The Detectives said their goodbyes and thanked Mrs Prentis for the coffee and biscuits. She said,

"You're welcome," moving the remaining biscuits to a place of safety.

When they got into the car and drove off, Jill said,

"What did you make of the two men on the downs?"

"Coincidence?" ventured James.

"Yes, it probably is, but what about that business with the van?"

"Jill, I really don't know. You heard what Prentis said. He couldn't be sure that the van wasn't just passing by."

Jill had to agree but added,

"2 a.m. is very late for traffic, but maybe we're looking for something that's not there!"

James was concentrating on the road but added quietly,

"You know Jill. If I was paranoid, I might think that DI North's casual behaviour fits a pattern. He apparently decides that the van is not

177

relevant, so just leaves it out. It's nothing we can pin on him, but it might be worth mentioning at our review meeting later."

"Yes. I don't suppose he'll blow up in front of Sandy Charteris," said Jill, hoping she was right.

Chapter Thirty-Seven

James and Jill got back to Brighton and grabbed a sandwich at a local delicatessen. They then sat in the car, preparing for the review meeting. They got back to the police station about 3.30 p.m. It gave them time to make sure the case files were in order and contained hard copies of all their interview notes for the past week.

James was pleased to see that a photo fit of the man, described by Sandra Temple, was staring out at him when he opened an envelope on his table. He had arranged for an officer to visit Sandra Temple and the results were positive. An electronic copy had been pinged to both his and Jill's laptop. The face on the photo fit was also quite a convincing match with the picture given to him by Tricia Braithwaite. James had commented that it was fortunate that the picture had not been a Picasso-type representation. They laughed that it could have been a bizarre face, all square angles and misplaced eyes.

"What's the joke, can anyone join in?" asked DS Jackie Read, as she strode into the room and got her laptop out.

"Just a bit of fun," said Jill.

"It's a laugh a minute, this case, isn't it?" Clearly it wasn't, if Jackie's demeanour was anything to go by.

"Coffee anyone?" asked James, trying to break up the exchange between the two Detective Sergeants.

Both said, "Yes please," and James went off to the coffee machine. When he returned with the three coffees and some Kit Kats, there was still no sign of DI North. It was nearly 4 p.m. when DCI Sandy Charteris walked into the room, carrying a takeaway drink. He looked at the three Detectives and helped himself to a finger of Kit Kat.

He picked up the photo fit and the drawing.

"Looks like the same mug!"

"Looks that way," said James.

Looking at Jackie Read, Charteris said,

"Where's DI North?"

"He went up to the office, sir. Said he wouldn't be long."

"Can you please give him a buzz and tell him the meeting is about to start."

"Yes sir," responded Jackie Read, obviously not relishing the task of poking a bear with a stick.

The bear strolled into the room, holding a cup of coffee and said pointedly,

"Where's the fire?"

Charteris looked at him.

"DI North. I'm in no mood for your attempts at sarcasm. I called this meeting for the usual time, which is as you well know, 4 p.m. It's now nearly 4.15, so let's just get on with it."

"Yes sir!" said North, with a heavy emphasis on the 'sir'.

Charteris obviously noticed the inflection but didn't rise to the bait.

"Now the first thing I want to say, is that DI Halstead and DS Trent will remain as part of this case."

North and Read shot each other a look. Jill noticed this less than subtle response. James was looking through his papers.

Charteris continued.

"They will stay at the safe house, again next week."

"Why is that sir?" asked North.

"Because I have just said so. Why do you ask, DI North?"

"Just curious sir. I wouldn't have thought it too onerous for our colleagues to commute from Lewes, now that they're in the swing of things."

Charteris looked as if he might explode. His neck was red and he steepled his hands, before giving a rather cold response to North's question.

"DI North. You are an Inspector. I am a Chief Inspector. No further explanation is necessary. So, let's get on with the review."

James felt that the belligerent North was lucky not to receive a full-on public bollocking for his impertinence. But North was making a fair point about the safe house; one which James himself had raised initially.

The review was going quite smoothly until Jill raised some queries. She was a bit wary about seeming to challenge North, who hadn't said much after his earlier rebuke. Jackie Read had been business-like but seemed to be miles away.

Jill started.

"We have found some discrepancies, which need to be cleared up. They may well be administrative errors or accidental omissions.

First of these is the evidence from Tricia Braithwaite."

Jill handed out copies of her interview notes.

"It seems that she was waiting for an officer to visit her to do a photo fit of the man she saw on the night of the burglary next door. The man was trying to get a van started. It then suddenly came to life and he got in as it sped off. DC Westmore did the initial interview and says he passed the file to you DI North. Apparently, you were going to sort out the photo fit, but nothing more was heard by Miss Braithwaite."

North looked daggers at Jill.

"Wait a fucking minute! What are you saying?"

Before Charteris could intervene, Jill replied,

"I'm saying the photo fit was never followed up. And I don't appreciate being sworn at DI North!"

Charteris spoke. "We are professional colleagues DI North. This is not an episode of The Sweeny. If anyone does the swearing, it's going to be me. Understand?"

North still looked daggers at Jill.

"We didn't have enough support on the case, when DC Westmore and I were the only officers doing interviews. The promised bodies were spirited away to the children's home enquiry. So, mistakes were made. Not big mistakes, just every day, minor errors."

"So, it was just an error?' DI North?"

"Just an error sir, caused by pressure of work," said North, glowering at Jill.

Jill continued.

"As it happens, Tricia Braithwaite is an artist and she made her own picture of the man," she said, handing the portrait to North, who barely glanced at it.

Jill carried on. "Then we have another error concerning the registration plate on a suspicious vehicle. A Susan Bolton saw a vehicle with the registration AE61 BUS, which has subsequently turned out to be a made-up plate. She apparently reported this to DC Westmore and he passed the information to you, DI North. Apparently, it wasn't followed up and…"

"Now what am I being accused of?" asked North, whose face had gone puce. "I've already explained about lack of resources and your remarks feel like some sort of witch hunt DS Trent!"

James spoke.

"Not a witch hunt. We just want to clean the files up and ensure that all the interviews are in order and any follow ups have been dealt with. No need to get so sensitive. You've given an explanation. DC Westmore told me that the files may have needed a bit of tidying up."

"Then why does it feel like you're ganging up on me? I'm an experienced DI. I don't like insinuations like this."

Charteris stepped in.

"DI Halstead is right. You've answered the queries and you say they are just errors or oversights. So calm down. DS Trent, have you any other issues to raise?"

"Yes sir, it concerns a Sandra Temple. She says a man called at her house and asked if she wanted a house alarm fitted. She was supposed to have a follow up visit for a photo fit. There was no follow up and…"

"Yeah, don't tell me. It's down to me again," said a belligerent North.

Jill looked up and fixed North with her gaze.

"I don't know who it's down to, but DC Westmore said he advised you and thought you were going to organise the photo fit."

North just shrugged.

"What can I say? I've messed up again. Don't you ever make mistakes, DS Trent?"

"Yes, sometimes. Nobody's perfect."

DCI Charteris looked at James. "Anything to add?"

"Yes sir. We now have the artist's picture and the photo fit and as we said earlier, they could certainly be the same man. I'm going to circulate both and see if anyone recognises the person. He's pretty distinctive with a 1970s look: long hair and a droopy moustache. Perhaps he's known locally."

North looked resigned now but made an effort to pour cold water on the photo fit.

"There are loads of long-haired blokes with droopy moustaches in Brighton. Must be left over from the hippy community. I can't see this being of much help. We'll probably get lots of look-a-likes if we go public."

"Nevertheless," said Charteris,

"We haven't exactly made much progress with this case, so let's go public and see what we get. I can get a couple of civilian support people on the phones in case DI North's prediction is correct."

He turned to Jackie Read.

"You've been very quiet. Have you anything to add to the discussion?"

Jackie Read seemed to snap out of some private thoughts.

"No sir, our side of this case hasn't turned up anything new. Everyone we have interviewed has had nothing of significance to add."

Charteris summed up the week's work, and then added,

"Hopefully we will get a lead on Mr 1970s. We carry on next week. All four of you are off duty over the weekend, so just try to relax and recharge your batteries for next week. Nearly all the follow up interviews are completed. I'll get everything collated and you can collect the revised case files first thing on Monday morning. Oh, Jackie and Jill. Are you both over the knifeman incident? No lingering anxieties, I hope. Any problems and I'll arrange counselling."

For the first time, Jackie seemed to cheer up.

"You're talking to the winners, sir. He lost big time. He's the one who'll need counselling."

Jill smiled as they all got up to leave.

Chapter Thirty-Eight

North and Read walked out to the carpark together. North was still in a bad mood.

"That fucking cow tried to skewer me. All that crap about missing information and actions. What the fucking hell are they both playing at?"

"Well, you must admit that your pressure of work explanation was a load of horseshit."

"Horseshit? Well thanks for your fucking support. We're supposed to be a team. You didn't say a word. Don't wind me up, you might regret it!"

"What's that supposed to mean?"

"Just watch yourself, that's all. Remember your illegal search of that prat, Carter's laptop. If that comes out, you might be for the disciplinary board!"

"What! And you get off scot free. Remember, you put me up to it. You supplied the sleeping pills."

"No need to worry about Carter."

"What makes you think that?"

"I know the bastard and he's shit scared of me,"

"You know him? How?"

"Never mind darling. Just keep your gob shut and stay out of things you don't understand."

"Or what?"

"Jackie, you're in over your head. Things can get very nasty if you stick your nose in my business. Just be a good girl and fuck off home. Next time you have a fight, you might not have that goody, goody cow to help you, and I can promise that you will be overmatched!"

Jackie was almost speechless and before she could think of a response, North got into his car and screeched out of the carpark, leaving her very shaken.

Just then, James and Jill walked past her to their car. Jill put her hand on Jackie's arm.

"Are you all right Jackie? You look terrible."

"Thanks for that Jill. No, I'm all right, it's just that DI North is such an arse. Enjoy your weekend Jill."

With that she turned and walked to her car.

James looked at Jill and glanced at the receding figure of Jackie Read.

"Wonder what that's all about?"

"Don't know, but whenever North is involved, there's always grief for somebody. I'm glad I've got a nice DI."

"Why thank you DS Trent. Come on, the weekend awaits."

"Yes, it's going to be really strange being in our own flats. No more late-night chats or shared hot chocolate."

"Tell you what, why don't we meet up for a Saturday night meal?"

"Sounds great James, any ideas where?"

"Well yes. If the weather's nice on Saturday evening, why don't we go to that Italian at Sovereign Harbour, in Eastbourne? If we go early evening, we might get a table outside next to the harbour."

"Sounds great James. It'll be a good antidote to all the washing and ironing."

Chapter Thirty-Nine

Early on Saturday evening, James and Jill were sitting at a patio table outside an Italian restaurant, overlooking the marina at Sovereign Harbour. It was a warm evening and nearly every table was taken. There were couples and tables with four people. There were also some family groups sitting around two tables pushed together. Although there were children, none were running around but the evening was young.

James had on a cream and blue, striped polo shirt with cream shorts and blue deck shoes. Jill was wearing a white t-shirt with navy shorts and soft white shoes. They were both glad they had opted for the sporty look instead of formal clothes, because their fellow diners were similarly dressed. It was the sort of evening that was ideal for alfresco eating. Jill had picked James up from his flat and they had driven to the restaurant in her little Fiat 500. James had not made any of his usual remarks about being a bit squashed, although Jill had been expecting him to say something.

They had ordered a bottle of Sancerre and were enjoying the evening. Jill was smiling at James.

"If it wasn't for our recent living arrangements, I wonder if we'd be doing this on our day off."

"Well, we've been out for meals before, but it's always been after work."

"James, I do worry about our professional relationship. This feels so comfortable and I really do enjoy your company."

"As long as you call me sir and follow my orders at work, we'll be just fine DS Trent," said James, laughing. Jill laughed too.

"You know what I meant."

Their starters arrived and they both tucked in. Jill proposed a toast.

"To our success."

"Our success. And," added James, "our survival!"

Jill frowned.

"Are you really worried that we might be in danger?"

James gave Jill a serious look.

"Perhaps, but we're a good team. We just need to watch each other's backs!"

They ate in silence for a while. Both had a sense of unease about some of the elements of the case; especially concerning Bob North.

"Tell you what Jill. No more talking shop. Let's enjoy our evening and forget we're cops."

"Funny, I was thinking the same."

Their main courses arrived and they sat, happily eating and enjoying the occasion. One of the family groups had become noisy, with three of the children leaving the table and running around. A well-built woman in her thirties was on her feet and calling for the children to sit down. People at the tables nearby were glaring at her and the children.

The woman stared them down and then said in a loud voice,

"Don't suppose you've got children!"

A woman at the closest table shouted back.

"I have but we taught them table manners!"

The well- built woman looked daggers. A man at another table joined in. "Look, we're out for a meal and a nice evening. If you can't control your children, why don't you leave?"

"Yes, we didn't come here to have noisy children running about!" said another woman.

A man who was part of the well-built woman's group, stood up.

"Watch your mouth," he shouted, to nobody in particular. Just as it was all about to kick off, the restaurant manager came over and asked everyone to calm down.

"It's too warm for arguing and fighting. Please, everyone, just enjoy your food and drink."

This impromptu speech seemed to do the trick. The man and the well-built woman sat down, as the three children returned to the table. Their ice cream had arrived and the children ate it quietly. They soon had the ice cream moustaches and were now little angels.

Fortunately, James and Jill were quite a distance away from the incident and were hoping that they would not have to get involved to break up a fight.

"I'm glad that all fizzled out," said Jill.

"Yes, it would have spoilt our evening," said James, sipping his wine.

They finished with chocolate sponge pudding and expresso coffee. James had asked the waiter to cap the rest of the wine for taking away. They paid the bill and decided to take a stroll around the marina. It was still quite warm, but Jill had bought a cardigan with her. James helped her to put it around her shoulders. As they strolled, they saw a cormorant, sitting on one of the floating platforms.

"That's very appropriate," said James, pointing at the cormorant, which was busy drying its wings by holding them out and flapping them.

"Why so James?"

"It's the code name for the security around here: Project Cormorant."

"Oh, yes, I've heard of it."

"They have beefed up security here to stop any illegal activity. Cameras everywhere, so we'd better be careful," he laughed.

Jill had linked her arm in his and they talked while they were strolling.

"How would you fancy a boat James? You could be Captain Halstead and take a trip up to the Eastbourne lighthouse."

"I don't mind boats but I wouldn't trust myself taking one out without an experienced crew member."

"I could be your First Mate."

"Do you have any experience?"

"Only the boating lake, when I was a kid."

"Great use that would be then."

They arrived at the locks and were in time to see one filling up with water. There were three boats waiting for the water level to rise. They stood and watched for a while and then headed back the way they had come. Unknown to them, the figure of Bob North was looking at them from the deck of a large cabin cruiser. He was standing next to another man who had a windswept complexion. North's eyes followed the pair as they walked by. He noticed that they were arm in arm and knew that he'd been right, when he'd made a crude remark about their relationship.

Jill dropped James off at his flat. Both really wanted to end the evening romantically but neither made a move. Jill pecked James on the cheek as he squeezed himself out of her little car.

"Ring you tomorrow about next week," said James.

"Yes, take care James."

As she drove off, James couldn't help reflecting upon how nice Jill looked. Coincidentally, Jill was thinking the same about James. They had another week of living under the same roof. Their close professional relationship was intact. Their personal relationship was something else altogether.

Chapter Forty

Monday morning found James and Jill driving to their temporary home in Brighton. They were in James' BMW. They got to the house after some traffic delays in Brighton. They dropped off their bags and put some provisions in the fridge. They had spoken on the phone on Sunday but had not arranged to see each other that day. Both had pottered around their respective flats in Lewes, although Jill had popped out to the local mini store, to get milk and eggs for the week ahead.

When they arrived at the Brighton police station, neither DCI Charteris nor their two team members were anywhere to be seen. They sat at the table in the meeting room and sorted through the case files. These had been updated and any previously missing information had been included. There was a hard copy of the photo fit of the moustachioed man. There was a photo of Tricia Braithwaite's picture sketch as well. It just had to be the same man.

While they were sorting out the files, DCI Sandy Charteris walked in. Takeaway coffee in one hand and a sheet of paper in the other.

"Morning, nice weekend?"

"Morning sir," said both Detectives in unison.

"Yes. Good weekend," said James.

"Good, good. As you can see the case files have been updated. Nothing missing now," said Charteris, with just a hint of something not said in his tone.

"Are DI North and DS Read, coming in?" asked James.

"They've been and gone. Collected their files and left."

"Oh," said James, surprised that they hadn't hung around.

Charteris looked as if he might say something about the flying visit but didn't. Instead he asked,

"Did you hear about the body of a man that was washed up on the beach near Eastbourne pier?"

"Yes," said Jill. "There was something on the local TV news, but they said the police hadn't released any details."

"That's right. There are photos of the dead man, and we have to decide about releasing a photo to the public. It's always a bit macabre when it's a death mask but fortunately, he wasn't bashed about much at all, so it's not too scary for the public. Got a photo here."

Charteris showed them. Both looked shocked.

"What is it? Do you know him?" asked a concerned Charteris.

"I would swear that this is the man who attacked Jackie Read, in her flat!"

"What! Are you sure DS Trent?"

"Well, about seventy percent sure, sir."

James Halsted looked at the image.

"I only saw the chap as the uniforms were taking him out of the flat but yes, it does look like him. Has it been circulated internally yet sir?"

"Not yet but I know a good place to start."

Charteris picked up a telephone.

"DCI Charteris here, is PC Standish on duty? OK, what about PC Moore? OK, can you send PC Standish up to the meeting rooms? What? Yes, now please, he'll have to have his bacon sandwich later!"

He turned to James and Jill.

"PC Moore, the second copper who accompanied the prisoner isn't on duty, but PC Standish is having his breakfast."

A few minutes later, an out of breath Geoff Standish came into the room. "You wanted to see me sir?"

"Yes, PC Standish, do you recognise this man?"

Standish gave the photo a long look.

"Dead sir? But yes, he does look familiar."

Then a lightbulb came on in his head.

"Yes sir, he looks just like the man who we took to hospital."

"And who subsequently escaped?"

"Err, yes sir."

"All right PC Standish, you can go back to your bacon sandwich."

"Yes sir, thank you."

Charteris was silent for a moment. Then he said,

"Right, I want you two to arrange to go and view the body. He had no ID and we have absolutely no idea where he came from or how he got in the water; but it's likely he came off a boat. Let me know if it's definitely the guy who attacked Jackie Read. I'll clear it with DCS Marsh. Just let me know once you've come to a conclusion."

James asked, "And our current job sir?"

"Multitask, DI Halstead. I'm sure you can fit it in."

"Might be an idea to ask DS Read if she recognises the dead man, sir," said James.

"Yes, I had intended to ask her, but she and DI North shot off this morning, before I could ask them."

Charteris, again, left something unsaid, floating in the air. He then turned on his heal and as he was leaving said,

"Ring me, if you turn anything up."

Chapter Forty-One

James wasted no time in finding out that Doctor Claire Grant had carried out two post-mortems on the body, which was still being held in Eastbourne. Claire Grant said she would meet them there later that morning to see if Jill recognised the deceased.

On the way to Eastbourne, Jill was wondering what was going on. Why had North and Read been in such a hurry? And why had Charteris seemed a little preoccupied when talking about them? James had shared her feeling of unease.

They arrived in Eastbourne at the mortuary and met Doctor Rosemary Grant.

"Hello Doc, err, Rosemary, we've arranged to see the dead man, from Eastbourne beach."

"Morning James, Jill, come with me. I hope you appreciate that I've come over from Lewes, just to see you."

"Very much so Rosemary. Great personal service."

Doctor Grant took them to see the body. They had a good look and Jill was now convinced.

"Yes, I'm ninety percent sure sure that this is the man who attacked Jackie."

"Have you established cause of death, Rosemary?" asked James.

"Yes, death by drowning. The only other features were two recently broken ribs and a possible sprained wrist."

"I'm one hundred percent certain now," said Jill

"What makes you so sure?"

"The injuries. I was there when he attacked Jackie. We both struggled to get a knife off him and that's why his wrist was damaged."

"And the damage to his ribs?" asked an incredulous Doctor Grant.

"Jackie Read sat down heavily on him and I knelt and sat on him! We had him trapped face down on a settee and held him down until reinforcements arrived."

"So, it was police brutality?" asked a half-smiling Claire Grant.

"No, it was self- defence," said Jill.

"Apart from those two injuries, the body was in reasonable condition. The man was wearing a poorly inflated life jacket and a waterproof coat. Both of which kept his body afloat but didn't save his life."

"Have you established cause of death, Rosemary?"

"An initial post-mortem suggested straightforward drowning with some evidence of hypothermia. A follow-up told the same story. No evidence of foul play. So not one for you and your colleagues James. Apart from identification."

"So he falls in the sea, fully clothed with life jacket that didn't save him?"

"Exactly so James. Probably fell overboard from a fishing boat perhaps."

They went back to the office and declined a cup of tea. Doctor Grant ran off a copy of the Post-Mortem and some associated notes.

"Good luck with the ID. I've had some fingerprints run through police records but no matches. By the way, did you ever get to the bottom of that death in the cellar case, Arron Kelp, wasn't it?"

James grimaced.

"No Claire. We've had to put it on ice, excuse the pun. We've been seconded to Brighton on another case. Now we've got this one as well."

"Good job you're top Detectives then," Smiled Claire Grant.

On the way back to Brighton, Jill rang DCI Charteris and confirmed that it was indeed the man who had carried out the attack. She told him about the injuries which matched. It wasn't murder but it was a strange situation, because of the attack. Could be a coincidence or something else.

Charteris confirmed that they were officially on the case, which meant finding out who the dead man was, which might in turn provide the answer to the attack on Jackie. James had listened to the conversation between Jill and Charteris. They were driving over the South Downs to Brighton, rather than via the bypass outside Eastbourne. James pulled into the carpark at Birling Gap for a drink and a sandwich. Before they got out of the car, James turned to Jill.

"Jill, I've got an idea. You know we thought the dead man looked a bit like the guy who was with Fancy Carter in the restaurant, on that first night?"

"The guy with the John Lennon glasses?"

"The very one, yes. Well I know it's a long shot but as we don't really have much to go on. Why don't we ask Mr Carter if we can see him?"

"And say what, James?"

"Well, I'm thinking that we could suggest that the dead man looks like his dining companion. We could gauge his reaction."

"Yes, I think it might be a good idea. We need to find out his address but I'm sure it won't be too difficult. Well I hope not anyway," said Jill, on an optimistic note.

DI North and DS Read were just returning to their car after another interview with a possible witness. For some reason, Bob North seemed to be in a better mood. More accurately, he was in less of a bad mood, which was his default position these days. Then Jackie Read's mobile rang.

"Yes sir. No, not much progress. Well, can it wait 'til our 4 p.m. get together?"

"Can I ask what it's about? Oh, really? Well yes. OK sir."

North was bursting to ask.

"What's that all about?"

"You know that body which was found on Eastbourne beach? Well it turns out that Jill Trent has identified him as the man who attacked me. Charteris wants me to have a look at a photo of him to confirm the ID."

"What! You know you can't say it's him."

"Can't say? What am I supposed to say, if I think it's him?"

196

"It's him Jack, take my word for it."

"How do you know? You haven't seen the photo of him yet."

"I know. Just accept what I say and remember what I told you about getting in over your head!"

"Bob. What's going on? I'm scared."

"So you should be. You asked me to get the bastard out of the way before he could be interviewed about attacking you. Well, I did what you asked. He escaped from the hospital and…"

"And now he's dead! Bob, I didn't ask you to kill him!"

"Don't worry, I didn't kill him."

"Someone did!"

"If you must know, he went for a boat ride and fell over the side."

"Fell?"

"Yes, fell. It's true Jack, nothing for you to worry about. Just an accident; that's all there is to it. A fucking accident."

Jackie Read looked as white as a sheet. She was trembling and wished she could just walk away from North, but he'd got her involved in something that was far more serious than just a computer data theft. Still trembling she looked North in the eye.

"What's going on? Just tell me the truth," she said, putting her head in her hands.

North put an arm around her shoulder, but she shrugged it off.

"OK, be like that. You want the truth? OK, you already know that the bastard who attacked you is an associate of Carter. He decided to teach you a lesson for conning Carter."

"He told me that before he attacked me."

"What I can't tell you, is how he's tied in with Carter. Just trust me that it wouldn't be in my interest, or yours, if the connection comes out. There's a lot more at stake than just your little computer theft. Just say that you don't recognise the bastard, when you see Charteris."

"But Jill, has said it was the man!"

"Difference of opinion. What can Charteris say? You don't think it was the man who attacked you. End of."

"No, not end of. Charteris has asked James and Jill to investigate and find out the identity of the dead man."

"Shit! Why is it always them? You know how straight they are. They'll go at this like a dog with a bone. Look, I've got to make a couple of private phone calls. I need to take out a bit of insurance, in case they come up with a name and address."

"What does that mean?"

"It means that you just do what I say. Spread some doubt. I can clean this up, but you need to keep your gob shut. You don't know anything, Jack. There are some heavy people involved and you don't want to find yourself taking a swim as well."

Jackie Read didn't answer. She was a tough woman and could look after herself, but she was scared. North was in deep. But she didn't know how deep or what it was. She didn't want to know. But she needed to know! She was a reasonably good Detective and honest; that is, until she stole from Carter's laptop. Why had she been stupid enough to do it? She had a sexual relationship with North and perhaps it was this that persuaded her to break the law. Why had she got so close to this bastard? She was a good police officer and now she was compromised.

Her thoughts were interrupted by North.

"I'm dropping you off in town. Get yourself a drink and wait 'til I contact you. We'll go into the office at the usual time and you'll just have to brass it out with Charteris."

They drove off and Jackie Read got out in Brighton. She went and sat in a coffee shop and silently drank her cappuccino. What was she going to do? North was capable of anything. She knew that North had a reputation for bending the rules but murder and dangerous people, seemingly capable of harming her, was a whole new ball game. She licked powdered chocolate off her top lip and was lost in thought. This was more than she had bargained for. More than she had ever imagined. But what to do?

Chapter Forty-Two

James and Jill got back to their room at Brighton police station about 3 p.m. James had intended to see if he could find a contact phone number for Carter. In what can only be described as serendipity, he happened to glance at some flyers on the police community notice board. There in glorious colour, was the face of no other than Fancy Carter, beaming at him. On the bottom of the show poster, in small print, was a notice which read, 'Fancy Carter, in association with Glee Productions'. James Halsted asked the Desk PC to see if he could find a telephone number for Glee Productions. James then joined Jill in the meeting room. She was busy typing up notes to add to the photocopies Doctor Grant had given them.

"Guess what? There's a poster for Carter in reception. And it's got the name of the company that promotes his shows."

"Brilliant! That's saved us a bit of chasing around," said Jill, smiling.

Ten minutes later, a PC handed James a note with a contact number for Glee Productions. James rang the number and spoke to a woman named Alice Preston. She was a little guarded at first, when James asked her for a contact number for Carter. James convinced her that he was, indeed, a police officer and if necessary, he would visit her office in person to get the information. She eventually gave him Carter's mobile number but said she would tell Carter what she had done. She added that Carter was back at the Devonshire Theatre in Eastbourne for two more nights: Tuesday and Wednesday this week.

James came off the phone and Jill said,

"What a masterful performance. You charmed her into giving you the phone number."

James smiled.

At 4 p.m., Jackie Read appeared in the room. She still looked worried and James was concerned.

"Jackie, are you all right?"

Jackie tried a smile, which could only be described as half-hearted.

"I'm OK, James. Just a bit tired, that's all."

Jill put her hand on Jackie's arm.

"If we can help with anything, you only have to ask."

"That's kind of you. I'll bear it in mind."

Before Jill could explain about the identification of the dead body, DCI Charteris came into the room.

"Afternoon everyone. Where's DI North?"

"Making some enquiries sir, he shouldn't be long."

Charteris handed Jackie the photo of the drowned man.

"Take a good look at this photo. Ever seen him before?"

Jackie Read took it and gave it a long hard stare. She held it in the light and then moved it closer to her face.

"No sir, doesn't look familiar, should it?"

"DS Trent thinks this is the man who attacked you in your flat."

"Really sir? Can't say I recognise him."

Charteris frowned.

"DS Trent, tell her about the injuries."

"According to Doctor Grant who did the post-mortem, he's got a sprained wrist and two recently broken ribs!"

Jackie Read tried to look relaxed but didn't feel it at all.

"Two broken ribs?"

"Yes, exactly the same as the guy we held down!"

"Well, I still can't see the resemblance but if you think it's him..."

"I'm sure it's him," said Jill.

James Halstead nodded his agreement.

"I only saw him for a brief moment, but I'm convinced it's the same man."

Jackie Read shrugged her shoulders.

"Sorry, we'll just have to differ." Looking at Charteris, she said, "Is that all sir?"

"Err, yes, I suppose it is. Can you ask DI North to pop up to my office when he comes in?"

As he turned to leave, he gave an almost imperceptible glance towards James and Jill, then was gone.

"I'm sorry, I don't recognise him. That's all there is to it," said Jackie, looking just a little guilty.

"Don't worry about it," said James. "You were in a stressful situation, at the flat."

Jill, shrugged.

"Jackie if you don't recognise him, fine. Just forget it."

There was still no sign of DI North and it was now a quarter to five. Jackie decided to call it a day and told them she would ring North from the carpark. She got outside and sat in her car. The interior was red hot, because it had been in full sun since she parked it that morning. She had walked to the station from the coffee shop, because North hadn't telephoned her. Getting very hot, she got out of the car and rang North. It went straight to voicemail and she left a brief message, telling him he was wanted by DCI Charteris. She got in the car, turned the air conditioning to maximum and with a worried frown, drove off.

James and Jill were still in the meeting room. Jill sat opposite James at the table.

"What did you really think about Jackie, not recognising the dead man?"

"Probably the same as you."

"She's lying."

"Afraid so, but the question is. Why?"

"If we knew that, we might make some progress," said Jill.

Before they left for home, James rang Fancy Carter's mobile. Carter answered after three rings and wasn't at all surprised that it was the police. Obviously, the woman that James had got the phone number from had alerted Carter.

"What do you want?" asked a brusque Carter.

"Just a few questions, Mr Carter. When would be the best time to come and see you?"

"No time really. I'm doing some shows at the Devonshire in Eastbourne. Can't it wait?"

"Afraid not, Mr Carter. Can you make a quick interview tomorrow morning, say 11 a.m.?"

"Well if I must. I've got a rehearsal in the afternoon, so it will have to be a quick interview. I'm staying at the Grand Hotel. Ask for me at reception."

Carter's reluctance to speak to the police, seemed to James to be a bit odd. The man was a well-known entertainer on the south coast and even had a poster on the notice board in Brighton police station. Why wouldn't he want to help the police? In the end, although he had somewhat reluctantly agreed to meet in his hotel suite, he hadn't sounded very pleased. The two Detectives decided to head for home. James had threatened to prepare a meal; one of his speciality dishes: salmon en croute. Well in truth, it was his speciality, frozen, pre-prepared meal.

They ate James's special dish, accompanied by fresh asparagus and new potatoes. They had decided to drink water instead of wine. After the dishes were loaded in the dishwasher, James had an idea.

"Fancy a walk to the seafront, to let the meal go down?"

"Yes, that would be lovely James. It's such a nice evening and too early to call it a night."

They had both changed into jeans and trainers. Both had t-shirts with hooded jackets. As they walked along the pavements, Jill linked arms with James. Once again, they looked like a young couple out for a stroll. In fact, that's exactly what they were, except that they were work colleagues. James liked the way Jill held his arm. They both knew that something was happening between them. If their bosses knew, they might be unimpressed but perhaps their feelings towards each other were inevitable. So far, it had not gone beyond meals and companionable togetherness.

When they got back, they both changed into their night clothes; Jill in her pyjamas and James into his jogging gear. They had a cup of drinking chocolate and as they were going to bed, Jill kissed James on the cheek and off they went to their separate rooms.

Chapter Forty-Three

The next morning, they allowed themselves a brief lie-in. They showered and had breakfast. They decided to dress up a little because Carter's hotel was a five-star establishment. James had his blue, lightweight, linen suit, with white shirt and open neck. Jill wore a moderately short, cream, summer dress with a light blue cardigan. They arrived at Carter's Eastbourne hotel and found a parking space at the front. They went to reception and asked for the number of Carter's room. James showed his ID and gave them his car registration. He assured the receptionist that he had a pre-arranged appointment with Carter, just to avoid any speculation.

The receptionist telephoned Carter and she nodded to one of the front door staff, to accompany the two Detectives up to Carter's suite. When Carter opened the door, it revealed a very spacious area, with a sea-view and balcony. There was a pleasant, fresh smell, which suggested that the place had been cleaned recently. A fresh sea breeze gently rustled the curtains. Carter led them to a seating area, which had a large comfortable-looking settee and an armchair facing it.

Carter motioned them to sit down on the settee. Carter took the armchair and looked apprehensive. James introduced himself and Jill, who slipped a notebook out of her bag along with a sheet of paper.

"Thank you for seeing us, Mr Carter. We realise that you are a busy man, so we won't keep you long."

"What's this all about?" asked Carter, his demeanour looking anything but the King of Comedy!

"I don't know if you remember, but last week on Monday evening, you were dining at a restaurant in Brighton."

"I dine at lots of restaurants in Brighton."

"Well last Monday evening, we happened to be there when you came in with a companion. You might recall that you had a conversation with a woman, who you thought you recognised."

Visibly shaken, Carter replied,

"Err, oh yes, I remember. Thought I knew her. Turned out I was mistaken. The old eyes aren't what they once were."

"Yes, as it happens, the woman was one of our party."

"Oh, I see. Is that why you're here?"

They both saw a trickle of perspiration forming on Carter's top lip. He quickly produced a large, theatrical looking handkerchief and dabbed his lip. He stole a look at Jill's crossed legs and quickly looked away, when she caught him staring.

"Is that it?" Carter asked, desperately trying not to look at Jill's legs again.

"No Mr Carter. I just mentioned the incident concerning the mistaken identity, to jog your memory. I'm sure that it's difficult to remember specifics, when you dine out so often."

Carter couldn't be sure if this was an attempt at sarcasm by James. He decided to ignore the remark because it had been said with innocent sincerity. Or at least he chose to interpret it that way.

Jill took up the questioning.

"Mr Carter, we are really interested in your dining companion. Can you tell us his name, please?"

"His name?" asked Carter, dabbing more moisture from his top lip and forehead.

"Yes, it would be of great help to us in an ongoing investigation," smiled Jill, ignoring Carters eyes, which were now firmly fixed on her legs.

James cut in.

"Surely Mr Carter, you know the name of your companion."

"What's he done?" asked an obviously worried Carter, not answering the question.

Handing Carter the sheet of paper with the photo of the dead man,

Jill asked,

"Do you recognise this man, Mr Carter?"

Carter was now leaking perspiration as if a dam had burst. With another theatrical flourish of his handkerchief, he attempted to staunch the river of liquid, running down his red face.

"Is this a photo of a dead man?" blurted a clearly distressed Carter.

"Yes, Mr Carter. I'm sorry to show you this without warning you first, but his body washed up on the beach, near here last Friday. Apparently, he drowned," said James, trying hard to sound neutral.

Jill kept up the pressure.

"We know this is hard Mr Carter, but we think this man looks a bit like your companion from last Monday. Perhaps you don't recognise him without his glasses! We think it's the same man."

Carter had staunched the flow of liquid but felt that he had been skewered. If he had been able to think it through, he should have denied that this was his companion and suggest that it was clearly a mistake. The only problem was that he would have to invent a name and then the police would be asking for an address. What a bloody mess!

The two Detectives were gazing at Carter, waiting for an answer. To add to his discomfort, Jill held the photo in front of Carter.

"Take your time Mr Carter. We just need to know if you recognise the man and we would still like the name of your companion."

Carter was resigned to defeat. "Yes, it's not a very good likeness but now I think I recognise him. He's Steven Daynes."

"Was he a friend or business associate, Mr Carter?" asked James.

"Just a friend."

"And his address?" asked Jill, pencil poised over her note pad.

"Err, I don't know," said Carter, somewhat implausibly.

"Phone number then," said Jill.

"I'm sorry, I don't know."

James was becoming a little impatient.

"Mr Carter. Are you asking us to believe that the man is a friend? You dine out with him, but you don't know where he lives or what his phone number is?"

"That's exactly what I'm saying. He was just a casual friend. He usually rang me and we would meet up somewhere."

"So, wouldn't his phone number be on your mobile?"

Thinking faster this time, Carter gushed,

"You see, I lost my mobile and had to replace it. He hadn't rung me since I got the new mobile."

"And you lost your phone between the meal, that Monday evening in Brighton and now?"

"Yes, that's right. I take it you didn't find his mobile?" asked a worried Carter.

"There was nothing on the body. It could be at the bottom of the sea. If we had the number, we may have been able to get an address, or bank account details from his service provider."

"Oh, I see," said a clearly relieved Carter.

"All right Mr Carter. You have at least confirmed that his name was Steven Daynes and it's the same man you were with at the restaurant," said James. "I think that's all for now. We're based at Brighton Police station at present. Here's my card in case you think of something that will help us."

Fancy Carter had regained some composure and still holding his flamboyant handkerchief he got up and accompanied the Detectives to the door.

When they got to the car they sat there for a while. James was rubbing his chin. Jill smiled.

"What are you thinking James?"

"That the only time he's lying, is when his lips are moving."

"I don't buy the fact that he doesn't know the address. He was trying to think it all through, on the hoof. At last, we've had a bit of luck. We now know for sure that his companion was the dead man. He could have just braced it out. At least we have a name, if it's real."

"The great Fancy Carter can't really afford a scandal. He probably thought if he gave us the name but nothing else, he couldn't be accused of withholding information. Although he clearly is," said Jill.

"He was certainly worried. He was sweating like a horse."

"Couldn't take his eyes off my legs."

"I didn't notice," said James.

Jill smiled.

Chapter Forty-Four

North had arranged for a day off. He had telephoned DCI Charteris at home the previous evening, saying that he needed some time to sort out a family problem. Charteris hadn't been exactly overjoyed to have his dinner interrupted and consequently, didn't bother to raise North's no show that afternoon. He thought that the old 'give someone enough rope' theory had some merit. He told North to inform DS Read and tell her to take DC Westmore out with her on interviews. When North had rung Jackie Read, she was on voicemail, so he just left a blunt message and hung up. He hadn't fancied having to explain why he had the day off. It wouldn't have been the truth of course, because he really had to move quickly. Jackie was asking too many questions.

North was relieved when Jackie just texted him, with a curt, 'OK'. He had a clean-up job and he had arranged for Terry Dalton to meet with him. Both men had arrived at a particular flat, very early in the morning. Despite the fact it was summer, both men wore woolly hats and had jackets, with collars turned up. North had a bunch of spare keys and generally, one normally fitted. It didn't always work and if they had to force the lock, it was touch and go whether or not a neighbour heard them. Fortunately, the bunch of keys trick worked, but not until the fifth key.

They entered the flat in Finsbury Road, not far from Brighton's Queens Park. North's training meant that they carried out a thorough search. They each had a dustbin liner, into which they put paperwork and anything that could help a police enquiry. Knowing what the owner of the flat did for a living, they thought some of his merchandise might be stashed away. They even checked the toilet cistern, with no luck. North also thought there would be cash, but if there was it was well hidden.

Where the hell was it?

Then, stuffed inside a biscuit tin, they discovered a large roll of cash, with a thick elastic band around it; all in twenties and tens. They didn't count it and Terry Dalton shoved it into his pocket.

There was a photo of a woman in a frame. North looked at the photo and put the frame in the bag. They were getting warm now with all the activity. They both had rubber gloves on, supplied by North. They were very careful not to make the property look like it had been ransacked. Although they had taken precautions against leaving forensic evidence, North didn't want a full-scale forensic investigation to be ordered. If the flat was left, just as if the occupant had gone out, it shouldn't attract too much suspicion.

When they had carried out a thorough search and made sure everywhere was tidy, North looked around the rooms. He hoped that they had done a good job. The cash had been a bonus. No point in leaving it for someone else to snaffle. He could imagine DI Halstead and DS Trent, discovering the cash. Then, bagging it up and recording it, to the last note. Of course, they wouldn't dream of doing anything else, he thought, with a sour expression. As he looked around, he reflected that he had once been an honest copper. But that didn't make you wealthy. Honesty was for mugs.

They left the flat unseen, as far as they knew. They walked some distance before getting into Terry's car, which had been parked in an adjacent road. Both men were sweating and threw their hats and coats into the boot along with their black bags.

"I'll get rid of all this crap," said Terry Dalton, as he started the car.

"Yeah, I don't want any of it found. Keep the cash."

"I intended to."

"I thought we might find some drugs as well as cash."

"You're the expert Bob. Thought you lot knew all the hiding places."

"On a raid we rip places up. Pillows, furniture, the lot. If we'd done that, my nosy colleagues would have a field day. Too much risk of leaving traces of DNA. Just have to hope we've not missed anything."

"Want me to drop you off at the nick?"

"Very funny."

Chapter Forty-Five

James and Jill had another interview lined up. This wasn't with a witness; it was with a burglary victim. The house was in Saffrons Road, Eastbourne. James had picked it up from the revised case files. Apparently, the victim, a Mr Chandra Singe, had seen an item at a local antiques shop. It had been in a window display, but the shop was closed. He had been back to the shop when it was open and told them it looked like his property. The proprietor had said Mr Chandra Singe was mistaken and just dismissed it.

The file note had explained all this, with a telephone statement from Mr Singe, outlining what had happened. They had a mobile number for Mr Singe and had told him that they would be in Eastbourne today and asked if it was convenient to see him that afternoon. Fortunately, he was able to see them.

Jill was looking at the statement sheet.

"As an expert on antiques, James, what do you know about a rare, late 19th Century Sampson and Mordan, silver, novelty, telescopic pencil? In the form of a squirrel, holding a nut."

"What do I know? Zero, is the answer. My expertise is limited to the bible box, which I saw on an antique show."

"I'm disappointed James. It says on the list of stolen items, that it's estimated to be worth £1200 to £1800."

"We're in the wrong jobs," laughed James.

They pulled up outside a very grand house in a leafy area. They were greeted at the door by Mr Chandra Singe. He was a tall, expensively dressed man, with a carefully manicured beard. They introduced themselves and were shown into a large living room. There was a glass-fronted display case which contained some antique looking glass vases.

Glancing at the cabinet, Jill said,

"These are very pretty, Mr Singe."

"Yes, they are. They're all from Czechoslovakia."

"Are they very valuable?" asked James.

Mr Singe, frowned.

"Moderately valuable. The only item of real value was a Pavel Hlava vase. The bastards stole it."

Jill was looking at the list of stolen items in her file.

"I've got it on my list. It's estimated to be worth £5000 to £7000."

"Yes, probably more in fact. Whoever robbed me knew the values, because it was the only vase they took!" said Mr Singe, with a sorrowful expression.

They all sat down. Jill had the case notes on her lap and her notebook open. James asked the first question.

"Mr Singe, you apparently saw a silver, squirrel pencil which resembled one that was stolen from you."

"Yes, it was in the window of Chambers Antiques and Collectables in Grove Road, not far from here. As the shop was closed on Sunday afternoon, I went back yesterday and spoke to Mr Chambers. He said I was mistaken and treated me as if I was some kind of con man!"

"Did he let you look at the squirrel?"

"No, he wouldn't unlock the cabinet. I was a bit foolish, because I told him that I had a very similar squirrel stolen. He just looked at me and told me to go away. Well, words to that effect. I should have just asked him to let me handle it, without saying why."

Jill held up her sheet showing stolen items and pointed to the photo of the silver squirrel.

"Can you confirm that this is the item you are talking about?"

Singe glanced at the photo.

"Yes, it's only 3.5cm high but worth a great deal of money."

"My listing says £1200 to £1800, Mr Singe."

Singe looked sadder than ever.

"Yes, I'm afraid so. Look, I've spent a lot of time and money accumulating antiques. My house insurance has cost me a fortune. I had to put in an alarm system at huge expense, before they would even consider insuring my collection. I had to photograph every single item and send my insurers a complete list with descriptions and estimated values. They are still hassling me over details and frankly, I think they are suspicious of me. It's monstrous!"

James could see that Mr Singe was getting really agitated and he was also close to tears.

"I'm really sorry to hear this, Mr Singe. We're working on the case and hopefully we will be able to catch the people involved and perhaps retrieve the stolen items."

"I know you are sincere DI Halstead, but I know the antique trade. Lots of stolen items end up on the continent. Most antique dealers are honest, like the cuddly ones you see on TV antique shows, but a small number aren't."

"Again, I'm really sorry, Mr Singe. We'll call on Mr Chambers to see what we can find out about his squirrel, if he's still got it. I do have to ask you one more question. Are you absolutely certain that the piece you saw in the window, was yours?"

"Not absolutely sure, but it's a rare item. What are the chances of two different examples being located in Eastbourne, let alone being almost, within walking distance of each other?"

"Yes, I see your point. I have to tell you, that without some kind of proof that the silver squirrel is yours, it will be difficult to bring charges."

"I understand but I just feel that the one in the cabinet is mine. I know that feeling is not enough."

"I'm sorry Mr Singe, but you're right. We'll do what we can. Here's my card. Please contact me if you think of anything that can help. I'll ring you if Mr Chambers is able to shed some light on how he obtained the squirrel."

They said their goodbyes and sat in the car.

"I can't see a reputable antiques dealer selling stolen goods," said

Jill.

"Not on purpose, that's for sure." They drove around the one-way system and were lucky enough to find a parking space. It was a bit of a squeeze for the BMW. Jill's Fiat 500 would have had room to spare. Her mention of this point made James raise an eyebrow, but he smiled. They walked along the road and found the antique shop at the far end. Fortunately, it was open. They entered and saw a flamboyantly dressed man, with longish hair, sitting at an old desk. He was involved with what appeared to be a drawn-out deal on something. His fruity tones filled the air.

"But they're just not worth that. No. I'm bloody serious. Look up the price in a book or online. No, no you're quoting a top retail price. I doubt you'd get anywhere near that at auction. No, look, I'm not a charity! I'll meet you halfway. Five hundred quid is my absolute top price. Don't scoff. If you think you can get more, go somewhere else. OK, let's leave it at that. The five hundred's on offer 'til this Friday. Any later, and I'm not interested. What? Well good luck with that!" He put the phone down, stood up and smiled at the two Detectives.

"Can I interest you in anything, Sir, madam?"
  "I was hoping you could help us. I'm DI Halstead, this is DS Trent."
  "Oh," said Ludo Chambers, his smile fading fast.
  "Are you Mr Chambers?"
  "Yes, Ludo Chambers. What seems to be the problem officers?"
  "I don't know if there is a problem, until I've asked you a few questions. I believe you had a gentleman in your shop yesterday asking about a silver squirrel pencil?"
  "Err, yes, said his name was Singe. Said he'd seen a silver Sampson and Mordan pencil, in the shape of a squirrel. Pointed it out in one of my cabinets. Said he'd had one stolen!"
  Jill held out the sheet of paper, with the photo of the squirrel.
  "Is this like the item he was interested in?"
  "Probably was, but I told him he was mistaken."
  "So, can you tell us where you obtained your silver squirrel from?"

asked James.

"Yes, I can."

Chambers went to his desk and pulled a large book from a side drawer. It was like a Victorian ledger. He put some spectacles on the end of his nose and flicked through the pages.

"Ah, here it is. One silver Sampson and Mordan pencil, in the shape of a squirrel. It was in a box of mixed items."

"Can you tell me where you got it?" asked James.

"Yes, it was from a car boot, over in Willingdon. I saw a box of what the stall holder thought, was a load of junk. Made him an offer and got the lot."

"How much did you pay?" asked Jill.

"It's a bit embarrassing. A tenner! In this game you make an offer and if the seller accepts it, you do the deal."

"But the squirrel is apparently worth a great deal of money!"

"To be honest, it's so small I only found it at the bottom of the box when I got home. Great find though."

"Great for you, it seems, Mr Chambers. I don't suppose you know the name of the seller?" asked James.

"Nah, it's all casual at car boots. I was just lucky. Sampson Mordan made lots of different designs. Silver pigs and the like. Good money to be made, if you can pick them up at a reasonable price."

With that, Chambers went to a display cabinet and got the silver squirrel out. He also got out a duck's head, an owl and a fish. He put them all on the top of his desk.

"These are all Sampson and Mordan. Worth a bit of money because they are silver and very collectable, but it's a niche market. Want to see my purchase records on these?"

James shrugged.

"No need, Mr Chambers. I guess Mr Singe was mistaken. Thanks for your time."

As he and Jill left the shop, Ludo Chambers immediately made a phone call, while staring through the window at the Detectives, as they disappeared down the road.

Chapter Forty-Six

James and Jill drove back to Brighton. They discussed the day's interviews.

Jill had been staring at the case notes.

"You know, this antiques game is full of people who seem to know what everything is and what it's worth."

"I suppose, if it's what you do for a living, you would be pretty clued up," said James.

"Yes, that's true. Mr Singe knew a lot about his collection and Chambers seemed to immediately know all about Sampson and Morden figures, including size and value," mused Jill.

"Yes Jill. And your point?"

"Just a thought. The people doing the break ins steal specific items. In Mr Singe's case they left a load of stuff behind and just took the most valuable items. Reading the case files and descriptions of stolen items, it's all relatively high value stuff: things like small bits of silver, or antique jewellery. Take that Czech glass vase. How did they know that one particular one was worth up to £7000? Apart from bible boxes, would you know which antique items were valuable, James?"

"Apart from bible boxes, no," said James, smiling.

"My point is, that the thieves were either experts or had an expert with them or had photos of the valuable stuff, with descriptions, say, on their mobiles."

James considered Jill's theory.

"Do you know, Jill? You might just have something. Let's assume it's a team. They could have an alarms expert, an antiques guy and perhaps, a driver. Or one of them could double up."

"It's a possibility James. We just need to get a break on the case to fit it all together."

They arrived at the Brighton police station about 4.30. The interview with Ludo Chambers and the traffic had delayed them. Despite this they were still the only ones in the meeting room. They followed their usual routine of updating files and interview reports. Jill had made some notes of the conversation with Chambers and she typed them up on her laptop. In the meantime, James was trying to locate an address for the late Steve Daynes.

He had tried the council, to see if he could get any information from the registration of voters' listings. He was amazed when the woman he spoke to actually had an address on file. She told James, confidentially, that Daynes was shown on another file, as owing council tax. The woman he had spoken to, was apparently sitting right next to a council tax recovery officer, who had overhead her mention the name. James reflected that in police work, most investigations were about wearing out shoe leather and a small part of the work was little bits of information just turning up. It didn't happen often but when it did, it was welcomed with open arms.

James looked very pleased with himself.

"I've only got the address of the late Steve Daynes," he said to Jill. "It's in a block of flats in Finsbury Road, Brighton."

"Great, James. I assume we'll be sniffing around there tomorrow?"

"Yes, we will. The council say that Daynes is the only name on the electoral register, so it's likely he lived alone. I'll organise a locksmith just in case."

"Any sign of our two colleagues?"

"Not a sign of them, or Charteris either."

"Come on, let's go home. What about fish and chips somewhere and a drink at a pub?"

"Sounds good."

They got back to the house, showered and went out to a fish and chip shop near the Brighton seafront. The place was busy on this balmy evening. Both were dressed in shorts and t-shirts, with trainers and hoodies. They really enjoyed just being part of the crowd and not having to ask endless questions and trying to gauge the truth. They both loved their jobs but they liked downtime. They were very aware that their lives had been somehow changed by virtually living together, rather than being alone in their respective flats. James had lived alone since his marriage break up and divorce. Jill had always lived alone and was never keen to have a boyfriend move in and upset her routine. One boyfriend had suggested living together but she had always resisted this.

Jill had felt almost relieved when her last relationship had ended. She thought her desire to live alone might have contributed to her break ups. In fact, there hadn't been lots of potential boyfriends clamouring for her attention anyway. Just three and none of them serious. In reality, she hadn't really found a man she wanted to share her life with. Living with James in the Brighton safe house was a nice experience. Of course, she wasn't living with him in the true sense. This was a work arrangement. They had a good relationship but they weren't lovers. They were colleagues. But nevertheless, she felt comfortable.

After fish and chips, they found a pub not far from the seafront. They managed to get a table and both had red wine. As they looked around there were lots of flamboyantly dressed men and a few women. Over in one corner, was a man who they were sure they had seen on TV. He was drinking and laughing with two other men and a woman. Either the jokes were really funny, or the drinks had been flowing for a while. The TV personality walked past their table, on his way to the toilets. He gave James and Jill a big smile as went by.

"I know him, but I just can't place him," said James.
    Jill laughed.
    "Whatever you do, don't ask him where you've seen him before."
    "Don't worry, I wouldn't dream of embarrassing you," laughed James.
    The man came back and re-joined his friends at their table. A fresh round of drinks had appeared and there was more raucous laughing and joking.

"Fancy a refill, or shall we call it a night?" asked James. "Let's call it a night."

They got a taxi back to their house. It wasn't that late, so they decided to sit and watch TV. They found nothing they were really interested in and switched the TV off.

"What a load of rubbish," said Jill.

"Sorry to talk shop but I think you are on to something when you were speculating on the team doing the burglaries. All the properties had the alarms turned off. Remember what Mr Singe said about his insurers insisting on house alarms in order to insure the antique collection. Fat lot of good, alarms are, if the crooks can disable them. None of the previous enquiries have turned up a bent alarm expert but somebody must have been involved."

"And the fact that they are selective and only steal the most valuable items, does indicate some expertise in antiques," added Jill.

"You know what? I think we should spread the files out on the floor tomorrow and have a good look at everything again."

"I'm glad you said tomorrow, James."

"We're visiting the late Mr Daynes' flat, tomorrow morning. We could come back here and have a good look at the case files later."

They both stood up to go to their rooms. They found themselves facing each other. James gently kissed Jill on the lips and she responded. They were locked in a long kiss. When they broke off, they each smiled, said nothing and went to their rooms. Both knew that the first move had been made. They could easily have taken it further, but something had stopped them. At that electric moment they both knew where this could lead. The attraction and desire, was mutual. Best of all, it felt natural. It was now becoming a question of not if, but when, they would take the next step.

Chapter Forty-Seven

The next morning, Terry Dalton was lying in bed. Alongside him was Angie. Terry Dalton lived in a rented flat in the Meads area of Eastbourne. Many of the properties were very expensive. It was, for want of a better description, a rather posh place, which nestled close to the foot of Beachy Head. He also had a six-year-old Mercedes convertible, sports car. He had no visible means of support, but he was never short of money. He always paid his rent on time and he seemed, on the face of it anyway, just a normal guy. His lifestyle wasn't flash and he didn't splash the cash, excessively. He'd got that advice from DI Bob North, who'd told him to just try and look like an average bloke. And not to do anything that attracted attention.

If DI North knew that Terry had got involved with the anti-hunt, animal rights activists, he wouldn't have been impressed. Terry only met these people occasionally, mainly through the lovely Angie who was currently sleeping next to him. He looked at her pretty face. He reflected that Angie was the perfect name for her, because she looked like an angel. Looking like an angel was as far as it went. She and her best friend Tracie were ferocious animal activists. The incident on Eastbourne seafront, involving the young lads throwing stones at gulls, was typical of the two young women. Their fellow activists, George and Sean, were committed to the cause but were not as bold as the two women. The lad who was whipped, by the snooty Isobel Massey, was also a member of their little group. It had been Angie who had asked Terry to teach the Masseys a brutal lesson. Terry had only done it because he fancied Angie. He wasn't particularly an animal activist, but he did get annoyed when people obviously needed a kicking but seemed to get away with things. He was just the man for the job. He belonged to a fitness gym in Eastbourne and bench-pressed heavy weights. Terry was by no means a big thick bruiser. He had brains to go with his brawn. Beating people up was hardly keeping a low profile though.

Terry was by nature, dishonest. He would, in his younger days, commit petty crime. He had been a doorman at a nightclub, at a time when they were called bouncers. His strength and willingness to give someone a good hiding had meant the nightclub had to let him go. The job was changing and beating up punters was no longer part of the job description. Three years ago, he had met DI Bob North. Terry had been suspected of an assault in a Brighton pub. He was a customer and he had objected to a couple of men knocking his drinking arm and spilling his beer. Had the men apologised and offered to replace the pint, the evening might have gone a lot better for them. They had chosen an alternative ending, which meant a visit to the local A&E with some broken bones.

A witness to the violent incident had followed Terry to a nearby flat, which he had shared with a mate. DI Bob North had visited Terry at the flat and after a long chat, had suggested that he could make the charges go away. The witness had a loss of memory and the two damaged men, somehow, couldn't identify Terry as their attacker. His association with Bob North had proved to be a lucrative one. He was now what could be described as, intelligent muscle. He watched North's back on occasions. He also did some work for some people North associated with.

In recent times, Terry had been involved in things that he could come to regret. If he were convicted of these things, he would certainly be facing a long prison sentence. But the money was good. Better than he could get earning an honest living. Bob North wasn't at all like any copper Terry had ever known.

While he was just lying in bed thinking, Angie slowly woke up.

"What about tea in bed?" she asked, still bleary eyed from last night's boozing.

"OK, lazy. Want some breakfast as well?"

"Yeah, great."

Angie had her breakfast. She then got up and went to the bathroom. She called out.

"I'm having a shower."

"I'll join you," shouted Terry, his facial expression a picture of anticipation.

Chapter Forty-Eight

James and Jill sat having breakfast. Jill had made poached egg on toast. James had marvelled that the eggs were perfect. He thought that he could never get poached eggs to come out like hers. As they sat and ate, they caught each other's eyes.

"Jill, about last night."

"Don't say anything, James."

"But I shouldn't have kissed you like I did..."

"James, I wanted to kiss you and I hope you enjoyed it as much as I did."

"Of course I did. It's just that we are work colleagues and I had no right to just kiss you. It's called sexual harassment."

Jill smiled.

"Oh, James you are such a lovely man. We both know, when the time is right, we'll take it further. I certainly hope so."

"So do I Jill."

"But not when you have poached egg around your mouth!"

James laughed.

"What would I ever do without you, Jill?"

"Go out with food on your face, I should think."

They both laughed as James poured the fresh coffee. Their feelings towards each other were mutual. No need for embarrassment or explanations. They finished their breakfast and were soon on their way to the late Steve Daynes' flat, in Finsbury Road. James had looked at the street map of Brighton and they had decided to walk instead of taking the car. The locksmith had been booked for 10 a.m. and was meeting them at the premises. They had both dressed down today, after their experience at the home of Arron Kelp. Jeans and light jackets were the order of the day.

When they got to Finsbury Road, the locksmith had evidently got the last available parking space, which was a fair distance from the block of flats.

He saw them arrive and got out of his van and waved. There was no external door entry system, which was a little unusual. They made their way up the stairs and James rang the front doorbell. They waited for about five minutes in case someone came to the door. James then asked the locksmith to get them into the flat. The locksmith had something in his hand and as if by magic, the door was unlocked. The locksmith did a little bow.

"Do you want a full lock change?"

James shook his head.

"Not at this stage. Will it lock again when we leave?"

"Yes, I've only opened it. If you come out and close the door, it'll just be locked again."

"OK. Thanks for that. We may need to do a lock change at some time but not today. Lots of paperwork involved."

The locksmith nodded and left them to it.

They walked inside and both had put on latex gloves and shoe covers, which Jill produced from her bag. They had an initial glance around; opened a few drawers and looked in cupboards.

"What do you think, Jill?"

"I think it's been professionally searched and things have been removed. It's too neat and there's no personal stuff on display."

"Yes, my thoughts, exactly. But of course, as ever, we don't know why."

"Makes me wonder if this is a cover up."

"By?" asked Jill.

"Oh, I don't know. But the question is, why are things are being covered up?"

James was frustrated.

"Let's just have a closer look at everything. People do make mistakes."

Jill nodded her agreement.

Still wearing their gloves and taking care not to touch too many surfaces in case they smudged potential fingerprints, they went around the flat, inch by inch. Nothing was revealed to them.

James stared around the room.

"The air vents! People often hide things in the air vents. Look there are two of them. No scuff marks, so whoever searched the place didn't look there."

"Another Sherlock Holmes moment, James," smiled Jill.

James carefully removed the front of each air vent, revealing absolutely nothing behind them.

"How disappointing. Perhaps Daynes had nothing to hide."

"Perhaps. Now, where else wouldn't people have searched?" asked Jill, looking around for inspiration.

"What about something stuck to the underside of the settee and armchairs?"

They carefully turned the armchairs over, but nothing was stuck under them. They then carefully manhandled the settee onto its back.

James scratched his head. "Nothing stuck under here either."

"But did you hear something fall down when we turned it over?"

"I heard a rustle," said Jill.

"The hessian hasn't been cut, so no one's looked inside. Look, there are four drawing pins on this side, holding the hessian in place."

James took out a little penknife, causing Jill to smile at the fact that he carried one; although she said nothing. He prised out the drawing pins and felt around inside

"There's something in here. We need to tip the settee this way a little. I'll come around your side. Both together. There! That's it. Something moved."

Reaching inside James retrieved a little exercise book. He held it in a gloved hand. He opened the book which contained names. Next to each name was what looked like passwords? There must have been about fifty names. Unfortunately, they were all first names, with no surnames. Jill produced a plastic evidence bag and James popped the book inside and sealed it.

"I think we've been really lucky to find this, but goodness knows what it all means."

"Clients, customers, contacts." suggested Jill.

"Yes, could be. Pity there aren't surnames and addresses but that would be asking too much."

"I think we should get a forensic team to do a sweep here. I know they won't be best pleased that we've been in first, but you never know what might turn up."

They closed the front door and left. As they walked down the stairs an elderly woman, who had obviously been waiting behind her door on the next landing, spoke to them.

"Are you friends of Steve?"

"No, we're police," said James, showing her his ID. "I'm DI Halstead and this is DS Trent."

"Oh, only I haven't seen Steve for a while, I wondered if he was all right. When I saw those two men early yesterday morning, I was a bit worried. I didn't like to call the police because Steve often has people coming and going."

"Can you describe the two men, Mrs-?"

"Sinclair and it's Miss. Miss Abby Sinclair. I didn't see their faces, but one was tall and big built. The other one was shorter but looked a bit stocky. I saw them through my spy hole. They were upstairs for ages and had two big dustbin bags. I thought it was a bit funny that they were wearing woolly hats and coats with their collars pulled up. It was really warm. Not the weather for hats and coats."

Jill smiled at Miss Sinclair.

"So you didn't see their faces at all?"

"No, I'm sorry. Is everything all right? Is Steve all right?"

"I'm afraid we think he's the man who drowned in Eastbourne, last Friday," said James, trying to say it as gently as possible.

"Oh, dear!" cried Miss Sinclair.

Jill stepped forward to comfort her.

"Why don't you have a nice cup of tea? I'll make it for you."

Abby Sinclair seemed to visibly shrink. Then in a soft voice she said, "Would you both like to have tea with me?"

"We'd love to," said Jill.

They had tea with the visibly distressed Abby Sinclair. James was reluctant to show her the death mask photo of the drowned man. He finally decided that he must get a positive identification.

"Abby, I want to show you a photo. I have to warn you that it was taken after death. It's not gruesome because there are no injuries. You can refuse to look at it, but we really need to know if it's Steve Daynes."

"I understand. I'm not really squeamish and I would like to help you, for Steve's sake."

"Can you please tell me if you recognise the man?"

"Oh dear, oh dear, it's Steve. It's Steve Daynes."

"Thank you, Abby. I'm really sorry to show you this photo and I know it's really tough for you. Would you like me to send a police liaison officer to see you?"

"No thanks. It's just sad that he's dead. I'm OK. It's a bit of a shock to see Steve looking like…"

They finished their tea and left a business card with Abby Sinclair. Jill had comforted her and by the time they left she had recovered her composure. Apparently, she had known Daynes as a neighbour for a couple of years and apart from having lots of visitors, he was no trouble at all. They went back to their house, puzzled by the book of names and the two men in hats and coats. Something was going on. But what?

Chapter Forty-Nine

When they arrived back at their house, James got on to the forensic team and explained what he wanted them to do. He asked them to get a locksmith to accompany them. It was arranged for the following morning. They had asked James, what specifically, he was looking for. He told them honestly, that he didn't really know but that he sensed that they might just turn something up. The man in charge had mentioned budgets and allocation of tasks but had relented when James explained that the occupant of the flat, was the dead man found in the sea at Eastbourne.

Jill had made coffee and spread all the case files out on the floor of the living room. James was very interested in the timeline of the burglaries. They were spread over a six-month period and covered quite a wide area. They looked again at the photos of the stolen items. With few exceptions, the photos revealed items that could be easily transported.

In nearly every case, house alarm systems had been deactivated and several of the victims had been away from home. Only two of the houses had not had a working alarm system at the time of the burglary. So far, there had been no evidence that linked any of the known underworld alarm experts to the burglaries.

Jill was sitting cross legged on the floor, checking and rechecking statements and looking at photos. James was stroking his chin and Jill smiled in anticipation of an observation.

"I think I've found something," he said, pointing to his completed timeline. "There's a period of five weeks, where there weren't any burglaries. Up 'til now, we've only been concentrating on the files marked for us to visit. We've ignored the ones that have been allocated to Bob and Jackie. If you look at all the burglaries across both ours and their set of task sheets, you can see a pattern. Each burglary is dated."

Jill looked across at James.

"What's the significance of that, do you think?"

"Perhaps none, but why break the pattern? For the rest of the period of activity, there was an average of one break in each week. There were a couple with gaps of a fortnight but then a gap of five weeks."

"Perhaps they were missing a member of the usual team. It would have to be the alarm expert or the antiques expert."

"Or maybe one person filled both roles."

"Possible but I can't really see one person doing both. They don't exactly fit together, do they? Don't suppose the TV antiques experts are also whizzes at electronics," said Jill.

"Yes, you're probably right but I do think the five-week gap is significant."

"James, are we really getting anywhere at all on this case?"

"Just bits and pieces and we need a bit of luck to unlock the clues. Talking of luck, let's have a look at the little book of names."

They both put gloves on and James got the book out of the protective evidence bag. They counted fifty-seven first names. There was nothing else in the book that would help them; nothing at all, to identify the people listed. What the passwords related to was anyone's guess at this stage.

Still pondering the significance of the book, James and Jill went to the Brighton police station. They arrived in the meeting room and both DI North and DS Read were sitting at the table. Jackie Read was updating the wall board using a marker pen and North was speaking on his mobile. The duo didn't look too happy. North was haranguing someone and Jackie Read gave the briefest of nods when James and Jill said, "Hi."

To break the ice, James said, "Coffee, tea?"

"Coffee, please," said Jackie Read, in an almost bored voice.

North just shook his head and carried on his phone conversation.

DCI Sandy Charteris was standing in the doorway.

"Black coffee, no sugar for me, please."

James came back five minutes later with everyone's orders. All five Detectives were sitting around the table now and Charteris motioned to North to wind up his phone call. North gave whoever he was talking to a curt,

"Got to go, bye."

Charteris told them that he wanted to get up to speed on any progress and he also had some news for them.

"Right, ladies and gentlemen. First a bit of news. We've had a response to the circulation of the photo fit. An anonymous caller has given us a name for Mr Seventies moustache man. Does Roland Meeks mean anything to you?"

A deadpan Bob North, shook his head.

"Did this person know where he lives?"

"They suggested Lewes. Said he'd got a lock up somewhere in the area but didn't know the location."

"Did they say how they knew Meeks?" asked North.

"No, and they hung up before we could ask any more questions. We couldn't trace the caller."

"Might be a time waster," said North, with a disinterested yawn.

"So, what's the next step sir?" asked James Halstead.

"I want you and DS Trent to have a nose back in Lewes tomorrow. Just ask around. See if anyone can put the name together with the photo fit. I still want you to be based in Brighton for the rest of the week, but we need to follow up the Lewes connection. And it's your patch."

James and Jill nodded.

"Right DI North. Any progress to report?"

"Not much sir. We've spoken to nearly all the witnesses now and nobody has had anything to add to their original statements. Bit of a waste of time really!"

"I'll be the judge of that DI North. DS Read, anything you want to add?"

Read shook her head.

"No, nothing sir."

DCI Charteris turned his attention to James.

"Right DI Halstead. Any news on your drowned man?"

"Yes sir. We now know that his name is one Steven Daynes. He lived in a flat in Finsbury Road. We've been there and had a look around. The place had been searched and we think items have been removed."

"What makes you draw that conclusion?" asked North, brusquely.

"Well, a neighbour saw two men leaving the flats carrying dustbin bags."

"And you think that suggests that the men had been in the dead man's flat, because they were carrying dustbin bags?" asked an unsmiling North.

"DI North, this is not The Spanish Inquisition!" said an impatient Charteris.

"Apparently," continued James, "the two men had tried to disguise themselves, or at least avoid identification. It was early morning, quite warm and they had woolly hats pulled down and coats with collars turned up. Bit suspicious don't you think?" James seemed to be directly addressing North and looking him square in the face.

"Could be just a coincidence," offered North, looking at Charteris in case another rebuke was forthcoming.

Jill took up the story.

"The fact is, that someone gave the flat the once over. They missed this."

She handed the little book to Charteris. It was still inside the evidence bag. "It's not been dusted for prints yet, but it contains lists of first names, with what looks like passwords, next to each one."

North looked a bit red in the face but didn't offer an opinion. Jackie Read looked at the evidence bag.

"What significance does this book have?"

"We don't really know at this stage," said Jill, adding, "We don't know for certain that the book belonged to him. It was inside the lining of the settee base. The names could be contacts but we've no idea what the passwords mean."

"They may not be passwords at all," offered Jackie.

"We're only speculating Jackie, but they must mean something."

"Perhaps they're all trainspotters," said North, trying to sound light-hearted.

In truth, North was inwardly cursing. All that bloody effort to remove possible evidence and they'd missed the book. He knew full well what the names and passwords meant. He just hoped his new colleagues wouldn't find out.

James filled everyone in on the forensic search booked for the following day. He assured Charteris that it could provide some information and acknowledged that the forensics budget was not unlimited. Charteris, just nodded.

Charteris looked around the table.

"OK so we've got the investigation of Daynes purely to establish who he was. And a nose around Lewes, to see if Rolland Meeks is the name in the frame for the photo fit. Anything else?"

Nobody spoke. James and Jill had decided to keep their theories about the timeline for the burglaries to themselves for a while. They felt a bit uncomfortable raising it at the meeting in front of North. For that reason, they hadn't updated the case board on the office wall.

"Nothing? Right, just carry on. I want to pick this up again tomorrow."

With that, he got up and left the room.

North threw his pen down on the table. Looking directly at James and Jill, he said,

"You two are fucking clever, aren't you? You come to Brighton and swan around. You make clever discoveries and whatever I say, Charteris takes your side!"

James was a bit taken aback.

"It's not a question of sides. We've been asked to join this team. And we're trying to help solve the antiques burglaries; same as you. So, I don't see any need for your aggression. As far as I'm aware, we're on the same side."

"As far as you're aware!" exploded North

Jackie Read interrupted.

"For, goodness sake Bob. Just drop it; you're making an arse of yourself again."

North stood up, knocking his chair over. James stood up as well.

"Look, Bob, I don't want to do this. Just calm down."

North didn't say another word. He gathered up his files and stormed out. Jackie Read just shrugged her shoulders and got her papers together.

Jill put a hand on her arm.

"Jackie, are you sure everything's OK?"

"Yes, it's just fine. I've worked with Bob for a while, on and off. He gets like this. He's like a bear with a sore head. I think he's under stress. Maybe something in his private life."

"Forgive me Jackie," said Jill, "but are you two in a relationship?"

"Are you two?" asked Jackie, as she walked out.

Chapter Fifty

James and Jill decided to have an evening in. James prepared his signature dish of pasta bake, followed by chocolate ice cream. They had a bottle of red wine but didn't drink it all.

After they had filled the dishwasher, they sat in the living room drinking freshly made coffee. There was a companionable silence. They had some smooth jazz playing softly and they were very relaxed.

Jill broke the silence. "James, this is just so comfortable."

"Yes, and I'm really enjoying the whole thing. This just isn't the same as our working relationship. Whenever we went out for the odd meal after work, it never occurred to me to think anything of it. What with my divorce and everything, I wasn't looking for a relationship. Since we've been thrown together, I'm really enjoying our free time together."

"I know, I'm thinking the same. North has us down as intimate friends. I wonder if others have the same opinion?" asked Jill, as she curled up on the settee next to James.

"I'm sure Jackie does."

"James, let them think what they want. I don't really care what they think."

"Yes, but we're still colleagues. We have to be careful not to blur the edges."

"Do you really mean that James?"

"No, I don't," said James, smiling.

"That's good, because I want a cuddle."

Jill got up and sat on James' lap. He put his arms around her and she felt warm and soft. They cuddled for what seemed like hours but in reality, it was about half an hour. James had wanted to hold Jill in his arms forever. He gently kissed her on the lips and she responded. If there hadn't been a ring at the door, things would have gone a lot further. The bell had jolted them out of their warm embrace. They smoothed their clothes and Jill ran her fingers through her hair.

James went to the door and saw Jackie through the spy hole. Being a police safe house, there was a CCTV system, but this was turned off because it wasn't currently needed. James opened the door.

"Hello James. I Hope I'm not disturbing you."

"Come in Jackie."

Jill greeted Jackie with a peck on the cheek. Jackie looked tired and drawn. Not at all like the fit athletic woman from last week. Her hair was tied in a ponytail. She wore a tight-fitting top which stretched around her curves and jogging bottoms.

"I know it's late, but I really wanted to speak to you." She plonked herself down in an armchair and looked a bit tearful.

"Brandy or coffee?" said Jill.

"I'd love a brandy. Make it a small one, I'm driving."

Jill poured everyone small brandies and they all sat sipping from their glasses. Jackie gave a little sigh.

"Jill, you asked me about my relationship with Bob North and I was rude to you."

"Oh, forget it Jackie."

"No, it was unforgivable and I'm sorry. I want to tell you something but before I do, I want your word that you won't do anything."

James looked worried.

"Jackie, we can't give you our word without knowing the nature of what you're going to say."

"Yes, I understand. We're all serving police officers and all that."

Jill looked directly at Jackie's face.

"Jackie, why don't you just tell us? Get it off your chest. You've looked really worried for a while now. Maybe we can help."

Jackie was biting her lip and her hands were trembling. She gulped down the rest of her brandy. She looked at the brandy bottle.

Jill felt sorry for her.

"Jackie, if another brandy will help, have one. There are two spare rooms here. You can stay the night to save you driving home." James nodded his agreement.

"Yes, I'd like that. If you're sure I won't be disturbing you."

James and Jill shot each other a glance. James topped up all three glasses because it looked as if it might be a long night.

"I've just got to tell someone and I trust you to listen and be fair. Where to start? First off Bob North and I have had a sexual relationship for a while. At first it was exciting, because we could be different people in private and not a DI and DS. Then Bob asked me to do something for him. He asked me to set up Fancy Carter. He wanted me to copy Carter's computer files. Don't ask me why, but I agreed. It was a bit to do with our relationship; I guess I trusted him."

"Anyway, I pretended to be attracted to Carter and booked into his hotel where he stays when he's doing his shows. To cut a long story short, I led him on. He thought he was going to shag me. He nearly did as well, although I would have stopped him. He came to my room, full of himself."

"I put some crushed sleeping pills in his drink. He didn't notice because I think he had popped Viagra and was all worked up. I thought the bloody sleeping pills weren't going to knock him out. It crossed my mind that the Viagra might override the sleeping pills, but it didn't and he ended up snoring like a pig."

James and Jill looked aghast and at the same time sympathetic but neither spoke, which encouraged Jackie to continue.

"I had managed to get the combination of his room safe, where he kept his laptop. Bit of luck really — doesn't matter how. I copied his files onto a flash drive and left Carter in my room to sleep it off."

"I went straight round to Bob's and we looked at the files. Only problem was that Bob didn't seem that interested in what was on them. I think he just used me to make a point. But I don't know what. Now he's holding it over my head, because I broke the law."

"The bastard!" said Jill.

"That's not the half of it. Carter thought my name was Christine, which is why he approached me in that restaurant. Bob sorted him out in the toilets. I think he roughed Carter up. The guy with Carter, in the round glasses, was a friend of his, and he was the one that attacked me. I am truly sorry I had to lie to you Jill and say I didn't know who he was. Before you came to the rescue, he told me he was going to cut me, for messing with Carter's computer."

"I was angry for being put in this position. Angry with Bob and angry with Carter. That's why I was extra rough on Daynes. I wanted to do him some damage. I wanted to really hurt him! When you got him arrested, I panicked and asked Bob to get him away from the hospital, so he couldn't implicate me with Carter. I wasn't thinking straight. I didn't know what his relationship with Carter was but I couldn't take a chance."

James looked concerned.

"So, North got Daynes out and what? Had him drowned?"

"I don't really know what Bob did. I got the feeling that he was a bit surprised that Daynes drowned. I'm sure that someone else is involved in this. I've heard him making calls to a mate. Don't know his name. That's it, you might want to arrest me and report me."

James and Jill really didn't know what to say. James eventually said, "Jackie, this is a terrible situation for you. I don't propose to do anything at this stage. We'll need to think this through. My head's spinning with everything you've told us. I suggest we all sleep on it and think what our next steps should be. I'm guessing that you've got no actual evidence against North?"

"You guess right James. He's a clever sod but he's up to his neck in something. I just don't know what it is."

Jill showed Jackie to her room. She came back to say goodnight to James. She looked into his eyes.

"Nearly James."

He kissed her and gave her a hug. "Yes, nearly."

They went to their rooms.

Chapter Fifty-One

The next morning, when James and Jill came into the kitchen, there was a note on the table. It was from Jackie.

Thanks for listening last night. I just had to tell someone. Sorry to rush off, but I've got things to do.

J.

"I bet Jackie wishes she could turn the clock back," said Jill.

"Yes, I feel a bit sorry for her. She's scared of North and now she's worried what we'll do about the information."

"James, why don't we share it with Lorraine Marsh. We're going to nose around in Lewes today. We could ask her advice."

"Yes, I was thinking the same. We can't just ignore the information, now Jackie's told us. I'll give Lorraine's secretary a buzz and see if we can drop in today."

An appointment was arranged for that afternoon. After breakfast James and Jill set out for Lewes. They didn't really have a starting point for finding out about Rolland Meeks. If only the informant had given his name or a possible location for Meeks. They decided to ask around in the town centre.

Jill had some copies of the photo fit and she and James visited some of the coffee shops and cafés. They even called in on a couple of early opening pubs. None of the staff at these places gave even a flicker of recognition when the photo fit was shown to them. The two Detectives had been walking around for about two hours and eventually came to a little coffee shop near the antique emporium, just over the river bridge at the centre of Lewes.

"Come on Jill, time for coffee and croissants."

"Just what I was thinking. Whose turn is it?"

"I'll get them, grab a seat," said James, reaching for his wallet, with a smile.

They sat at a window seat and ate in silence. Jill looked across at James.

"You know if Jackie hadn't turned up last night?"

"I know what I wanted to happen and it would have changed things forever."

"Is that a bad thing, James?"

"No. Not a bad thing. We'd just have to take care at work, that's all."

"Let's just see where it takes us. Agreed?"

"Agreed."

They finished their coffee and were looking out the shop window.

"Look," said Jill. "Isn't that my old wrestling partner, Oz?"

"Yes, and he's heading our way."

Oz came through the door and immediately recognised the two Detectives. He came over to their table.

"Well, if it's not my old fighting partners."

"Hello, Oz," said James, a little apprehensively. "Can I get you a coffee?"

"Well, I don't know if I should risk being seen with you but yes, I'll have a large Americano, if you're buying."

James got the Americano and refills for him and Jill.

"What are you up to now? Still looking for poor old Arron's killer?"

"It's ongoing," said Jill.

"Translated, you aren't doing very much."

"Not exactly," said James. "It's still a live investigation but we've got a couple of other cases on the go. Besides, we shouldn't really discuss it with you. No offence intended!"

"None taken. You were very fair about the assault."

"Mainly because you missed with your punch." smiled Jill.

"My back's OK now, in case you were wondering," said Oz, retuning Jill's smile.

Oz noticed the photo fits on the table. "Who's that mug shot?"

"It's a man we would like to interview," said Jill.

"Let me have a proper look."

Oz reached into his pocket and took out a pair of glasses and put them on the end of his nose.

"Only for reading," said Oz, with a half-smile. "Hang on. I know this mug. It's Ratty Rolland Meeks."

James was amazed. "Is this a coincidence, or what? We've spent a couple of hours asking around and you suddenly appear and know who he is."

"Not such a coincidence. He was a friend of Arron Kelp!"

James and Jill were dumfounded. James was the first to react.

"A friend of Arron Kelp! Are you sure?"

"Course I'm sure. They used to do some buying and selling together. I think Ratty was an old drinking mate of Arron's. Not in the two boozers you know about. They always met up at the Railway Tavern. I saw them there a few of times."

James was really interested now.

"Buying and selling what?"

"Old junk mainly. Well old junk as far as I was concerned. I told you about it when you questioned me after our little punch up. Arron knew a lot about antiques and the like. You know Antiques Roadshow type stuff."

"Was he an antiques expert?" asked Jill, making a few notes.

"Old Arron knew a bit about most things, but antiques was his game. That's why he wasn't short of a bob or two."

"And what about his mate, Rolland Meeks? Did he know much about antiques?" asked Jill.

"Nah. He knew sweet F.A., really. His game was electronics. He used to sell some of those gizmos that they use for breaking into cars. Shouldn't really tell you that but you can get them on the internet, nowadays. No big deal really."

"That is, unless you get your car stolen," mused James.

"Well, each to his own. He's strictly small time. Haven't seen him for a while. Guess Arron's death put an end to their little partnership. Look, I've got to go. Have to be somewhere. Thanks for the coffee. This doesn't make us mates."

"Just one more question Oz," said James. "Do you know where Meeks lives?"

"He's got a lock up, round the back of Convent Field. Think he dosses down there most of the time. Don't know if he's got a proper place somewhere else. That's all I know. It's what Arron told me, that's all. Bye now, got to go."

Oz walked out of the coffee shop and James and Jill just looked at each other in disbelief.

"Do you believe in fate, Jill?"

"Call it what you like James. This is a big coincidence."

"If it's all true it links Arron Kelp with Rolland Meeks."

"And one was an antiques expert, the other was into electronics."

"Kelp was missing for over a month and it coincides with the lull in burglaries."

Jill was still trying to come to terms with what could be described as serendipity.

"James, if this fits together the way it looks like doing, we've made some progress at last."

"Do you remember when we interviewed Oz after his night in the cells?"

"Yes."

"Well, do you also remember when we asked him if Arron Kelp had any friends; he said no, except for the big bloke."

"I wonder why he's telling us about Rolland Meeks now," said Jill.

"Who knows? It's just one more bit of the puzzle."

"We'll need to ask Oz about his temporary memory loss, at some stage."

James looked thoughtful for a moment.

"What James?"

"I'm wondering if Oz was the anonymous caller. It really is a massive coincidence that he found us in the coffee shop and then saw the photo fit."

"Maybe so. But why now?" asked Jill.

"I just don't know," said James with a frown.

"Do you want any more coffee?" came a voice from the counter.

"Err, no thanks," said James, "nice coffee."

The man behind the counter gave them a look that said, you've been sitting there a long time, nursing empty cups!

They got back to the car and drove in the direction of Priory Street, which was near Convent Field. They travelled along Ham Lane and there across the field, were a couple of large sheds. They finally got to a small courtyard which had some larger business units surrounding it. There was a woman painting the doors of one of them. As the two Detectives pulled up and got out of the car, she gave them a wary glance and carried on with her painting.

"Hello," said James, trying to look friendly. He showed the woman his ID.

"I'm DI James Halstead and this is DS Jill Trent. We were wondering if you know a gentleman named Rolland Meeks."

"Yes, I know Ratty Meeks, and he's no gentleman."

"Why do you call him Ratty?"

"You know, Roland Rat! From the old TV kids' show."

"Oh, yes, I remember. Quite famous, wasn't he?" said James.

"Rolland Rat was but Ratty Meeks is just a strange man. Looks like he never left the 1970s."

"Any idea which unit is his?" asked James.

The woman pointed to one of the larger buildings at the other side of the courtyard.

"It's the one with the faded, red door. I haven't seen Ratty for a while now. His van's not there. Could be inside. It's a big old unit. Don't know what he stores in there. Think he sleeps there sometimes."

"You don't know where he actually lives, do you?" asked Jill.

"No, he doesn't talk very much. He moves things in and out. Cardboard boxes mainly. He's a furtive sod. Goodness knows what he gets up to. Could be an Aladdin's Cave in there."

The Detectives thanked the woman, who carried on painting. They walked up to the faded, red door which was locked with a large, expensive-looking padlock. One of those with rows of numbers instead of a key.

Jill handled the padlock and tugged it just in case it wasn't secured.

"These are the kind with hundreds of different combinations. We could be here for a week trying numbers, without getting in."

"We could but what about that window up on the side?"

"If we could borrow a ladder, we might be able to get in. The window isn't shut properly."

They asked the woman if she had a ladder, but they were out of luck. Then James thought they might be able to stand on some wooden boxes that were stacked nearby and get access. James moved a couple and placed them under the window.

"Up you go Sergeant," said James, with a broad smile.

"Why me?"

"Because you're lighter than me and I'm the Inspector."

Jill smiled. "OK sir! Are you sure we can break and enter legally?"

"We saw an unlocked window," said James, reassuring himself that they had due cause to investigate. As a precaution, James got two pairs of protective gloves from his car boot, just in case a scene had to be preserved.

James helped Jill on to the wooden boxes which creaked a bit under her weight. In truth, he wouldn't put Jill at risk, but she was very agile. Jill managed to get the window open and disappeared inside. She stretched her legs to stand on a wooden, mezzanine floor and walked down some steps. It was very dingy and smelt musty. In one corner was a bed with a sleeping bag on top of it. There was an old armchair that had seen better days. Next to it was an antique coffee table, with a bronze table lamp on top of it. Jill pressed a switch on the lamp and it came on, illuminating what was obviously a living area. The light revealed an extendable aluminium ladder. Jill took the ladder up the steps and called out to James.

"James, I've got a ladder. I can push it out of the window for you."

"Hang on, while I move the boxes. OK, push the ladder through the window."

Within a few minutes, James had joined Jill inside the industrial unit.

"Looks like Meeks camps out here," said James. "Yes, all mod cons. Well, at least there's electricity. What's that humming sound?" asked Jill, looking around.

"It's coming from the far side. Looks like a cupboard."

They walked over to the door and the humming got louder.

James turned the handle on a wooden door, which wasn't a cupboard at all. It was a room. They both cautiously entered. There was a light switch on the wall, next to the door. James switched it on and the room was bathed in light. There were two large, commercial type chest freezers, which were the source of the humming.

"Wonder why Meeks has got these," said Jill. She gently lifted the lid of one of the freezers. There were packs of what looked like frozen meat. Each was wrapped in a polythene bag, secured with a plastic clip. She picked one of the bags up and unclipped it.

"Oh my God!" shouted Jill, as she threw the bag down.

"What is it?"

"It's a dead cat!"

"What?"

"There must be a dozen or more!"

James looked horrified. "Meeks must be the cat kidnapper."

He opened the lid of the second freezer and revealed another scene of horror. There was a dead body of a man, surrounded by more dead cats, in plastic bags.

They both remained motionless, almost not believing what they were seeing. Staring at them, was a frozen version of the face in the photo fit. Jill was the first to speak.

"It's Rolland Meeks!"

James pulled the photo fit from his pocket.

"Yes, looks just like this image. Long hair, droopy moustache but very dead!"

"So, what have we got? Another retribution killing. Meeks kills cats, someone kills Meeks," said Jill.

James looked doubtful.

"Arron Kelp killed his dog by starvation and the same thing happened to him. Looks like Meeks killed all these cats and froze them. Someone did the same to him. It can't be that simple. Oz said they were friends and business partners. Bit of a coincidence that they were both the victims of retribution killings, don't you think?"

"Yes James. Maybe we're supposed to jump to that conclusion but I agree, it's all too easy."

"Let's call it in and get a forensics team here. We need Claire Grant, if she's on duty."

They made the arrangements and asked for some heavy-duty bolt cutters to be brought along. They both climbed out of the window and sat in the car.

"On the plus side, I think I've solved the cat kidnapping case," said Jill.

"Yes, I expect Lorraine Marsh will give you a gold star when we see her later."

"I never imagined that I would solve the missing cat case like this. How grizzly. Those poor pussies!"

The forensics team arrived about an hour later, along with the pathologist, Doctor Claire Grant. The process began. There would be photos of the dead body and surrounding area. Dusting for fingerprints and all the usual Scenes of Crime activity. The body of Rolland Meeks would be removed for a formal autopsy. Sergeant Rosemary Mires had been seconded to the Detective's team, when James and Jill had left to work on the robbery case and was pleased to be out of uniform. She was now revelling as Scene of Crime Officer for this murder scene. Because she had everything organised and under control, James and Jill headed to Lewes police headquarters to meet with DCS Loraine Marsh.

Neither had fancied having lunch after the macabre death scene. They met Lorraine Marsh in one of the meeting rooms. She was sitting on a comfortable settee and James and Jill each took an armchair. A coffee percolator was on the go and there were even a few biscuits.

"I heard about your gruesome discovery this morning. I guess it solves the missing cats' case but opens up a whole new one."

"Yes Ma'am, it does," said Jill

James was still deciding whether to have a biscuit. He still didn't fancy eating. Deciding against it he looked directly at Lorraine Marsh.

"We're developing a theory about the death of Rolland Meeks and Arron Kelp. We think the two are linked somehow. It looks like retribution for the killing of animals, but we think it's a bit of smoke and mirrors. We're thinking that the two dead men could have been involved in the antiques burglaries. We've been told that Kelp was an antiques expert. It's entirely possible that he was the person who had identified the most valuable items in each burglary. We think Meeks was an electronics expert, who might have disabled house alarm systems."

"There's a timeline that suggests that Kelp's absence coincides with a pause in the burglaries. All theory at the moment but it looks a possibility."

"And you think someone killed both men? For what reason?"

"Ah well, that's an unknown at present. That's what we still have to find out," said James, sipping his drink.

"Jill. Have you anything to add?"

"No, DI Halstead has pretty much covered everything we know so far."

"OK. Now what did you want to see me about?" asked Lorraine Marsh, leaning back in her seat.

James told Lorraine Marsh about the conversation with Jackie Read and the incident involving Fancy Carter; plus, his association with Steve Daynes. He also said that Jackie Read was frightened of DI North. When James finished speaking, DCS Marsh just sat and said nothing for what seemed like an age.

"You do realise that I should flag this up and instigate an enquiry? But I'm going to advise the ACC, mainly to cover my backside and subject to his agreement, I'm not going to do anything at this stage. This Daynes character was somehow spirited out of hospital and is now dead. The fact that he drowned in the sea and it doesn't look like murder, means that we don't necessarily have anything we can pin on DI North. Jackie Read asked North to get Daynes out of custody. But we would only have her word for that, if we confronted North."

James and Jill gave her a look but said nothing.

"I know you are wondering why I'm handling it in this way. There are much wider implications here. I want the both of you to keep an eye on Jackie Read. If you think she's in real danger, I'll get her taken to a place of safety. But at the moment, it's vital that we keep her and DI North in play."

"Can I speak freely Ma'am?" asked James.

"Yes."

"Ever since this started, I get the feeling that we're in the middle of something. Staying at the safe house. Working on the antique burglaries and investigating the death of Steven Daynes. We all know that some of this is not exactly normal procedure. There must be a bigger picture, which we aren't aware of."

Lorraine Marsh sat forward and looked first at James and then at Jill.

"I assume you share the same views as James?"

"Yes, I do Ma'am," said Jill, meeting Marsh's gaze.

"When I came to see you for a midnight visit, you both raised your concerns about what was really going on. I know that I didn't give you a satisfactory response and I do really appreciate that some things do seem to stray outside of recognised procedure. I told you that ACC, Trevor Johnson, had given me specific orders and so far, nothing has changed. He wants a discrete presence in Brighton. You know there are whispers about DI North and I don't know to what extent DS Read is involved. What you have told me about North, asking Read to do something illegal, is worrying but it kind of fits a narrative. Plus, the drowning of Daynes raises some question marks! Please just carry on working on the burglaries. You have already made more progress than was previously the case. Just pursue it. I want you to firm up on your theory and when you're ready, present it to Sandy Charteris in private. Don't share it with North and Read yet."

"So, we just keep at it until we have something concrete to report?"

"That's about the size of it. Look, I've told you as much as I can but please trust me. There are elements to this affair that I'm just not at liberty to tell you. As I've already said, I'm aware that procedures are being stretched. By the way, I know I'm asking a lot of you. I want you both to stay in Brighton for another week. Are you both able to do that? Or is it a problem?"

James responded.

"If you think it will help, then I am happy to stay."

"That goes for me too," said Jill.

"Good. Just remember that I have your back. If anything goes wrong, you are acting on orders directly from the ACC and me."

"That's a great comfort Ma'am. Nothing in writing, I take it?" asked James, half smiling.

"If that's all, let's finish there, shall we?" asked Lorraine Marsh, with the briefest of smiles and no response to James' question.

James and Jill got up and left. On the drive back to Brighton, James glanced across at Jill.

"Are you sure you don't mind spending another week with me?"

"I'll just have to put up with it," said Jill, as they shared a grin.

Chapter Fifty-Two

When James and Jill walked into Brighton police station, the Desk Sergeant called them over and handed James a folder. It was an interim report on the forensic investigation at Steven Daynes' flat. They went to one of the vacant interview rooms. They both sat at the interview table and James took out the report. It made interesting and surprising reading.

Interim Report
4a Finsbury Road

An extensive search was carried out at the above address. Multiple fingerprints were recovered and will be run through the police database.

There were minute traces of cocaine on some surfaces and a sniffer dog was deployed. This led to the discovery of a disguised cubby hole; cut in the kitchen worktop, located underneath a microwave. Inside the cubby hole was a half a kilo of cocaine and one kilo of cannabis. Both have been removed for analysis.

Located under the drugs was a package containing £10 540 in cash.

All items have been allocated reference numbers. The notes will be tested to establish that they are legal currency.

At this stage, the multiple fingerprints suggest that the occupant had many visitors. It is probable that drug dealing was occurring at the property.

This conclusion must be viewed as speculation at this stage, until the tests and investigation have been completed.

Alexander Lavern

SOCO
Ext 3431
Brighton Office.

"A cubby hole under the microwave? Some Detectives we are!" said James.

"Can't win them all. The drugs element is unexpected. Wonder how well Carter knew Daynes?" replied Jill.

"Guilt by association is difficult to pursue but it does beg the question about North's interest in Carter."

"Yes, it makes you wonder if the interest in Carter's computer was really just some sort of ruse or something more significant," said Jill.

"We might have to speak to old Fancy Carter again," said James, closing the folder.

They made their way to the meeting with DI Charteris. Jackie Read was sitting at the large round table and North was on his mobile phone, as usual. Charteris entered the room and sat at the table.

"Good afternoon everyone. Who wants to start?"

North ended his phone call.

"We've finished the witness interviews on our sheet. Nothing more to report. No sightings of possible burglars or vehicles."

Charteris looked at Jackie Read.

"Anything to add, DS Read?"

"No sir."

"DI Halstead?"

James had to be careful what he said. "Nothing directly on the burglaries, sir. We've completed most of our interviews and the files are up to date. There are some outstanding visits for three addresses. We've been working on the case of the drowned man, Daynes."

He handed Charteris the interim forensics report.

Charteris looked at it carefully. "Drugs?"

"Yes sir. But as you can see, we won't know the full facts until the investigations are complete."

North was staring at James across the table. He didn't say anything, but he didn't look happy.

James continued.

"We also discovered a body in Lewes. It is thought to be Roland Meeks. At least it does look very much like the photo fit. I haven't got the autopsy report yet, but it looks like murder."

Charteris raised an eyebrow and North continued his gaze at James. Then North suddenly spoke.

"What makes you think it was murder?"

Jill answered his question.

"He was found inside a chest freezer, with a load of dead cats, wrapped in plastic bags. We think he had been kidnapping and killing them, for some reason."

"Looks like someone did the same to him?" said North. "Sort of tit for tat killing?"

"Could be," said James, not wanting to mention the link with Arron Kelp.

Jackie joined in.

"So, could it be some animal activist nutter?"

"It's a possibility," said James, trying to avoid opening up the discussion.

Charteris was resting his chin on his steepled fingers by now.

"So, you've got two bodies on the go DI Halsted."

"Yes sir."

"Right, if you need any additional help, you can use DC Westmore. I want you and DS Trent to continue with the burglaries investigation as well."

"Yes sir. We've got a couple of leads to follow up, but DC Westmore will be a handy resource."

All the time James was talking, North was watching him like a hawk.

"DI Halstead and DS Trent will be staying on in Brighton for another week," announced Charteris.

North and Read exchanged glances. North's face suggested that the news was not exactly welcome but he said nothing.

The meeting broke up at 5.30.

James and Jill made their way to the carpark and were about to get into James' BMW, when Jackie Read approached them.

"Another week then?"

"Yes," said Jill. "Are you OK, Jackie?"

"Yes, I'm OK. I've not been arrested yet, at any rate!"

"Just take it easy Jackie. I don't think you need worry at this stage. No need for a Federation Rep just yet," replied Jill.

Jackie nodded and walked away. North was lurking in the carpark, smoking a cigarette. Jackie's brief chat to the two Detectives had not gone unnoticed. He had a long final drag and stomped on the dog end. He had something to do later that evening and he was almost looking forward to it.

Chapter Fifty-Three

James and Jill got back to the house a little after 6 p.m. They had decided to order a takeaway and then go out for a stroll afterwards, as it was a pleasant, warm evening. Summertime at the seaside, when the weather was warm, was very pleasant. After showering and changing into shorts and t-shirts, they took delivery of a Chinese meal.

They then decided to walk to the Brighton seafront and drop into a pub for a drink. As they strolled along the road, Jill, as was now usual, hooked her arm into James' arm. They were just chatting about everyday things and were talking about food provisions for the following week. Jill was concerned that she hadn't been going to the gym regularly and asked James if he would like to accompany her sometime soon. He agreed to go next week. They would both be going home to their respective flats for the weekend before joining up again on the following Monday.

Jill looked at James as they strolled.

"James, we're practically living as a couple now. The weekend will be very strange."

"Doesn't have to be. We can meet up like we did last weekend."

"I'd like that. Why don't we go out for a drive somewhere and have a meal?"

"Any more meals out and we'll both have to spend a lot of time in the gym," laughed James.

They had a couple of drinks in a pub near the pier. Then they made their way home. They both felt a bit tired and were flopped on the settee, in a companionable silence. It was very late and they both stood up to go to their rooms. James kissed Jill passionately on the lips and she responded. She put her arms around his neck and he felt her warmth. Reluctantly, they went to their separate rooms. The moment would come but not yet.

****

DI Bob North rang the doorbell at Fancy Carter's Brighton flat. Carter answered the door, wearing a red silk dressing gown. His faced showed fear but he tried to hide his feelings.

"Hello Fancy, hope I'm not disturbing you. I heard that your short engagement in Eastbourne was over, so I thought you might want to discuss our previous meeting."

"I'm very tired. I was just going to bed. How did you get into the building?"

"Oh, it's a piece of cake getting around door entry systems! You look very fetching in your silk dressing gown."

"What do you want?"

"What I want, is an answer to my question. Who are you working with in the drugs business?"

"You know I can't tell you."

"Did you know that your mate, Steven Daynes is dead? Made a surprise appearance when he was washed up on Eastbourne beach. Upset the sunbathers, I hear!"

Carter sank down into an armchair. He had nothing left. He seemed resigned to his fate.

"I was told he was dead."

"Yes, very dead. I wouldn't be surprised if you got a visit from some colleagues of mine."

"They've already interviewed me. I'm surprised you didn't know. Anyway, they've got nothing on me."

"I know but guess what. The forensics team found cocaine, cannabis and ten grand, in cash, hidden at Daynes' flat."

"Fuck! But all they know is that Daynes is just an acquaintance of mine."

"You and I both know that's a lot of fucking shit. You, my fat friend, are up to your fucking neck in this."

"What can I do? I'm not going to talk, whatever you do to me, because I'll end up dead!"

"Right, that's what I wanted to hear."

"But you said you'd fit me up if I didn't tell you."

"Let me tell you instead. Your business partner is Ryan Ledbetter!"

North's statement hung in the air. North liked it that way, because he was old school. He often threw out statements and would then keep completely silent, to force the other person to say something. Often, they would blurt out some information, just to break the silence.

"If you know that, why all the threats!" blurted Carter, both relieved and frightened at the same time.

"So, it's true, then?"

Carter was defeated. "Yes, it's true."

"Well, that wasn't so hard, was it?"

"But…"

"I just wanted to see what you would be prepared to do, to save your own skin. I know all about your late mate Daynes. I know it's big business for you. The lovable King of Comedy, is a drug dealer. If you want to carry on in business, all you have to do is keep your gob shut."

"How do you know all this? Why haven't I been arrested?"

"Because it's only me who knows."

"But you're still police."

"Very perceptive. I'm also pissed off watching bastards like you getting rich, while I have to work for relative peanuts! Ever wondered why Ledbetter insists that you only supply certain customers with drugs?"

Carter didn't answer and just looked puzzled.

"Don't strain yourself trying to think of the answer. You supply certain customers and my people supply another lot. It's all split into areas. We do half each!"

"Your people?"

"Yes, I've got a network of small-time dealers; so you see if Ledbetter gets arrested, we lose our importer. Then the whole thing goes down the toilet, for both of us."

"I knew there were other players and I thought Ledbetter had carved out his own area to avoid a turf war," said a surprised Carter.

"There are other players and it's a big enough business for all of us. Your mate Daynes almost blew it all apart. His fucking contacts book is in the hands of the police but it's not going to be of much use, it's just lists of first names. They could be anybody. The clever sod also put a password next to each name. They probably mean absolutely nothing, but my smartarse police colleagues will spend time trying to make sense of it. Your old mate had a sense of humour. I cleared his flat out and took all his papers just to slow the inquiry down. Didn't know the bastard had special hiding places though!"

Carter was trying to process all this sudden and surprising information. It could all be a double bluff. The look on North's face told him otherwise. This man was a hard bastard and not a person to cross. Carter could see that there were going to be changes to his life. But what?

"How do you know so much about Daynes and his book of names and passwords?"

"Because Ledbetter told him to do it. The names are regular small-time dealers and users. I don't suppose many of the names are real anyway. Just a way of keeping track and making sure that regulars get priority supplies." "Where do we go from here? What do you want of me? If it's money, I can let you have some. Name your price."

"This isn't a shakedown. You're going to need a new distributer now that Daynes is dead. I'm going to introduce you to someone who can help. I want you to hand over your drugs to him from now on. He'll do the rest."

"If I cooperate, where do you fit into it?"

"There's no if. You will fucking cooperate. I'll tell you where I fit in. I'm your new partner. No need to tell Ledbetter. I'm taking over your patch. You just carry on as usual. Provide the funding and storage and I'll do the distribution. Is that all clear?"

"Yes," said Carter, with a resigned expression.

"Good boy. Now remember, if my colleagues speak with you again you stick with your story that Daynes was just an acquaintance. You've got no idea about any drugs. They can't prove anything and if they push it, speak to your solicitor. I'll be in touch soon, otherwise your druggy customers might go elsewhere, and I won't like that one bit."

North left a shattered Carter and made his way back to his car. He got a pay as you go mobile phone from his glovebox, inserted a sim card and rang a number. It was picked up after only three rings.

"It's all fixed. There's no way on earth he would give your name to the police. No, I couldn't get the contacts' book. It's not my fucking fault. Batman and Robin found it and it's in the evidence room now. No, I can't get it out. Not without raising suspicions. It's not that important. I know all the dealers anyway. I'll smooth things over. Don't worry. Look, let's meet up soon. Take a nice cruise and have a chat. Yeah. That'd be great. Sunday about 11 a.m. See you then. By the way I think you shouldn't contact Carter for a while. He's a bit hot with my smart-arsed chums. Give him a wide berth for now. I'll tell you when things cool down. Yeah that's my advice. Stay in the background. Bye."

North removed the sim card. He smiled to himself. He had hoodwinked Ledbetter, who had been concerned that Carter might talk now Daynes was dead. He could take over Carter's patch on the pretence of helping. Ledbetter wasn't all that smart. If his goons got involved, Terry would deal with them. As double crosses go it was very clever

Then his mood changed. He would have to do something about the oh-so,

clever James Halstead and that cow of a Sergeant of his. He still didn't see why they had to stay in Brighton. Something wasn't right but he didn't know what. Jackie Read was too friendly with them. Perhaps it was time to sort her out as well. Nothing was going to get in the way of him making enough money to retire to Spain, even if it meant drastic action. Or to be more precise, some even more drastic action.

Chapter Fifty-Four

Saturday morning found James and Jill back at their respective flats; back to the grind of housework and feeding washing machines. They had arranged to go to Jill's gym that afternoon. James had been signed in as a guest and he was on a running machine next to Jill. She was gliding effortlessly, at a slightly higher speed setting than James. After the workout they went to the club swimming pool. James was wearing a very loud pair of swimming shorts, which attracted some looks from fellow swimmers. Jill had a subtle, black, all-in-one costume. James privately thought she looked absolutely stunning. They swam about twenty lengths of the pool and then relaxed in the jacuzzi.

They had a meal at the health club restaurant and planned their Sunday together. It would have been so easy to both go back to either of their flats and just fall into bed. The fact that they didn't, was a combination of their working relationship and an unspoken, shared view that it was too soon. Virtually living together for the past fortnight had unlocked their feelings. James was still recovering from his divorce and Jill had decided that up 'til now, she didn't want a serious relationship.

Living in close proximity to James had changed her mind. She liked the fact that he was old fashioned. She liked the way James would blush, when encountering women with a lot of flesh on show. She smiled to herself when she thought about the women, drinking on Eastbourne pier. Several had worn low tops, which barely covered their breasts. She knew this had embarrassed James. Walking arm in arm with him, off duty, had seemed so natural. They both felt completely relaxed doing this. And of course, there were the goodnight kisses, which also seemed natural, yet in a sense, out of place. They were colleagues. James was her boss. All very confusing but at the same time wonderful.

James also had confusing thoughts. Jill was his trusted DS. She was clever and brave. She had looked lovely in her swimming costume and he just couldn't help looking at her. She was becoming very important in his life. His divorce was over, except for custody of the missing cat. It was time for him to move on. He knew he was starting to fall in love with this attractive woman. He so wanted to take it to the next stage. He felt that Jill did too. And yet, they were in the middle of a murder enquiry, a possible drugs trade related death and the antique burglary investigation. It was almost as if he and Jill, were the only Detectives available. In his experience, one pair of Detectives would not normally be asked to investigate so many cases at once. The ongoing investigation at a children's home had swallowed up lots of resources. He still had some nagging doubts about the orders he'd been given.

What were he and Jill really supposed to be doing in Brighton? What was going on with DI North and DS Read? Why was the ACC taking such a close interest? Why not just bring in Professional Standards to investigate? If North wasn't a case for Professional Standards, who was? So many questions and problems and he was falling in love with his DS! What a difficult but at the same time, wonderful phase his life had entered.

They had both returned to their respective flats on Saturday night. James had told Jill that he wanted to take her out on Sunday morning and that it would be a mystery destination. They met up bright and early on the Sunday. Jill had collected James in her Fiat 500. He had suggested that they both wear trainers and for Jill to bring some sun cream. They were wearing their usual shorts, t-shirts and hoodies.

"If this is a mystery destination, why are we in my car?" laughed Jill. "And why the sun cream?"
    "Just be patient and head for Eastbourne seafront."
    "OK boss. Should I have got my bucket and spade as well?"
    "Don't be cheeky."

They found a parking space not far from Eastbourne pier. James paid for six hours parking.

"We don't need the car for what I've got planned. I thought your little Fiat would be easier to park on the seafront."

"This is intriguing."

"Walk this way," said James.

"Yes sir."

Jill held onto his arm as they strolled to the pier. James then took Jill's hand, boarded an open top bus and paid for two tickets. They went upstairs and two of the front seats were unoccupied.

"It's the hop on, hop off, bus trip."

"It's not going to do my hair any favours," laughed Jill.

"Nor mine but at least we have the windshield in front of us."

"So where are we going?"

"Well the reason for the footwear, is that we're going to do a bit of walking."

"Sounds good."

The bus made its way along the spectacular Eastbourne seafront and then began a sedate climb up a winding road, to the top of Beachy Head. They got off at the stop nearest to the popular country pub.

"Right, breakfast here and then a nice walk," said James.

"What a lovely idea. Breakfast's my treat. No arguments!"

"Would I argue with a lovely lady?" asked James, instantly a little embarrassed by what he had just said to her.

"Thanks for the compliment," smiled Jill, thinking how relaxed James seemed.

They had a light breakfast of coffee, toast and marmalade. The views from the pub windows were spectacular. Lots of tiny white dots were scattered over far off fields. It was only the fact that they were moving around, that meant the white dots were sheep. After breakfast they set out for a walk. They went to the cliff edge but not as close to it as some other walkers. The sea views were magnificent. On the horizon, were several large container ships. They were too far away for proper identification, but the towering decks suggested containers, piled high.

They then set out towards the redundant Belle Tout Lighthouse, which was situated high up on the cliffs. The building had been moved back from the crumbling cliff edge, in a massive feat of engineering. It was now a private guest house. How long it would be safe from falling into the sea, was another matter. Laughing and talking, James and Jill breathed in the fresh air.

"Do you know James? I could stay up here with you forever."

"Wouldn't it be lovely? How an earth can we be dealing with dead bodies and burglary, in such a glorious part of the country."

"Somehow the day job seems at odds with all this," said Jill.

They stopped and James took Jill in his arms and held her close. They kissed and hugged each other. Then, as if it was a completely natural thing for them to have done, they carried on walking.

"James, I don't know if it's the location or the fresh air but I'm finding it hard to go on like this."

"Oh," said James, looking alarmed.

"James, I have to tell you. I love you."

"I'm so happy you feel that way because it's been driving me mad. I love you so much."

"Now I've got tears in my eyes."

"Tears of joy, I hope."

"Yes, yes, tears of joy."

They hugged again but this time their kissing was intense. They found a nice secluded area and took off their hoodies and used them to lay down on. They both lay side by side in silence, holding hands and never wanting this moment to end.

"Wouldn't it be glorious to make love in the open?" whispered James.

"Yes, it would until we saw the headlines in the paper if we got caught," laughed Jill.

"Yes, it would be a moment of madness. Can you imagine what DCI

Charteris would say?" laughed James.

They stayed there for what seemed like an eternity. In that moment they were so close and they both knew that things could never be the same again. They were in love; they just wanted give in to their instincts. Jill sat up.

"James, what are we going to do?"

"I think we should keep it under wraps until we finish our investigations." "If this were a novel or a film, we would just make love and to hell with everything else! But this is real life and as much as I want you, I think we should wait. You must think I'm really straight-laced."

"James, I think you are a lovely, old-fashioned man and I agree with you. Just think how fantastic it will be when we can just let everything go and spend all day in bed together."

"It's a date for the future then."

"Of course it is."

Brushing grass off their hoodies, they continued their walk. They eventually came to Birling Gap and the large tearoom at the top of the cliff. Although it was heaving with tourists and holiday makers, they found a table outside and had lunch. The odd annoying wasp dive-bombed some of their fellow diners but they were mainly after sugar and cakes, not James' and Jill's toasted cheese and tomato sandwiches. Although their glasses of wine did get some unwelcome attention.

After lunch and a comfort break, they waited for the hop on hop off bus. Although lots of people got off at Birling gap, the top deck was fairly crowded. They managed to get seats nearer the back of the bus. They sat and enjoyed the panoramic views over the South Downs. The bus made slow progress on its way down into Eastbourne and eventually it stopped at the pier. James and Jill got off and went back to Jill's car. Fortunately, the sun had been masked by white, fluffy clouds during the day, which meant that they had not ended up with bright red faces. They ended their wonderfully romantic day by having fish and chips.

They both knew that a perfect end to the day would have been spending the night together. They had already settled that particular thought for the time being and reluctantly parted company when Jill dropped James off at his flat. James had arranged to collect Jill next morning to spend their third week at the Brighton house.

Chapter Fifty-Five

Later that evening James got a call on his mobile, from Doctor Claire Grant.

"Hello James, hope I'm not disturbing anything but I wanted to catch you before you go back on duty."

"No problem Claire. What is it?"

"I wondered if you would drop in and see me first thing tomorrow morning. You seem to be giving me a lot of work lately and I want to talk with you about your latest dead body."

"Very amusing Claire. Can you tell me anything now?"

"Only that Rolland Meeks was definitely murdered. I'll give you the gruesome details tomorrow."

"OK, see you about 9, if that's all right?"

"That's fine James. Night."

James rang Jill and told her about the change of plan.

They were both curious.

At 9 a.m. the next morning, the two Detectives met up with Doctor Grant.

"What can you tell us, Claire?"

"Well James, as I said last night. Definitely murder."

"And the murder weapon?"

"No weapon, just bare hands. His windpipe was partially crushed by someone with massive power. Most likely a man, I would say."

"Any signs of resistance?" asked Jill.

"None at all. If I were to speculate, I'd say Meeks was lifted off his feet by his neck. Nothing under his fingernails, except dirt. No skin tissue etc. No evidence that he fought his killer."

"How long had he been dead?"

"About a week, I'd say. He was frozen solid and well preserved. You have a brutal murder on your hands. As I've said, the killer would be a particularly strong individual and, in my opinion, judging by the damage to the neck, extremely dangerous. I've copied a full set of photos for you. Would you like to see the body?"

"Err, no thanks. I've already seen him frozen. I'd like to hold on to my breakfast."

"OK James. I'll email my autopsy report to you and send over a hard copy file later."

"Thanks Claire."

"By the way, rumour has it that you two are still living together in Brighton. What's going on?"

"Special case. We need to be close to developments."

"You sound like a politician being interviewed at the BBC!"

"It's the truth Claire. No big deal. We go where we're told."

"If you say so. By the way Jill, you're looking full of the joys of spring. Got a new boyfriend?"

"Now that would be telling," said Jill, throwing a quick look at James, which didn't go completely unnoticed by the good doctor.

"Must get going; thanks for the information Claire," said James, as they were making for the door.

Claire Grant smiled to herself as she thought what a lovely couple these two would make.

They arrived at the Brighton house and put some milk in the fridge. They had replenished some of the supplies during the previous two weeks. It wasn't the only police safe house in the Brighton area, but it was certainly a comfortable place and better than a hotel. They were also able to claim reasonable expenses.

James opened a door to a room that contained the case files. It was about the size of a single bedroom and was locked by a combination coded keypad. It was out of bounds to anyone staying at the house for their own safety and was used only by police officers. It had a secure telephone line and a secure internet access. James and Jill had been using it to set up a visual crime board, with photos of Kelp and Meeks and notes written with a marker pen. Under normal circumstances they would have used the dedicated room at Brighton police station, but their investigations were shrouded in unknowns. The suspicions surrounding DI North and to a lesser extent DS Read, had meant that a similar case board at the Brighton police station was purely based on the burgled properties and witness statements, for cross referencing purposes. Nothing on Arron Kelp and Roland Meeks. There was also a big question mark, with the words 'Big Bastard Terry?' written underneath it.

The words 'drugs connection', were written next to Steven Daynes' name. Alongside this was 'address book?' There was an all too obvious connection between the deaths of Aron Kelp and Roland Meeks. The word 'RETRIBUTION?' with a question mark, had been written in large capitals next to the two names. The discovery of drugs would certainly mean that the drugs team would take over the Daynes case. The board showed the possible timeline for the antique burglaries. Also, on the board was the antique dealer Ludo Chambers. The only connection here was that he dealt in antiques, as did Kelp and Meeks. They had both agreed that this was tenuous, but they had included it anyway. There was another big question mark with 'disposal of stolen antiques', written underneath it. Perhaps the Silver Squirrel in Chambers' shop was a red herring. Why would he sell stolen goods? Mr Singe must have been mistaken.

"You know Jill, we need to sit down and brainstorm this information. We've stared at it and discussed it, but I've got a feeling we're missing something."

"Yes, there's definitely a gap here. Pity we're not seeing the full picture."

"That's it," shouted James.

"What have I said?"

"The full picture. Remember the discussion with Mr Singe? He said insurance companies want pictures of items being insured."

"Yes, and the case files on all the burglaries have photos and values attached."

"Exactly. I'm thinking that the insurance people would want a definitive value for each item with at least one photo. Jill, let's have a look at some of the case files and specifically the photos."

They got several files out and spread them on the desk. James was looking very closely at each of them. He was rubbing his chin, doing what Jill laughingly described as his Sherlock Holmes impression.

"So, what exactly are we looking for James?"

"Have you noticed that most of these photos are very similar, in terms of distance from the camera and settings?"

"Yes, I guess you're right. But how does this help us?"

"Well, I was wondering if the valuations and photos were done by the same person."

"I think I'm with you James. There have been over two dozen burglaries and that raises the question of how did they know which properties to rob?"

"Exactly. Inside information!" said James again, stroking his chin.

"I think we need to get some help on this. I think we need to get DC Westmore involved."

"Only problem, we don't know what his relationship is with North," mused Jill.

"Yes, I know, but don't forget that he made no attempt to cover for North when we spoke about missing bits of information, in the case files."

"Won't he find it a bit strange that we've left some information off the case board at the station?"

"I don't like doing this, but we can use DC Westmore on a need-to-know basis. When you think about it, that's exactly what's happening to us."

Jill nodded her agreement.

"Sandy Charteris offered us Westmore. If he thought there was a tie up with North, surely he wouldn't have suggested it."

They agreed to involve DC Westmore. James rang the Brighton police station to find out where he was. Westmore was working in the office all day and James asked him if he could come to the safe house that morning.

Charteris had already mentioned to Westmore that he may be needed. James and Jill spent the next half hour discussing the burglary case and speculated about the deaths of Steven Daynes and Rolland Meeks.

DC Westmore arrived, carrying his laptop and some files. They poured him a coffee and the three of them settled in the living room. DC Westmore looked a little apprehensive and was obviously wondering what this was all about. James had just told him on the phone, that it was part of the investigation into the burglaries. The case files were on the large coffee table in front of them and there was a slight atmosphere in the room.

James and Jill had noticed it and wanted to put Westmore at his ease. James opened the conversation.

"Relax Peter, this isn't the Spanish Inquisition."

"Sorry but I was wondering what's going on."

"What, with the case?"

"Err, no not exactly. Can I speak openly sir?"

"Go ahead, this is an informal setting. Get it off your chest."

Peter Westmore fidgeted and drained his cup.

"Thing is that everyone at the station is wondering why you and DS Trent are staying at this house, when you both live not very far down the road at Lewes."

James didn't answer straight away. He and Jill exchanged glances.

"The truth is, that we have been asked to stay here by our boss, DCS Lorraine Marsh. She wants us as close to the investigation as possible."

"With respect sir, that doesn't really explain what's going on."

"What do you think is going on, Peter?"

"The rumour is that you are carrying out some kind of investigation and that the burglaries make a convenient cover!"

"Really?"

"Yes sir. That's what people are saying."

"Do these people say what they think we are really investigating?"

"Not specifically sir."

"Care to speculate."

"I've probably said too much already."

"Don't stop now, Peter. Just spit it out," said James, eyeing Westmore.

Peter Westmore looked as if he wished he was somewhere else. He sat in silence and James and Jill said nothing. They both looked at Westmore, who, despite knowing all about silence being a great interview technique, just had to speak.

"Some people are saying that it has something to do with DI North and DS Read."

"Why would they say that Peter?"

The dam suddenly burst and Westmore blurted.

"Some people think DI North might be bent! They think he cuts corners and associates with some dodgy people."

After a slight pause, James responded.

"Don't we all know some dodgy people? It's part and parcel of the job. We come across all kinds of characters."

"Look sir. Nobody has got anything concrete on DI North and if they had, they would call in Professional Standards, wouldn't they? Maybe you and DS Trent are under cover Professional Standards officers. Work with North and see what turns up. Jackie Read is his partner, in more than one sense."

"What does that mean?"

"That they're close, personally."

Jill gave James another glance but said nothing. She wondered what colleagues might be saying about her and James and whether DC Westmore was really only referring to just North and Read.

James didn't respond immediately to Westmore's blurted speculation. He looked directly at Westmore and in a calm quiet voice, he spoke.

"Peter, I can't comment on station gossip and speculation. I appreciate that you wanted to get it out in the open and I commend you for your candour. DS Trent and I are not in any way involved with or working for Professional Standards. We have been directed by our boss to work and stay in Brighton. This is our third week and we are trying to make some progress on the burglaries." "I want to ask you a question now."

"Go ahead sir."

"Can I trust you?"

"To do what, sir?"

"To work closely with us to solve the burglaries case and bring those responsible to justice."

"Of course, sir. I'm not a bent copper!"

"Never thought you were. I don't want our investigation compromised."

"Is that clear?"

"Yes sir. Perfectly clear."

James had made a decision, based on his instincts about DC Westmore. He and Jill took Westmore into the secure room and went over the whole case with him. Westmore immediately noticed the case board on the wall He had seen the one at the station because he had worked with Jackie Read, when North was off. He wondered why there were two boards but didn't say anything. They discussed the burglary timeline with Westmore and they told him about their theory, that Kelp and Meeks were part of the robbery team. Westmore agreed that Kelp's disappearance could be the reason for the gap in burglaries in the timetable.

Westmore agreed with most of the theories and had a few suggestions himself.

"OK Peter. What I want you to do, is find out who did the valuations for the owners of the antiques. There's no mention of this in the files."

"That's because we got the photos and valuations from the victims. They provided copies for our case files. We didn't think to ask where the valuations came from. We assumed that the owners had just provided the information for their respective insurers and any valuation queries were dealt with by the insurer's experts."

"It'll take a bit of time to contact all the victims. If there's nothing else, I'll get onto it straightway."

"Thanks Peter. Let me know what you find out. You've got my mobile number," said James.

"Bye sir, DS Trent," said Westmore as he left.

"I agree with you James, that Peter Westmore is one of the good guys."

James looked a bit pensive.

"You know Jill, it seems that there's a general opinion that Bob North is bent. I really do wonder why there's been no official investigation. Why leave it to us?"

"If I knew that Jill, I'd be a happy man."

Chapter Fifty-Six

DI North and DS Read were sitting in North's car. They had been rounding off some minor details with witnesses and were now drinking take away coffee and eating sandwiches. North had been a bit more cheerful since the weekend.

"What are you up to Bob?"

"Up to? I'm not up to anything."

"What was that business with Carter's laptop really about?"

"Nothing darling. Just a bit of fishing. I've already told you to forget it ever happened. If anyone finds out it's your word against Carter's. I guarantee, he'll never press charges and without that, you can stay well clear of any manure."

"I'll never understand you. You sail very close to the wind and one day, you'll slip up. You could be out on your ear, with no pension, no nothing."

"Fuck the pension. It's peanuts."

"What does that mean?"

"It means, darling, that I don't need to rely on a pension."

"Bob, I'm not going to get dragged into anything illegal. I'm thinking of looking for a transfer to another force."

"Another force? Don't make me laugh."

"I mean it Bob. I'm thinking of applying to the Met in London."

"The fucking Met. Do you really think you're cut out for it? There's a lot of violent bastards in the big city. You won't like it. Believe me."

"Well, I don't like this. Not when you talk about money and not needing a pension."

"Forget all that crap. Do you know how long it is since we had a bit of 'How's your father'?"

"No, I don't and it's not going to happen again, ever!"

"You bloody bitch! Things were all right between us until Batman

271

and Robin came on the scene."

"If you mean James Halstead and Jill Trent, I don't know why you hate them so much."

"Because they're so fucking honest."

"And that's a bad thing for coppers?"

"It is if you want to get rich and get out."

"Money again."

"Yeah, money. Lots of it. Let's get going."

****

Meanwhile, on board Ryan Ledbetter's boat at Sovereign Harbour, in Eastbourne, Simon Wells and Ludo Chambers were sipping wine. They were seated inside the large cabin and Ryan Ledbetter was annoyed. Ludo Chambers had just told his two business partners about the antique silver squirrel pencil, which had attracted the attention of the police. He had thought it was amusing but Ledbetter disagreed.

"So, you take a stupid chance and try to sell a stolen item in your shop. Ludo, you are a Class A prat."

Chambers laughed.

"Don't hold back Ryan. Say what you think."

"I think you took a risk that didn't need to be taken."

"And I thought I could get more for it than the knockdown prices we get in France. Besides, I told the police that it was from a car boot fair. You know, the old box of rubbish, hidden gem and all that!"

Simon Wells smiled.

"Yes Ludo, the old private purchase. No names. Just an amateur clearing out the loft."

"That's not the point," said Ledbetter. "You two are in the trade. You know you can't directly sell stolen items. You could have buggered things up."

Ludo was serious now.

"I could have buggered things up?"

"Ludo, you are such an arsehole. Things have got a bit tight lately and you two do nothing but moan," sneered Ledbetter. "Anyway, we're out of the stolen antiques business, as of now."

Simon Wells looked startled.

"Out of the antiques business? But why? It's worth a lot of extra cash to all of us. I thought we were just giving it a rest, not giving it up."

Ledbetter gave Wells a stern look, which frightened the two antique dealers.

"A lot of questions are being asked about the burglaries, so my contact tells me. So just listen for a minute."

The two antique dealers felt like naughty schoolboys. Ryan Ledbetter was not a man to cross. He had made his money in various, questionable ways. He even owned a nightclub in Brighton and some of his associates were not people they would want to socialise or be in business with. In fact, they were probably best avoided.

"Listen to me, both of you. We've had a good run and so far, the police haven't got anywhere with their investigations."

"How do you know that?" asked Chambers, pouring another glass of wine and offering the bottle around.

"I know, because I got it from the horse's mouth. Apparently, there's a couple of smart-arse Detectives on the case. They've been moved to the Brighton team, looking at the burglaries. The point is, that they are the worst kind of cops. They're honest, so can't be paid off."

"I bet it's the two Detectives who came to see me about the silver pencil."

"So, if we're out of the antique business, what are we going to do instead?" asked a less than cheerful, Ludo Chambers.

"There's no 'we'. Our partnership is at an end. I'm concentrating on my other business."

"The cannabis business?" asked Simon Wells.

"Which has provided a nice income alongside the antiques trade. But my other interests are expanding and believe me, you don't want to know."

The two antique dealers looked crestfallen. They had no idea what

Ledbetter was really in to. But it was obviously far more dangerous than antiques smuggling!

"But our association has worked well for all of us," said Ludo Chambers.

"Yes," snarled Ledbetter. "As I've told you both many times, I took all the risks and you two sat on your arses and just supplied the network of contacts in France and Jersey."

"But you never got caught," whined Chambers.

"No, but I came close. Do you realise how tight things are on the south coast nowadays? I've told you this before but you obviously need telling again. Project Cormorant is a twenty-four-hour security system. Cameras everywhere and day and night patrols. If it wasn't for inside information, I'd have gone down the pan a long time ago. And there's the security in Jersey and France. What with all the terrorism threats and people smuggling, things are very tight now."

"For old times' sake, surely you can tell us what your other business is," said a resigned Wells.

"I could but I won't. That way, you can't talk to the police or drop me in it."

"Ryan, we are old mates. We wouldn't dream of doing anything like that," said Ludo Chambers.

"Wouldn't dream of it? If for one minute, I thought either of you would ever drop me in the shit…"

The sentence hovered in the air. Both men knew that to drop Ryan Ledbetter in the shit would be fatal.

Chapter Fifty-Seven

James Halstead contacted DCI Sandy Charteris and told him that they were working on a few aspects of the burglaries, which they didn't want to share with North. Charteris agreed and told them to check in with him the following day. James also told him that he was using DC Westmore. Charteris didn't comment.

James telephoned his team at Lewes. Rosemary Mires answered the phone.

"Hi Rosemary, anything for me?"

"Yes sir, we found a few interesting items at Meeks' lock up. His driving licence was at the back of a desk drawer. There's a Lewes address on it. I've had it checked, but it's a dead end. He apparently moved out a year or so ago and obviously didn't notify the licence people. No mobile phone or any other items of interest."

"Pity. I had hoped we could get some of his contacts from phone records."

"There was one interesting find. We found two car number plates stuffed down the back of a cupboard. AE61 BUS!"

"Brilliant! That confirms a theory we're working on."

"I was just preparing a report on the crime scene. Forensics came up with a big fat zero. No prints, apart from Meeks'. I'll email it to you, later today, if that's OK."

"Yes, that's fine, Rosemary."

"Oh, and sir, would you tell Jill that I've been in touch with Roy, from the RSPCA. He's arranging to have the dead cats removed. He was talking about reuniting them with their owners, from photographic records and microchips."

"Sounds a bit macabre. Anything else? Are the team OK? I've neglected them of late."

"Nothing else. The team are fine. They've plenty of ongoing cases to investigate and they've all got photo fits of Rolland Meeks, plus his driving licence photo. They've been asking around about contacts and known associates but nothing yet."

"OK, thanks Rosemary. Be in touch."

Jill was still staring at the case board on the wall, when James came back into the room. He told her about the frozen cats and Roy's heroic intentions. Jill was appalled but admired Roy's dedication.

One the way back to the house, they dropped into a supermarket to get some salad bits. Jill prepared a tuna salad. They sat at the kitchen table and talked as they ate. Jill was sipping a glass of wine and saying that she really must go to the gym tomorrow evening. When they had finished the meal, they cleared everything away and sat on the settee in the living room.

"Jill, I hope you're OK with our personal situation."

"What, not sleeping together?"

"Well, yes, but put that way, it seems a bit naff, doesn't it?"

"James, I'm in love with you and it would be simple and wonderful to jump into bed with you and forget everything else."

"You know I feel the same. If we do, it'll just complicate our investigation. I'm not sure I would be able to concentrate on the case anymore."

They both laughed. Jill moved really close to James on the settee.

"Nothing to stop us being close, is there James?"

"Nothing at all."

They watched a David Attenborough wildlife documentary. It was a repeat but they found it enthralling. When it was time for bed, they kissed for a while and with admirable self-control, reluctantly went to their separate rooms.

The next morning while they were having breakfast, James got a call on his mobile. It was DC Peter Westmore. He asked if he could come to the house, with the results of his investigation into the antiques valuations and photos. They arranged to meet at about eleven o'clock.

Westmore arrived at precisely eleven o' clock. They sat in the living room and Westmore got some papers out of his shoulder bag.

"I was surprised how quickly I was able to get the information you wanted. I rang round all the burglary victims, yesterday evening. I thought the evening would be the best time to catch them all. Anyway, it turns out that twenty out of twenty-five had used the same valuer. William Topperfield antiques. He does insurance valuations and takes photos of the items, which is included in his service."

James sat forward.

"That's interesting, all twenty used the same company."

"Yes, but apparently William Topperfield didn't visit them in person. He sent another antiques expert to do the actual valuations and take photos. Topperfield then did a follow up in person, with the valuations and photos and gave them an invoice. Several of the people I spoke with said Topperfield was charming and that they were pleased with his work."

Sipping her coffee, Jill asked,

What about the rest of the victims?"

"Well, of the remaining five, I could only make contact with one of them before I left the office. The others all went to messaging. I asked them to contact me but as of this morning, no response. My office phone's being covered, so my team will ask any callers about the valuations and photos. One of the burglary victims, here it is number ten on the list, was different to the others."

"Different?" asked James, pouring another coffee and offering a top up to the others.

"Well it's a bit of a strange story."

"In what way Peter?" asked James, as he topped up Peter's cup and then Jill's.

"Bit of a coincidence really. A Mr Sean Morris got his valuations from an antique dealer called Mathew Stilgo. Apparently, he's a mate of Mr Morris and did it at mate's rates."

"And why is that strange?"

"That's not the strange part at all, because Mathew Stilgo is a bona fide expert. The strange part is that DI North visited Mr Morris in connection with an incident in a Brighton club. It seems that Morris was in some sort of altercation outside the club and was punched by some guy. He wasn't seriously hurt. A patrol car was passing and the assailant ran off. The uniforms took Morris home, after he declined hospital treatment. They reported it and a couple of days later, DI North turned up to take a statement."

"OK, so normally a DI would probably not get involved," said James.

"No. He or she would delegate to a DS or a DC," mused Jill.

"I know I'm probably imagining things that aren't there, but Mr Morris said that DI North took quite an interest in his collection of antique watches, which were on display in a cabinet. The very same watches were subsequently stolen in a burglary a few weeks later."

"And you feel that this was what?"

"A bloody coincidence, sir."

Jill smiled a Westmore's forthright view.

"Did he tell DI North what the watches were worth?"

"Not only did he tell him, he showed him the valuation documents and photos. There were seven watches in all. Most very old. I've looked at the file on Mr Morris's case and the total value was over eleven thousand pounds!"

The three looked at each other. James said in a calm voice,

"We are either looking at a coincidence or something else that we can't prove. At least not at the moment. DI North has almost certainly written up his visit and filed an interview report. He could justify his visit."

"He probably could sir, except that I've checked the file both online and for hard copy. There's no record!"

James said nothing. He just looked from Westmore to Jill.

"I have to get back to the station," said Westmore. "I've got an interview to do on a case I was already working on. Sorry, but it's been in the diary for a week."

"Yes, that's fine Peter. And thanks for your quick results."

"I thought you would want to speak with William Topperfield. His contact details are here," said Westmore, handing over a typed sheet. "His business address is the same as his home address. He lives above his shop."

"Thanks again Peter. Stay in touch and let me know about the other victims when you make contact."

Chapter Fifty-Eight

A phone call to William Topperfield established that he was available that afternoon. The two Detectives arranged to visit him at his shop at two thirty. The shop was in Lewes. James and Jill had a bite to eat. Afterwards they spent some more time looking at the case board and throwing around theories, which didn't really get them very far.

They set out for Lewes and had to park a little way from Topperfield's premises.

They walked to the end of the road, which had antiques shops and showrooms on either side. At the very end was an impressive shopfront. There was a large, ornate sign which read: William Topperfield Antiques. Underneath was another sign: Valuations and house clearances.

They entered the shop and the door triggered a brass bell. A man was at the far end of the shop, which was packed with glass cases, full of objects. There were some very old-looking teddy bears, staring glassy-eyed from behind the counter. On the floor was a bright red, vintage, child's pedal car. It had a price tag of £2000 on it.

At the far end of the shop was a tall man. He had, what could be described as, a foppish look. He wore a dark blue, velvet jacket with a carelessly placed, red handkerchief hanging from the top pocket. He wore red trousers and had long, fair hair with sideburns that could grace a Charles Dickens character. He could have been aged anywhere between fifty and sixty.

James stepped forward. "Mr Topperfield?"

"Yes," said the foppish man.

"Good afternoon. We spoke on the phone earlier today. DI Halstead and this is DS Trent."

"Pleased to meet you," said Topperfield, offering a hand with gold rings on three of his fingers.

James shook hands. Jill did likewise but felt that Topperfield held on just a little too long and she was glad when he let go.

"I'll just close the shop. Not much trade after two p.m. normally. Won't you come over here and sit down?" He indicated a much-worn leather settee and an equally worn armchair. James and Jill sat down on the settee and seemed to become engulfed in the soft leather. Topperfield was equally engulfed in the armchair.

"You mentioned some valuations on the phone, Inspector. How can I help you?"

"We have a list here of twenty valuations that you carried out for insurance cover." James showed him a copy of a sheet that Westmore had helpfully typed out. It showed names and addresses.

Glancing at the sheet, Topperfield said,

"Yes, I remember some of these names and addresses. Is there a problem?"

"We'll come to that in a minute, Mr Topperfield. I understand that you have a colleague who carries out the initial valuations."

"Yes, that's right. He writes down the valuations and photographs them if the client so wishes. They all do, because it's a free part of the service."

"Can you tell us, who did the valuations on these addresses?" asked Jill.

"Yes, most certainly." Topperfield got up and rummaged through an old desk, behind the counter. He came back with a large book. He put on a pair of old-looking spectacles He took the typed sheet from James and spent the next ten minutes talking to himself as he compared the names on the sheet with his book. When he had finished, he looked over the top of his spectacles.

"Yes, I can tell you, that all the addresses were attended by Mr Kelp!"

James and Jill shared a glance.

"Mr Arron Kelp?" asked James.

"That's right, Arron Kelp. Really knows his stuff. I was most upset that he just seemed to up and leave. Haven't heard from him for ages. Why, is there a problem?"

"I'm sorry to have to inform you that Arron Kelp is dead."

"Dead!"

"Yes sir. It was in the local newspapers and on local TV. I'm surprised you didn't know."

"I didn't. You see I've been in the USA for the last seven or so weeks; only got back last weekend. Arron wasn't the same after his animal abuse conviction. Said people were really nasty to him. I told him I was disgusted that he had killed his dog. Despite this, I was minded to help rehabilitate him. I didn't want to pressure him to do any valuations. Told him to take some time to reflect. How did he die?"

"He was found locked in a derelict cellar, without food or water."

"What a terrible way to go!"

"Did you ever meet a man named Rolland Meeks?" asked Jill.

"Rolland Meeks? No, I don't think so."

She showed him the photo fit of Meeks.

Topperfield studied it, with glasses on and then off.

"You know, I did see Arron talking to a man who looked a bit like this. I remember thinking that he had the same, long hairstyle as me. Don't see that very much nowadays. Seventies throwback. But I didn't know his name and it was only on the one occasion."

"Where were they when you saw them talking?" asked Jill

"Right outside my shop. Arron was about to enter when this man tapped him on the shoulder."

"Did you hear any conversation?"

"No, I was too far away. I was dealing with a customer and just happened to glance over her shoulder and saw them in the doorway."

"How did they seem? Were they friendly?" asked Jill, getting a little frustrated.

"Hard to tell really. They just had some words and the man walked away. Arron entered the shop, nodded to me and went to the back of the showroom. That's all I can tell you. Sorry. Is it important?"

"We can't really say at this stage," said Jill, with a reassuring smile.

"I think that's all for now, Mr Topperfield," said James.

"You didn't tell me why you've got all these names and addresses Inspector."

"They have all been burgled and the valuable items were taken."

"Oh dear! I don't know what to say. I hope you don't think I'm involved."

"No, I don't Mr Topperfield, but if you intend to leave the country again, I would appreciate it if you would let me know. You can reach me on this number," said James, handing him one of his business cards.

Topperfield said nothing but looked worried.

When they were walking back to the car, Jill said,

"So, it looks as if our theory about Kelp was right."

"Yes, but it doesn't explain why he ended up locked in a cellar!"

"I guess we aren't looking at Mr Topperfield."

"No, I think he's just been duped. Seems like a typical eccentric. I'll get Peter Westmore to check out his USA story, but I believe him."

"Are you up for the gym later? We could have some food there afterwards."

"Yes Jill. I know you miss your workouts. It will use up some energy in case we're tempted to do any other strenuous activity."

They both laughed.

When they got back to the house, Jill typed up the interview with William Topperfield and updated the case board in the secure room. James had agreed with Charteris that they had no need to report back to Brighton police station. They got changed and went to the gym. As they drove, they didn't notice a black van pull out behind them. It kept a discrete distance and pulled into the health club car park. The two Detectives went to their respective changing rooms.

The man who had been driving the black van hadn't got out. He was just sitting there watching.

Later, after a strenuous work out and a less than healthy meal of jacket potato with cheese topping, James and Jill were about to get in their car.

Suddenly, the man who had been sitting in the black van approached them. He had a baseball cap pulled down over his eyes and sunglasses. Without speaking, he punched James hard in the stomach. James went down, winded from the heavy blow. The man immediately grabbed Jill, who tried to kick the man. He had enveloped her in a bear hug and lifted her like a rag doll. He carried her to the black van. The rear doors were already open. He threw Jill inside, locked the door and quickly drove off. James, gasping for air, had regained his feet and was desperately trying to get the registration number of the van as it disappeared from view. Grabbing Jill's handbag from the ground, he jumped into his BMW and sped off after the van. When he got outside the carpark there was no sign of it. He did his best to remain calm, but he felt a massive sense of panic.

He phoned the Brighton police control centre and told them that his DS had been abducted. He gave them the vehicle plate number: EA62 HMW and could only say it was a black van. He then contacted DCI Charteris and quickly explained what had happened. Charteris immediately spoke to the police Inspector, in charge of the traffic division. She confirmed that she would issue instructions to all mobile units to stop and detain the driver of the van.

Despite his training and experience, James was distraught. He blamed himself. He should have put up more resistance but the blow to his stomach had winded him. It had been so easy for the man to snatch Jill. When he had calmed down, he again contacted DCI Charteris with a full description of the attacker. A big man, with a baseball cap and dark glasses. Wearing a white t-shirt, blue jeans with trainers.

Jill had tried to open the doors of the van, but they were locked. There were no windows, so she had no idea where she was. As her hands and feet were free, she thought she might have a chance to escape once the doors were opened. Suddenly the van seemed to pull in somewhere. She heard the driver get out and the sound of a door opening, with a groaning squeak. The driver got back in and the van moved forward. She then heard the door squeak again as it had obviously been slammed shut.

Despite being an experienced police officer, Jill was apprehensive and in truth, a little scared. She was ready to make a move as soon as the van doors were opened. She knew that the man was big and incredibly strong. He had lifted her up as if she weighed nothing.

The van doors suddenly opened. In front of her was a brute of a man. The baseball cap had been discarded and replaced with some kind of Special Forces balaclava. All she could see was the man's eyes. His massive arms were heavily muscled, as he stood back and stared at her.

"OK, you bitch. If you think you're tough, have a go. I don't normally hit women, but there's always a first time."

"What do you want? Who are you?"

"Yes, like I'm going to tell you my name!"

"I'm a police officer."

"Tell me something I don't know. Your mate wasn't much use, was he? One punch and down he went."

Jill was scared of this brute of a man. She considered having a go and kicking out but even if she got lucky, she didn't know if the door was locked. She was still inside the back of the van, so could only see a large, wooden door and part of a wall.

"Step out you bitch," shouted the man.

Jill slowly got out of the van and stood up. She was wearing shorts and a t-shirt, with gym trainers.

"Nice legs!" said the man, obviously leering at her from behind his masked face.

Jill felt very uncomfortable that his eyes were all over her.

"I know, instead of fighting, you and I could have some fun. Bet you'd like that. Make a change from your boss, wouldn't it? Bet you have a lovely time at your safe house."

Jill got ready to fight. If this brute tried to rape her, he wouldn't get away scot free. She could still hurt him, even though he was so strong.

"Relax bitch. As much as I know you'd enjoy it, that's not why you're here."

Jill glanced around. They seemed to be inside some kind of wooden barn. There was an opening high up on one of the walls. Bales of straw were piled up in one corner. There was a bunk bed, a small table, with two bottles of mineral water on it and a bar of chocolate.

"All mod cons, darling. Hope you'll be comfortable here for a few days. Toilet arrangements are a bit primitive," he said, pointing to a bucket, with a toilet roll next to it. Jill said nothing.

"Might even be back later, so we can get to know each other. We'll see. Can't promise anything." He laughed, got the van keys out of the ignition and locked the van. He turned and opened the large door, just enough to squeeze out.

Jill heard what sounded like a chain being threaded through something metallic. Then she heard an engine start up and the noise became distant. She sat on the bunk bed and was worried about James. She knew he would be beside himself with worry and would probably hold himself responsible for her abduction. Jill eyed the bucket and gave a bit of a shudder. Not the best of toilet arrangements!

She stood up and walked around the barn. She checked the wooden walls to see if there was a weak point but found none. She looked up at the window, but it was too high to reach. There was nothing to stand on. Jill went over to some bales of hay. She attempted to move one, but she could only budge it a fraction. The bales were large and must have been put there by mechanical means. The light outside the window was fading. She looked around for any form of lighting. There was nothing. She had no means of lighting a fire either. Even if she had, the heat and smoke would most certainly kill her before she could burn a hole in the wooden wall.

Meanwhile, James was in Sandy Charteris' office.

"This waiting is driving me mad," said James.

"Me too, James. No sightings of the van yet and it's going to be dark in another hour."

"I want to be doing something but where to start looking?"

"Brighton's a big place. She could be anywhere," said Charteris.

"Heard there was a problem," said a voice through the open office door.

It was DI North.

"Your DS has gone missing, I hear. Be a bit lonely at the house tonight!"

James jumped up but Charteris got up and grabbed his arm.

"DI North, you've got a fucking wicked mouth on you and one day someone's going to punch it!"

"That someone would be me, you bastard," said an angry James.

"No offence meant. No point in having a disciplinary for assaulting a fellow officer."

"It would almost be worth it," snarled James.

"DI North, I suggest you piss off before you regret opening your big mouth. And if you do get hit, you won't have a witness. Do I make myself clear?" shouted Charteris.

"Oh, it's like that is it, sir! Well I was just going home. Have a nice evening."

North was gone before James could break away from Charteris' grip on his arm.

Chapter Fifty-Nine

Jill walked around the barn. She couldn't just sit and wait. She had no idea what that gorilla intended to do to her. Her apprehension had now given way to anger. She stood near the bales of hay and felt a draught, which she hadn't noticed before. There was still some light coming through the high window, but it wouldn't last much longer.

She climbed onto the nearest bale of hay. They were piled two high. Jill moved over them towards the draught and looked down at a gap between the bales and the side of the barn. What she saw suddenly raised her spirits. Whoever had stacked the bales had misjudged the distance and the bottom bale had damaged two wooden slats in the wall. She managed to slip down between the bales and the wall. One of the wooden slats was broken and the other was cracked. It was a confined space, but Jill managed to get both her feet against the cracked wooden slat. She used every ounce of her strength. Her leg muscles were strong, from all her gym work. Suddenly the wooden slat gave way and broke. Jill managed to force both slats open until there was a gap in the wall. It looked like a tight fit to squeeze through. She tried to put the nightmare scenario of being wedged between the bales and the wall, to the back of her mind. Jill manoeuvred her body into position to slip through the gap. She managed to get her legs through and then had to contort her body to get out completely. Finally, she was out. By now it was dark. She had no idea of the time because her wristwatch and mobile phone had been in her handbag. She had no money. She didn't know where she was and whether the big man would return and catch her. Jill soon realised that the barn was isolated. There were no other buildings in sight. There were open fields and she could just about make out a wooded area in the distance, because it was picked out against the twilight sky.

She had to make a decision about which direction to go in. She had to move away from the barn. Jill was confident she could probably outrun the big man because of his bulk. But she didn't want to have to do that because one trip in the dark and it would be all over. Jill had been in this situation before. She had been on a training course where the participants had been dropped off in a rural location and had to find their way back to a given point on a map. It had been difficult but at least there had been four or five colleagues to encourage each other. Jill snapped out of these recollections and headed for the wooded area. She was very careful where she trod and despite a couple of stumbles, she made good progress. As she reached the woods, she noticed the rear of a car. Someone had parked there. Jill was cautious in case it was the big man.

She trod stealthily and edged towards the car. The front windows were wound down and cigarette smoke was wafting out. Jill got closer and saw that there were two women sitting in the front of the car. There was no sign of anyone else. She decided to take a chance and approached the car. One of the women gave a startled cry of alarm.

"Where the bloody hell did you come from?" she said, in a slightly strangled voice.

"I'm sorry to make you jump, but I need to use a mobile phone."

"Oh, yeah! Then you run off with it."

"It's not like that. I'm a police officer."

"Show us some ID," said the other woman. "Anyway, why are you dressed in a t-shirt and shorts? Is it standard police wear these days?"

"Look, I'm in trouble. I was grabbed by a man and locked in a barn. I've just escaped and I really need to contact Brighton police."

Both women looked Jill up and down. They looked at each other and then one of them said to Jill,

"Get in the back love, we'll drive you into Brighton. Which nick is it? The central one?"

Jill nodded and jumped into the back of the car. She hadn't realised how tired she was. She was also thirsty and hungry. She hadn't risked drinking the bottled water or eating the chocolate in case they were drugged.

"Thanks. I really appreciate the lift. Where are we by the way?"

"Just outside Brighton," said the woman, who was driving.

"I bet you're wondering what we we're doing parked in the woods?" said the other woman.

"Err…"

"Don't take any notice of Kay, she loves to embarrass people," said the driver. "I'm Mandy by the way. We're partners. Here, take my mobile and make a call if you want. Jill almost grabbed the phone and quickly rang James on his mobile. He picked up at the second ring."

"Jill, are you OK? I've been worried sick. The whole force is looking for you."

"Yes, I'm safe and unhurt. I'm getting a lift to the station. Where are you?"

"I'm with Sandy Charteris. In his office. I'll come out to the carpark to meet you." Jill thanked the two women as she got out of the car. She threw herself into James' arms and they hugged. DCI Charteris just looked at them and they broke off the hug. Charteris recovered his composure.

"Jill, what the hell happened?"

They went inside and sat in Charteris' office. Jill had a rug over her bare legs and she was drinking a large mug of chocolate. James was sitting near her looking both concerned and relieved at the same time. Jill told them the full story and said she would write it up for the files. She had kept one piece of information to herself because she wasn't sure what it meant. She trusted Sandy Charteris and quietly said,

"I think we've got a security problem. The man who grabbed me has inside information. He knows about the safe house!"

Charteris looked deeply concerned.

"It's information known primarily to the police. Your temporary home is going to be sold off in a few months' time, because we're buying a new property the other side of Brighton. Nevertheless, your house is now compromised. The main point is that nobody outside the police should know about it. What did the man say?" asked Charteris.

"He said, 'Bet you have a lovely time at your safe house'."

James didn't react. Then said,

"Someone has leaked it to this man. For all we know, he's been watching us."

"Certainly looks a possibility, James," said a worried Charteris.

James was concerned about Jill. She looked tired.

"I think Jill needs to get some rest."

Charteris nodded.

"I'll get a patrol car to make a regular drive past the safe house. The secure locks will deter any break-in attempts and you only need to hit the alarm and the control centre will have a car there very fast."

James and Jill drove to the safe house. Jill was relieved to be reunited with her handbag. James was really concerned about her, but Jill said she wanted a shower to get the dirt from the barn off her. James felt really sorry for her. He went to his bedroom, showered and changed into his jogging suit. He was sitting on the settee, lost in thought, when Jill came into the room. She was wearing pyjamas and her hair was a bit damp. It looked better without straw in it. She plonked herself down next to James.

"I was so scared James. The man was so big. I thought at one stage he was going to rape me!" She had a tear in the corner of her eye.

"Jill, I'm so, so sorry, I didn't stop him. I…"

"Don't James. It wasn't your fault. He was so bloody powerful. It would've taken a lot of coppers to overpower him."

"I've let you down. One punch and it was all over. Despite my training."

"James, you are sweet. Please don't blame yourself."

"Jill, there is one thing. The man who attacked you was big and strong. Just like the man Oz described."

"Yes, I thought that too. Arron Kelp's friend."

"Big coincidence. Why would he want to grab you?"

"I don't know. But now I'm safe here with you. That's all that counts at the moment."

With that, Jill sat on James' lap and snuggled up to him. James caressed her back and kissed her gently. She felt warm and comfortable. For the first time since her escape, Jill felt completely safe. She was so relaxed after her shower and the exertions of escaping from the barn. Jill fell into a gentle sleep. James didn't mind at all. This lovely, precious woman was cuddled up to him. How could he have let her down? He wanted to hold her like this forever. James was content, listening to Jill's soft breathing.

After about an hour, he spoke gently into her ear as he rubbed her back. Jill stirred and smiled. James helped her off his lap and walked her to her bedroom. He stopped at the door and gave her a soft kiss on the lips.

Jill walked sleepily to her bed and drifted back into sleep. James got into his own bed and smiled with relief that Jill was safe and unhurt.

The scene at Bob North's flat wasn't pleasant. North was standing drinking his third whiskey of the evening. The massive figure of Terry Dalton was pacing up and down. He was drinking a bottle of lager and gesticulating with his free hand.

"How many times do I have to tell you? She got away. That's all there is to it!"

North was angry.

"I told you that fucking bitch was clever. You should have tied her up. But oh no! You just left her to wander around and look for an escape route. Very fucking clever! What is it about you? You didn't tie that prat Daynes up either."

"I didn't think there was any way to get out of the barn. The window was too high. The door was padlocked from outside and I took the key out of the van and locked it."

"It's a wonder you just didn't leave the key in the van. She could have driven out through the fucking wall then!"

"Look, I'm upset as well. I was going to go back and have a bit of fun with her tonight."

"The whole idea of grabbing her was to break up their little team. Halstead would've been distracted and looking for revenge. It would have given us a chance to tie up some loose ends. Instead, we've alerted them. It won't be easy to disrupt them now."

"I could grab her again."

"Are you fucking mad? You got away with it once. But as much as I hate them both, they're smart and straight. Two things that make them dangerous to us."

"Well, where do we go now?"

"We just leave them alone for a while and get on with our new expanded business. I think we can trust Carter. He's shit-scared of Ledbetter and won't cross him. The next shipment is due in two days."

Chapter Sixty

James and Jill were eating breakfast when James' mobile rang.

"Morning sir. Well yes, that would be nice. Are you sure? That's really great. Thank you."

"Good news, James?"

"Good news if you fancy a day off with me."

"Really?"

"Yes, Sandy Charteris wants you to take a day off after your kidnapping. He said you can file your report tomorrow. I gave the photo fit guys a description of the big bloke, yesterday. Baseball cap pulled low and big dark glasses. Built like an 'outside toilet'."

"What do you want to do today, James?"

"Why don't we take a drive up to the south downs? We could have lunch at a pub and get some fresh air."

"I would love to do that."

"And don't worry about that big bloke. Next time, I'll be ready for him. Between the two of us we should be able to take him."

"Yes, James. No match at all. Two to one."

"Seriously Jill, are you sure you're OK?"

"Yes. I'm very tough."

They drove up to the top of Beachy Head, found a parking area and were a little dismayed to see a ticket machine. Nothing's free any more.

They climbed up the hill from the carpark and from the top, the car looked like a toy. They strolled along the cliff tops and saw a group of students, making their way along a well-trodden path. They reflected upon how lucky these young people were to be able to enjoy the fresh air and be apparently carefree. They walked for a couple of miles before sitting down by the side of the path. They both wore their off-duty casual gear. The usual shorts and t-shirts with hoodies and trainers. They felt nothing like cops! They felt like lovers. Boyfriend and girlfriend, enjoying each other's company and feeling very close.

The trauma of yesterday's events was still at the back of their minds but neither mentioned it. Jill laughed because she had fallen asleep on James' lap the previous evening. He told her that he had enjoyed every minute and that he had watched her sleeping. They eventually got back to the car after a long walk back down to the carpark. They drove to the Tiger Inn, a lovely old pub in a picturesque setting, in East Dean. They managed to get a table outside in the gardens. After lunch, they had a stroll around the village. When they got back to the Brighton house, they were both tired. James prepared his pasta bake special, washed down with a merlot.

They spent the rest of the evening watching a TV police series and laughed that they couldn't get away from the day job. They both drifted off to sleep on the settee, woke up, past midnight and went to their rooms.

****

Ryan Ledbetter had set out for a night crossing to France. He had a couple of companions. They were thickset men in their late thirties. Brian Taylor and Stuart Crowe worked for Ledbetter at his Brighton club. They were doormen but their modern title was security assistants. They were adept at sorting out any trouble at the Brighton club. Their shaven heads and well-muscled shoulders were normally enough to deter troublemakers. On the odd occasions when it didn't, they reverted to old fashioned methods, which meant a quiet word round the back of the club. Both men were heavily involved in Ledbetter's business activities and ran his club, when he was away on his sailing trips. They were more than just hired muscle.

Ledbetter was an experienced sailor and ensured that his vessel had all the appropriate lights showing. The modern navigation equipment made it easy to travel on the seas, by both day and night. Just a rich businessman out for a trip; perhaps a bit of night fishing. Their real reason for this night excursion was a bit riskier than just a pleasure trip or fishing. It was something that Ledbetter had done many times, with a very clever twist.

Ledbetter never drank alcohol on these trips. His two companions had a bottle of coke each, because Ledbetter had strict rules aboard his boat, whenever he was at sea. When in harbour, it was a different matter altogether. But just now, it was a dry trip.

Chapter Sixty-One

The next morning, DCI Sandy Charteris rang James and suggested that they have their meeting at the safe house, rather than at his office. By the time he arrived, James and Jill had finished breakfast and were dressed for work.

"You seem to have settled in quite well. This may well be the last week you stay here."

"Really sir?" asked a surprised James.

"Yes. After what happened, I was wondering to myself just how safe this house really is."

"The man snatched me from outside the gym. Not from here."

"I know, but he knows about this house. We'll give it some thought, after we discuss the incident and your investigations."

Jill had typed up the whole story about the kidnap, before breakfast. She gave Charteris a hard copy of the report, which she had printed off in the secure room. Charteris was unaware at this stage of the case board on the office wall. They took him into the room and he stared at the board.

"You have been busy. The board back at the station looks a bit bare, compared with this."

"We didn't feel ready to share some of this. The only other person who's seen it is DC Westmore," said James, feeling a little sneaky.

"It's OK James, I told you to be careful what you report. We all know that DI North is up to something."

"Sir, how long are we going to keep this up? I mean, can't you step in and hand it all to Professional Standards?"

Jill looked at James, then at Charteris. She wondered whether James had overstepped the mark with Charteris.

After about a minute, Charteris spoke.

"James, I've told you how sensitive this is. You know the orders on this come from the top. If they wanted North investigated officially, they would do it in an instant. They obviously don't."

James just shrugged his shoulders.

"Yes sir. In the meantime, we just plough on?"

"Yes, you just plough on. Now talk to me about your theories."

They went through the whole case. Charteris just sat on an office chair and didn't interrupt. He nodded at some of the points and even looked slightly surprised at others. He was particularly interested about DI North, apparently not recording an interview with the man who had his antique watches stolen. He hadn't actually commented. He merely shook his head.

When the briefing ended, he steepled his fingers and looked over the top of them.

"So, let me get this straight. You think Kelp and Meeks, were part of the antiques robbery gang. Kelp did a number of antique insurance valuations on behalf of Mr Topperfield. Coincidentally, all the people he visited became robbery victims. The car number plate, AE61 BUS, was found in Meeks' lockup. You think the big man, seen with Kelp in Lewes, could be the man who kidnapped you, Jill. You've no idea what the connection is between the two. You think that DI North is somehow involved in the burglaries, based entirely on his apparent poor case management. You have nothing concrete and when I broached it with him recently, he put it down to pressure of work and administrative errors. I do wonder why North didn't think about the connection between the valuations. He's an experienced Detective. Looking for patterns or common factors is second nature!" Charteris was on a roll now. He raised a hand when James tried to speak.

"The apparently accidental death of Steven Daynes, the man who attacked DS Read and the two of you beat up. Sorry Jill, detained, has no proven link to the burglaries? You say he does have links to Fancy Carter, who to my knowledge has pretty, heavyweight solicitors. Since the discovery of drugs at Daynes' flat, the drugs team are taking over the Daynes case. Does that sum it all up?"

"Yes sir," said James. "There's a few loose ends. We're waiting for DC Westmore to make contact with the remaining four burglary victims to confirm who did their insurance valuations."

Charteris had made up his mind.

"I think it's time to put the cat among the pigeons. I want you both to come to the office this afternoon and update the case board with everything you've told me. Include your query about the big man and his apparent friendship with Kelp."

"But won't that alert DI North? If he's in any way involved, he may be forced to do something."

"Yes, he may James." Charteris turned and looked at Jill. "You've not said much, Jill. Are you sure you're OK to carry on? Do you want a word with the police counsellor?"

"No sir, I'm fine. I was a bit shaken up but I'm over it now. I just want to solve the case."

Attempting to lighten things up, Charteris said,

"Are you two getting on all right, living under the same roof? It can't be easy, living with your boss." Charteris gave a sort of half smile which indicated a lot more than he was saying.

"No problem at all Sir. DI Halstead is fully housetrained." Jill smiled.

Charteris returned her smile and James shuffled his feet but said nothing.

After Charteris left, Jill called across to James who was sitting at the kitchen table with a case file.

"Do you think DCI Charteris was implying something, James?" "What do you mean?"

"James Halstead, you know exactly what I mean."

"Oh, that you and I are more than colleagues, you mean."

"Yes."

"Well are we, Jill?"

"You know we are. I love you James." Jill walked over to James and kissed him on the lips. She was wearing a nice summer dress, which showed off her slim figure. James put his arms around her waist, as she stood in front of him. Jill put her arms around his shoulders. They both felt a charge of sexual electricity. James's mobile rang. He desperately wanted to ignore it, but he released Jill and answered it.

It was DC Peter Westmore. Two of the remaining burglary victims had used Topperfield for valuations. Two had used Ludo Chambers.

When the call had ended, James and Jill looked at each other. They had been so very close to making their relationship intimate. Both knew it and accepted that the moment had gone. Jill said mischievously,

"James, there's no escape, you know."

"I know Jill. It's like they say in books. If you wait for a long time, the sex is just great, when it happens."

"I'll hold you to that, DI Halstead. What books have you been reading?"

That afternoon James and Jill arrived at the Brighton police station and set about updating the case board. They included everything they had, including some question marks underneath points of speculation. When they finally finished, they sat down and had coffee. DC Westmore had helped them to put everything together. It was very impressive.

At around four p.m., DI North and DS Read walked into the room. The updated board immediately caught North's eye and he stood in front of it rubbing his face. Jackie Read looked at it too. North was about to say something, when DCI Charteris walked in.

Gesturing towards the case board, he said,

"Impressive, isn't it?"

North was clearly agitated.

"How comes all this extra information has suddenly been put up? I didn't know about any of this!"

"DI Halstead and DS Trent have been working on some theories. I asked them to update the case board. Any observations, would be appreciated."

North was red in the face.

"My first observation is that we were supposed to be working as a team. Why wasn't this stuff put up on a daily basis? I feel as if DS Read and me have been excluded. I'd like to remind you sir, that this was my case originally and…"

Charteris cut him off.

"DI North, you aren't in competition here. DI Halstead and DS Trent were specifically asked to join the investigation team. I've let all of you have your head on this case and at last, it seems we are making some progress. What's your problem?"

"My problem?" shouted North, 'is that the team hasn't been working. We haven't communicated, except when there are suggestions that I've cocked something up or misplaced a file. I don't call that team working!"

James and Jill just looked at North. They didn't speak. Jackie Read was about to say something, when Charteris turned to her.

"DS Read, have you an opinion on what's been said?"

Jackie Read spoke very softly.

"No sir, no opinion."

North was getting more and more wound up.

"Thanks a bunch, Sergeant!"

Charteris ignored the outburst. "Now that we've heard your views DI North, what do you think about the theories and connections?"

North composed himself and standing by the case board he spoke.

"So, we think Kelp and Meeks were part of the burglary gang. The big guy seen with Kelp, could have been the same person who grabbed DS Trent. The link between Kelp, Topperfield and the break ins could be significant or a coincidence. The two valuations by this Chambers guy breaks the connection somewhat, because the people who engaged him were also robbed. Suppose you think he's involved in the burglaries as well?"

"It's possible," offered Jill.

North scoffed at her remark. Charteris didn't comment but maintained a firm expression as he looked at North.

North, who had been relatively calm, suddenly noticed a question mark with a note under it, which said, 'Mr Morris, Antique watches, fight outside club. No record of DI North interview reports on file. Need to resolve.'

North's demeanour suddenly changed.

"Oh, I see. Another fucking cock up from good old DI North," he shouted, bits of spittle forming on his lips.

Jackie Read stepped in and grabbed his arm.

"Calm down, Bob. I'm sure there's an explanation." She looked at James and Jill.

"Might have been an idea to have asked DI North about it, before putting it up on display!"

James who had been quiet, responded.

"It was just something that cropped up during our research. Perhaps you're right Jackie. We could have asked about it first, I suppose."

"You suppose?" said a slightly calmer North. He then walked over to the round table and sat down. He was joined by Jackie Read. Everyone was looking at DCI Charteris, who had, as was his habit, steepled his hands.

He looked around the table.

"I for one think that we've got a bit closer to the truth. The safe house has been compromised, because Jill's kidnapper mentioned it when he was holding her. If it's the same big man who may be involved in the burglaries, then someone is clearly getting rattled."

"That's a big 'If'," said North. "This so-called big guy might well have been known to Kelp, but I see no actual link between that and DS Trent's apparent kidnapping."

"There's no apparent about it!" said an annoyed James. "Jill was grabbed and anything could have happened to her, if she hadn't escaped."

North gave a sharkish smile.

"Sorry, DI Halstead, I've obviously hit a nerve."

DCI Charteris was becoming fed up with the sarcastic comments.

"Look, all of you. This is supposed to be a team. And DI North, I don't much care for your attitude. I suggest we call it a day. I'm stopping these 4 p.m. meetings, because I don't see the need for them now. Just get together if you feel you have anything to contribute. Otherwise, use your mobiles. Is that clear?"

All four nodded and stood up to go.

"By the way, the Drug Squad have got an interview booked with Norman Carter tomorrow at ten thirty. He's coming in with his solicitor to discuss his relationship with the drowned man, Steven Daynes. I want the four of you sitting in the viewing room. I've given DI Freeman a copy of your interview with Carter," he said to James. Nodding towards Jackie and Jill, he added, "As this Daynes was involved in the knife attack, you have an interest."

"Do you need me there, sir?" asked North. "I've got a meeting lined up with one of my informants, tomorrow morning. Might have some important info on the burglaries."

Charteris seemed to think for a minute.

"OK DI North. You can give it a miss, but I want the rest of you there."

Chapter Sixty-Two

North went straight to the carpark and got his throwaway mobile out of the glovebox of his car. He inserted the sim card and rang.

"You know who this is. Don't mention my name, just listen. I hear you're being interviewed tomorrow, by the Drug Squad. They'll want to know about Daynes. Just a friendly reminder to keep your fat gob shut!"

"Yes, I know you've got your solicitor involved. Just remember that you know nothing of your mate's activities. I saw the statement you gave Batman and Robin. Just stick to it. You don't want to go for a late-night swim, do you?"

"Calm down, I'm just reminding you. There's a lot at stake. Don't fuck things up for me. I make a bad enemy!"

North clicked off and removed the sim. Jackie Read slipped into the passenger seat.

"Bob, you must be mad to keep having a go at everybody. Jill could have been raped or killed. You've no right to trivialise it."

"I don't really care what happens to the bitch. Her and her lover tried to set me up. Missing interview notes. What a fucking joke!"

"Charteris won't put up with your insubordination for ever. He'll break you and you'll be gone."

North turned and looked Jackie in the eye.

"Listen Jack. I'm thinking of walking away from all this. The job, Brighton, everything."

"Where would you go and what about your pension?"

"Fuck the pension. I already told you I don't care. I'm not short of a bob. Thing is Jack, how would you like to come with me?"

"Come with you, to where?"

"Jersey first off, then Spain. I've got a place out there."

"I didn't know about that. How long have you had it?"

"Doesn't matter. Don't give me an answer now. But I need to know in the next couple of weeks. I've got something on the go and then I'm history in this place."

Jackie was dumfounded. She hadn't expected this at all. She and North had been in a relationship for a while and at first it was good. She had really fancied this rough diamond in the early days of the relationship. The sex had been great and they had shared a few laughs along the way.

In recent times, North had changed. He'd been distracted. The incident with Fancy Carter's laptop had spoilt things. She no longer trusted North because he had used her. Looking back, the laptop thing had been weird. North had told her that Carter always kept the laptop locked away and took it with him on stage engagements. Having seen the copied content, she couldn't see why. She had deep regrets. She had been unprofessional. She had got too close. What a mess!

Her thoughts were suddenly interrupted by North.

"You've a lot to think about, Jack. Just let me know what you decide. Perhaps we could rekindle our relationship. We've not had any 'How's your father', for a while. I might get fed up with waiting."

Jackie didn't answer. She got out and went to her car. North drove off. Jackie was lost in thought for another few minutes and then left the car park.

James and Jill decided to spend the evening in. It was James's turn to cook, so he opted for take away pizza. Jill told him he was cheating but she really fancied a pizza. They had showered and changed into their sports clothes. The pizza delivery man arrived and James had double-checked him through the spyhole in the front door. They ate on their laps and drank Jill's favourite merlot. James got some chocolate ice-cream from the freezer and after clearing everything away, they sat on the settee, drinking wine and listening to some smooth jazz. They were both feeling a little tired. Jill laid on the settee, with her legs over James' lap. He gently massaged her legs as they relaxed.

"Don't worry James, I'm not going to fall asleep on you tonight," Jill laughed.

"You've still got some scratches on your knees."

"It was from scrabbling around on bales of hay."

"I know. Jill, I'm so lucky to have you. I really do love you and I know I've said it before but, I was so scared I'd lost you."

"I was thinking of you all the time. I was worried that you would be worried sick about me," said Jill, with a little tear in the corner of her eye.

"Thank goodness it turned out all right," said James, gently rubbing Jill's knees.

Neither had discussed North, either in the car, back to the house or before they had eaten.

"Jill, what did you make of North's behaviour?"

"A man under pressure. I'm convinced he's bent."

"Me too. My instinct is that something's about to break. He was almost manic when he saw the piece about missing interview notes."

"I felt sorry for Jackie. They obviously had a good relationship at one time."

"You know Jill, I'm worried about her. I think North is the sort of man who could do just about anything, if he felt cornered. He's a real brute when his temper's up."

"She's a tough lady, James. You saw what she did to Steven Daynes. She goes to the gym and she's fit. She's a stone heavier than me and Daynes was lucky she didn't do him more damage than just a couple of broken ribs."

"I know, but she had you to help her. Imagine if North really kicked off. Or that big guy grabbed her, like he did to you."

"Yes, he picked me up like a rag doll."

"Don't, I still have nightmares about what he could have done to you, my precious Jill."

Jill sat up and kissed him. James responded. They were locked together for ages and then, reluctantly, they both went to bed in their respective rooms.

****

The next morning James, Jill and Jackie, all sat in the viewing room, watching Carter and his solicitor, waiting, in interview room four. They had been there for ten minutes

Fancy Carter looked nervous. His solicitor, Justin Bale of Bale and Ambrose, was a middle-aged man, with longish, silver hair and heavy black-rimmed glasses, perched on the end of his large nose. James was quite relieved that the Daynes case was now in the hands of the Drug Squad. He had enough on his hands, with the two so called retribution killings. There was also no evidence that Daynes had been murdered but the drugs haul found at his flat definitely made it a case for the drugs team.

Two Detectives entered the room. DI Freeman was a smartly dressed woman in her mid-thirties. She had short, dark brown hair and wore a blue business suit. Her unsmiling demeanour suggested that DI Freeman was a no-nonsense police officer.

DC Layne was younger and had shoulder length, black hair, tied in a ponytail. She wore a green dress and had a writing pad in front of her. She had a softer expression than her boss.

DI Freeman looked directly into Carter's eyes. Carter felt intimidated but didn't react.

"Mr Carter, you are not here under caution. It's a purely voluntary interview and you have chosen to have your solicitor present. You can choose to leave at any time. This interview is not being recorded on tape. We will take notes and send you a copy, as requested by your solicitor. Do you understand this?"

"Yes."

"Mr Carter, would it be correct to say that the late Steven Daynes, was known to you?"

"Yes."

"Can you tell me how you knew him?"

"He was a casual acquaintance."

"I have here, notes of an interview between you, DI Halstead and

DS Trent."

She passed a copy to Justin Bale, who cast his eyes over it, made a couple of brief notes and placed it in front of Carter.

"You told my colleagues that you didn't know where Steven Daynes resided and you didn't have a contact telephone number because it was on a mobile, which you lost. Is this correct?"

"Yes."

"Are you aware of what Steven Daynes did for a living?"

"No."

"What would you say, if I told you that a quantity of Class A drugs were found hidden in Steven Daynes' flat?"

Justin Bale leaned across and spoke quietly into Carter's ear. He then looked at the two Detectives and spoke in a posh fruity voice.

"Mr Carter is extremely surprised to hear this information." Carter just stared ahead and didn't engage the Detectives.

"So, you have no idea why Steven Daynes, would have a quantity of drugs in his flat?"

"I think you will find that I have already provided you with an answer to your previous question Detective Inspector. To recap, Mr Carter is extremely surprised to hear that drugs were apparently found in Steven Dayne's flat. He therefore cannot be expected to speculate about the reason," said Bale, getting a large, red handkerchief from his pocket and loudly blowing his nose into it.

"Mr Carter, can you tell us anything more about your friend?"

"Casual acquaintance, Inspector," replied Bale, shoving the red handkerchief back into a pocket.

DC Layne spoke.

"Mr Carter, have you any idea why Steven Daynes, would be in the sea, fully clothed? Was he into sea fishing?"

"DC Layne, given that Mr Carter was only a casual acquaintance of the deceased and didn't have intimate knowledge of his activities, it's most unlikely that he could answer your question," said Bale, in a condescending voice.

"Thank you, sir," said Layne, with an unconvincing smile.

"Unless you have anything to add, Mr Carter," said Freeman.

"Nothing to add," said a slightly relieved Carter.

"In that case, I would like to thank you for your cooperation. DC Layne will email you a copy of her notes, from this informal interview. Mr Bale, if you or Mr Carter have any comments on the notes, I would appreciate it if you would let me know. DC Layne will see you out."

James Halstead looked at Jill and Jackie.

"Well, that was really illuminating."

"As the old saying goes, he was only lying when his lips were moving," observed Jackie.

"And that solicitor is as slippery as an eel," said Jill.

DI Freeman and DC Layne entered the viewing room.

"What a performance that was, Linda," said James.

"Yes," she shrugged. "Move along, nothing to see here. DC Layne will email a copy of her notes to you, James. In the meantime, we'll just keep on digging."

"Any progress with the notebook we found at Steven Daynes' place?" asked Jill.

"Nothing we can use. Just a load of Christian names and what appear to be passwords. Of course, it could be a client list for drug customers or perhaps dealers but without surnames or any other notes; it could be anything. Got to go now. Keep in touch."

The two Drug Squad Detectives left. Jackie Read watched them disappear.

"I wouldn't want to piss Linda Freeman off."

James and Jill nodded, in agreement.

Chapter Sixty-Three

Later that day, DI North was with Terry Dalton. The two were sitting in North's car near Birling Gap, on the South Downs. They were making plans.

North wore a worried expression.

"We need to get out, Terry."

"Why, what's happened?"

"Things are getting a bit too hot. Batman and Robin are putting things together. They suspect you're involved in Kelps' murder and the kidnapping of the lovely Jill."

"Yeah, shame she got away. I would've enjoyed a rough and tumble in the hay with the bitch. They've no idea of my identity, have they?"

"No, not yet. Time to move on though. Are you set for tonight?"

"Yeah, everything's ready. My mate's looking forward to some night fishing."

"You've got to get to the buoys before daylight."

"No problem. What about Carter?"

"He's always got a lot of cash stashed away. He'll buy the merchandise and then we can make a move. Look, I might take Jackie along with us. She's thinking about my offer to take off with me."

"Glad you said that Bob. I want to bring Angie along."

"How big's the fucking boat?"

"Big enough for five or six people."

"And your mate can get us across the channel?"

"Yeah, piece of piss. Don't worry. He's been back and forward for the last three years. He runs fishing trips in the channel. The coastguard ignores him now."

"Let's hope so. I don't want to go through all this trouble, just to get stopped and searched in mid channel."

"Stop worrying. Your mate Ledbetter's been doing the cross channel run for ages and hasn't had a sniff from the coastguard."

"He's had a lot of info from me on the 'Cormorant' security systems that's why, but I can't fix the coastguard!"

"Anyway, I'm bringing Angie along when we leave for the continent."

"She'll need to keep her mouth shut about the trip."

"Don't worry, I'll tell her it's a surprise boat trip. Give her a bit of spending money and she'll be as good as gold."

"You need to keep an eye on her."

"What about Jackie? Can you trust her?"

"If I can't, you might have to make sure she doesn't talk!"

"I've already killed two people for you."

"Not for me. For us! Kelp got greedy and Meeks got careless and what was all that cat killing about? The sick bastard!"

"Almost made me heave when I saw all the dead cats in his freezers."

North didn't respond. Then Terry looked earnest.

"I'm not killing anyone else. Especially Jackie Read."

"You would have hurt Jill Trent."

"Hurt her and had fun with her but no way would I have killed her."

"Just forget about Jackie. I'm sure she'll come with me, so it won't be a problem."

Later that evening, James and Jill had gone to the pictures and had a fish and chip supper in Brighton. They were both thinking about life after the safe house. Charteris had told them that this was definitely their last week there. He also told them to deploy all the security devices. The three weeks had gone quickly and, in that time, they had fallen in love. What would it be like to go back to their respective flats? How would their love affair develop? Their professional and private lives were merging.

Ryan Ledbetter was returning from France and was sailing along the south coast, just off Eastbourne, near the foot of Beachy Head. He slowed down and called out to his two companions, who were out on deck. Brian Taylor and Stuart Crowe, each held red buoys attached to lobster cages.

Inside the cages were packages wrapped in heavy duty, waterproof plastic bags. At a given signal, the two men heaved their lobster cages overboard. The buoys bobbed around in the foam and Ledbetter increased the throttle, until the cabin cruiser was making headway, towards Sovereign Harbour, where the boat was berthed. Ledbetter was wary of the security provided by Project Cormorant. He couldn't risk entering the harbour with the goods and getting searched. The contents of the waterproof packages, currently sitting on the seabed inside the lobster cages, would almost certainly send him and his men to prison. He smiled because he was too smart for the authorities.

Ledbetter entered the harbour lock and the keeper waved to him from high up near the lock gates. The keeper was an honest man and a previous attempt by one of Ledbetter's associates to 'buy' him had failed. The associate had been arrested, but the lack of witnesses had meant a successful prosecution was out of the question.

Ledbetter and his men sat in the comfortable lounge, on board the cruiser. All three were sipping malt whiskey and celebrating another, potentially profitable venture.

"Right. Just after dawn, my mate Charlie will go and collect the lobsters," said a grinning Ledbetter.

They all laughed. Stuart Crowe was curious.

"Don't the security people patrol the inshore areas twenty-four hours a day?"

"Yes, they do, and I get a heads up about schedules but here's the thing. Human nature works in our favour. It's called familiarity. Charlie has kept his little fishing boat on the East Beach for donkey's years. The security people know him and his boat and don't give him a second glance. One time the winch on the beach got stuck, just as he was hauling his boat up. And would you believe it? Two security guys helped him to free the mechanism and get his boat up. The big laugh was, that two kilos of cocaine were still inside the lobster cages. They were well covered up but they didn't know they were helping the drugs trade!"

The three men laughed and poured some more whiskey.

Much later, about 3 a.m., a fishing boat was making its way along the shoreline. It was approaching the location of the red buoys. Terry was shining a torch and because his mate had put lobster cages in this spot himself over the years, it was fairly easy to locate the two they were seeking. His mate was named Dave. He was Terry's fishing friend and had two things going for him. He would do anything if the money was right and he knew how to keep his mouth shut. There were rocks under the sea in this location, which meant that lobsters were often found here. Terry hauled the two buoys into the boat. He smiled when he saw the lobster traps. The entry hole to the cages had been blocked off with wire, to prevent lobsters from getting inside. There was very little room, beside the plastic packages anyway.

Dave gave a little laugh.

"I'd love to see Charlie French's face when he comes looking for the buoys."

"Charlie French?" asked Terry, looking puzzled.

"He keeps a fishing boat along the beach from me. He'd do anything for money, no matter how bent it is."

"Just like you, you old bastard."

Dave just smiled as they made for shore.

The fishing boat made its way to the East Beach and Terry helped to winch the boat onto the beach. The winch was the key to launching and recovering boats from this area. Night fishing was a regular activity. Terry looked around and made sure that nobody was in the vicinity. His car was parked around the back of some fish-processing sheds. He walked to his car and when he was satisfied there were no security people lurking, he went back to the boat. He retrieved the plastic packages from the lobster cages and put them inside a holdall. He nonchalantly strolled to his car and he was soon heading out of Eastbourne and onto the bypass. He picked up the Brighton road and drove at a sensible speed, to avoid attracting attention from police patrol cars.

He made a few detours, to make sure he wasn't being followed. He eventually arrived at Bob North's flat, where he and North sat in the lounge and congratulated themselves for a lucrative early morning's work.

Bob North laughed.

"Can you imagine Ledbetter's face, when he finds out the coke has gone?"

"Yeah, he'll be looking for blood!"

"As long as it's not ours, I don't give a fuck!" laughed North.

Just before dawn, a little fishing boat made its way along the coast, close to shore. Anyone watching from the beach, would have seen the little boat making several passes near the shoreline. Whoever was on board seemed to be searching for something; apparently without success. This continued for an hour. The fishing boat started to move out further from the beach and then turned and headed back along the coast.

Ryan Ledbetter was snoozing in his cabin. His two companions were in another part of the cabin cruiser. The whiskey had taken its toll and both men were snoring. Ledbetter was jolted awake by the ringtone of his mobile.

"What? I don't fucking believe it! Can't find them? Did you look in the right place? I know you're not fucking stupid, but the buoys can't just drift away." He threw his mobile onto his bed and stormed into the cabin where his two men, were awake but groggy.

"What's all the shouting, boss?" asked Brain Taylor.

"The fucking buoys weren't there for the pickup."

"We secured them boss. You saw us doing it. No way they can't be there!"

"No way unless some bastard took them and the drugs with them."

"But who would know? And besides, nobody would be stupid enough to cross you, boss."

"Nobody stupid, but somebody clever."

"What do we do?" asked a barely awake, Stuart Crowe.

"We go looking and I know where to start."

Ledbetter grabbed his mobile.

"Bob, it's Ryan. I know what time it is. Time we had a little chat. Meet me at my club at eight this morning. I'll tell you what for, when I see you. And Bob, it's not a fucking request!"

Chapter Sixty-Four

Bob North did as he was told and turned up at Ledbetter's Brighton club just after 8 a.m.

Ledbetter was alone in his office.

"Drink Bob?" He asked, nodding towards a row of spirits on a corner cabinet.

"Too early for me Ryan. What's this all about?"

"It's about the cocaine."

"How much did you bring over?"

"Four kilos."

"After cutting, we could make it stretch into a big profit."

"Yeah, except. I don't have it."

"What do you mean?"

"I mean, that some bastard has stolen it."

"Stolen it?"

"You heard."

"Any idea who?"

"That's why you're here."

"You want me to find out, who?"

"Let's not fuck about. Apart from me and my two associates, the only other person who knew about the drop, is you!"

"Me? What are you fucking getting at? Do you really think after all this time working together, I'd double-cross you, Ryan? Do you think I'm fucking mad or something?"

"I could get my boys to ask you."

"Yes, and the answer would still be the same. And Ryan, I don't like being threatened. I'm a copper."

"Yeah. A bent copper. You've had your cut from every drug deal and the same goes for the antiques trade. I've even let you buy drugs from me to sell, so don't give me all that copper shit."

"So, what are you saying?"

"I'm saying that some bastard is going to pay for stealing from me. Nobody does that to Ryan Ledbetter."

"Aw, come on Ryan. This isn't a gangster movie."

"No, it's more serious. You find out who's got my drugs and I'll deal with them. I want some results, otherwise cop or no cop, my men will be asking you some questions. Do I make myself clear, Bob?"

"Crystal, Ryan. I'll get back to you," said Bob, not wanting to antagonise Ledbetter.

It was still early and Bob went back to his flat. The cocaine had been stashed at a nearby lockup. Terry had gone home and Bob was preparing for his exit. He needed to convert the cocaine into hard cash. He knew just the man to go to. No other than the self-proclaimed King of Comedy, Fancy Carter. He was of course aware, that Carter had been informally questioned by the Drugs Squad over his association with Steven Daynes. He also knew that the police had no hard evidence that Carter was involved with the deceased or that he had any connection with drugs himself. North had to play this carefully. He needed to find out whether there was any surveillance on Carter. Those drug squad bastards were capable of anything. In truth he was a little intimidated by DI Freeman. She was nobody's fool and had made some important drug busts in the past. The last thing he wanted was to have her on his case, before his great escape to the easy life. He hoped that Jackie Read would agree to go with him. Although he would sacrifice anyone to achieve his goal, he would only deal with Jackie if he really had no choice.

James and Jill were up early and eating breakfast. They had discussed the end of their stay at the safe house and had been a little down at the prospect of not sharing a home together. They both felt a little embarrassed because they hadn't broached the possibility of living together at either of their respective flats. They had considered the possibility, privately, but neither had mentioned it out loud. The time to say something was probably approaching fast and they both knew it.

Just as they were about to leave for the office, Jill's mobile rang.

"Hello. Oh, hi Roy, how are you? Great. Yes, I'm fine too. The cats? Yes. I hope it all went well. I bet it was really sad for the owners. Yes, I suppose at least it gave them closure. Really? Have you got it? Roy, just hold onto it. We need to meet this morning. In the same coffee shop will be fine. My Inspector will definitely want to come along as well. Have you reported it to my colleagues in Lewes? No, that's OK, I understand. What time? Yes, great. Look forward to seeing you. Bye."

"What was that all about?" asked a curious James.

"You're not going to believe it but that was Roy, the RSPCA Inspector. He's been reuniting frozen cats with their owners, by trying to match them with photos, cat collars and microchip information. Guess what? One of the owners found a note, inside the bag containing their cat."

"A note?"

"Yes. A note. It's from Rolland Meeks."

"What's it say? I confess I killed your cat?"

"Better than that. It's a confession about the antique robberies. It names, names."

"Did Roy read it to you?"

"No, he's a bit wary. Didn't want to say too much over the phone."

The two Detectives met up with Roy at the coffee shop. They managed to grab a corner table and were soon sitting with cappuccinos. Jill introduced Roy and James to each other. Roy made a joke about the 'Two Js', which raised a smile from everyone.

"We've got a colleague named Jackie, at Brighton Police station, so that makes three 'Js'", said Jill, biting into a croissant and brushing the crumbs off the front of her jacket.

Then it was suddenly serious. Roy took a plastic envelope out of his shoulder bag and handed it to James.

James examined it briefly.

"You've looked at the contents, Roy?"

"Yes, sorry. I didn't know what it was. I haven't told anyone about it. The cat owner saw it through the wrapping around her cat and just pulled it out and gave it to me. She didn't look at the contents, because it was sealed inside the plastic bag, in an envelope."

James and Jill looked at the note. It was on two sheets of foolscap and written in spidery, but legible handwriting.

In case I don't make it, I want to tell you all about the antique robberies. My mate Arron Kelp was killed because he got careless, according to Terry. He was our valuations man. He really knew his stuff. But he started taking the odd item from our haul and sold them to a fence. Terry and the boss found out and Terry locked him in a basement to die. Terry said it served him right for what he did to his dog.

We sell the antiques on the continent, to dealers who don't ask questions. There's a man with a boat at the Eastbourne harbour. He takes the stuff across. There are two antique dealers, who have the contacts abroad. They take a cut for arranging the sales. I don't know their names, but I heard Terry talking to the boss on the phone about a guy with a funny name. Ludo, I think it was.

Don't know the name of the boss. I do know he's a copper. Me, Arron and Terry do the break ins. I'm writing this because Terry had a go at me. I made a silly mistake. I was seen by someone. Terry told me there was a police computer image of me, called it a photo, something. Said I'd put everyone in danger. Said there were two smart-arsed police Detectives asking questions. Even said my van number plate had been seen.

I'm sorry about the cats. I can't help it. Can't stop. Don't mean to kill them. I keep them all safe in the freezer. I know Terry and the boss will want to shut me up. Terry could go down for murdering Arron and now I think I'm next. This note is my bit of revenge in case they kill me. Rolland Meeks.

James and Jill were astounded.

James shook Roy's hand across the table.

"Well done Roy. Guess our forensics team missed this note. It ties up a lot of loose ends. Sorry we can't discuss it with you."

"I understand. I was a bit frightened because, supposing this Terry bloke finds out I've found this note?"

"Don't worry, Roy," said Jill, in her reassuring voice. 'We won't mention your name or occupation. It's possible that you might have to give evidence about finding the note at a future date, but if there's a trial, obviously, it will mean we have the suspects in custody."

"Err, OK, Jill," said a barely convinced Roy.

Chapter Sixty-Five

James called DCS Lorraine Marsh and arranged to see her as a matter of urgency. They met in her office and presented the note from Rolland Meeks.

"This note kind of confirms your theories about the antique robberies. It does explain how the antiques were disposed of. It's all very vague, concerning names."

"Yes Ma'am," said James. "But we've met a man named Ludo. We think it refers to Ludo Chambers. Can't be many people with that name. If we could question him and put a bit of pressure on him, he might give us some names."

"Yes James, but as we know, the note doesn't constitute evidence. Chambers could just deny it and there's nothing we can pin on him. I'm more concerned about the link to a police officer."

"Yes, and this bloke Terry. If he did kill Kelp and Meeks, we've got a dangerous man out there. I wouldn't mind betting that it's the same man who abducted Jill. If that's the case then she had a lucky escape," said James, looking directly at Jill.

"That's a lot of speculation but I can see the link, because of the comment about smart-arsed Detectives. It's you and Jill!"

"Thanks Ma'am," said James.

"This is deadly serious because it confirms an internal source and explains the compromised safe house."

James leaned back on the comfortable settee.

"Ma'am, don't you think we've got enough now to bring a case against DI North?"

DCS Marsh didn't reply straight away. She stirred her coffee and held the spoon between thumb and finger.

"Yes, we probably have got enough to ask Professional Standards to look at it. I can't make that decision. I have to refer it upwards to the ACC. DI North has always sailed close to the wind and I think it's time to clip his wings. I want you to speak to this Ludo Chambers character. See if you can get him to open up. He might be willing to give us the name of the police officer. I want you to move out of the safe house by the weekend. In my view it's no longer safe, if somebody is tipping off criminals about it. I know you're using the full security measures at the house, but I'd be happier if you weren't there. I'll talk to DCI Charteris. I'm aware that he's already told you that your time there is up, but just get out before the manure starts to fly."

James and Jill both nodded. This was it. The end of their time together.

"I'll keep you in the picture about DI North, when I've spoken to the ACC. In the meantime, watch your backs! Is that all?" James wore a quizzical expression, which Lorraine Marsh picked up on.

"Come on James. Say what you're thinking."

"It's just that I still have the feeling that Jill and I are in the middle of something. I can't put my finger on it, and I know your orders for us to stay in Brighton came from the top, but…"

"No 'but', James! We've discussed this so many times already. I don't make the orders. I'd say that you've achieved something. You have both made real progress on the antique burglaries. Before you joined the Brighton team, the investigation was going nowhere."

"With respect, Ma'am, there's a bit more to it than just the burglaries."

Lorraine Marsh fixed both Detectives with a stare.

"Yes, there probably is. I'm sure when the time is right, it'll all come out. Until that time, I suggest you just try to make sense of the Meeks' letter. Do I make myself clear?"

James nodded, as did Jill.

That afternoon the two Detectives were on their way to see Ludo Chambers at his shop in Eastbourne. They had considered telephoning him first but had decided to catch him unprepared. They were still convinced that something was going on with the ACC, DCS Marsh and possibly DCI Charteris. They couldn't understand why Professional Standards hadn't been called in to investigate North. The evidence was circumstantial but there were lots of small things that seemed to add up to something bigger.

They grabbed a parking space, not far from Ludo Chambers' shop. They saw him through the shop window, sitting at his antique desk with his feet up. As they walked into the shop, Chambers, glanced at them. His face suddenly wore a concerned look, as he hurriedly finished his phone call and stood up.

"I'll have to complain to the Chief Constable about police harassment," Said Chambers, half smiling.

"We just wanted a chat, sir," smiled James.

"Not that bloody silver squirrel again?"

"No sir," said Jill. "It's about another matter."

"Do I need my solicitor present?" said a half joking Chambers.

"I don't think so. At least not at this stage, sir," said James.

"What is it you want, Chief Inspector?"

"Thanks for the promotion, but it's Inspector," said James, flashing his ID. "You'll remember DS Trent. We wanted to ask you about the sale of antiques on the continent. Do you know anything about that particular market?"

Ludo Chambers looked worried, despite desperately trying to hide it.

"Yes, I know a bit about it. I sometimes go across to France and Belgium to buy and sell."

"So, would you have any contacts in those two countries?"

"Yes," said Chambers, desperately trying to anticipate the line of questioning.

"Could you provide me with any names and locations?"

"Not really, Inspector. It's mostly people who trade in the street markets. In any case, I'm just on first name terms."

Jill stepped in.

"Just like your purchase of the silver squirrel, from a car boot fair. No real details, just casual transactions?"

"Not quite, Sergeant. It's a bit more business-like than car boots. These are proper traders at licenced street markets."

Jill nodded and looked at James, who said,

"Your name came up in connection with a case we're investigating, Mr Chambers. Not to put too fine a point on it, the case involves stolen antiques."

"Stolen antiques? I'm a member of the Antique Dealers' Association, not some cowboy trader. I take great exception to your insinuation."

"Why do you think your name came up, sir?"

"How the fuck should I know?" Chambers lowered his head. "Err, sorry about the foul language but I don't like your questions. Perhaps I should ring my solicitor for advice."

"Oh, just one more question," said Jill.

"Do you know a man named Roland Meeks?"

"Roland Meeks? No, I don't think so. Why are you asking?"

James smiled.

"No more questions. At least for the time being. We may have to ask you to attend a formal interview at some stage. We're based in Lewes and Brighton, but we can arrange for it to be in Eastbourne, if it's more convenient. We'll let you know sir. Thanks for your time."

As soon as the Detectives left and Chambers had watched them walking down the road, he immediately grabbed his mobile and made a call.

"Simon, can you talk? Well listen up. I've just had a couple of Detectives in my shop. What do you mean, 'so what?'. Just listen. They were asking questions about my contacts on the continent. Why worry? Well you better start worrying because if I go down, I'm taking you with me old chum! Fuck Ryan! I'm not going to prison for him. Yes, I know, he's a bastard but when push comes to shove, we've got to look after ourselves. OK, let's meet up tonight and discuss it. OK, right, see you then."

Ludo's brash, almost devil may care demeanour had disappeared. He worried that the two Detectives knew more than they were letting on. He was frightened of Ryan Ledbetter but frightened of prison as well!

James and Jill knew that they didn't have enough on Chambers to formally interview him yet, but he had seemed rattled by their questions. There were other questions that they could have asked him, but they had decided to let him sweat. Maybe he would crack and then whatever was going on might be revealed. They made their way back to Brighton and DCI Charteris confirmed that it was their last night at the safe house. They went back to the house, earlier than normal and decided to go out for a meal. Not a celebration, more a recognition that something had come to an end.

They decided to go to the restaurant where they had accompanied DI North and DS Read. It seemed like a lifetime ago but it was only three weeks. They had only just sat down, when to their surprise Jackie Read walked in and came to their table.

"Hello Jackie.' Said Jill. Do you want to join us?"

"Err, no. Err, no thanks. Have a nice evening."

James and Jill looked at the retreating Jackie, as she disappeared outside.

"What do you think, James?"

"I don't know. Bit strange."

"Perhaps she was meeting a man here and we cramped her style."

"Yes, that might be it."

Jackie Read was on her mobile.

"Change of plan. We can't meet at the restaurant. I'll explain when I see you. Plan B. See you in the usual layby in half an hour."

Chapter Sixty-Six

James and Jill got back to the house later that evening. They had strolled along Brighton seafront and were now sitting on the settee together. Jill was in her pyjamas and James in a jogging suit.

Jill smiled. "James, there's something I've been meaning to ask you. Do you always wear jogging gear for bed?"

"No. I normally wear nothing at all. What about you?"

"Naked as the day I was born," laughed Jill.

"So, we're both nudists in bed."

"Looks like it."

"Why are we doing all this small talk?" asked James, suddenly looking serious.

"James, have you locked the front door?"

"Yes, it's the first thing I do, after your little adventure with the kidnapper. And the security systems are all set as well. Nobody can get in. Why?"

"Just checking. Can you excuse me a minute? I need to go to my room. Be back in a tick."

Jill got up and left. James picked up a magazine and started to flick through it. He was engrossed in an article about historic Brighton. He was vaguely aware of Jill coming back into the room. He looked up and was open mouthed. Jill was standing there, just wearing her knickers. James couldn't help but stare at her.

"Like what you see?"

James was unable to reply. Before he could get any words out, Jill came over and sat astride his lap, facing him. James threw the magazine on the floor and he kissed Jill's breasts. She moaned with pleasure and looked into his eyes. She then got up and started to pull his jogging bottoms down. James took his t-shirt off and was down to just his boxers.

Jill tugged his boxers off and James didn't feel even slightly embarrassed. He sat back down on the settee. Jill pulled her knickers down and kicked them off.

She sat back astride his lap and he was soon deep inside her. They kissed and Jill thrust her breasts into his chest. They had no inhibitions. They had waited so long for this moment and nothing could stop them now. Jill had the most glorious orgasm as James thrusted ever more quickly. Suddenly, he exploded inside her and they held each other tightly. The sheer joy made them both a little tearful. The long wait for this moment, had heightened their lovemaking to a level which neither had experienced before. Jill just sat there and held on to James. They were locked together in a tight embrace.

"I never want to let you go. I love you so much. I could just stay here forever," said Jill, still tingling.

James caressed her back. "I've wanted you ever since we moved in. I have never felt like this before. I really am in love with you."

"Sorry to jump on you James, but when you said you slept naked, I just had to make love to you."

"Don't apologise. It was over so quickly; we need to slow down a bit next time. Let's go to bed. My room or yours?"

"Mine I think."

They showered together and washed each other. James enjoyed drying Jill with a large, soft bath towel. When they were both dry, James wrapped the towel around them both as he pulled her close. They started kissing and the towel fell away.

"Oh James, you've recovered very quickly," said Jill, with a lascivious look.

They both laughed as they fell into bed together.

They had taken their love affair to the next stage. Now, they would have to make plans for the future, when they left the safe house. The long wait for intimacy now seemed a little foolish. There had been so many times when they had wanted to fall into bed together, but something had stopped them. Was it duty? Perhaps it was more than that. Whatever it was, didn't matter now.

Chapter Sixty-Seven

There was no love at all for Fancy Carter. He was standing inside the very lock up building, from which Jill had escaped. Bob North and Terry Dalton were standing in front of a worried Carter. North had telephoned him earlier and had insisted that they meet that night. Carter, who had been expecting to meet his new drug distribution partner, was apprehensive. Terry had collected him from his flat, in North's car.

The large figure of Terry Dalton loomed menacingly. North wasn't in the mood for niceties.

"Listen you fat slob. I'm giving you the same deal as the one you've had with Ledbetter. Same price. Cash in hand. You get four kilos of pure cocaine. If you cut it, you can make a fair profit."

"Look, Mr North, I can't cut it or distribute it without Daynes. He had all the contacts."

"That's not my fucking problem."

"But you said you'd get me a replacement distributer."

"I know what I said," snarled North. "Things have changed. I've got to get out fast. I want one last chunk of cash. Not as if you haven't got the money!"

"But I have to be careful. I've already been questioned by your lot. I know they think I'm involved with Daynes. They might even be watching me!"

"They're not fucking watching you. Do you really think I wouldn't know? Grow up Carter. Now what about the cash?"

"I can only get my hands on £30,000."

"Where is it?"

"Stashed in a hiding place at my flat."

"And that's it? That's all you've got?"

"Yes, that's it. You don't realise how difficult it is to put that much cash together without raising suspicion."

"I've seen your bank records you bastard. Plenty of money going in and out."

"It's legal money. I buy and sell fine art."

"Yeah, if you can call dealing with that prat, Chambers, legal." "It's all above board. Receipts and everything. The tax man takes a share."

"Look! I haven't got time for all this crap. Let's go get the cash. We'll bring the merchandise along and do the swap. I can't afford to hang around. We'll do it now. Tonight."

"Is Ryan involved?"

"Fuck Ryan."

"Fuck me, Bob? You must be getting desperate," said a voice from behind them.

Standing there with a smile was Ryan Ledbetter, flanked by his two heavies, Brian Taylor and Stuart Crowe.

"I've heard the whole thing Bob. I knew you were involved and now, I want my fucking drugs and your hide."

Taylor and Crowe lurched towards North. They had made a fatal mistake of ignoring Terry. Crowe was stopped short by a massive punch in the face, as Terry stepped in front of North. Crowe hit the ground with blood spurting from his shattered nose. Taylor was momentarily distracted by this and Terry elbowed him, on the side of his head. He staggered sideways as a hefty punch from Terry caught him square on the jaw. As he was going down to join his bloodied friend on the ground, Terry caught him full in the face with another ferocious punch. Ledbetter couldn't believe what had just happened to his henchmen. Neither man would get up any time soon.

Ledbetter pulled a knife from his coat and raised it, intending to stab Terry. Suddenly there was a loud bang, followed by a second one. Two crimson patches appeared on Ledbetter's chest. He went down with a disbelieving look on his face. His eyes were dead and so was he. North just stood there with a revolver in his hand. The smell of cordite filled the air. Carter was horrified and clasped his hands over his red face. Terry looked at North in astonishment.

"A fucking gun?"

"Yes, a fucking gun!"

Carter was unable to move. He still had his hands over his face. He looked at North. He was terrified.

"You must be mad, you're a copper. How are you going to get out of this? It's cold blooded murder."

"Yeah and you're an accessory." Pointing to Terry's van, which had been there since Jill's abduction, he said,

"Terry, stick a rag in the petrol tank. Be quick about it!"

Terry did as he was told. North still had the revolver in his hand. Ledbetter's body was on the ground near the van. Blood from the two bullet wounds had now turned his whole front a sort of brownish-red and was pooling under his body. Ledbetter's two heavies were still down and groaning. But they were incapable of getting up.

North hustled Carter out of the lock up and put him in the back of North's car. Carter didn't resist or say anything. He just sat there with a look of absolute shock.

Terry carefully ignited the rag that was sticking out of the petrol tank. He closed the doors as he quickly got out. They were about thirty yards away, when there was the sound of an explosion. Bob North and Terry Dalton didn't look back. North just drove. Carter was feeling shaken and terrified because he was a witness to the cold-blooded murder of three men.

North had the drugs in the boot of his car. They went to Carter's flat, where he produced £30 000 in cash. It was the proceeds of lots of drug deals, over a long period of time. Carter was a careful man and his legitimate art dealings and his illicit drug business were entirely separate. Both activities cross-funded each other. Money laundering through a legitimate business. Who would suspect him? Well, perhaps now, after the drug squad interview it might be time for him to get out. He really didn't want to buy the drugs from North. Carter was about to say something when North grabbed the front of his jacket.

"Listen carefully, you fat bastard."

"You're up to your neck in all this. You can do what you want with the coke. Just keep your head down. If you go to the police, I'll kill you. Understand?"

Carter, having seen the shooting, believed North was capable of anything. He just nodded and looked at the floor. He had four kilos of coke and no means of selling it on without Daynes. The King of Comedy no longer had anything to laugh about.

Chapter Sixty-Eight

The following morning James and Jill woke up. James got up to make a drink and he and Jill had a cup of tea in bed. They just sat up sipping their tea and feeling absolutely wonderful. Jill had the duvet around her waist and was bare chested.

"In the films, the woman always has the bed covers pulled up to her chin. Glad this isn't a film," he laughed.

Jill laughed too. She reached for the TV remote and switched on the news. There were several items of national news. There had been tremendous thunderstorms in Scotland, due to humid conditions. The weatherman explained about cold upper air meeting mild humid air. The Home Secretary had made a gaffe but had managed to put the blame on civil servants.

Then, the local news came on. There was a report of a fire just outside Brighton. The fire services and the police suspected arson. Apparently, a vehicle fire inside a lockup had ignited the whole building. Fire and forensic teams had been investigating and the remains of three bodies had been discovered. The police had not released any further information and the case was described as ongoing.

Jill had no idea that the burnt-out building had also been her prison. She had only seen the area in the dark and the TV shots didn't really provide a wide-angle view of the surroundings. They finished their tea and had another shower together. The shower had led to another urgent lovemaking session. After breakfast they loaded their bags into the car and set off for Brighton police station, to meet DCI Charteris. He was sitting in his office and looked at the two Detectives as they entered.

"You two look very chipper this morning."

They both felt they were blushing. Did it really look obvious that they had been having sex this morning?

"Oh. Just happy to get back to normal, sir," said James, hoping he didn't look as embarrassed as he felt.

"Did you see that fire on the news, sir?" asked Jill, hoping the change of subject would change the discussion about their 'chipper' appearance.

"Yes, some of our people were out there all night. Bad business. Three dead. No ID as yet. We're having to rely on dental records but as you know, it's a drawn-out affair. By the way, do you know where DI North is this morning? I couldn't raise him on his mobile or at his flat."

"No sir,' said James.

"Not only that, I can't raise DS Read either!"

"Perhaps they're in a signal black spot," said Jill, hoping her redness had subsided.

"Well, if you do hear from them, tell them I want a word, will you? Thanks for your contribution to the antiques case. I'm asking DI Linda Broadbent to follow up on the antiques angle. She's very knowledgeable in that area. I couldn't bring her in before because she was seconded to the children's home case, which is now just about concluded. Thanks for your notes on the Ludo Chambers interview. DC Westmore showed me a copy of the report you emailed him. Slippery character, Mr Chambers."

"Very slippery sir," said James. "We're going to just tidy up a couple of loose ends back at Lewes."

"I'm sure Lorraine Marsh will be glad to get you back."

"I think our team coped without us sir. Sgt Rosemary Mires was seconded to help out."

"Yes, I hear she's applied to get out of uniform. The experience with your lads and lasses, probably gave her the taste for Detective work."

James and Jill set out for Lewes, wondering what had happened to North and Jackie.

Jackie was with North. They were sitting in his car near the old fishermen's sheds just off the East beach at Eastbourne. Jackie had decided to go with North. She had her passport and a suitcase. North had been pleased that she had decided to join him. He didn't want to leave her behind, especially as she had been suspicious about his activities. He was feeling confident that this woman was now back in the fold. He didn't intend to tell Jackie about the drugs or the murders of Ledbetter and his two henchmen. That would have turned her away from him and he would have to shut her up. North didn't totally trust Jackie and was a little surprised that she had actually agreed to join him, especially as his plans had been brought forward. He thought any decisions could wait until they were in Spain. If she played up, he would sort it.

North decided to take a chance with Jackie.

"Look Jack, I'm letting you in on something. You've been asking me lots of questions. I've got a secure strongbox in a Jersey bank, stuffed with cash, under the name of Michael Norton. And a bank account in Spain under my real name."

Jackie looked at Bob North but didn't say a word.

"The look on your face is a picture, Jack. We've also got company. A guy named Terry and his tart."

"Bob, why are they coming with us? I thought it was just the two of us?"

"Look Jack, don't start. Terry's a business acquaintance. We've worked together for a long time."

"What do you mean, business acquaintance? You're a copper. How can you be in business? We've discussed this before. You'd have to declare it to the higher ups, to get permission."

"Forget all that crap, Jack. I told you I've not been relying on police pay. We've made a fair old bit of money."

"Enough to have an account in Jersey, under an assumed name and another in Spain."

"Don't worry darling, the one in Spain is in my real name."

"All legitimate and above board."

Jackie didn't say anything. Just then a big man tapped on the car window. He had a large holdall and was accompanied by an attractive, young woman.

North and Read got out of the car.

"Terry, Angie, this is Jackie." Everyone gave a nod.

"We have to wait 'til later. We're going in that fishing boat," said North, pointing towards a fishing boat with a wheelhouse perched on top of it.

"Looks a bit small to cross the channel," said a worried Angie.

North looked irritated but managed to smile.

"Nah, it's plenty big enough. Dave, the guy who owns it is a mate of Terry's. He's nipped across to France in it for years. Terry's been out in it night fishing, loads of times. Haven't you Terry?"

The big man just nodded, as he put an arm around Angie, who still didn't look that convinced.

"We've got a few hours before we go. Got to wait for the tide. Let's go for a drink and some food. There's a place just along the path, near the boats."

North hadn't told Jackie or Angie that their destination wasn't a recognised French port. Terry's friend Dave had been involved in smuggling and other illegal activities on and off. He knew lots of isolated parts of the French coast. A few years back it had been booze and cigarettes. He had also smuggled cash for people he knew well. He had built a false bulkhead with enough room to hide cash and drugs. Dave was just the kind of man that North would find useful. A man who took a commission for a service, with no questions asked. Dave had, on some occasions been intercepted by French coast guard patrol vessels but his luck had always held. He had even smuggled illegal immigrants from France and had landed them near Seaford. Yes, just the kind of man North would like.

North had a contact in France who would arrange to get them into Spain. The cash in the Jersey strong box could wait. North had gone to a lot of trouble to set it up and it was his emergency fund in case things went wrong. He hadn't intended to tell anyone about it but because Jackie Read was now back in the fold, he couldn't help bragging how clever he'd been.

Chapter Sixty-Nine

James was sitting at his desk in Lewes and going through the cases under investigation by his team. Jill was at her desk on her computer. Because of what had happened between them, it was a little strange to be back in their office, doing everyday things. Jill had taken a coffee into James and he had smiled as he thanked her. It seemed all very formal. They were tying up some loose ends on the antique burglaries case, before sending the information to DI Broadbent. The note from Rolland Meeks had been a significant breakthrough. Two suspected members of the robbery team were dead. A third member was still at large and was most likely responsible for the demise of Kelp and Meeks. The main problem was that nobody had been able to describe his facial features. They only had the general description from Oz, who had described the man as 'a big bastard'. Jill's attacker was also a good fit for this description, but she hadn't seen his face. Just his physical size.

James was reading a file when DCS Lorraine Marsh appeared in the doorway of his office. She looked a bit flushed. Pulling the door shut, she said,

"Right James. You were wondering what's been going on. Now you're going to find out. I've just had a phone message from Jackie Read." James looked quizzically, at Lorraine Marsh.

"Yes James. She's in a bit of trouble. She's in Eastbourne with DI North and a man named Terry. There's another woman with them as well. She couldn't say much but North is making a run for it, on tonight's high tide."

James still looked puzzled.

"I'll explain everything later. I want you to take some uniformed back up and go and arrest North and his companions."

"Any reason why you want me to lead this, Ma'am?"

"Yes, it's connected to the case you and Jill have been working on and you know Jackie Read."

"They're hiding in one of the fishermen's sheds next to the east beach. Take care James. North is a dangerous man."

"Yes Ma'am, but what about the local police in Eastbourne. They're already in the vicinity?"

"James, I want you to lead on this. I've already ordered two teams of uniformed officers and they will meet you in the carpark."

"Is there no other information. Couldn't Jackie Read be more specific?"

"Afraid not. Jackie was in the toilets at a waterfront café. She couldn't get away from North for too long. Now get organised and keep me informed."

With that she was gone.

James told Jill, who was as puzzled as James about Jackie's role in all this.

They organised the uniformed officers into two teams of four, in two police cars. James and Jill went in James' BMW. They all wore stab proof vests, which was standard procedure for this kind of operation. The plan was to park up, away from the fishermen's sheds and walk up to them. They arrived at the location, just under an hour later. They parked out of sight of the fishermen's sheds. The two teams of four made their way to the sheds. James and Jill followed closely. Although everyone was wearing protective vests, none of the officers were armed because there had been no indication of any firearms when Jackie Read had telephoned. She had told them it was DI North, a guy named Terry and a young woman. Otherwise a specialist firearms team would have been deployed.

They were soon in sight of the sheds and there were several to choose from. Then, Jill spotted North's car and parked next to it was a Mercedes sports car. She phoned the office to get a PNC on the number plate. After about ten minutes her phone, which was turned down low, vibrated. Jill listened, said, "Thanks," and rang off.

"The car's registered to a Terrence Dalton. Address is in the Meads area of Eastbourne."

"Expensive area," said James.

The two teams of uniforms converged on the shed, with the cars outside. James stepped forward and tried the door. It was locked. Some of the police officers went around to the rear of the shed, which backed onto the beach. There was no sign of anyone. James pulled everyone back. They retreated to a safe distance away and stepped behind an old lifeboat, which was high and dry on the beach. It had clearly seen better days. There were 'keep off' signs on the boat. It was really just a rotting hulk.

James thought that perhaps North and his companions might still be at the café. He didn't want to risk an arrest where there could be families with children. He decided to wait to see if they came back.

Suddenly, a young woman appeared from a shed, which was about three along from the one where the cars were parked. North was cunning; not parking right outside the shed he was actually in. The young woman unlocked the Mercedes and got something from inside. She then stopped and lit a cigarette, gave it a long drag and walked slowly back towards the shed that she had emerged from. The sheds were quite large because they were used for processing fish. Not all were now in use, but at least two appeared to be up and running, because there were company names displayed on the walls. Plus, an unmistakable fish smell.

The young woman finished her cigarette, threw it down and stomped on the butt. She disappeared inside the shed. Jill thought she could be Terrence Dalton's girlfriend, because she had opened his car to get her cigarettes. James issued his orders. He wanted the uniformed officers to surround the fisherman's shed. He and Jill would walk in through the door, backed up by two uniforms. They all walked quietly towards the shed. James and Jill stepped inside. There were four figures sitting at an old table at the far side. James called out,

"Police officers. Stay where you are!"

North was surprised and angry. He jumped to his feet.

"What the fuck are you doing here?"

"I'm here to arrest you."

"For what, having a meeting in a fisherman's shed?" he said, with heavy sarcasm.

"I'd like all four of you to walk towards me with your hands in the air."

Jackie Read immediately broke away from the group and walked towards James.

"Come back here!" shouted North. "You've fucking betrayed me, you bitch!"

Jackie Read kept walking and was almost level with James, when a gunshot rang out. Jackie Read staggered and fell against James. There was blood on the back of her shoulder. James had caught her as she fell but he had a bloody patch on the top of his left arm. Jill rushed to his side as Jackie slumped, almost in slow-motion, to the floor. The two uniformed police officers moved forward and North waved a gun in their direction. The noise of the gunshot had brought all the other police officers running inside the shed.

"I've got five more bullets. If any of you are feeling heroic, just keep coming."

Jill was almost in tears at the sight of James holding a bloodied arm and obviously in pain. He managed to compose himself.

"Give it up Bob. You've got no chance."

Before he could answer, the young blond woman broke away from where North was standing and rushed towards the police officers. She was crying and obviously terrified. North fired again, intending to hit James, but the terrified Angie had run across his field of fire and was hit in the back. The huge figure of Terry Dalton ran to his fallen girlfriend. He picked her up like a rag doll and caressed her. She was limp in his arms. He gently laid her down on the ground. The big man had tears in his eyes as he turned towards North.

None of the police officers moved.

"I didn't mean to hit her," shouted North.

"You bastard," shouted Terry, who was beyond all reason now. His eyes were filled with tears, but they were wildly intense. For such a big man, he moved surprisingly fast. North understood Terry's intentions and fired at him. The bullet hit Terry but didn't stop him. North fired again and Terry was covered in his own blood. He was suddenly on North. The big man had his huge hands around North's neck. North fired again at point blank range but it didn't stop Terry from crushing North's windpipe. North was unable to do anything. He went down and sprawled at Terry's feet. Terry was gushing blood all over North's limp body. He turned away and just about made it to Angie's crumpled body. He tried to cradle her in his arms, but his enormous strength finally gave out. He fell forwards and was locked in a deathly embrace with his girlfriend. There was blood everywhere.

Jill was trying to help James who was still conscious. One of the police officers had gone for a first aid kit from his car. He came rushing back as Jill managed to remove James' blood-soaked, stab proof vest. She placed a large lint pad over the wound in his arm. She was tearful but was still trying to be professional. Jackie Read was laying on her front. A police officer was trying to staunch the bleeding from the top of her back. Another officer had summoned medical help and soon the sound of ambulances filled the quiet seafront. DCS Lorraine Marsh who had been on route to Eastbourne appeared and came upon the harrowing scene. James was sitting on the ground, with Jill trying to tend his bloodied arm. Jackie Read was still laying on the ground but her eyes were open, and she was moving, despite being covered in blood.

Close by, lying in a pool of blood, was a big man in a death embrace with a young woman. Further away was the sprawled body of DI Bob North. There was blood on the front of his jacket, but it was all from Terry. North's head hung at an angle and a revolver was clutched tightly in his dead fingers. Lorraine Marsh was horrified and knew that there would be an enquiry. Politics and wider issues crossed her mind; but that was for another day. Her immediate concern was for her officers.

After James and Jackie had been tended to, they were taken by ambulance to Eastbourne hospital. Amazingly, neither had life threatening injuries but it had been a close-run thing. A few centimetres either way and it would certainly have been a different story for Jackie. She had been incredibly lucky that no vital organs had been hit.

The forensics team carried out their usual investigation. Photographs were taken of the three dead bodies, before Doctor Claire Grant authorised their removal, for post-mortem examination. Jill had insisted on going in the ambulance with James, clutching his hand all the way to the hospital and then reluctantly parting with him while they operated on him.

Jackie Read also underwent surgery. The bullet that struck her had passed right through her and hit James upon exiting. This had taken the momentum out of its flight, but it was still potent, as it had glanced his upper arm and tore his flesh.

Chapter Seventy

Four weeks later, James was sitting in DCS Lorraine Marsh's office drinking coffee. He even dunked a biscuit. To hell with it breaking off and falling into his drink. Jill was also there, as was Jackie Read. She had made a miraculous recovery, thanks in part to her fitness levels, but she still had to take things easy for a while. Lorraine Marsh had asked them all to come in for a de-briefing. James and Jackie were not yet signed off for active duty but they were fit enough to come into the office.

Lorraine Marsh looked a little apprehensive. The reason was soon clear, when the Assistant Chief Constable, Trevor Johnson walked in, clutching a takeaway coffee. Everyone was about to stand.

"Please, remain seated. No need for formality. Sorry about bringing my own coffee, I didn't know if you had your own machine or you used the station coffee. So, I took out some insurance," he said, indicating his cup. Everyone laughed politely. The only person not to laugh was DCI Sandy Charteris. In fact, he was stony faced.

"I've asked Lorraine to get you together, because I feel I owe you an explanation." He first addressed James and Jill.

"I know you thought it irregular to be asked to stay in a Brighton safe house, but I wanted you both to keep an eye on DI North. We thought the ambiguity of your presence might unsettle him. We knew he was into something and now we know what it was. We found £30 000 in cash in the boot of his car. He had a passport with a false name, to access a bank account and strongbox in Jersey. He had £250 000 in total. He had another account in Spain with £200 000 and a modest villa. All, no doubt, from the proceeds of crime!"

"How could he get that much money together sir?" asked James, dunking his second biscuit.

"We think his primary source of income was from a drugs network.

He was certainly involved in drug dealing across the area. He was also up to his neck in the stolen antiques business. Before you both joined the burglary investigation team, very little progress had been made. That was in part, down to North. He was obviously stalling the case. DI North was also providing information on the coastal security system. He had a contact in project Cormorant; movements of security teams, that sort of thing. You probably know that the system watches costal movements both offshore and, on the beaches, and we had thought it was pretty secure. We've arrested a man on suspicion of being North's contact in Cormorant and he broke down and confessed to everything. We believe North was working with a man named Ryan Ledbetter, who has since disappeared. Ledbetter has a large boat moored at Sovereign Harbour at Eastbourne. From all accounts he was definitely involved in drug smuggling and distribution."

"We were also fortunate to have DS Jackie Read working with DI North. She works for Professional Standards and was their inside person. I was approached by them and asked to cooperate in their investigation. The brief was to get close to North and find out what he was up to," He nodded towards Jackie.

"Look guys, I'm so sorry I couldn't let you into it," said Jackie. "That night I came to see you both, was really difficult. I had to pretend to be scared of North. In the end I didn't have to pretend. I wanted to make absolutely sure I could trust you. My job makes me very cynical and watchful. I guess I was a bit bitchy with you at times, Jill. It was all an act."

"You were very convincing, Jackie," said Jill.

"You were very kind to me. You also acted properly by reporting me to DCS Marsh. It was the right thing to do. I knew you were both honest cops, but in my job, I have to check everyone out."

"It was difficult Jackie," said James. "We didn't want to drop you in it, but we couldn't just ignore what you told us about Carter and the laptop."

"I've been under cover for a long time. I got close to North. Too close. I'm not proud about that!" she shrugged.

Sandy Charteris still wore a grim expression.

"I have already voiced my views on this whole affair, sir," he said, addressing ACC Trevor Johnson.

"For the sake of clarity and to answer any questions that James and Jill might not want to raise here, I have to say that I'm a bit pissed off. I wasn't told that Jackie was undercover. This omission has made me look a bit foolish and I regret that, Sir."

"I know you felt you should have been told but my agreement with Professional Standards was, that I would limit the information to myself and Lorraine."

Sandy Charteris didn't reply. There was an awkward silence.

Lorraine Marsh who had been quiet, looked at James.

"James, I'm really sorry about your injury. You too Jackie. If there had been any indication of a firearm, I would have assigned an armed unit. The gun must have come from one of North's friends. The young woman who was killed, was an innocent victim. She was just with the wrong man. I really do regret that."

Jackie Read looked at James.

"I'm really sorry — I didn't know about the gun. I knew that North was capable of violence, but I just didn't think he would be armed. The young woman, Angie, paid a terrible price and some of us had a near miss."

ACC Trevor Johnson rounded off by thanking everyone and the meeting broke up. He hadn't expanded on what Lorraine Marsh had said and he didn't offer any response to what Jackie Read had said. Although, he had frowned when she mentioned getting too close to North. Then, rather abruptly, the ACC thanked everyone again and left the room. James felt that there were still elements to this whole episode that had been left unsaid. He thought it wise not to raise any questions at this time because the ACC had not encouraged any further questions. James also felt a lot of sympathy for Sandy Charteris. If he had been aware of Jackie Read's true identity, he might have played things differently.

James had only been home for two weeks after his hospital treatment. Jill had stayed with him at his flat ever since. Their lovemaking had been gentler than the explosive encounters at the Brighton safe house. James had stiches in his upper arm and although the wound was healing nicely, he had to take care. They had decided to live together at James' place and Jill had arranged to rent out her flat, complete with impressive railway noises, via a letting agency. They wanted to stay together. Jill could have lost her wonderful man and she was determined to hold onto him.

There was an ongoing investigation of Carter, by the Drugs Team. Ludo Chambers was placed under surveillance. His association with Simon Wells was noted but nothing more. Forensic work on the human remains found in the burnt-out lockup, was ongoing. Some of the stolen antiques had surfaced in France but most had disappeared, leaving insurers to pay out on the losses.

The fact that Jackie Read was working for Professional Standards had surprised James and Jill, not to mention a very pissed off Sandy Charteris. The explanation by the ACC about their stay at the Brighton safe house, when they only lived up the road in Lewes, had still been a little perplexing. If it was to unsettle North, it had worked. It had nearly cost Jill her life. Although it seemed to break accepted protocol, James and Jill had no complaints about the unforeseen romantic outcome.

Jackie Read had moved on, no doubt to another undercover placement. She had learnt a valuable lesson about not getting too personally involved. James had wondered if her intimacy with North had tarnished her career. He would probably never know. It had also occurred to him and Jill that Jackie Read might well have been a false name.

North's criminal activities had certainly tarnished the reputation of the police. The ACC and DCS Lorraine Marsh had been asked to account for their actions. Questions about their orders concerning two Detectives staying at the safe house had been raised. The involvement of Professional Standards was also being reviewed. ACC Trevor Johnson took early retirement on full pension and DCS Loraine Marsh moved to another division, keeping her rank. Sandy Charteris was promoted to

Acting Superintendent. Perhaps there were other elements to the whole affair. If there were, then nothing ever came out.

James and Jill would have to sort out their professional relationship in line with police policy. But their private life was already sorted, thanks to the safe house. Although they were both questioned during the enquiry, neither had any blame attached to them. They had solved two murders and made a major contribution towards resolving the antique burglaries. Life for both James and Jill would be different now.

Printed in Great Britain
by Amazon